THE DOLL WITH
A BRUISE

Interact Publishing Limited

About this book

Shona believes her mysterious bruise connects her to a beheaded woman found in a fenland ditch.

'Coincidence, exaggeration and attention-seeking,' says the shrewd police inspector.

So Shona investigates: recognising a link between her bruise and an iconic Celtic cross from a Scottish isle; discovering a woman in her village that no-one realises is missing; obsessing over the doll that shares her bruise.

Nothing makes sense.

Is Shona going crazy?
Or has she been targeted by a serial killer and marked for murder?

The truth is... far... far worse.

CONTENTS

The Doll with a Bruise

by J. L. Dawn

Copyright © 2019 Interact Publishing Ltd
All rights reserved.

ISBN: 9798655415386

Dedicated to Cath who helped me write my first novel

1 SHONA

A Murder
by S Patterson

Tuesday night May 21 2019

Octopuses are hard to love. They kill almost anything you put in a tank with them, including other octopuses. They're notorious escape artists, they're smart and they rip lives apart. I don't make them happy.

I think of them as male, perhaps because they remind me of my time with Boy – except that I lived with Boy for over 15 years (octopuses aren't that long-lived) and he managed not to kill me in all that time. We successfully procreated and then he escaped. See, smart!

I work with a lot of cephalopods: octopuses, cuttlefish and squid make up 30% of the population of our laboratory aquarium. Our lab's newest resident was already housed when I started my night-shift. He was an algae octopus, Abdopus aculeatus. He came with a reputation for escaping – earning the nickname 'Gone Puss' in his previous aquarium – and for being 'uncooperative'. Our lab hadn't officially named him, so 'Gone Puss' it was.

I tried to make him happy, even feeding him first on my rounds. There were 28 live experiments I had to note and report on, and over 50 of the 130 tanks required me to feed their occupants at night, including most of the cephalopods.

Two hours into my rounds, I caught my left arm on the feeding trolley and yelped. Zebra fish mobbed to the side of a tank to stare, nudging fins. Thumb-sized bob-tailed squids, so cute I refused to devise any experiments to do on them, glowed with concern. My three-day-old bruise was no longer tender but the wounds that had been left on my psyche were another matter – bloody, raw and on the verge of turning gangrenous.

Normally I coped well with the night-shift – four nights a month – that gave me time alone; time to think in the low blue light and watery soundscape of the six long rooms. The routine was cathartic and the specimens fascinating. I was fortunate to do a job that made use of my biology degree and challenged me. Four nights a month were worth that. Time lost with Harry on those four evenings was made up at the weekend when I went full-on super-mom.

A phone stood on an empty desk. I dialled '0'.

'Hey, Shona.' A yawn. The security guard on reception. The only other person in the building at night. I'd woken him.

'Hey, Leroy.'

'Was there er... anything...?'

'A lot of fish.'

'Woh, yeah.'

'There's a new octopus here. I don't think he's happy.'

'Maybe he needs a lady octopussy.'

'Wouldn't end well. Chances are he'd tear her into bits and eat her.'

'Wo-oh, nightmare,' said Leroy. I could tell he was already losing interest.

'Most species of octopus die after sex. When they do mate, he ups and leaves. She has to care for the fry on her own. She stops eating. Either way he kills her. Males and females eh? Can't live with each other, can't live without.'

'Octopuses?'

'The issue isn't that you make each-other miserable; that's manageable – normal, even. The problem comes when one of you points that out; putting it out there, means you've got to deal with it.'

'Shona? er... you OK?'

'Great.'

Would I be phoning if I was OK?

'Only normally, you don't –'

Normally...

This Tuesday, I craved human conversation – even Leroy's – rather than be left alone with my own thoughts. They had a disturbing habit of stomping around my head, as though they owned the place.

As I returned to my workstation I checked the 50-gallon tank. Octopus: one, still all too present. Every centimetre of Gone Puss was in motion; every limb crept, spread, twisted and gyrated. His sac of a body heaved against the glass, trying to force a way through. Everything moved apart from his coin-slot eye. As I drew level with his tank, he spat out the pellet of thawed shrimp from the same feeder tube I had pushed it into two hours earlier.

Cephalopods often take time to adjust to the dead shrimp we substitute for the live prey they corner in their reefs, but Gone Puss was a seasoned aquarium inmate. He had no excuses. No, he was determined to register his animosity towards me personally. Gone Puss was setting out the terms of our relationship. The pellet was a flaccid reminder that his ancestors developed in the world's oceans 230 million years before my mammalian ones pitched up.

His hunting instinct had discerned that my life signs were edging to the wussy side of wimpy – octopuses, inanimate objects and children have an unerring sixth sense about these things. Even from within his tank, he had correctly identified me as something he could prey upon.

'Missed,' I snarled back. I let the pellet lie. I couldn't even retaliate. Octopuses are the only invertebrates given special protection by the Government under the licensing of animal experiments.

Smart? They've got a lobby group.

Normally, I didn't mind the nights. Normally, I didn't let rejected morsels of un-breaded scampi unhinge me.

I sat and typed with stabbing fingers.

My laptop keyboard beat out a word, but it was nothing to do with the experiment notes I was employed to make.

S U C K E R!!!?!

Three goes to spell it correctly. I stared through it.

A burst of 'Flower of Scotland' burbled from my mobile. It was a text. Anonymous, that was rare. It would be marketing; some clever scam; to click or n... I clicked.

'Recognise this, Sho?' read the sparse text. The words were followed by assorted emojis and a pared down link. Another click, a video clip opened. The title read: 'Doll Killer murder victim – police appeal for help'. It was dated 28th February, nearly three months ago.

I twisted the phone and hunted around to increase the volume. The footage was zeroing down onto a map of fields, waterways and scrubland. A presenter's voice was speaking...

'Police are appealing for help in identifying the headless woman found dead yesterday morning in a drainage ditch in fenland close to Whittlesey. They believe the murdered woman was in her mid-30s. She had light-brown hair. Her hands were also missing, cut off at the wrist, displaying obvious similarities to The Doll Killer murder. Her only identifying mark is a distinctive bruise on her upper left arm...'

A graphic flashed up on screen. I dropped the phone on the desk. My hand clutched at my left bicep. It was my bruise, similarly faded, horribly familiar, only the one on the screen was rendered on something that bore no resemblance to living flesh.

I recalled the 'headless handless woman' case from earlier in the year. 'Doll Killer' headlines swirled.

I reviewed the emojis: three yellow Munch heads gaped their fear at me, a cool silver knife cut a fitting end to the trail.

Who sent this? Who even knew I had a bruise? I was too ashamed to have mentioned it, to have done anything but hide it away under long-sleeved tops. Too horrified by the memories it evoked.

Why would any...? I blocked the sender and dialled 0 from my office landline. After four rings I concluded Leroy wasn't at his post; maybe in the loo, more likely outside snatching a fag. The rush of water refreshing a tank – through the jumble of pipes criss-crossing the ceiling – made me jump. Behind me, things thrummed in the creepy pump room – domain of the sullen maintenance engineers – where I had yet to discover a light-switch.

The two bruises were identical. I knew it because I had studied mine in the mirror for far too long, seething at its origins. Both bruises bore too close a similarity to a Celtic cross to be explained by coincidence. Not just any cross, but St Martin's Cross on Iona. Both must surely have been inflicted the same way.

Why would I share a bruise with a corpse? And why, on God's good Earth, was it shaped like an iconic Eighth Century Celtic cross from a sheep-bitten isle.

It had seemed a mad coincidence when I first discovered my bruise. Now, it smacked of sinister cultural branding. It was as if St Columba himself had sailed up the Cam to label me a sinner. No argument here; even a Glaswegian 'Proddie' knows better than to quarrel with a Saint.

This was my 'Madonna in the toast' moment. It must be a sign. Convert or...

And there it was. A simple sickening logical step: there was only one other person who could tell – who would know – the two bruises were the same. My bruise had been inflicted by the murderer. This text was from the Doll Killer. I must have been alone with him? Which begged the question: shouldn't I already be dead?

Another thought: I was alone at night in a dark workspace with only a truculent, probably under-nourished octopus to protect me. I looked up. Like Leroy, Gone Puss had vanished.

Calm down. Think, Shona. Could there be any other explanation?

I retraced the steps that led to my bruise; a chain of events from a week ago, events that may have cost me my closest friend, events culminating in the word on my laptop. It had started with 'Bruise Night.'

* * *

And that had started with Harry, last week – a lifetime ago. His dad, Boy, was enjoying a six-month cycling sabbatical leaving me juggling a football starlet and a full-time job. My wounds over Boy peddling away from parental responsibility had hardly healed when Harry ripped them open again with the unthinking callousness 11-year-olds specialise in.

'Dad's got Candi with him,' Harry said.

It was as if a shadowy abomination had wormed from his innocent mouth. It slithered towards me across my kitchen floor-tiles.

'No. No, I don't think so. Candi's at work. Or in her cottage I expect.' Me shoring up fortifications before they plummeted moat-wards.

'I just saw her, in the background in Dad's Skype,' Harry waggled his new expensive guilt-edged phone at me. 'I thought he'd gone on his own. Candi's with Dad in Patagonia.'

It made sense to Harry. It probably made sense to everyone but me. Why wouldn't Boy take his fresh, so-o much younger, emotionally needy squeeze with him on his triumphant sabbatical? Why wouldn't he want to share his tent, his (doubtless tandem) bike, his smoked Patagonian boar meat sarnies... with her?

And why wouldn't Candice jump out of her shapeless sweaters at the chance to park her job for six months for an all-expenses-paid vacation of a lifetime with the only man she'd ever managed to snare?

It even made sense that Boy had decided not to tell Harry or me he intended taking her. It was undoubtedly a kindness. The unwarranted outrage welling up within me now, perfectly vindicated Boy's decision to keep me in the dark. 'Oh, it's nice he's got some company,' I said to Harry...

'He's bloody gone and taken Madame with him!' I said to Lotte.

'Who? Boy? Candi!? What? To Patagonia?' she replied, suitably shocked before guffawing. 'You've got to hand it to her, Shona.'

'Believe me I'd like to – backhand!'

I had parked Harry in front of his X-Box and grabbed the phone to dilute my pain by letting it ripple out into a diminishing puddle of close friends. Does this quack remedy reduce anyone's suffering and trauma? There was no statistical evidence that sharing my latest humiliation around worked as medication. Any chance of even a placebo benefit was doomed; Lotte was undoubtedly the last person in the village you would go to for sympathy. Still, we had shared a lot recently; mainly dating tittle-tattle and bottles of Sauvignon Blanc.

'She's got her hooks into him and she's not letting go,' Lotte thoughtlessly laughed again. 'I should have pushed Shouty in her direction after we separated. It would have kept him from creeping back.'

Shouty was Lotte's former husband. I had often enquired, but never found out, how he came by his nickname. For some reason 'post-orgasmic triumphalism' kept suggesting itself as an answer. As far as I was aware, he had no intention of creeping back.

'I expect you had too much respect for his good taste.'

This drew another deranged peal of mirth from Lotte, 'Shouty doesn't have any taste, Sho; at least, not where women are concerned. He married me for god's sake. The fact is, I barely knew Candi back then and from the handful of times our paths had crossed, I assumed she was asexual.'

'You're not making me feel any better,' I bleated.

'God, sweetie, no, I'm sorry. Fancy Boy taking her out there with him. I always believed Patagonia existed for people to get away from women like Candi.'

'It's not far away enough.'

'I know what you need...'

Lotte had seen her opportunity. She re-pitched her Saturday night out.

Lotte and I had grown close since I had returned to the village from the 'Big House', as Harry had christened it. We were back in the 3-bedroom cottage Boy owned in the heart of the village, across the paddock from the church. It was the same cottage Harry had known as 'Happy Home' for the first two years of his life.

Lotte wasn't formerly in my inner circle. An acquired taste, she would accost strangers as if she had known them all her life and, if she wasn't in sight, you'd take her laugh for the mating call of an exotic macaw.

We were both single parents with young boys, who played for the same under-12 village footie team, and now formed a two-woman dating-app mutual support group. Lotte was engaged in an ongoing (so far five-year) pursuit of a new man to replace Shouty's indeterminate (but presumably raucous) role in her life. I had two-and-a-half years of half-hearted scanning, swiping, emoji-ing and infrequent dating behind me.

Lotte was a rare presence at the school gate or footie touchline. As director of sales for some engineering outfit up the A1, she spent her time on other pitches. However, we had been part of some overlapping social circles beforehand, we were of a similar age, we both enjoyed a drink, and were loud and garrulous enough that we would inevitably gravitate together halfway through any evening. Several garden parties and village functions had resounded to the chorus of my manic jackdaw chuckle interspersed by Lotte's booming hoots. So it was that we latched onto each other while constructively abusing the referees in our sons' matches.

Our dating and matchmaking objectives were at opposite ends of the spectrum, our online profiles wildly different, but we both ended up dissatisfied. Lotte required constant break-up advice as yet another suitor, who had been bedded and found wanting, needed to be let go. I craved ceaseless reassurance that it wasn't my fault that the only men ever attracted to me were dull, not remotely in Boy's class, and impossible to fancy.

'Shouty's mate's Cambridge party is on this Saturday don't forget, Sho.' Lotte had been trying to wrangle a 'yes' out of me for over a week. 'It's guaranteed to dispel all thoughts of Boy plunging through the Patagonian –' suppressed giggles delayed her sentence until she finally managed to yelp, 'bush.'

'I don't know, Lotte; masked balls don't really sound my thing. I've got Harry to find a sitter for.'

'All taken care of, sweetie; Harry's round mine with Ollie. I've rustled up a spare aunt for the night. Anyway, it's a "Masquerade" not a ball, according to the invite Shouty's mailed through. I hardly imagine people will be judging you on your dancing.' She let the innuendo dangle indelicately.

'Sounds like an orgy to me.'

'Only if that's where you want it to go. Big house in posh Cambridge; it's completely respectable...' she hooted again, '...until it's not. You can wear that clingy red number we bought when you hit nine and a half stone. I've booked a cab, darling. Don't make me go on my own.'

✳ ✳ ✳

The cab revved into the large drive five minutes early, scattering Lotte's meagre gravel. I yanked at my scanty hemline, but still earned disapproving looks from both Ollie's aunt and Harry. I ruffled Harry's hair at the door. He pulled away in the prescribed 11-year-old manner. It was a text-book pull away; he must have been studying YouTube videos on technique. Ollie broke ranks to run to Lotte and give her a hug around the waist, earning a lingering kiss on his forehead.

Lotte was travelling light. She handed me a slim purse to plop into my large shoulder bag, which contained everything I could think of, snatched-up in a panicky exit from our cottage. The only thing Lotte carried was a stylish black filigree eye mask. It wouldn't disguise her at all. A red velvet Viennese mask topped by a fountain of scarlet feathers (the better to hide behind) nestled in my bag.

A tall smart-ish man stood by his large silver car, which I vaguely registered as German and expensive. I caught him appreciating the efforts we had put into our outfits. He was momentarily embarrassed to be spotted leering, but had the rare good sense to smile it away. Lotte in full battle dress looked a decade younger than her 39 years. She gave a gravel-scrunching twirl in her heels. I imagined I heard a nauseated harrumph from behind us as Lotte's front door banged shut.

'Nothing to stow?' asked the driver.

'Stow?'

'Bags? Cargo?'

'It's not a cruise,' squealed Lotte, walking up to him. 'We're your cargo.' She cupped his chin, 'And you are?'

'Brandon,' he seemed conflicted; calculating how much he'd endanger his tip if he pulled away; how much he'd imperil his morals if he didn't.

'Mm-mm and what lottery did we win you in?' Lotte let him go and whisked a creased invite from beneath one lace sleeve. Had it sprung from her cleavage, I thought, Brandon would have melted away into the warm evening air.

'The Uber lottery.'

Lotte laughed, 'Your mission is to ferry us to this address in Cambridge, and ensure that someone from your crew is around to bring us back safely, Bran, no matter how well lubricated we appear.'

Brandon studied the address on the scrap of invite.

'Do you know it?' asked Lotte.

'We have this thing called Sat-Nav.' He rubbed his chin, imagining goodness knows what, but it awaited us at the address he held between finger and thumb.

'Witt-y boy.'

* * *

Cambridge City centre is 25 to 50 minutes away from our village, depending on traffic. Tonight, it was light and the venue was on our side of the city. We would arrive too early. Lotte enticed Brandon with a drink and a bigger tip if he would detour to a gastro pub in a village on the city outskirts and chaperone us while we indulged in a quick sharpener. The bar was busy, but we didn't cause as much of a stir as I feared. Lotte fished her purse out of my bag, and packed Brandon off to the bar with a £20 note while we chatted.

'It's got to be weird going to this kind of party when your ex-husband's there.' I said. I wouldn't have wanted Boy lurking in disguise, watching me cavorting around a little too desperately in an indecently short red dress.

'Why?' returned Lotte, 'I'm grown-up and Shouty's getting there. He relayed our invites don't forget.'

'Suppose you don't recognise him in his mask. Ye gods, suppose I end up snogging him.'

Lotte was momentarily thrown by this image. 'You have spent the last three years complaining that there's no-one out there for you, Sho,' she said. 'Shouty's quite the catch – MPSD, don't forget.'

I stared, uncomprehending.

'If you have to ask, you can't afford him.' Lotte's comeback was polished by use.

I had to ask. It stood for: Minor Public School Darling.

I stopped myself from saying I wasn't yet sad enough to start picking up Lotte's cast-offs – there was a goodly selection – and changed the subject to Lotte's sales team.

'How's what's-her-name doing at work now?'

It was safer territory with Brandon around.

'The what's-her-name who can sell, or the one who can't?'

'The one you want rid of.'

'Ah, prudish Penelope' (Lotte didn't pronounce the final 'e'). 'As useless as ever. We had a set-to this week. She claims her sales are below par because she won't wear heels, skirts and a come-hither smile.'

'It's good that she's got principles,' I provoked, as Brandon jinked his way back with a tray of drinks. He'd bought a non-alcoholic beer for himself. I approved.

'Lenecia and I have principles too,' insisted Lotte. 'There's a line, we draw it, but behind that line we're well presented, smiling, captivating and utterly professional. Both of us are pulverising our targets too.'

'What do you reckon, Bran?' I asked. 'Should pretty girls smile at customers to get on?'

'I'm relentlessly charming.' He held out some change to Lotte who shook her head and tossed her purse back in my bag.

'It's all part of the job and I need the tips.' He pocketed the change.

'Ever turned a ride into a ride, then?' Lotte nudged me.

'Only twice,' said Brandon, after a telling hesitation, shifting on his bar stool.

'You do need the tips,' laughed Lotte.

'Lotte, you're embarrassing the laddie,' I scolded lightly. I could see Brandon hadn't known how to take her comment. He was older than I'd initially thought; probably late 20s; tall with dark tousled hair and long slender hands ravaged by a ruinous nail-biting habit – as if a Perspex drawing pin had been hammered into the back of each fingertip.

'I'd put him in my sales team,' Lotte tapped Brandon's knee as a peace offering. 'But the board won't let me sack Penelop. They go on about the "post-Weinstein climate". My conscience is clear; I've never told her to wear heels or skirts; just get sales. People don't buy from people with a face like a wet weekend; they buy from people they get on with.'

* * *

We rocked up at the large house detailed on the invite two drinks later. A brief negotiation over our leaving time ended with my insistence there was a car outside by midnight. Brandon logged my mobile number and said whoever picked us up would text when they arrived.

'Three Proseccos at least', Lotte calculated. She used a variable measure of how many drinks she'd need before she found a man desirable, while crises were measured on The Gin Scale.

'He's sweet on you.' I delicately removed my mask from my bag.

'I reckon he fancies his chances more with you,' she said, manoeuvring her mask over her piled-up raven hair. 'We'd better get another drink in you, in case Bran picks us up.'

'I don't need three drinks to realise a man is attractive enough,' I responded primly.

'No,' said Lotte, 'you need three drinks to realise you are attractive enough.'

She rearranged her modest cleavage to maximum effect and tottered up the steps. She took an exaggerated breath. 'Tits to the fore! Tonight, Shona, my darling, you are not leaving unless you've pulled, but –' she looked me up and down, adjusted my mask slightly, twisted me from side to side so my clingy dress flared. She nodded approvingly.

'Hope you've got a hammer in that sack thing? You'll need it. You'll be fighting them off tonight, girl.'

She was right – in the worse possible way – but there wasn't enough own-brand gin in Waitrose to measure the crisis that awaited me behind that door.

❋ ❋ ❋

It opened to reveal a tall man in a crimson high-waisted velvet jacket. His nose, jaw and forehead were concealed by a Phantom of the Opera mask. It didn't disguise his leer.

'Lotte and Sho,' announced Lotte. 'Primed and ready for any-thing.'

'You'll do wonderfully,' Phantom drooled, bowing us in.

A companion in a ruffled white shirt and Day of the Dead half-mask manoeuvred two tall glasses in one hand. Fizz arced into them.

I glanced around. People clung to walls, the party was still to take off. Women were in a minority.

The Phantom peeled Lotte away from my side. A pair of revellers corralled me. One hid behind a spiky black bird mask, the other sported an elaborate Venetian affair in black, white and gold. It covered three-quarters of his head and a neatly trimmed brown beard jutted out beneath. Either could have been Shouty.

Soon the house was buzzing. Music blared. My companions were replaced. I barely saw Lotte, except once. She asked for my bag, probably to reclaim her purse. As she handed my bag back, she whispered something in my ear. I couldn't hear but it sounded salacious. She departed, glass in her hand, a raucous laugh in her throat.

Bolstered by nervous drinking, I chatted to anyone and everyone, little worrying if they were kindred spirits, let alone my next life partner. A short man with foxy headgear and busy hands scuffled close. A horny crimson devil with a generous supply of passable red wine moved him on. A barely disguised academic pinned me by a drinks table determined to wow me with his wit and intellect. I couldn't hear a word he said.

A tall man appeared at my side, pushing a glass of red at me. A cheap plastic cloak, Zorro hat and full-face plastic mask demonstrated minimal wardrobe effort. Still, his wine plumbed deep hints of rustic peasantry with stirring notes of Spar special shelf. I nick-named him 'Asda Man'.

Lotte had disappeared with the Phantom host. I was several drinks to the good and not short of wolfish company and then...

... and then I woke up in a strange, barely lit, bedroom. I was alone, apart from a collection of coats, a burgeoning headache, and the vaguest impression that someone had just left my side. There was no memory of how I'd got there.

I groaned, struggling to sit up, likely to throw up? The only light was cast by a retro lava lamp. My hair bunched painfully. Investigating fingers found my mask askew, hoisted up over my forehead. To my horror I found the top of my slinky dress down around my waist, while one red bra strap had escaped its shoulder.

Someone knocked on the door and giggled. I hurriedly tugged my mask back down, frantic not to be recognised in this compromising position. As the bra-strap was swept back over my shoulder, I caught my left bicep and swore – it was unaccountably tender. I hauled the top half of my dress back into place.

A masked male head pushed around the door, 'Are you going to be long?' it asked and disappeared before I could muster words. A woman cackled.

Rational thought was impeded by a fog of disorientation. I knew I hadn't been raped. Checking down below confirmed the assault's limits: pants, in place; tights, undisturbed. No man living could have got my tights down and back up without me knowing.

That I couldn't be sure of the level of intimacy I'd been involved in, curdled my mind, that I couldn't recall my complicity in it, terrified me.

My bag lay sprawled on a coat on the bed. I hauled it up by

one strap. More of its contents spilt out, joining others already on the bed. I scrabbled a pack of tissues and a hairbrush back into the bag. A tiny pristine notebook, which went everywhere with me, followed suit. A rubber-banded pack of dog-eared business cards, which I had long since given up using, made a break for the far side of the bed – two had escaped the band. I urgently retrieved a slim torch.

My overloaded make-up bag was further away and slightly open. I panicked and felt inside for its hidden zip. It opened to reveal a credit and debit card still in place. My battered phone was still at the bottom of the bag. I'd been semi-ravished, possibly assaulted but not robbed. My automatic relief at this, evaporated to be replaced with a surety that I'd rather it had been the other way around. Make-up items were hastily re-packed. I felt over the bed and coats to ensure I had everything. The final escapee, a plumy-crimson John Lewis lipstick, was located and bagged.

I stood up, immediately wobbled and slumped back down. One heel was on and the other off. In the half-light I saw it close to the door, but had to sit for a moment while my head lectured me on the impossibility of vertical as a viable state. The vastness between the bed and the door taunted me. I forced balled knuckles into damp eyes but only encountered sequins and feathers.

'Hurry up,' urged a male voice from outside. 'We're losing the moment here.'

I pushed off from the bed, made the near-irreparable mistake of trying to scoop up my shoe on the way to the door, lost balance and careered into it. A howl came from the other side, followed by an explosion of cackles. I yanked the door hard to dislodge a chair that had half-fallen against it, and rushed, confused and embarrassed, outside. I didn't glance at the amused couple, lustful and eager to take over the room.

* * *

I hunted high and low. No sign of Lotte or Asda Man, although I was far from certain he'd been involved. I did find the man in the Day of the Dead cossie on the stairs, chatting to a woman. She appeared to have dressed as a cross between the blue Teletubby and a highway woman. I seriously doubted she could stand, let alone deliver, but didn't feel ready to lecture anyone. Her legs resembled Tinkie Winkie's in his later years, but Day of the Dead was beyond caring.

I asked him if he had seen my friend in the black lace dress. He pointed to a room at the far end of the landing. He just wanted me gone. I went to knock. A couple on the wall told me they had 'bagsied' that room next. I knocked again; no answer. I tried the handle; locked. I called Lotte's name; first quietly, then loudly, finally tearfully. The couple left, their desire trumped by my wretchedness. Still nothing. I tried Lotte's phone, but she wasn't picking up. It confirmed my suspicion that she'd left it at home. I slumped down. Party-goers took one look and moved along.

I don't know how long I had been sitting there before I received the 'Flower of Scotland' burble. A text said my car was outside. It couldn't wait long. I called for Lotte one last time, then left.

A Prius, silver naturally, waited. Its yawning driver gazed laconically towards the house. I negotiated the steps and a carousing couple with exaggerated care and begged to be taken home. The driver woke me at my village outskirts. I credit-carded him with a tip for his flagrant disinterest. I made it safely inside without removing my mask.

'Bruise Night' still hadn't finished with me, though. I groggily put the kettle on, wrenched off the mask, gingerly prodded at my afflicted arm and went upstairs with a plan to shower and be sick, ideally not in that order.

The final shock of a traumatic Saturday night awaited me in my bathroom. As the light flicked on, I caught sight of myself in the mirror. A word had been scrawled in lipstick – my plumy-crimson lipstick it turned out – across my forehead. I didn't feel any inclination to admire the subtle pigmentation, sheer coverage and glossy finish, and hope John Lewis aren't anticipating a testimonial, but the letters in the mirror were clear and legible:

ЯƎʞↃUƧ

I spelt it out: 'R. E. K. C. U. S'.

REKCUS that I had driven Boy away and into the youthful arms of Candi.

REKCUS that I had wrapped myself up so tightly in work and parenting that – three years on from that rift – I still had no new relationship to show for my time at the online dating coalface.

REKCUS that the only date to have laid hands on me since Boy, seemed to have found me on 'Murderous Matches'.

And I'd let him get to second base!

2 LINDI

April 2018

A phalanx of reception desks waited beyond the three sets of double doors. A colony of receptionists, or – more likely – educational administrative executives, clucked and crowed to each other. Idle conversation was off-limits at Lindi's factoring office. She'd had to beg time off to answer the school's summons.

The women's chatter ceased as the doors swung back behind Lindi. Heads bobbed up, flicked towards her, faces made solemn. They're expecting me, thought Lindi. It is serious.

'Ms Sandbrook called me to come in,' she approached the desks.

'Yes, she's waiting for you in her office, Mrs Khan,' said one of the receptionists.

'It's Mills,' said Lindi.

'Mrs Mills?' the reception party exchanged rattled glances.

'Ms Mills,' said Lindi.

'You're Ashal Khan's mother?'

'Ash's mother, yes.' Lindi tired of the game. 'Please, Ms Sandbrook said it was urgent, just point me to her office.'

The short empty corridor registered few life-signs from the student body: a bloom of variable art on crinkly paper pegged to wires, a distant hum of hive voices and a stale polish scent infused with over-groomed, under-washed adolescence.

Ash slouched, resolutely aslant, in one of the upright chairs outside Ms Sandbrook's office. The polished student, delivered by Lindi's car that morning, had corroded, something tribal bubbling through. The school secretary greeted Lindi and asked her to wait. The headmistress would be informed.

'I know you're not hurt, Ash,' said Lindi. 'What's it about?'

'Nothing, mum. Waste of everyone's time.'

The secretary returned. Ms Sandbrook was still with the Government people. She would see Lindi shortly. The secretary departed, ostensibly to get Lindi a tea, more likely to avoid awkward chit-chat.

'Government people?' Lindi rounded on her son.

'From some anti-Muslim agency or other,' said Ash.

'Anti-Muslim? You're not Muslim. Please, Ash, I need to know.'

'I don't know who they are.' Ash was irritated, not yet worried. 'I had an argument with one of the guys in class.'

'Argument? A fight?'

'No.' Ash straightened in indignation. He had never been the kind of pupil to get into fights. 'If I'd been in a fight, it would all be sorted by now. There's ten of those every day. I had some verbals with a wanker called Ratcliffe. He said something spectacularly racist, as usual. For once, I had a go back, he reported it, then all this –' a dismissive hand jerked upwards.

The Headmistress's face poked around the door. 'We're ready for you now, Mrs Mills,'

Lindi didn't bother to correct her. Both she and Ash rose.

'Not you, for now, Ash,' said the Head. 'Just your mother.' She waited for Lindi at the door, 'Thanks for coming in. I know you had reservations about time off work.'

'New job,' said Lindi. They had first met in A&E after Ash had fractured his arm in a gymnasium accident two years ago. The school expected Lindi to sue. She didn't. They caught up at parent evenings. Lindi was impressed by both Ms Sandbrook and her Ofsted-ratings, 'an inspirational leader', responsible for the school's 'can do culture'. Ash was viewed as an asset, a straight 'A' asset. He would burnish the school's record at his forthcoming GCSEs.

The large office teetered towards the opulent, its heavy desk centre stage. Lindi was led towards a functional plastic chair borrowed from outside. She imagined ancient chewing gum welded beneath its seat rim. It was perched at the end of the desk. She was cast in the role of 'naughty pupil', here to be lectured.

Across from the Head, two plush visitor chairs were already occupied. A man in his late 30s in a sleek suit, blue, slim-cut, beyond most Luton budgets, gave the barest nod. Lindi was a necessary part of this process, but not an important one. A younger woman in the season's belted trouser suit offered an unsought uncertain smile. Neither got up. Lindi became overly conscious of her own outlet jacket – last season's clearance three years ago – and her workaday dark skirt. She felt drab and out-gunned and wished she'd washed her hair.

'This lady and gentleman are co-ordinators from a specialist government initiative that supports schools in dealing with possible ideological issues.' The Head's wording was careful. Lindi was immediately reading between the lines. 'It just so happened that they were already here today, presenting to staff. I asked them for advice after Ash became involved in an incident.'

'I see.' She didn't.

After fuller introductions, Lindi gleaned that one of the pair doubled as a police officer; she was unsure which.

The man turned towards her. 'I understand you're bringing up your son alone?'

'That's right.'

'Where is Ashal's father?'

'My husband, Ayan, had to return to Pakistan.'

The pair's glance was more disquieting for their efforts to disguise it. 'Is he politically active?'

'No… well, yes, in a way.'

'I see. Is Ashal involved on social media?'

'Not especially.'

'So, more inclined to follow others then?'

'Why am I here? What's Ash done?'

The man rushed to explain. Practised phrases welled out from some ingested pamphlet of scrupulous, committee-approved wording: '…rise of extremist voices… set up by the Government… preventing people being drawn into terrorism… protect students from radicalising influences…'

Lindi concluded the reason she had been persuaded from work was to appreciate how serious and far-reaching this process was, how inexorably it would grind forward from here.

She interrupted at the first opportunity. 'What was this incident?'

'We're getting to that.' His pause underlined the gravity. 'Another pupil reported to school staff that Ashal threatened to put his name on an Isis death list.'

'And you believed him?' Lindi asked evenly, turning from the co-ordinating pair to the Head.

'It's not relevant whether I believe him, Mrs Mills,' said the Head. It had been 'Lindi' last time the two had chatted to discuss Ash's A-level choices. 'We're tasked with reporting any incident of this nature to the authorities. We have a statutory duty' – she dusted the words with her discomfort at the obligation – 'to do so as soon as it is brought to our attention. We aren't given any leeway.'

'We have the specialist training required to address these problems,' said the man. 'That's why we're here. We're part of a four-pronged –'

'What does Ash say?'

'He denies those were his words,' put in the Head.

'So, it's one boy's word against another,' said Lindi. 'Or are there other witnesses.'

'None have come forward and I haven't asked for any,' said the Head.

'Why isn't this other boy in the room outside?' asked Lindi.

'No one is suggesting the second boy said anything to lead us to believe he is being radicali -'

'I am. I'm suggesting he said something radical that initiated your incident. That seems as much of an allegation as has been levelled at Ash.'

'We're not about to discuss another pupil with you. Our attention is focussed on Ashal,' said the man. 'You don't seem to be taking it very seriously consi –'

'I have left my workplace under duress and driven across town to be here. Believe me; I am taking this situation extremely seriously.'

The man wrestled his frustration at being interrupted. 'It's our job to investigate –'

'Support,' the younger woman took over from her co-coordinator. Lindi reassessed the pecking order. 'Support, not investigate. We're here to offer our help. Any assistance our expertise provides, to you and Ashal.'

'It's Ash.' Lindi was more inclined to believe the man's explanation of their role. 'He hasn't been Ashal for years.'

'My mistake.' The woman pushed at papers in her lap. 'But I still hope you'll both accept our support.'

'I won't thank you,' said Lindi. 'Doing so would mean I accept your willingness to demonise my son.'

'Ha-hardly 'demonise!' said the man with an unconvincing half laugh. 'The question is, could Asha... your son be at risk of radicalisation? Should we be taking steps to safeguard him?'

'That isn't the question.'

'What?'

'The question is why have you focussed on one boy when two were involved in the incident? The answer is because you're pre-conditioned to look at general statistics, not investigate specific facts.'

The man simmered with indignation, allowing Lindi time to add, 'I don't blame you; your job is much easier if you define situations as simply black or white. It's just, in this case, it's led you to the wrong conclusion.'

'Which is?' asked the woman.

'That if two boys have words about the Middle East, it's always the one with a Muslim surname who's the danger to society.'

* * *

Lindi warmed the second half of last night's Thai. A heap of official reading matter had jostled around on the back seat of her car as she and Ash argued their way home – the residue of the meeting. It now littered the lounge table. It wore the labels 'Prevent, Prepare, Pursue and Protect' on it. Lindi noted The Home Office had paid as much attention to alliteration as policy.

Ash refused to accept the situation was serious. The more vehemently he rubbished the incident and the backlash it had provoked, the more Lindi knew he had said something provocative and careless; that he regretted his words.

When Ash had later been invited into the Head's meeting, no one had asked what he'd said to Ratcliffe. He was quizzed about which mosque he attended. What websites he looked at. Whether he and his father were of Sunni or Shia faith. He refused to answer half their questions, others he didn't understand. Lindi wished he would say, 'I don't', 'I don't know'.

Instead, Ash retaliated, 'Talk about an over-reaction. This is worthy of a third-world dictatorship.'

Lindi felt momentarily proud of her son, then she caught the Head's eyes raised to heaven and realised Ash had dug himself in deeper than the Head could pull him out. Lindi hadn't taken a backwards step in the meeting either. It was where Ash got his guiding principles from. Too late Lindi grasped that – regardless of the rights and wrongs – only humble pie would satisfy the well-meaning but well-clawed bureaucratic monster Ash had awoken.

Ash disappeared to the upstairs of their tiny semi as soon as they were home. Lindi knew he would be Googling the hell out of the monster's track record and powers. Ash's response to a challenge was to arm himself with every shred of information he could. It wasn't much different from Lindi's own inclination.

'There's a stunning irony here,' Ash had slipped into the room. She knew he was seething that he hadn't had a chance to explain himself, to admit or deny guilt. The anti-radicalisation pair's questions were about form-checking, not establishing the facts.

Their comments on the process were euphemistic. It would keep him on the right path, they said. Hook him back from the extreme edge, they meant. It was voluntary, they said. He'd be on a watch list if he refused, Lindi heard.

'They believe I've been radicalised,' Ash continued. 'They're convinced I'm a practising Muslim, yet first stop on their programme is a meeting with an Imam.'

'You've brought this on yourself, Ash. I don't know what you said…' she left it there, not adding, but we both know you said something.

'It's that twat Ratcliffe, Mum. He's pathetic, no friends, no brains. "Paki this", "Jihadi that". I usually ignore him. The one time I have a go back…'

'Ash, you'll be the death of me.' Lindi served up dinner in their living room. They ate on their laps. She flicked on the TV – news reports of Taliban bombs in Afghanistan – it went off.

'If we fight this, Ash, it will just drag on. The reality is that the sooner we say fine, accept their programme, go through the motions and emerge with a signed certificate saying: "cured of extremism", the sooner they can pat themselves on the back and add you to the stats proving their prevention policy works.'

'It doesn't work. Or, no-one can prove it does.'

'Only then your life will return to normal.'

'Mum, you know it's crap, don't you?'

She tapped his arm, 'I know you, Ash. I know you didn't mean anything by it.'

'Good to know, but I meant their policy and operation is crap. According to what I've read, 80% of the referrals they investigate are bogus. Human Rights lawyers say it's policing thought-crime, like in 1984.'

'Go through a few of their hoops. What harm can it do?'

'But I didn't do anything.'

'It's not me you have to convince.'

*　*　*

After dinner Ash returned to the holistic teenage world of bedroom, phone and laptop. Lindi gingerly stirred the literature occupying her coffee table.

She opened a pamphlet. Passages on 'religious ideology', 'allegiance to British values', 'the counter radicalisation process', blurred before her. None of it relevant to Ash.

Her fingers lingered over a photograph. It showed a girl in a burka holding a gun and staring out across sand dunes and a ruined city. The article was about a mother. She had been oblivious to her daughter's involvement in extremist politics. The girl went missing. Next, the mother learned that her only child had caught a plane to Turkey. A smaller smudgy picture showed a girl close to the border with northern Syria. Names had been changed, models used. The article felt typical, more than actual.

Ash wasn't a practising Muslim, nor was his father, but, like his dad, Ash was becoming distant from her.

Ash was only upstairs, but his phone and computer meant he could be a world away. She tried to limit his time on them, but they represented his social life, his hobby, his educational homework portal, his revision tools.

Ash's life was on screens. She wasn't part of it. Until their move to Luton, they had always been close. That was no longer true.

She tossed the missing girl's story back on the pile.

How well did she know her son?

** 2002 **

Lindi escaped from South Yorkshire to London to study mathematics. She planned to teach the subject.

Ayan was unearthed in a nightclub, at the end of her first year at uni. She was barely 19. She, and a handful of university girl-friends were reeled-in at a club by a group of men. Lindi assumed they were City or advertising types. They were brash, expensively-suited and presumptuously eager to put the girls' drinks on their lengthening tab. The club wasn't outrageously pricey, nobody was drinking champagne, but the drinks fell beyond a student budget. The girls had gambled on finding male benefactors inside.

The men were in their late 20s. They were all white apart from one, the least attractive or insistent of them was a plump, darker-skinned, bearded man. Lindi found herself entertaining him at the bar while his friends danced with her friends and drank to excess.

Ayan turned out to be better company than she expected. He was unceasingly cheerful, self-deprecating and confidently spurred the conversation forward. Smartly dressed – not showy – Ayan was merry on the drink but didn't share his friends' mission to get shit-faced. He didn't press drink on Lindi. In her experience 'get them blatted' filled the first three chapters in the male dating strategy book. When Lindi said 'no more' she meant it. It usually took an age to convince impoverished amorous students of this fact, let alone wealthy businessmen.

The four other men peppered their conversation with their careers, their things, their influence, their affluence. A hunger to impress so deep-rooted it no longer required conscious effort. Ayan, in contrast, treated conversation as a joint enterprise, interested in teasing out her stories, smoothly embroidering them with his own.

There was something old-fashioned and chivalrous about him. She badgered him to say what he did job-wise.

'I'm the one-and-only UK agent for a massive Pakistani paint corporation,' he laughingly told her. 'I don't have a company car, not even an office.'

'What?'

'I'm pretty sure I haven't been trusted with a company phone, nor do I have a single client that I'm aware of, 'though it's been a while since I checked.'

Lindi had never heard of the company.

'I'm not surprised. It doesn't do business in the UK. It only employed me because my mother insisted.'

Drink and laughter exploded out of Lindi. Ayan flourished an immaculate hankie. Lindi mopped, then stopped and read out two initials, on its corner, 'AK'?

'Ayan Khan; AK – like the machine gun,' Ayan rattled off a laugh.

His mother had made Ayan's employment part of the deal when she sold off his father's paint factory, he said. Brought up in Karachi, Pakistan's most populous city, Ayan had also been schooled in the UK. These friends had been fellow students at Oxford.

At the end of the evening, Ayan asked for her number and she gave it. He intrigued but wasn't date material. Some of her friends were picked up by the men they had danced with. The only thing Ayan picked up, was the bill.

3 SHONA

Wednesday morning May 22 2019

My mind stalled, clutching at explanations for the anonymous text. Tuesday night's lab work took a back seat – didn't stop it nagging. Before my official finishing time I tracked down Leroy. He agreed to keep an eye on me as I scampered to my car.

A lethargic student in his early 20s, Leroy security guarded to stay on top of university fees. We had exchanged 'Hey's for the first time on my night shift a month previously. His agency specialised in guards that I summarised as 'cheap, creep and asleep'. Leroy ticked two of these boxes, but creeped me out less than his more disturbing predecessors. He didn't hang near my desk trying to impress me with his lack of small talk, he didn't have a manic stare that put aquaria inhabitants off their food, and he did have an IQ higher than most things in the tanks – with the possible exception of Gone Puss.

Leroy yawned as I correctly identified my car – the only one in the dimly lit lab car-park. He resisted the temptation to rib me for being scared of the dark. Something in my expression said, 'don't mess with this woman; she's too close to the edge and has probably been sniffing tank-cleaning chemicals.'

Two new work rules were drawn-up as I sprinted to my car:

1. park closer to the lab;

2. stay away from sinister shrubs.

I drove home as if Tam o' Shanter's hellish legion was suckling at my exhaust fumes. My early departure and record-setting drive home led me to spook Caitlyn. She scrambled around guiltily when my key turned in the door 15 minutes ahead of time. I concluded that she had been transgressing one of the three rules set down by her father, Hugo, when he gave permission for her to baby-sit on school nights:

1. no boys,

2. no binging,

3. and no practising any games at which he could still beat her.

'Isn't that a bit restrictive, Hugo?' I'd enquired.

'Hardly,' he replied, 'she beats me at everything but FIFA.'

I acquiesced; sometimes female emancipation comes second to child-sitting demands. I ignored the hastily re-assembled cushions, Caitlyn's red face and breathless, 'Oh hi, Ms Patterson', and rushed upstairs to check on Harry. He was safe asleep.

A quick glance around revealed no sign of murderers. Neither could I spot any hidden youths, chocolate wrappers or evidence of undue FIFA activity. I paid Caitlyn, watched apprehensively as her tiny torch surveyed the narrow paving on the 120-odd metres up the lane to her home, waved her safely in, double-locked everything and breathed out.

Sleep had changed its shift patterns since the party on Saturday night. The wee hours of Wednesday morning barely featured on its new roster. When, finally, sleep came, it drenched me in incoherent dreams. Wakeful periods left me entangled in the logic that:

taunting text + identical bruise = warning.

No innocent ways you could end up headless offered themselves. Inevitably, every theory led back to one question – whether I had been unconscious in a bedroom with a murderer on Saturday night? Sound sleep only clocked-on 40 minutes before the alarm clock insensitively stuck to its regime. I finally roused myself to bundle Harry into the car (we had missed the school bus) and drove him to big school in nearby Arlston. Harry deposited, I called Lotte.

I hadn't heard from her since 'Bruise Night'.

She hadn't returned home on the morning after the hateful party. Rising on that Sunday, I had kept myself busy – too busy to check on my tender arm. I wanted the previous night's events scrubbed from my mind just as all evidence of party graffiti had been scoured from my forehead. I hadn't been in any state to drive to Lotte's house. The walk was only ten minutes.

The door was opened by Ollie's sour-faced aunt. She was apparently expecting someone else – someone she was going to have a ruck with – Lotte.

'Where's your partner in crime?' she asked. The word 'crime' came after she had dismissed other more accurate terms. 'She was supposed to be back late last night. She's not phoned. It's really inconsiderate.'

'Sorry,' I said, 'I came home earlier than Lotte wanted to. She must have stayed in Cambridge. I think Shouty was at the party, perhaps...'

The aunt's eyebrows twitched at the mention of Shouty, who I assumed must be her brother. 'Oh crap, I do hope not. Lotte's not still hankering after Scott, is she? The poor woman really has to move on.'

This sounded to me like a serious misreading of the dynamics of Lotte's relationship with her ex-husband, but I got out my phone.

'Put it away. Lotte won't have risen yet if she was partying hard last night. Well done, you, on having better discipline.'

'Hardly!' I had forsaken my friend, condemning her to an awkward night in Cambridge. 'Actually,' I said, 'I don't think she had her phone with her last night. I can look after Ollie, if you have to be somewhere. He and Harry are both at footy this morning.'

'Thank you...?'

'Shona,' I filled in. Harry and Ollie joined us, tousled from the sleep-over.

'...Shona, but I'm staying for lunch anyway. It's just I'd be happier knowing where Lotte was and what time to expect her. I'll take Oliver to the game.'

And she did. I didn't chat to her much, because I'm Harry's team's coach. I have to spend my time bawling encouragement, reminding eleven budding Messis that not everyone can play on the wing, bringing my culinary talents to the half-time oranges, shooing excitable parents off the pitch and ensuring that my False Libero© formation is being faithfully executed.

When I brought Ollie on in the second half, I did smile enquiringly at his aunt, who glanced at her phone and shook her head.

She collected Ollie at the end of the game, a narrow 2-3 defeat brought about by a ridiculous penalty decision and the ref ignoring a nailed-on red card tackle.

'Are you worried?' I asked. 'Can I do anything?'

'No,' she smiled. 'Thanks anyway. Her phone's still off. It's what I'd expect. If she's stayed round Scott's, she'll creep in late tonight after their inevitable argument. I'll call him again when we get back to the house. Well done out there by the way. Good game.'

'Mad penalty,' I confided. We were out of earshot of the ref. 'That's what cost us.'

'Oh, I didn't see it.' She had come over all José Mourinho. 'Didn't we win?'

* * *

Still no word the next day either. I'd tried Lotte's mobile on Monday and slipped a 'call me' note into her letterbox. No response. I concluded she was blaming me – quite reasonably –

for forsaking her in Cambridge, phoneless, with only a skimpy frock and whatever she'd had in her skinny purse. I decided to let things lie.

But that was before the anonymous text. Now, I just needed to hear Lotte say, 'Sod off, Shona, you cow!' I rang but her phone was off. She could be in a work meeting. I left a 'let me know you're OK,' message and hung-up.

Her silence heightened my anxiety. My anger had been focussed by the ominous text. Someone had likely drugged me, definitely molested me, gratuitously 'Sucker'-ed me and – I now reasoned – bruised me to mimic a murdered woman. They had done their utmost to undermine what brittle confidence I retained three partner-less years after my split from Boy. It felt personal and it felt like a message.

I determined I had to identify my attacker and take them down. The text suggested he was linked to this murder. Surely that required the police to investigate. I drove to Linbourn, a town where I could picture a small anonymous police station. I parked nearby. It was closed. A red notice said I should travel to towns at least an hour's drive away. Modern policing clearly didn't budget for situations like mine.

I hoped the murderer wasn't closing in while I dithered.

In case he was, I used the nearby yellow police phone to report my presence, explain that I had been recently attacked, possibly by someone connected to an unsolved murder and tacked on my belief that I could be his next target. I figured I had to lay it on pretty thick. They'd have to prioritise me ahead of any Linbourn jay-walking activity. Stay there, they told me, and took down my name and number.

About 12 minutes later, still unmurdered, I saw a police car approach. Two uniformed officers got out. One confirmed my identity, while the other unlocked the police building before I was ushered inside. Introductions gave me their names: Sergeant Anthony something-French; and PC Joanna Angus. I remembered her surname because it was Scottish. She was bonnie, despite trying not to be.

'How long is it going to take?' the sergeant surveyed his watch.

'Twenty minutes, er... half an hour,' I stammered. 'If you have another murder you need to get to?'

They hadn't.

The PC left to put a kettle on. I was in a room with a bare table. It didn't resemble interview rooms I'd seen on TV, so much as Harry's bedroom after a sleepover. Apart from the table, every surface was crammed – books, bags, papers and files. Bins over-flowed with food wrappers. Dog-eared 'no comments' hung in the stale air.

Hard chairs were indicated, and the sergeant's phone put on the table to record my story. I felt nervous and about to be judged. After some turgid preliminaries ensuring my personal details were properly logged, the sergeant asked which murder I had information on.

'The woman found north of here who had her head and hands cut off. The murder was nearly three months ago.'

'The one the press labelled "The Doll Killer?"' Interest perked up. The PC started making notes.

'The one with the bruise. I can't remember the details. I was attacked on Saturday in Cambridge and received a bruise on my arm.' I pointed.

'OK.' Interest tangibly evaporated. 'Can we see?'

I showed them, already feeling that this was going embarrassingly wrong.

'It's not very clear,' said the PC.

'Almost nothing there,' added the sergeant.

'It's faded,' I admitted, 'but even now you can see the similarities to the bruise on the dead woman's arm; the one you asked for *any* information on.'

They exchanged uncertain looks. The PC pulled up something on her phone and they both studied it. The sergeant was unconvinced. The PC asked me to move my bruise into the light and took pictures of it.

'Who gave you the bruise?'

'I don't know, I'm afraid.'

'Where were you when you were attacked; Cambridge I think you said?'

'In a house. It was a party. I don't have the exact address with me, but I'll get it for you.'

'But you didn't know the man – I assume it was a man...?' he noticed my hesitant look and continued not unduly incredulously, '...or wo-man, who attacked you?'

'I was unconscious. I think I'd been drugged.'

'You know it's too late to test for that now?'

'Yes, I know; flunitrazepam doesn't stay in the system for more than 12 hours.'

'Flumiga-what?'

'Oh er, Rohypnol, I mean, the date-rape drug. It can sometimes be detected in urine for longer, but 72 hours at most. I looked it up.'

'Had you been drinking at the party?' asked the PC.

'Yes.'

'How many drinks?'

'A few,' I confessed, feeling thoroughly wanton, 'four... probably five.'

'Five?'

'Maybe six.'

'Beer?'

'Spirits, gin, and some wine.'

'Go on.'

I told them about waking up in the room; about the state of undress I was in; about the masks. I answered questions effectively confirming that I had no memory of how I had got to the room, no idea how long I had been unconscious, no notion of who might have been responsible, that there were no faces I could identify, that I didn't know the host, and that I hadn't mentioned the attack to anyone at the time.

'Not even your friend, who was there with you?'

'No, I had to go home without seeing her again. I left her there,' my voice caught. 'I've not seen her since.'

I told them about the word 'Sucker' having been revealed when I took off my mask. I noticed the look that passed between them and interpreted it as, 'yup!'

'When did you realise you had the bruise?'

'Not until Sunday night.'

'So, it was hardly painful?'

'I was aware my arm was really tender but it's a hard place for me to see and what with football, then tennis in the evening, I hadn't seen it. I examined it in the mirror in the changing room after tennis. I was wearing a shorter-sleeved shirt.'

'Did you show anyone?'

'Only Harry, my son, I think.' He'd seen it on the way home.

Harry had been playing tennis as a junior in the village for several years and occasionally with me on a friend's garden tennis court. Recently, I had taken him to play with the seniors. Harry is up for almost anything.

'And you first saw the bruise around what time on Sunday?' The sergeant dealt in details, dates, places.

'It hurt after tennis. I looked at it in the mirror, around 7.30pm. It was really dark and vivid.'

'Could you have picked up the bruise playing football?' asked the sergeant.

I told him, no, I only coached.

'Do you mind if my colleague recaps?'

PC Angus launched into it, barely referring to her notes. 'You don't know for sure when you got the bruise, but the party seems a good possibility. You can't tell us who was at the party or identify anyone apart from your friend, because they all wore masks. We'll have to come back to the address but west side of Cambridge. You can't remember going to the bedroom, or who with, but you have stated that sex seemed an expected ingredient of this party. It was about coupling up. You had a lot to drink, which has to be a consideration, and you weren't in a position (or state really) to report the attack immediately after you awoke.'

I had my wrists out ready to be cuffed by the time she put her notebook down. Damn it but their cunning questioning had been too much for me. It was hard to be sure who was 'good cop' and who was 'bad cop' but it was all too obvious who was 'not much cop'. I was all but ready to plead guilty to criminal time-wasting in the first degree.

'Looking at this purely from a prosecution point of view.' My attention was dragged back to the sergeant. 'It could be presented that you had too much to drink, became pliable, and were persuaded upstairs by a man or men...'

Oh god! Or men?

'...he was likely trying to seduce you as he considered this a party for swingers. He may have rough-handled you sufficiently to cause your bruise, but when you passed out, he gave up and left; or he may have been disturbed. There is nothing like enough evidence to convince us, let alone the public prosecutor, that your bruising is pertinent to a more serious crime. I think it was probably accidental.'

The sergeant had been playing with his spiky hair but now spread his hands in a 'that's that' gesture, sat back and stared me down.

'I would suggest you have had a narrow escape, Miss Patterson. You could have suffered a more serious sexual or physical assault; you could have been robbed. The person involved had the time and means to assault you. Had he been even an opportunist criminal he would have found and taken your phone and credit cards. I am sure that having a word scrawled on your forehead is genuinely upsetting, but it is not a crime.'

'Not even graffiti-with-menaces?' Why do I come out with this stuff?

The pair shared a smile. 'We'd have to prove the property damage came to over £2,500,' said the PC.

The sergeant moved to switch off his phone, but I had a card left to play; the Deuce of Texts.

'I agree with your summary.' I stayed his hand and put my own phone on the table next to his. 'Which is why I didn't report it at the time. I put it down to experience, but late last night, someone anonymously texted me. The text pointed out that my bruise was inflicted on the exact same spot as on the murder victim's arm and sent me a link to a report of that murder with a picture of the bruise.'

I displayed the text for them to see. PC Angus entered the TV broadcast link on her phone and they both watched it.

'It may be innocent,' I said, 'but it is, at very least, in awful taste and in the context of a murder investigation, I thought it was worth bringing to your attention.'

The sergeant nodded. 'You don't know this number?'

'It's not in my contacts and I've checked my phone book at home.'

'No follow-up calls?'

'No, but then I blocked it immediately.'

'There could still be an innocent explanation,' said the sergeant.

'Granted,' I said, 'but...'

'Go on.'

Everything had spun right around. It was testimony to my low spirits that I felt so good about low-ranking police officers believing I could be a murder target. I milked it. The last time I'd enjoyed this much rapt attention, was the village Under-12s half-time team-talk against Atletico Biggleswade. Although that, I recalled, had led to 'Shorts-gate'.

'Even if my bruise was identical to the murder victim's,' I continued, 'that murder was nearly three months ago. I vaguely remember the grisly decapitation headlines, but the police bruise appeal had completely passed me by. Whoever sent this text seems too interested and too knowledgeable.'

PC Angus picked up the baton. 'Whoever sent it had to know about your bruise and find out your phone number –'

'Yet not know me well enough to be on my contacts list.'

'Are you usually "Sho" or "Shona"?'

'Shona, I'm not keen on Sho, but...' something occurred to me. 'A handful of close friends do call me Sho, and Lotte is one of them. She'd probably have introduced me at the party as

Sho.'

'So,' the PC bit, 'the texter could have heard you being called "Sho" at the party.'

'If the text came from someone at the party...' I realised I had missed out on a career in policing; I was good at this stuff. 'It had to be the person who attacked me. I was wearing three-quarter length lacy sleeves; no-one would know I had the bruise, unless they inflicted it.'

'If it was the person that assaulted you,' the PC built on my theory, 'they would have been able to access your number when you were unconscious. We can run this phone number.'

The sergeant stood up. 'Please give us a moment.' He wanted to rein his colleague in. They left and shut the door. I sidled up to it and listened. They spoke quietly but it was a small police station.

'What do you think, Jo?'

'I think "five-to-six drinks" actually means ten-to-twelve.'

'Probably, but that doesn't explain the text.'

'It's got to be worth putting a name to the mobile, Sarge.'

'No, we should hand it over to the murder team.'

'That DCI from Derbyshire's running it; the one who's always on the telly. He'd eat her for breakfast.'

'Inspector Hossein.'

'Yeah, loves the sound of his own voice, but he's good... isn't he?' the PC sought confirmation.

'Comes across well on TV. Uses the media brilliantly I'd say, and I think he gets results. Let's call this in to his team.'

'I've never done a murder,' she sounded wistful.

'And if we screwed this up, you'd keep that proud record.'

'Come on, Ant. Suppose it's nothing. Shouldn't we at least –'

'Suppose she is the next target and he gets to her while we're checking things out. He's killed two already and serial killers don't usually stop.'

Had he said 'two'? I'd not really focused on that.

The voice suggested the sergeant was returning. 'Plus, she fits the target profile: white, slim, mid-30s.'

I was impressed by 'Ant'. The sergeant was clearly sharper than I'd realised; he knew I'd be listening.

'Miss Patterson,' said Sarge, on entering, 'I'd like to stress that this is most likely nothing to worry about, but I'm going to pass on everything you've told us to the murder inquiry team. If they want to follow up, I imagine you'll hear from them very quickly.'

We tidied up some details. I had remembered the name of the road the party was in and described the house's location. Sarge produced a card with his contact details on on. Policemen had business cards, who knew?

'In Merseyside these must be bizzies' cards,' I said. No-one laughed. 'Sorry, that was probably murder-inappropriate, it's just –'

'It's OK, I know,' Sarge said.

'Nerves,' I said.

He told me to call if I thought of anything else or noticed anything alarming. I imagine he meant a man with an axe hiding behind a bush.

A pouty PC Angus noted my movements for the day. She asked if I had another number as they would hang onto my phone. I asked why?

There was a pause before Sarge said, 'In case there are other things on there that may help.' He promised he'd get it back to me promptly. I gave them Harry's number. I'd pick up his phone from home, I thought.

I thought wrong.

4 LINDI

May 2018

Lindi cajoled, threatened and negotiated with Ash until he signed up for the anti-radicalisation programme. Within weeks she realised her mistake. The programme and Ash were incompatible.

Forced to take more time off work, Lindi agonised about what to put on Dafiyah's absence form. The consequences of her 'honesty first and last' policy starved her of sleep. Informing her department head (a Muslim) that Ash was on a list of potential extremists must scupper her six-month probation period.

Early on in Ash's prevention programme Lindi attended a meeting to determine Ash's Muslim influences. 'Not having any' didn't fit the tick-boxes. Lindi's protestations that Ash was not and never had been Muslim didn't impress the interviewers. She was effectively telling them, you're wasting your time, our time and tax-payers' money here. It wouldn't wash.

'Ash's not into religion,' she said. Ash had given up protesting or contributing at all. 'If anything, he's Christian. We at least celebrate Christmas, which is more than we do any Muslim holy days or festivals. His father wasn't a practising Muslim either, and he's been out of Ash's life since he was seven.'

'That's eight years. And he's been resident in Pakistan all that time?'

'Yes, in Karachi.'

'So how do you know he's not practising now?'

'Because I'm his wife. The only time we ever went into a mosque was for our wedding.'

They ticked something. Lindi suspected it was 'Father a practising Muslim.'

'Could you describe your friends, Ash?' His friendship group was small – four of them – all better than average academically, none of them sporty or social. Their religious beliefs had not been proffered.

Unless Lindi drove Ash, which she would happily but was rarely called upon, it was hard for him to see friends outside of school. That left his phone and computer. These were private spaces as far as Lindi was concerned. They had been for the last 18 months.

'What sites do you look at online, Ash?'

'Porn, mainly.'

Lindi couldn't catch her astonishment. Did she really know her son so little?

'Why did you say that, Ash?' she asked on the way home.

'That's what they'd think, anyhow.'

'They will now.'

'They'd be more suspicious if I'd said homework and school stuff.'

Ash was invited to visit a mosque with one of the prevention agency's local managers. It would include a tour and a private talk to an Imam. It was made clear that Lindi didn't need to attend. She was torn; thankful that she didn't have to invent more time-off excuses for Dafiyah – who was losing patience with them – anxious that Ash's growing contempt for the intervention process would cause offence and create waves.

She elicited what promises she could from him regarding his behaviour, checked his socks for holes and handed him over to the agency.

When she returned from work, Ash was already home. She

readied herself for a diatribe of complaints about what a waste of time it had been when he should have been revising. More concerning was the discovery that he had been engaged by the visit to the mosque.

'I should understand what goes on in them at some point,' he told her. 'The Imam was cool, not preachy, for which much relief. He asked what questions I had about the Muslim religion. I thought, "go for it" and asked all the ones they never feature on the news.'

'Such as?'

'What really went on in Syria? Why Muslims hate the west? Where Isis came from? All sorts.'

'And?' Lindi's internal warning bell seemed to be clanging from some Arabian minaret.

'Long story short: Syrians are mainly Sunni, so Assad's minority regime is propped up by Shia Iran. The rebels – Al Qaeda, Isis and the rest – are bank-rolled by the Saudis. The BBC gabbles on about "fake news" but in all their reports on Syria, have they ever mentioned that?'

'Did he offer any answers?' Lindi tried to keep the dismay out of her voice.

'He said the media's always looking for simple answers but there aren't any. If you think it's about religion, you're ignoring the region's politics. If you focus on the politics you're underestimating the religion. Find out for yourself, he said.'

'This doesn't sound like the agency programme. Did Mr Norton attend this session?'

'Yeah, he was there, with one of the cops, drinking tea with the worshippers, doing their community thing. But the Imam took me round on my own and I chatted to him one-to-one.' Ash saw something in her expression. 'Don't worry, Mum, he didn't convert me; but it was good to be treated like an ad...' he rethought the word, 'like someone with half a brain for a change and not have to skirt around real issues.'

'So, what do you believe now?'

'I don't know,' Ash said adding, after a moment's thought,

'not in god, anyway.'

** 2002 **

Ayan phoned, inviting Lindi to choose a time and venue for lunch. Taken by surprise, Lindi agreed. She'd taken a temporary summer job in London; her friends weren't around, and she was socially and financially constrained. She picked a place close to work. The bar was cheap (so she could go Dutch) and she wasn't drinking. Ayan moved uncomplainingly from beer to water with no reduction in his vivacity.

He was different from the men in Lindi's life, mainly students up to this point. He was rich for one thing, but you barely guess it from his dress or chat. He was childishly indifferent to his wealth. He was unstintingly generous, never ostentatious.

They had been going out as 'friends' for two months when he arranged a mid-afternoon rendezvous in a hotel off the Kings Road. On arrival he introduced her to his mother and eldest sister. They were waiting in the lounge, pouring tea, draped in armchairs surrounded by trophy shopping bags. Lindi couldn't see any obvious gaps in their collection.

The two women were over from Karachi and, Lindi was delighted to discover, she liked them both. They didn't conform to her narrow experience of Pakistani women – Sindhi shawls, cloaks and head-scarves glimpsed on trips into Rotherham and Barnsley, a handful of hard-working quiet girls on her degree course. For a start they were in smart western dress, bare-headed, paler skinned than Aran and spoke English without a discernible accent. Lindi was soon revealing details of her life without ever being aware how they had been drawn out.

Ayan's mother was called 'Ammi' by her children and Lindi was encouraged to do likewise. Ammi hadn't remarried after Ayan's father's death eight years ago. Both her children teased her about the number of suitors she attracted. Lindi could believe it; Ammi shared her son's slight plumpness but was a well-groomed and handsome woman.

Naasira was the eldest of three sisters. Lindi guessed

mid-30s. She hadn't married and was a successful lawyer in Karachi. 'One of the best-known lawyers in Pakistan,' Ayan boasted. Naasira practised family law and involved herself in high profile women's rights cases.

Lindi craved the approval of these intelligent and worldly women. She was surprised that she set such store by it. They were impressed with her choice of a maths degree, quizzed her on her plans to teach and mock-taunted Ayan about taking a lead from his new friend in the career stakes. Lindi sensed a gentle edge to this jokiness, but it was also clear that the two women cut Ayan plenty of slack.

After two rounds of tea, Ayan helped Naasira take the shopping swag up to their hotel rooms. It was a pre-planned tactic. Lindi had been out-manoeuvred. She prepared herself for an 'and what are your intentions towards my son?' conversation. It wasn't necessary.

'Ayan was 21 when his father died unexpectedly,' said Ammi, 'little older than you are now. He was over here at university at the time.'

'I lost my dad six years ago,' said Lindi.

'Ah, then you know that it rips out the spine of the family. Ayan is our eldest son. He stood to inherit everything: our big house in Karachi, the company, the financial assets of the family. It was a lot of responsibility for so young a man. You know him a little. How do you think he would cope?'

'He'd find it hard.'

'You are an honest young woman. Yes, it was too much. He came home immediately of course; as did my second-eldest, Rahana, who was studying in America. We spoke together as a family. He said he didn't want to take it on. I understood. I think we all expected it. We agreed that he would sign everything over to me.'

'He told me you'd taken charge of the company.'

'I see his decision as a sign of strength, not weakness. Most young men would have been too proud to ask their mother for help.' Ammi smiled. 'I don't know much about you, Lindi –'

'Ayan and I haven't known each other long. We're just friends.'

'... but I do know he's proud of you. Usually, I don't get to meet his girlfriends.'

'We're not really boyfriend and girlfriend.'

'I can tell, but perhaps one day you might be.' Ammi forestalled another qualification from Lindi. 'I just wanted to say that if that happens and you make each other happy, you will make me happy too. Ayan is nearly 30. He has made his life here for now and he needs some good people in that life. I think you are a good influence. His family love him very much. And we'll love anyone he loves and make them welcome.'

'This is too soon, Ammi.'

'I mean nothing by it,' said the matriarch. 'I just didn't want you to think we wouldn't approve, that's all.'

5 SHONA

Wednesday afternoon May 22 2019

Feeling weirdly satisfied with my morning's work, I drove home, grabbed a coffee and hunted for Harry's phone. After a cursory search, I concluded that he must have taken it into school – something both I and the school expressly forbid him to do but which, everyone knew, was pretty well inevitable. I daren't phone to check. If it was on, he'd get into trouble.

From my landline I called Helen, Harry's grandmother. My own dear mum had died of cancer when my brother Martin and I were in our late teens, but Helen picked up the slack.

Helen was a long-term widow and one of our nation's most qualified and decorated Grans. Since Boy was one of six children (and the last to sprog), Helen had already skilled-up on every Gran badge going long before Harry came into this world. She was in her late-80s but had never down-sized from the four-bedroom family home into which Boy had almost certainly been born 56 years ago. All her other grandchildren were already out in university, work, married life and whatever constituted the world these days, which meant Harry got oodles of unrestricted Helen time.

She had never taken sides when Boy and I split-up. My change in relationship status went uncommented on. Helen still treated me like the daughter-in-law I had never legally been.

When Boy had headed off to the land of the hog-nosed skunk and Magellanic tuco-tuco, he left me with a major headache. He had looked after Harry on the four nights a month I worked. Harry would decamp to 'Big House', as he still called it, to stay with his dad. I took satisfaction from the knowledge that it played havoc with Boy's workaholic life-style.

I needed another child-care solution. I was in no position to give up my job and desperate not to cause waves at work. I even took legal advice to see whether I could stop Boy from going. My need for Boy, I reasoned, was greater than any tuco-tuco's. Apparently, this didn't stack up as a legal argument.

We discussed it like adults, at least until Boy suggested that Candi could step into the breach – she could come down for four nights on those weeks to look after Harry, he said. After which I discussed it like a traumatised three-year-old whose favourite toy has just been broken. Clearly, with what I now knew about Candi joining him on his sabbatical, that idea would have had as much chance of flying as... well, as Candi, before she slimmed down.

My first week of nights coincided with both Boy's departure and Harry's half-term. I took it as holiday and whisked Harry away for a week's skiing. This had the added benefit of giving Harry something to fixate on other than his father deserting him for six months to spend quality time with ugly skunks.

It also meant we didn't have to live through the chaos that occurred whenever Boy thought he could scoot off anywhere with zero planning and expect things to go swimmingly. It typically involved me finding his passport on the morning of his flight and despatching extra sets of emergency underwear to various parts of the world, where they would turn up too late having aroused suspicion at customs.

All Candi's job now, I reminded myself. For the next night-shift week, I negotiated with Hugo to allow Caitlyn one late night with a promise that I'd be back before 12.30. For the rest I'd put upon Harry's friends' parents, grabbing a night here, two there. I had yet to organise anything for the rest of this week. Initially I had intended imposing on Lotte, but I shelved that notion.

Helen had volunteered to help with Harry's child care while Boy was away. I hadn't taken her up on it, as she was 40 minutes' drive away from the village and half an hour from Harry's school. I had checked last week whether she was still willing, and she assured me she was. I piled all Harry's survival essentials: X-Box, Captain America jim-jams, superhero-branded unhealthy cereal (an occasional treat), tooth-brush and expensive toothpaste to fend off deleterious effects of said cereal. Helen didn't do panic, but I felt I'd better drop round late morning to check if she needed any help. I'd take her out for a spot of lunch. I bought dinner for Harry and her on the way.

Helen and I dropped into a village pub for lunch. She quizzed me about work, Harry's football and schooling in that order. Having Harry for three nights would be fun she said. She offered to drive him back up to school the following morning. I'd get caught up with 'those dreadful commuting idiots on the A1', she said, whereas she'd be going against the flow and could shop in Arlston. I was nervous (she was in her 80s after all) but she had to drive everywhere as her village had few facilities and, so far, hadn't admitted to any accidents. I said, OK we'd try it. I'd drop Harry off around 4pm that afternoon but would have to scoot straight off to work after.

I asked her if she heard from Boy much and she said he phoned her once a week. I wanted to ask about Candi, but this was negated by the fact that I so didn't want to ask about Candi. I hoped Helen would volunteer something definitive about Boy having Candi with him. She didn't. She worried about him being out there with a load of 'Grouchos' for company – could have been a reference to Candi – but said he seemed to be having a 'fine' time. I sensed Helen had dialled down to 'fine' from such options as 'brilliant' or 'thrilling' out of respect for my feelings.

Family holidays with Boy just before our split, had been 'grumpy' and 'hurtful', but I imagined 'scintillating' was probably the right kind of word to describe expeditions with unencumbered Candi.

I took Helen home and stayed for a tea. We chatted about her children and many grandchildren. I didn't mention that I was involved in a police hunt for a serial killer who had likely attacked me, so left in good time to get to Harry's school before kicking-out time.

❊ ❊ ❊

On picking Harry up, I asked if he had his phone on him. He said it was at home, finally admitting that it was under his pillow. Why on earth is it there? was the question that formed in my head, but I knew the answer – midnight texting.

You're only 11, Harry; I wanted to say.

Nearly 12, Mum.

Please don't interrupt when I'm only thinking and not actually speaking, I thought. OK, so you're nearly 12 but I won't have you enjoying a more active social life than me after the hours of 11pm. Right?

But Mum...

Instead of voicing those thoughts I said, 'You and Helen can call up Dad while you're with her; she'd like that.'

'You haven't brought my phone,' he said. Like it was my fault!

Having dropped Harry off with Helen I raced back home; pulling into the top of my road at a creditable 4.35pm. As I passed Benedicts bar I noticed the afternoon crowd had spilled out on to the pavement opposite the church. Considering it was a working day and late in the afternoon, I was taken aback at how many people were there. My car sparked some interest. I saw Hugo and another neighbour chatting outside his house. They broke off talking as I drove past.

Some 200 metres on was the reason for the excitement. Two

cars were pulled up outside my cottage. One was a monstrous traffic police SUV with chequerboard yellow and blue markings and a set of lights atop it – thankfully not flashing. The other was a sleek dark blue BMW shoehorned on to my tiny drive.

The sight of the police car caused tremors of inexplicable guilt. Two uniformed policemen were leaning on it conversing with two suited men (almost certainly cops) standing by my cottage. I parked behind the BMW and got out.

The younger of the two plain-clothes policemen put away a phone he'd been checking and hailed me. 'Miss Patterson? Shona Patterson?'

I nodded.

'You're late,' he said.

'Sorry, I've been dropping my son off with his Gran,' I felt even guiltier. 'I didn't know you –'

'We've been trying your phone since late morning,' he said. 'We've left plenty of voice and text messages.'

'I'm sorry, my son's phone was –'

'Your timetable said you'd be back from your son's school at 3.40. These two gentlemen,' he pointed to the traffic cops, 'have been trying to track you down at the school and ascertain what had happened to you.'

Christ! Not content with making my neighbours wonder what crime syndicate I headed up, the school mums would now have me down as the Ms Big behind the great tuck-shop swindle.

'Well I'm here now,' I said.

The second, older, plains-clothes policeman lifted himself away from the side of his car. He was sharply suited in black with a thin black tie and grey shirt. A tightly trimmed moustache hugged his lip with an equally restrained beard mirroring it below. I hazarded it was 'anchor' style based on a beards-briefing Lotte had given me two weeks ago.

He removed one hand from his trouser pockets to peer ostentatiously at some techie watch. He called across to the traffic cops, 'You can go, guys. Thanks, and sorry to have called you away from your other duties.'

'We understand, sir,' said one of them with a nod to me. 'If you thought she was in danger, you can't take any chances.' They both turned back to their car.

'This is Detective Chief Inspector Hossein. I'm DS Grant.' The first detective flashed ID from an inside pocket. 'We're from the Derbyshire police. We'd like a word with you please, Miss Patterson. Inside would be best.'

As I nodded, I heard faltering steps behind me. A chubby man with a camera was running awkwardly down the slight hill towards us from the bar. 'Shona,' he shouted to me, although I'd never seen him before, 'Shona Patterson? Can you tell us why Mr Toakley has been arres –'

'No, she can't,' Grant was snappish. 'And if you take any pictures I'll book you for invading her privacy.'

The camera lowered but the man addressed the other policeman, 'What about you, DCI Hossein? Is this anything to do with The Doll Killer?'

Hossein ignored the question and walked around his car to the door in the centre of my cottage. He crossed his arms and leaned one shoulder against the wall. He looked way too cool to be a cop.

'Sir, do you need us to send him on his way?' asked one of the uniforms, gesturing towards camera guy.

Hossein shook his head and called to his DS. 'Grant, find out what media he works for, and why he's here. Defuse him, then join us in the house.' Dark eyes flicked from me to the door, 'Miss Patterson.'

'Er... that door doesn't open,' I said, conscious that I was messing with his 'cool'. I ran around the other side of his car to my small gate. Leading him through the back garden to the functioning door, I fumbled with my keys.

'What's this about?' I dropped the keys and they landed by his highly polished two-tone chestnut shoes. He stopped me bending down – perhaps worried I'd spot specks of dirt on the shoes – and retrieved the keys himself.

'It's that one,' I said. He took over.

'Your bruise,' he said. We were close, and he smelt of exotic spices.

As we entered my scruffy lounge, I asked if I should put the kettle on. He ordered coffee with two and a splash for Grant, herbal tea for himself. He joined me in my tiny kitchen and scuffed around, hands back in their pockets.

His black hair was swept back, fluffed up, trained to flop to one side. That kind of training came in a tube, I reckoned. He was tanned and seemed more like a Bollywood star than someone who could lock me up – although we'd already established he was good with keys. He wouldn't be the young male lead but the hard-bitten late-30s hero. I could imagine him duffing up hoodlums without ever taking his hands out of his pockets. A sultry shake of his flop of hair and a couple of jiggly dances and there'd be heroines swooning all over the screen.

He was out of my league, but Lotte might have a chance. I found myself wondering what dating apps police used; not Tinder or Grindr obviously but maybe one called 'Ploddr' or 'Cuff'er'. I'd hardly seen his hands; was there a wedding ring? Then I remembered PC Angus talking about DCI Hossein having me for dinner – or maybe breakfast. That invoked an image involving marmalade and handcuffs. I erased it. I needed to be on my game.

Grant came in and Hossein returned to my lounge. Grant was a mini-me of his superior, but not carrying it off. His dark hair was also swept back but gelled more tightly to the sides, his beard was two razor-free days beyond designer stubble, and he wore a grey three-piece and dark gold tie.

'Which paper?' I heard Hossein ask as I lingered, dangling a teabag over the bin by the door.

'Local rag,' said Grant. 'Lives ten minutes away and a guy in the pub tipped him off, he says. Apparently one of the arresting officers mentioned your name and his mate put two and two together and got on the blower.'

'How did you leave it?'

'I've got his card and promised we'll call him first, but only if he's discreet until he hears from us.'

'Well done,' Hossein approved. 'Is he a stringer for any of the nationals?'

'Dunno.'

'We'll put him in touch with Vicious Doberman on the Mail.'

'You mean Victor Dobson?'

'Yeah.'

I entered with a tray. They were sitting on my dented armchair and stained sofa. A phone lit up the coffee table, ready to record my answers.

'I have to leave for work at 5.20pm,' I said.

'No. You need to call in and tell them you'll be late. We've driven down from Peterborough this afternoon, and waited nearly an hour for you,' said Hossein. 'We're going to get this done. Can we see your bruise?'

I pushed up my sleeve to reveal the fading bruise. They studied it, measured it and Hossein took a picture of it. I saw Grant give a slight shrug that morphed into a 'maybe'.

Grant flicked over some pages in a notebook and made a start. 'Do you know a Mr Chester Makepeace Toakley?'

'Yes,' I guessed, 'but not by that name.'

'Toke?'

'Yes.'

'What can you tell us about your relationship with Mr Toakley?'

'We play tennis together occasionally,' I said.

'Was he your boyfriend?'

'Lord, no!'

'He says you dated.'

'He's ly.... he's exaggerating.' There was a silence, I plunged into it, 'We had one drink... two drinks, once after tennis. I only ever see him at tennis.'

Like me, Toke played for the village tennis team. He was a good-humoured livewire and a regular at the village bar, Benedict's. You'd find Toke in the middle of the voluble group closest to the bar. He was a bachelor with means.

We had gone for a drink a few months after Boy moved out and we had got on well. It was a seminal moment for me. It brought home a fundamental truth about my post-Boy universe. During that drink I realised that someone whose company I enjoyed, someone that I had a sport in common with, someone who was well regarded in most of the social circles I eddied in, was still a far cry from anyone I wanted to go out with. I simply didn't fancy him. I'd had an entertaining evening with Toke and ended up depressed as hell.

'Do you think he'd like to develop his relationship with you?'

'I don't know. He's never suggested that.'

'Would you recognise Mr Toakley in a mask, if he had he been at the party last Saturday night?'

I thought. 'No, not given all the noise and –'

'All the drink?' suggested Hossein. I nodded; my reputation quivered then sank a notch.

'How would you describe Mr Toakley?' Grant was driving the interrogation.

'A bachelor.'

'Given his age, do you think there's a reason for that? Is he a loner?'

'He's a socialite; not a sociopath. By the sound of it, your officers arrested him in the pub today. He's a regular there. He's gregarious.'

'He wasn't in there on Saturday night,' said Hossein.

'You think he was at the masque party on Saturday? You think he was the man who attacked me?'

'What do you think?' asked Grant.

'It's possible,' I hesitated, 'but it could have been anyone. I was unconscious – only for a short while,' I added hastily, but too late. My reputation slipped again.

'Mr Toakley says he wasn't at the party. We haven't yet had a chance to check his alibi, but he seems confident it will pan out. He says he knew this party was going on in Cambridge, he knew you were going, and he knew it was a party for swingers, if that's the right term.'

I tried to pretend I wasn't familiar with the term, but my reputation was now firmly established. 'How on earth would he know?'

'Apparently a close business associate, Mr Scott Hadleigh, told him.'

So, Shouty and Toke were 'business associates'?

Grant checked his notebook. 'It seems clear Mr Hadleigh thought that you being there and "available" would entice Mr Toakley to attend.'

'I wasn't "available".'

The notebook claimed otherwise, 'Mr Toakley was told quite explicitly – we've seen a text – that you'd be "up for it".'

Hossein added, 'But he also says he didn't go.'

Aaagh! Why had I put myself through this? If DI Hossein was married, he could tell his wife; about this raving harlot he'd interrogated, who couldn't pull, even when squeezed into a flimsy scarlet dress and advertising herself as 'up for it'.

'Did Toke say where he was?' I asked.

'He said he'd planned to go but a client called, and he had to attend a meeting in Ely,' answered Hossein.

'We're checking it out, along with his business interests.' Grant moved on. 'The police in Cambridge have tracked down one Edward Gresham, who hosted the party you went to. Not surprisingly, he doesn't have a guest list, says he knew fewer than half the people there and barely recognised anyone. He doesn't remember the masked characters that you described to police officers this morning. He specifically didn't remember 'Asda Man'. He had no idea that you had been attacked.'

I was surprised that they were taking my report (taking me) so seriously.

Grant nudged the phone towards me. 'Given everything you've heard; do you believe Mr Toakley is capable of molesting you in the manner you described?'

'Yes,' I said slowly, 'maybe.'

'He's your anonymous texter, said Grant. 'Initially, he denied sending you a text at all,' 'which was pretty stupid because we had his phone. We just scrolled down and showed him it.'

'How would he even know about my bruise?'

'He saw it at tennis, he says. That he suggested to a...' notebook sheets supplied a name. '...Hugo Burrell that you'd been branded after signing up for some weird sect.

'Burrell replied that, knowing you, it was more likely you'd signed up for weird sex. That was why it stuck in Toakley's mind.'

Hugo Burrell was Caitlyn's dad. He was a social tennis player. His younger daughter, Aileen, was the same age as Harry and she had been his closest playmate up until the age of five. Hugo, I could happily have made a play for, but he was blissfully married – naturally – to lovely clever Esther.

Grant's pen was poised. 'Is it likely that he texted you about your bruise just as a joke, as he claims?'

'It's a bit sick, but yes, he specialises in rubbish jokes. But, if it was innocent, why deny it? And I'm surprised he recognised the bruise as being from your murder appeal – it was months ago.'

'He claims he was throwing out old papers, saw the picture and texted you. He thought he'd be on your list of contacts.'

'No, I've never had cause to call him.'

'You're on his contacts.'

'My number's easy to get,' I said, before realising it sounded like further evidence of my loose morals. 'It's on the tennis club's information sheets.'

'So is Toakley's.'

'What about his calls last Saturday night?'

'Wiped. He claimed it must have happened when he was deleting some pictures from an ex-girlfriend. He isn't very tech-savvy.'

Hossein took over. 'What do you know about the murder in Whittlesey?'

'I can remember some headlines from the time. When was

the body found; late February?'

'On the 27th of February.'

'I knew she'd been beheaded. I remember that she'd had her hands cut off too and that she was found in the fens. I've only seen her bruise from Toke's text. That's it. I was away skiing when she was killed.'

'Did the description of the woman in the text sound like any friends in the village, perhaps acquaintances you share with Mr Toakley?' asked Grant.

'No, I don't think so.'

'It is now nearly 12 weeks since her torso was found,' said Hossein. 'The investigation can't proceed unless and until we identify this woman, which is the start point for any murder inquiry. That's why we responded to your lead.'

'How did she die?' I asked. I don't know why I wanted to know, but I did. I was starting to feel a bond with this woman, whose killer I thought I'd met.

'We're not sure. We believe she was decapitated post-mortem, meaning –'

'I know,' I cut in, 'after she was killed.'

'Yes.' Hossein continued, 'Or she was already unconscious when the fatal blow fell. If it wasn't post-mortem, then the first blow would likely have been fatal. If she died by some other trauma, then she was beheaded within a very short space of time. She was beheaded by a heavy short-bladed weapon, probably with a slight curve.'

That was a lot of detail. I sensed Hossein enjoyed displaying his professional knowledge.

'Like a meat cleaver?'

'A butcher's cleaver is likely. It took four or five chops to take the head off, between C4 and C5.'

'The cervical vertebrae,' I was desperate to impress, 'halfway down her neck.'

'Opposite her adam's apple,' so was Hossein. 'Five chops may not sound a professional job but, to us, that indicates the murderer knew what he was doing. It hints he wasn't fazed by the situation. He may have killed before.'

'Did he chop from the front or the back of her neck?' I asked. They stared.

'Why would you ask that?'

'Most people would do it from the back, but the neck snaps easier from the front. If he'd done it before he might know that.'

'How do you know that?' Grant was suspicious.

'I read too much life-science-related stuff,' I explained.

'Right again Miss Patterson,' said Hossein. 'It was from the front, suggesting some proficiency or specialist knowledge. The wrists were chopped at the same time, but definitely post-mortem. Again, a clean job. Our tests on the body revealed several things but not how she was killed.'

'Presumably by a blow to her head,' I said. I was a natural at police stuff.

'Or possibly cut wrists, but that's less likely. The fact she was found in ditch-water messes with the forensics.'

'Was the bruise administered post-mortem, too?' I asked.

'We can't be sure; bruising varies hugely from one person to the next. The histological examination, that means –'

'Microscopic examination of tissue,' I interrupted. 'Biologist, remember.'

Grant gave a short laugh. 'The two of you should get together. The Guv could write a PhD thesis on this bruise.'

'Suffice to say,' said Hossein, 'that our best guess is that it occurred very close to her death – possibly within an hour – but we can't tell if it was before or after. Apparently, the dark blue pigment in a bruise can last distinctly for many days in the living and forensic science still has no accurate table for dating post-mortem bruising.'

'Why bruise her after she's dead?' I asked.

'Good question and one that leads us to believe the bruising happened prior to her death, but it most definitely wasn't administered by accident. You're convinced your bruise looked like hers.'

'It was identical,' I said.

'Mr Toakley isn't so sure. He says it was a similar size and a round shape, but, it could be, he's now trying to downplay the connection.'

'In case it links him to the murder. But if it wasn't the same, why send the text?'

Grant answered, consulting his notes, 'He says: he "wouldn't have dreamt of sending the text if he'd really thought they were similar". He meant it as a joke. He hadn't intended to scare you.'

'Was the woman sexually assaulted?' I asked.

'Too many questions.' Hossein had indulged me long enough. 'Describe your bruise to us.'

'Easy, it's a St Martin's cross.'

'What's that?' asked Grant.

'A cross superimposed on top of a circle.'

'Anything else?'

'Right,' here was my chance to explain my certainty. 'I bruise easily; I'm pale skinned, and a woman – more fat, less collagen – but the bruises don't come out straight away –'

'Typically 12 to 48 hours,' said Hossein, 'shorter when it's a bony part of the body.'

'Yes, but back of the arm, fairly fleshy and deep bruising... anyway, after tennis, it had only just emerged. In the mirror it was dark, really hard-edged and distinctive. I could clearly see the circle bit wasn't as vivid.'

'Who else was playing with you at tennis?'

'Apart from Toke and my son, Harry; Hugo, who's just up the road in Lychgate Cottage and Kotryna Webb, from the butchers.'

'How do you think it was inflicted?'

'What I thought on Sunday evening was that someone had thumped me really hard with a piece of St Martin's Cross jewellery from Iona. They're commonly sold as pendants. My mum had some stuff. It was done deliberately, like the "Sucker" they wrote on my forehead. They were marking me.'

'Draw a St Martin's Cross,' said Hossein. He had hunted one down on his phone screen and shared it with DS Grant.

I unearthed a notebook from my handbag and drew it, making the cross chunkier, the circle behind it thinner and showing the five distinctive bosses.

'That's it,' agreed Grant. He copied the term down in his somewhat larger notebook. 'How come you know so much about this cross, Miss Patterson?' His question smoked with suspicion.

'I'm Scottish. I was born and brought up in Glasgow, but my Mum was a MacInnes. She came from the Highlands and was always filling my wee head with stories of the Isles when I was growing up. My brother was named after the St Martin's Cross.'

'They called him, "Cross"?' said Grant. We all stifled our laughter. Hossein was either checking his dates on 'Plodder' or flicking through images of the cross on his phone. He showed one to Grant, who gave a nod of previously unseen enthusiasm.

'Good looker?' I inquired.

He showed me. It was the cross.

'You said your mum has this kind of jewellery?'

'Had. Mum had a lot of Celtic jewellery and stuff when we were kids, but she's dead – a long time ago.'

Grant changed tactics and started quizzing me about family and relationship stuff. My brother would have been a prime suspect if he hadn't lived in Canada.

Grant queried Boy's unusual name. He was the first boy after four daughters, I told him, it was a family nickname; it stuck – even after he was joined by a younger brother.

They went through the details of my life with Boy: the breakup, his affair with Candi, the fact they were both in Patagonia (Grant had heard of Patagonia but thought it only existed in legend), and my relationships with men since. This last bit didn't take long.

Eventually, at Hossein's sign, they stopped and stood. Grant picked up his phone, tapped the screen and tucked it inside his jacket.

I was already late for work but asked, 'What now?'

Grant was about to give some perfunctory answer, but Hossein stopped him.

He turned to me. 'There are three questions that I need to be able to answer "Yes" to, for me to feel I haven't wasted a vast amount of police resource on your report, Miss Patterson.'

This didn't sound a good way to end our first assignation together.

'Go on,' I said.

'Question two: is there anything other than the jokey text to link Mr Toakley to the attack you say took place at the party last Saturday night? What would you answer?'

'Is it up to me to have a view? You deal in evidence.'

'Let me put the question another way: Mr Toakley is currently in a cell in the bowels of Cambridge Police Station. Is he a sufficiently proven danger to society? Is the text enough evidence to pursue a case against him? In short, should I keep him there?'

'Let him go,' said a quiet voice.

'Right, so we discount the text. Question three: is there enough evidence to link the attack you say took place in Cambridge last Saturday to the murder of an unknown woman outside Whittlesey three months ago? There is a bruise that you tell us was identical, but – now we've discounted the text – is that enough?'

'It's not enough,' I said.

'I agree. Thank you for your time, Miss Patterson; your identification of St Martin's Cross may prove to be useful.'

'We only had it down as possibly Celtic,' added Grant. I think he was trying to be nice. His boss wasn't. They got up to go.

'What about question one?' I asked.

'It's irrelevant; we've already got two "nos",' replied Hossein, pulling the creases out of his suit jacket and inspecting it for evidential deposits from my sofa.

'You've made me late for work. I still have concerns I

could've been marked for death by a murderer.' The calm in my voice surprised me and I knew full well I wasn't going to like his answer. 'Please tell me what question one was.'

'OK, question one; are you a reliable witness?'

'Why; what else could I be?'

'You could be a woman who's had her life turned inside out for the last three years, who's seen the father of her child and long-term partner run off with a younger woman and recently whisk that replacement away on a holiday to a land so exotic, DS Grant thinks it's mythical. You're a woman who's had no luck replacing that relationship hole in her life and who's had a recent upsetting experience when she got out of her depth at a party where all the other guests were consenting adults,' Hossein stressed this last word more than was remotely necessary.

But he wasn't finished. 'A woman who took a jokey text the wrong way and either subconsciously, or knowingly, exaggerated the facts and the two bruises' similarity to get us to take her attack seriously, or maybe just to get herself some attention.'

'That's harsh,' I mumbled.

'Yes,' he agreed, 'but I'm responsible for utilising every second of my 50-strong team to bring a possible serial killer to justice. My men and women are under fire in the media and I'm under pressure to put the perpetrator behind bars in case he kills again. I'm paid to ask and answer those questions.'

'I take it the reliable witness answer's a "No" then?'

'As I said, it's irrelevant.'

As they made their way to the door, DS Grant paused and rummaged around in his suit pockets, 'I nearly forgot,' he said, 'handing over my phone, 'The Sergeant at Linbourn gave me this to return to you. He says to call if there are any developments.'

'Thanks. Sorry I wasted everyone's time.'

'Well, had you answered your phone and confirmed that you knew Mr Toakley, and would have believed his explanation, a whole lot of police resource would not have been expended,' said Grant. 'But the St Martin's Cross reference had passed us by.'

'Do you want us to keep your name out of the papers?' asked Hossein, as if it had been a passing thought.

'Please,' I sighed, 'I really don't want…' what: to look a fool, be seen as even more of a victim? '…to worry my son.'

'Fine,' Hossein was already walking out of my door and life, 'just don't talk to them yourself, then.'

'I won't; I promise.'

I was about to close the door when a thought occurred, 'What about Lotte? I mean Mrs Hadleigh; Scott's wife, Charlotte? Did you track her down?'

Hossein shrugged, 'I think the police at Linbourn did. They were looking into her whereabouts. Call Sergeant… what's his name?'

'Sergeant de Clerc.'

They left.

6 LINDI

June 2018

'Ash is a bright lad, he's socially engaged, he's open-minded about the programme.' Ali Hassan was an 'intervention provider'. He'd joined a meeting Lindi had fought for with Mr Norton, the de-radicalisation programme's local co-ordinator.

'That's kind of you to say,' said Lindi, 'You agree then, Ash shouldn't be on the programme or have a black mark against his record?'

Norton flicked papers. 'Your son did threaten to put a pupil on an Isis death list.'

'Ash has always denied he said that. It's one boy's word against another.'

'It almost always is,' said Norton. The office in the borough council building was sticky, the chairs hard, designed to ensure meetings didn't overrun. 'Radicals don't usually confess. Mostly, they don't even see it themselves, but professionals can pick it up.'

'Mr Hassan's a professional,' said Lindi, 'you heard what he just said about Ash.'

'I need to add, Mrs Mills, that Ash is typical of children who end up on the radicalised path,' Hassan stole away her argument. 'They're bright, otherwise they wouldn't question the status quo, they're usually coming late to their religion, often they've suffered a family loss – in Ash's case the separation from his father. Ash is having a crisis of belonging, wondering – probably for the first time – whether he identifies as Muslim.'

'Critics say your programme is too focussed on Muslims,' said Lindi.

'We are equally active in right-wing extremism,' Norton's response came with practised speed.

'But,' Hassan added, 'the simple fact, Mrs Mills, is that 98% of suicide bombers since 9/11 have been Sunni Muslims. That's people who share a religion with me and your son, responsible for 33,000 deaths.'

'Ash isn't Muslim. Your programme was the first time he had been in a mosque.'

'I know,' said Hassan. 'It's not usually people embedded in a religion, who are radicalised. Even MI5 recognises that being born into a religious family immunises you against extremism. Newcomers to Islam are usually the most radical.'

'Ash having a family connection to Islam doesn't make him an extremist.'

'No-one is suggesting he is,' Hassan smoothed her labels away. 'We're trying to ensure he never becomes one.'

Lindi felt as if she and Ash were lost in the belly of a twisting serpent, every argument she made only seemed to tie Ash more closely to the damning statistics of radicalisation.

'Surely, what you described would apply to a huge number of teenage children.'

'Exactly why we've trained 18,000 local staff to spot signs of radicalisation,' said Norton. 'In the past two years, UK-wide, 500 people have come through our more in-depth de-radicalisation process.'

'I read that.' Lindi's research showed only 5% of people on the programme were recommended for more intervention. 'But it's voluntary. Serious extremists would surely refuse to go on it, or just walk away.'

'That's still 500 possible atrocities or potential suicide

bombs defused,' said Norton.

'How would you ever know?'

'We never will,' said Hassan.

❋ ❋ ❋

Lindi's mobile had to be off at work. She respected the reasons; her office's business was largely done over the phone. However, she had to give the school a contact number; she gave the company's landline.

Ms Sandbrook called through before lunch. It was a hectic day with Lindi's team chasing down their monthly target. 'Mrs Mills,' the Headmistress started with warning calm, 'I'd like you to collect your son from my office now please. I'm suspending him forthwith.'

'But Ash has got a physics exam,' said Lindi. 'This afternoon.'

'That's as may be, Mrs Mills. I don't want him in my school a moment longer.'

'Physics is an A-level choice for Ash. You can't stop him sitting the exam.'

'Don't tell me what I can and can't do to safeguard the children under my care.' All pretence of calm cast to the winds. 'I have just been required to haul your son out of a lesson he shouldn't even have been in. I have children in tears. Your son is disrupting my school.'

He never used to before you blew-up the Ratcliffe incident out of all proportion, thought Lindi. Dafiyah was passing through the office. Her boss's attention had been drawn to this conversation. Lindi had no alternative but to plough on.

'This sounds very serious, Ms Sandbrook. You had better explain what Ash has done so I can determine if I must leave work to collect him. I'd ask you to take into account that I may well be walking away from this job if I do.'

Dafiyah marched to Lindi's work-station. Her grimace held a warning.

'He has been inciting religious discord in an R.E. lesson.' The Head's tone softened an iota, 'Ash has no need to be in school during exams, except for times when he is sitting one. If you undertake to come and collect him now, only delivering him back when the Physics exam starts at 2 o'clock, I will let him take it. As for the rest of his GCSEs, I don't want him on school premises unless he's in the exam room.'

'That's impossible,' said Lindi. 'The school buses are time-tabled for the beginning and end of school. I have to be at work.'

'You have a tough decision to take, Mrs Mills. Now, I need to know whether you are collecting him or whether I ask one of my staff to drive him to you, wherever you work.'

Lindi glanced up at Dafiyah. Her boss gave a despairing shake of her head, 'Go'.

* * *

Ash's school made much of its willingness to welcome, and ability to integrate, children of all faiths and any race. When Lindi chose a short-term let in the school's catchment area, it was nothing to do with its inclusivity aspirations and everything to do with an improving GCSE record. Lindi had once planned to be a teacher. She took her educational research seriously.

Ash was a bright student, an all-rounder, flourishing in arts, excelling in sciences. The school took Ash on when he moved into their area and didn't protest when Lindi's new rental fell outside the primary catchment zone. It was still on school bus routes.

'Inclusivity' and 'integration' cropped up everywhere in the school's brochure but Lindi had observed that 'integration' ended beyond its glossy pages. Playground groups were defined by race, religion, sex and age – probably in that order. It was noticeable outside the school-gates too, among the waiting parents – nearly all of them, mums.

The self-imposed playground segregation was underlined, probably reinforced, by an extended uniform range. It allowed Muslim girls to wear the hijab, while Sikhs, and Hindus, Pakistanis and Bangladeshis could wear school-branded versions of their traditional dress. Birds of a feather flocked together.

The irony wasn't missed by Lindi, wife of a Pakistani: the painstakingly crafted uniform policy undermined the politically engineered brochure promise. The big picture sacrificed because no-one could admit to the existence of the everyday reality of the tribe.

The pupils' behaviour wasn't driven by racism. Humanity packed down with those who shared its beliefs, aspirations and dress code. Luton was one of three UK towns where the 'white British' ethnic group was in a minority. Single faith schools served different religious factions. Inclusion was good in theory, but didn't play well in practice – given a chance you opted out.

Lindi's school-gate observations were relevant because Ash had swapped tribes. Her son had straight blue-black hair. He would not have stood out among the Pakistani and Muslim boy groups on the playground. However, his three closest friends all ticked the white British ethnicity box, so that was where he'd hung out. Lindi imagined it was why Ratcliffe baited Ash. He saw Ash as an interloper straying from his own herd.

However, Ash was, for the first time, to be found among the Muslim boys. He was more demonstrably engaged in group interactions too. Had this happened prior to Ash attracting the de-radicalisation programme's attention, Lindi would have been overjoyed – she wanted her son to have the broadest social circle. But now it just fuelled her concerns. The programme had awoken curiosity in the Muslim side of his heritage. She worried he was being defined by a new label.

On her way to the school Lindi guessed at what might have

happened if Ash was offered the chance to speak out in an R.E. lesson and give his new opinions air.

Again, she found Ash seated outside the headmistress's office. Again, he seemed unfazed by the attention.

'This has probably cost me my job Ash,' she said, on entering.

He shrugged. 'It was a crap job anyway.'

'Possibly, but we need it. More importantly, it's threatening to cost you your GCSEs.'

'Seems like an over-reaction. A-Hoy invited me into the lesson. He set up the debate.'

Lindi remembered Mr (call me Tony) Hoy, the R.E. teacher, from fourth year parents' evenings. Young, probably in his first teaching job, sprouting assorted piercings. She doubted any of his pupils was convinced by his homage to street cred.

'Why would he invite you in?'

'A friend, Rashid, said I should go. I asked, and A-Hoy said, "fine". He seemed keen.'

'Why go at all? You had a Physics exam at two. You should have been revising.'

She had spoken without thinking and deserved the derisive glare Ash gave her. He passed Physics exams in his sleep, literally scoring 100% in the last five modules he had brought home to Lindi.

'Rashid said the lesson was "Faith verses Society". It sounded interesting.'

'Do I know Rashid?'

'No, he's in the year below me. He's cool.'

The headmistress's door opened. The secretary stepped out. 'Ms Sandbrook has five minutes free now, Mrs Mills. Please go in.'

The Head was working through a sheaf of papers, glasses on. She raised her eyes but not her pen as Lindi and Ash entered. Mr Hoy wasn't present.

'Ash hasn't had a chance to tell me what happened,' Lindi moved to one of the seats.

'This is not about that, Mrs Mills. I don't plan to justify my decision. I only need to discover if it's possible for you to organise things to ensure Ash enters this school only when his exams start and departs the moment they finish. I won't have him interacting with other pupils.'

It was hammered out that Ash would wait in the nearest cafe, 1,000 metres away when Lindi was at work and school buses didn't fit with his exam timetable. His shrug confirmed he would not talk to other pupils on school premises.

'Leave us please, Ash,' the Head said after five minutes. 'I want a word with your mother.

'You may be aware, Mrs Mills,' she began, 'that Ash has become a beacon for Muslim activity in this school.'

'No. What does that mean?'

'His opinions are sought out and, I'm afraid, carry weight. He has apparently focussed attention on another boy in his year, Damien Ratcliffe.'

'Apparently?'

'Damien says he is being bullied by Muslim boys in school.'

'Bullied by other boys; not by Ash?'

'But Ash has put them up to it, according to Damien. If you still have any influence over your son, I'd ask you to use it, to make this bullying stop.'

'Is there any more evidence than the last time that Ratcliffe isn't just making this up?'

'This time, I have witnessed the name-calling. The boys call Damien, "Lemming". Previously, he says, only Ash used that name for him. I believe Damien.'

Lindi was initially confused by the absurdity of this, but then she worked out the genesis of the nickname. The obscure humour sounded like Ash's mind at work.

The Head stood. 'I think it would be best for everyone if Ash found another school immediately after his exams.' She put out her hand.

'I agree.' Lindi stood. She didn't respond to the quickly withdrawn hand. 'But I don't agree that Ash is radicalised.'

'You don't know the particulars of what went on in Religious

Education, Mrs Mills.'

'Because you've made a point of not telling me. I've had to draw my own conclusions. You're aware why Ash's interest in the Muslim faith has been heightened. I believe he was actively encouraged by Mr Hoy to engage in a debate. The topic was a poor choice for fourth years in a multi-faith school, and forms no part of their curriculum –'

The Head tried to comment, but Lindi talked over her. 'Faith or society – really? It's too divisive for either government or media to tackle. The debate was designed to highlight insoluble rifts in our community. Ash's insight goes beyond the platitudes of news coverage and he gives his opinion honestly when asked. It was likely be upsetting for children.'

'I have pupils here that have lost entire branches of their extended family to Syria and Muslim extremism,' the Head retorted. 'One girl fled the room in tears and had to be sent home.'

'Then it's even more ridiculous that your teachers are encouraged to frame discussions around toxic subject matter just to polish their liberal sentiments. You know better than I how long the school exclusion procedure takes, once started, Ms Sandbrook, and how messy it gets. I expect your full support in finding Ash a place in a suitable school or I will be bringing recent events here to wider attention.'

'Take care, Mrs Mills. We are merely following policy.'

'"Only following orders," doesn't have a strong record as a defence.'

'How dare you?'

'This is my son's life. Your willingness to side with a white pupil over one with a Pakistani and Muslim heritage is threatening to ruin it. I dare a lot. Do we have a deal?'

'Get out!' The Head pointed to the door.

As Lindi walked towards it, she heard, 'I want your son out of my school. For that reason, only, I will not stand in the way of his approach to a new school.'

'Thank you,' said Lindi under her breath. She didn't turn

around.

Ash survived his GCSE exam timetable but Lindi's probation period at work was unlikely to continue. A break clause was coming up in their rental. Lindi couldn't commit to staying there. It was providential, then, that her old work mail, which she no longer used, forwarded an email from someone she hadn't seen or spoken to for nearly six years.

** 2003 **

Ash's 'Pakistani heritage' played often on Lindi's mind. A month after her meeting with Ammi and Naasira in the hotel, Lindi allowed herself to ease into a relationship with Ayan. She was seduced by the family as much as the man. After the hotel meeting, Lindi – an only child – yearned to be part of that cultivated world. She admired the strong, warm, capable mother and found a role-model in Ayan's brave, intelligent, mould-breaking sister.

Lindi had been too focussed on her education to chase boys at school and the kind of boys who pursued girls, found Lindi too serious. That changed at university with two short casual flings.

When she started staying over in Ayan's well-appointed flat, Lindi was still seeing a Mancunian engineering student, Connor. He was bright, but intent on screwing up his chances of a first-class degree, plus just screwing. Women, laughs and lager were more attractive than revision and practicals.

Two years into his foundation course, Lindi couldn't see Connor getting his studies back on track. She didn't approve or condemn. Connor was fun, darkly handsome and popular. It was flattering he spent time with her. She didn't fuss when other girls came and went. Casual suited her and meant emotions didn't get in the way of her studies.

Ayan was the most care-free person she had met, but Lindi knew a relationship would be serious for him. She stressed that, although sex was going to be a fun part of their time together, it didn't mean they were going steady. She was candid about wanting to keep other relationships going. Ayan laughed it off, fine by him.

Except sex wasn't fun, it was difficult and often ended in dissatisfaction. Ayan was an attentive eager lover but he couldn't cope with condoms and Lindi had stayed off the pill. Any awkwardness caused wasn't down to Ayan. He quickly recovered from the embarrassment and jokingly blamed himself; never Lindi. However, she wanted to give their relationship every chance and grew increasingly frustrated for him.

At uni, Connor was encouraged into her bed more often, perhaps to persuade herself she wasn't the problem. She wasn't; it was the silken scrap of rubber that Ayan had rarely used and always struggled with. A few times things worked out, but by then, they were so anxious that the climax was all about relief – at least, on these occasions, it wasn't the 'hand' kind.

After two months Lindi went on the pill. Ironically that led to Ash. She knew she was the only woman sexually involved in Ayan's life. She still used condoms with Connor, for obvious reasons. However, the pill was not yet an automatic part of her routine. Its early days included small alarms, panics and stomach upsets that compromised its effectiveness.

As well as Ayan's improving sexual hit rate, there was one occasion – just one – when Connor's drunken fumblings didn't include the application of his 'love-glove'.

Sod's law dictated that at some time – either through Lindi's forgetfulness, allied to Ayan's enthusiastic thrusting, or Connor's tipsiness combined with Lindi's more relaxed sexual regime – she became pregnant. Looking back, it felt as if one stray sperm was so determined to 'be' that it ripped up her carefully mapped-out life plan. The sperm became Ash. Lindi resolved to love him all the harder.

When university medical staff told Lindi she was pregnant, her response was disbelief, before she recalled the confusion of missed pills. She had a decision to make. She decided to involve Ayan.

They were going out two or three nights a week. Sometimes,

when Lindi's revision allowed, Ayan took her away on week-ends. Often, she stayed a night or two at his flat. Connor had drifted out of the picture.

Lindi set everything out before Ayan; including the small possibility (she genuinely thought tiny) that Connor could be the father. When she finished, Ayan became thoughtful.

'This is serious, Lindi,' he said. 'We both know I don't do serious.'

Lindi swallowed. It was as she expected. 'It's my stupidity. It's not your fault and certainly isn't your problem.'

'And yet you have told me. You didn't have to.'

'No, I really did. I haven't told Connor and I won't. The child is almost certainly not his. He's no longer part of my life. Right now, you are.'

'Do you want to bring up this child?'

'I think so, but I can do so alone, if that's the way it is.'

'Would you want to do it together?'

'I always knew Connor wouldn't be part of my future. I was wondering whether you might be. I know this is not in your plans. You have no obligation to do anything, Ayan. It would turn your life upside down.'

'Leave it with me. I need to think it through.'

And somewhere in all that lay the truth about Ash's Pakistani heritage: it was a lie.

7 SHONA

Wednesday night May 22 2019

I rushed teeth, reapplied deodorant, changed blouses, grabbed my handbag and followed the two policemen out of the door. They'd be going nowhere until I shifted my car. I was below my usual presentation standards for the lab, but I was already late, so if I ruined Leroy's preconceptions about how glamorous his co-worker really was, it couldn't be helped.

Hossein and Grant weren't waiting for me; they'd walked up the road and were talking to Hugo by his gate. I didn't wave; just drove away.

Leroy's head was already nodding on to his chest when I arrived at the lab. I parked close to the doors.

I gave Gone Puss my jauntiest 'still here then' smile, vowed I'd feed him last tonight, grabbed my stuff and toddled off into the distant reaches of the aquarium.

About an hour into my routine, I heard my desk-phone going distantly. I was about to feed some small cut-throat trout. Opening the top of the tank had already sparked pandemonium. I wouldn't make it back to my desk in time. The phone stopped but went again after a few minutes. I couldn't think of anyone I wanted to speak to – except Lotte or Harry and they wouldn't call on the lab number.

An hour later, I returned to the room containing my workstation. Leroy was sitting at my desk reading something green and stapled that was probably his course notes. Gone Puss was studying the soles of his feet. These were up on my desk, but sluggishly removed when he spotted me approaching.

'Hey, Shona,' Leroy yawned. That was usually the extent of his conversation and just saying it nearly always wore him out. Tonight, though, he had more. 'I phoned you.'

'Sorry,' I said, 'I wouldn't have made it back. I was up to my neck in drugged zebra fish.'

'Woah really!?' Leroy was likely picturing me smoking reefers (pun intended) with a bunch of small semi-transparent fish. The effort briefly brought him to full consciousness. 'That sounds like a thing. This guy turned up for you at the front door.'

'What did he want?' I turned around from eye-wrestling Gone Puss to face Leroy.

'You. He was angry, I'd say; maybe drunk. I wouldn't let him in. You aren't allowed visitors, unless...'

'Unless I have a blue visitor chit with three signatures,' I exaggerated to hide my anxiety.

Leroy's forehead knitted.

'Four siggies if the visitor is drunk.'

Leroy wasn't sure but left it. 'This guy drove in fast, parked right out front, not in a space, like. Hammered, super-hammered on the door; you can bet I wasn't about to unlock it. He punched the buzzer and said he had to speak to you right then. I tried to call.'

'Did he leave a name? Or a message? Anything?'

Leroy shook his head. 'I told him you must be busy. We left it, say, a coupl'a minutes. I called your desk again; nothing. I told him your rounds usually took two hours or so. He smacked his fist into the door, stormed back into his car and drove off. Lots of revs. Angry guy.'

'Oh,' that didn't sound good. 'So, no idea who it was?'

'Your husband maybe?' Leroy hazarded.

'No,' I said, 'he doesn't sound like anyone I'd want to marry.'

'I wouldn't,' Leroy agreed. 'Looks like I'll be seeing you to your car again tonight.'

'Looks like.'

Here was a chance to put my recent interrogation experience to good use. Under my relentless inquisition Leroy made the following statement: the car was probably a big saloon, maybe an old-fashioned one; it was either grey or white. The guy was average height, sort of old with short blonde hair, but still looked fit.

I probed. 'What do you count as old, Leroy?'

'Well, he was at least over 40.'

I decided to end my questioning there before my bad cop side took over.

The instant Leroy left, I slumped against the wall, turned my head to the ceiling and swore. I was shaking but it was probably 50% tiredness.

Toke, I thought, broadly fitted Leroy's description (allowing for his zoning out on attention to detail). I had never told Toke where I worked. His hair was short but turning silvery. I had seen his car parked outside the tennis club on many occasions but never been in it. I couldn't remember the make, but it was a slightly older saloon and the colour was silver and would probably appear grey in the dim car-park lights.

The anger didn't sound like Toke. His temper tantrums were usually limited to a bit of racket abuse if he missed a simple volley at the net. Maybe spending the afternoon in a police cell suspected of murder ranked beyond being love-40 down on your own serve in a deciding set against Camworth. He must have been released from his cell, tracked me down in Cambridge (god knows how, the lab is hardly in a prime location) and come around to remonstrate with me for putting him in DCI Hossein's sights.

I couldn't blame him for being outraged; all he'd done was text a typically stupid joke to me and I'd fingered him for murder – he'd just caught me on a bad week. Despite that, I was in no hurry to explain things or run into him in the mood Leroy had described. I thought I'd let him cool down, before I unblocked him from my phone.

Peeling myself off the wall, I noticed Gone Puss's appraising gaze. I interpreted it as him thinking, 'just evolve another 230 million or so years and your race will stop being so stupid.' Or he could have been demanding, 'Shrimp me'.

I finished my rounds, feeding him last.

Returning to the desk, I phoned Gran Helen. She put Harry on promptly and we chatted. He told me he'd beaten Helen at draughts and pairs (his current favourite card game). I told him not to let his Gran wear him out and got a warning 'Oh Mum' for my efforts.

I asked if they'd called his dad. Harry said they'd tried him an hour ago, but he wasn't answering. Patagonia was four hours behind, which meant it would be late afternoon there. What would Boy and Candi find to do on a sunny afternoon on a Patagonian beach, I wondered. The same thing that sea lions and lionesses found to do, perhaps?

I spoke to Helen to check she was enjoying having her grandson over and still up for the next two nights. She was.

Next, I tried Lotte's phone. It rang three times and I finally got through. 'Hi Lotte.'

No answer.

'It's Shona,' I said. No answer. Lotte may be angry with me, but she never gave anyone the silent treatment. The word 'silent' didn't figure in Lotte's vocabulary.

'Lotte?!' The call clicked off and my phone clattered to the desk. A chill ran through me. My phone felt contaminated by the call, as though it had connected me to something cold and dark. I let it lie there while I ran through some possible explanations – the first one to come to mind didn't bear thinking about. OK, there were other explanations. Most likely Lotte was still pissed that I'd abandoned her. I'd call her office first thing.

I opened up my laptop and entered a search, 'murder in Whittlesey'. Google whisked up 27,800 results. I clicked on the first one, 'Headless woman found', which was dated 27th February from BBC headlines.

'Cambridgeshire Police are reporting that the body of a headless woman was found on farmland this morning, close to the market town of Whittlesey. The body, which was discovered by a dog walker, is also rumoured to be without hands, drawing inevitable links to the murder of an unidentified woman, discovered in October, in gravel pits close to the village of Billington in Derbyshire. That murder is still unsolved.'

I moved to a follow-up report from the 28th February.

'There has still been no announcement about whether police believe this latest murder could be the work of the same killer. They are appealing to the public in and around Whittlesey to get in touch if they have seen anything suspicious. 'The Billington murderer was nicknamed, "The Doll Killer" by the press after a headless and handless child's doll was found alongside the body. 'Detective Chief Inspector Dani Hossein of the Derbyshire Police, who is in charge of investigating the Billington murder, said it was too early to connect the two murders but was keen for the public to call in. "It's rare for a woman to vanish without trace in the UK. If you know of a woman in her 30s, a friend or relative, who has recently disappeared without explanation I urge you to get in touch. If we have a report, we can quickly check and determine whether she is this murdered woman."'

The Peterborough Evening Telegraph offered a juicier, 'Doll Killer strikes in Whittlesey' link, dated the 28th of February.

'The naked body of a mutilated woman found in a drainage ditch outside Whittlesey yesterday, is almost certainly linked to The Doll Killer murder in Derby just four months ago, writes Chief Crime Correspondent Steve Shelby.

'While police refuse to be drawn on similarities between the two murders, this reporter can confirm that a mutilated doll was found by the Whittlesey body. The murder south of Derby in October was also of a woman left naked, headless and handless and in that case

too, a child's doll was found close to the body. That doll was a macabre double of the victim, without a head and hands.

'A dog walker reported the second victim's body yesterday morning in a drainage ditch that leads into the Old Nene between Whittlesey and March. DCI Dani Hossein of Derbyshire Police is now leading the investigation into both murders. He told us: "While we can't confirm a definite association, the similarities between the two murders are striking and we are looking at the possibility that this new woman was brutally slain by the same killer. She was aged early-to-late-30s, around 5'7 – 5'9 inches tall, sandy-brown haired and well nourished. She was neither homeless nor destitute. This woman must be missed by someone."'

Another link from the 1st of March, led to a clip of a TV reporter standing by a ditch bank. 'The discovery of a headless woman's body near Whittlesey, on Wednesday, has led to the hunt for a serial killer,' she said.

'The finding of a beheaded doll has led to the inevitable inference that it is the work of "The Doll Killer", responsible for an identical murder south of Derby five months ago. Both victims were white Caucasian women in their 30s. They were naked, and had their heads and hands removed – chopped off – to avoid victim identification. This was highlighted by DCI Dani Hossein in this morning's press conference.'

The newscast was replaced with footage of DCI Hossein. He was standing in front of a row of desks, behind which other people sat. An empty chair in the middle of the desks showed where he was supposed to be. He held a microphone and was addressing a roomful of reporters.

'The killer has gone to extreme lengths to make it hard to identify these two women,' said Hossein. 'They have removed their heads to leave them faceless and prevent us from using dental records or hairstyle evidence, such as cut or dyes. He chopped off their hands to leave us without rings, fingerprints, or nail residue. He removed the body from where she was killed (probably indoors) and placed her in standing water, again to disrupt our forensics. This strongly suggests that if we identify the woman – either woman – the killer believes that identification will lead us straight to him or her.'

'Could the killer be a woman?' barked a throaty voice from the audience.

'It's unlikely for many reasons, but we can't categorically rule it out.'

'Is it definitely a serial killer?' shouted the same reporter's voice.

'Mr Shelby, please let me continue and there will be time for questions at the end,' Hossein responded. He went on, 'the only clearly identifiable mark on this latest woman's body is this distinctive bruise on the bicep of her left arm.'

A large image of a discoloured arm appeared on a screen behind Hossein. On it was my bruise, the thicker cross distinct and sharp, the circle thinner and clearly fainter, the bosses on the cross barely visible but hinted at. 'This bruising happened close to the time of her murder. If you recognise either the bruise or the implement that may have caused it, please contact us at the phone number we have given out –'

… so DCI Hossein can pop round to humiliate you, I finished, clicking the clip off.

I was falling behind with my work and started in on that instead. I didn't have to be back early tonight, so called Leroy to find out if I could stay an extra 30-40 minutes and catch up.

'That's cool, Shona, I'm on until 1am. Then Reynard takes over.'

What the hell kind of name was Reynard? I was in no state to cope with anyone remotely foxy.

'That's great, Leroy. Maybe you could be around at 12.30 to see me to my car.'

'No worries.'

I departed under Leroy's watchful eye just before 12.30am. An old blue van, presumably Leroy's, was parked by the furthest hedge. He had every right to be ashamed of it.

Leaving the car park, I kept tired eyes out for any silver saloons. I hoped the lateness of the hour would ensure Toke, or whoever I'd angered, would be tucked up in bed, fury dissipating.

There was little traffic in the Science Park backwater where our lab was tucked away. I hit the M11 for one junction then turned off. One set of car lights behind me was tugging at a loose corner of my paranoia. 300m behind, it wasn't gaining or falling away. I had an idea it had come off the M11 after me. I sped up. The gap didn't widen.

There was a railway crossing ahead and only one chance to turn off if the gate was down. As soon as I saw it wasn't, I floored the accelerator. I didn't want to get stuck behind that barrier. Two headlights followed. I hit the Linbourn by-pass and turned on to a dual carriageway. In my mirror I saw my tail turn too. There was only that one car behind me; still keeping pace.

Most of the suspicious activity going on here, I knew, was being created by my panic. I didn't want anyone following me home tonight. The vibrant lights of a garage beckoned. I dived in, slowing at the furthest pump, where I could see the carriageway. Keeping the engine idling and flicking off my lights, I awaited the imminent relief of seeing the suspect vehicle driving past and ahead of me into the night. It didn't. Nothing had come in behind me either.

The subdued lights in the forecourt shop meant no staff and no help there; self-service only. I felt like a sitting duck. If only I'd invested in the satnav with 'Evasion' or 'Getaway Driver' mode. I edged to the exit and on to the slipway. Peering back along the road revealed no sign of the other car.

Lights still off, I accelerated, away from the garage, on to the road and immediately into the outside lane. I was convinced another car had started up from back beyond the garage but this time there were no headlights following. The turning right across the opposite carriageway was upon me and I shot over it, earning a startled extended toot from an HGV coming the other way.

There was a small hotel 50 yards down this lane. Two lights

marked its double gate. I swerved again, this time into its wide frontage, spraying gravel before parking up alongside three other cars in front of the darkened building. I cut the engine immediately. I ducked down in the seat.

After 20 seconds I heard a car pass on the road. What now? I could get back to my village this way, following my pursuer through some winding lanes or I could go back onto the carriage way and take my preferred route over the chalk ridge. If it was Toke, of course, he knew where I lived and could just be parked up at home waiting for me. It occurred to me then that my nightmare scenario would be if he wasn't there. If, instead, there was just a dark cottage, a gate to my tiny silent garden and no way of knowing whether anyone was in it, skulking behind the over-fertilised hydrangeas. I knew I couldn't face that.

If Toke was there, I reasoned, I could just apologise, explain that the police had over-reacted and take whatever vitriol he needed to vent. How bad could it be? Except that, scuffling around in my head, like a rodent you suspect is lurking in your attic, was one guilty fact: when DS Grant had asked me if I thought it was possible Toke had assaulted me, I'd said 'yes'.

I needed help. It was 1.15am. I called Hugo's landline.

'Who's this?' a female voice furred by sleep.

'Esther, I'm so sorry. It's Shona. Is Hugo there?'

'Shona? What time is it? God! Shona, what's wrong? What do you need?'

'Could you just spare me Hugo for a moment? I'm worried someone may be waiting at my cottage.' I sounded so wussy. I imagined the deluge of shrimp pellets I'd get if Gone Puss ever got to hear about this.

'He's not here, Shona. He's up in London.'

'Oh Esther, I'm so sorry to have bothered you. Don't worry about it. I'm just being pathetic.'

'No it's fine. You must be frantic. Try Webby.'

I hesitated, 'Yep, good idea.' I so couldn't call Webby. Both men were close friends with Toke, but Hugo would laugh and joke and find a way to defuse the situation; Webby would be intimidated. Man-up Sho.

Sneaking back out onto the dual carriage way, I was driving into the village seven minutes later. As I drove past the church, I saw external lights on outside one of the cottages and Esther waved me down.

'Let's be quick,' she said as she jumped into my car. She was dressed in a massive coat with unfastened trainers; pyjama bottoms peeked out below.

'Esther, you're a life-saver.'

'Possibly literally, from what I hear.' A black weighty torch thudded into one palm. Esther was packing. 'You've stirred up the whole village, girl.'

'Oh god.'

'Where's Harry?'

'At Helen's. He's with his Gran in Welwyn.'

I pulled up on the drive. No silver cars were in evidence. Like a (not-very) special task force unit we hutched up the wall to my gate. Esther swung the torch around the corner to check the path and garden for assailants. Silent, she beckoned me forward with her free hand, then abruptly spread her palm back towards me – freeze! My heart was in my mouth. There was an ominous sibilant sound. I noticed that Esther's rigid body was quaking. A few fretful moments later, I realised that the hissing sound was Esther, wheezing with suppressed laughter. We opened the gate and moved to my door. Before we got there, unreliable sensors coaxed the outside light into life. I finally relaxed, unlocked and we went in.

'Do you need me to help you look around?' asked Esther.

'I'm sure it's OK.'

But we romped quickly round my small cottage. Esther turned down an offer of coffee.

'The village featured on the TV's Anglian News,' she said. 'It's about The Doll Killer murders, is that right?'

I groaned. 'The police say not.'

'They spoke to Hugo; asked him about some bruise you had.'

I showed her: 'Hardly anything to see now. Oh Esther, they sent the hunkiest cop I've ever met to interview me. He thinks I'm an attention-seeking fantasist.'

Esther gave me hug. I was close to tears. 'We all could have told him that,' she said.

'And there's an octopus at work that's got it in for me,' I wasn't sure whether I was crying or laughing.

'See,' said Esther, 'you're clearly not a fantasist. Everyone knows those octopi have got their tentacles into everything.'

I told her about Toke's text, about the angry confrontation earlier at work, about the car that I thought had been playing cat-and-mouse with me on the dual carriageway and that I worried might be waiting for me. I didn't mention the party or Lotte, but Esther did. She asked if it had anything to do with that saucy gathering Hugo had told her I was going to. I said 'probably' and left it at that. She told me that Hugo had found out two golfing mates were in London. He was going in tomorrow anyway, so went up to have a drink with them.

'Couldn't wait to tell them about being quizzed by the Filth, I expect' Esther served up with relish. 'By now he'll have them believing he's the village Godfather.'

We scanned the street through my window. It was empty, so Esther made to go home. At the door, she hesitated, 'Shona, you're shook up, and I probably shouldn't say this, but tomorrow morning, tell the police about being followed home.'

'I was imagining things,' I said.

'Probably, but there was a vehicle pulled up about 50 metres further on from your cottage. I only noticed because it moved when I stepped out to wait for you; after I put on our outside lights. It did a three-point turn and drove off quietly towards The Grange. It didn't ever put its lights on.'

'What colour?'

'Dunno, but dark, I think, not silver. Be sure and lock up.'

8 LINDI

July 2018

The email was from a former book-keeping client, Marcus Compton. The last time they had seen each other – the last time they had communicated – was when Marcus had sacked her.

Marcus's small internet marketing company struggled, survived, then thrived in a specialist niche. Lindi had been its part-time book-keeper. As the company grew, Marcus needed the extra credibility a top accountancy company would bring to impress bigger clients signing bigger contracts.

Lindi and he had parted on good terms. Her life had changed since, she wasn't looking forward to the catch-up small-talk, but she called the number on the email.

'Ms Mills, thanks for reaching out. How're you doing?'

The question she'd dreaded, 'Not as well as when we parted, Marcus, but surviving.'

'How's Ash?'

'Academically at the top of his game, but it's a difficult age. You've got that to come.'

'I'm sure.'

'What do you need, Marcus?'

'A smidge of finance work doing.'

'I feared as much. I don't run my book-keeping company any

more.'

She told Marcus that she'd lost her biggest client a few years back and was now working at a factoring company. He wasn't put off.

'Factoring yuck! Any chance you could fit in some work at weekends for me? Maybe take some holiday. I'd make sure it's financially worthwhile.'

'My holiday was used up getting Ash through his GCSEs. Last time I looked, Westons handled your accounts, Maz. There's nothing I can do for you that they can't throw five times more resource at.'

'For ten times the cost.'

'You stopped using me because you needed accountants with clout and credibility, what's changed?'

'I'm selling up.'

'Then you definitely need Westons. Your buyers won't take anything I do seriously.'

'Westons have done all the due-diligence. The deal's done, effectively. But I still need your help, Lindi.'

'I'm in Luton.'

'Yeah I heard –' he stopped.

'How did you hear?'

An embarrassed chuckle. 'Truth is, I checked.'

'Didn't your checks show I no longer do book-keeping?'

'Er...yup, they did, actually.'

'So, if you knew that...?'

'Let's meet up.'

'Are you still in Arlston? That's 40-45 minutes from me.'

'Yes,' he said, quickly adding, 'I'll come to you.'

'Really, Maz, don't waste your time. I'm going to be looking for a new job soon. I won't have time for that, Ash and freelancing for you.'

'No problem. When can you meet? Be good to catch-up anyway.'

They arranged a meeting for the following weekend.

* * *

They met in a cafe. Lindi had warned him she wouldn't have long. His call and the mysterious proposal that came with it, caused her to reflect on her circumstances. Ash needed a new school and they would need a reason for his change. She felt sure she would be sacked at the end of her probation period. Ash's problems had disrupted her hours. The forthcoming tenancy break meant they could leave their home if she wanted to. She had zero ties to Luton.

It was unlikely Marcus had enough work for her, but he must want her specifically – book-keepers weren't hard to find. Any commute to Arlston and back during rush-hour was awkward and she was several years out of book-keeping.

Marcus arrived late. It was a trait. He spotted Lindi, stabbed a finger towards her and strode to her table. 'Lindi Mills,' his bonhomie intimidated the quiet cafe, 'still keeping to the pirate code?'

He had borrowed this phrase from a popular movie and turned its 'he who falls behind, gets left behind,' maxim into his company's mission statement.

A scruffy pad and pile of papers thumped onto the table before he sauntered to the counter.

'I honestly don't have time for a catch-up, Marcus,' she said as he flung well-meaning innocuous questions across at her – only the answers were hurtful.

'Still all-business Lindi. That's what I love about you.'

Armed with coffees he began his pitch.

Lindi stopped him. 'Let me start.'

She told him she was about to lose her job, that she wanted to move Ash to a new school, that she was happy to work or live in Arlston and get back up to speed with book-keeping.

'But,' she said, 'I'd need enough of a commitment from you to pay my rent in the short term plus the time, and ideally contacts, to build up a client list again.'

She finished with, 'You want someone for weekends and holiday breaks. If you're selling up, it's inevitably short-term. Our respective needs aren't compatible.'

'Hold on,' he scratched his head and lifted a pen, 'let's just work on that.'

Marcus looked good, slimmer, with just a few curls of grey in his thick dark hair. He was the person Lindi had worked most closely with during her professional life. The period when she had done his books was chaotic and exciting. His company serviced a fast-changing and developing online industry. Traditional suppliers struggled to adapt old business models and cost structures, while a handful of disruptors conjured new ways to find customers.

Lindi and Marcus complemented each other. Marcus cut corners, pitched hard and adapted his company on-the-fly if he won the contract. Lindi thought things through and flagged-up issues no-one else brought to Marcus's attention. Recognising what he needed from her, she designed flexible spreadsheets. In this way the profit on his contracts reflected reality and not the guess-timated fudge Marcus would have previously settled for.

The two of them, often alone, worked late on deals. Being emotionally buoyed by success, or exhausted by the detail of nailing a pitch, brought them close. It could have escalated into more than just a business relationship – but only if they had been different people.

After Lindi's briefing, Marcus went silent. He doodled meaninglessly on his wad of papers. If you didn't know him, you would assume he was making notes or summing calculations. Lindi knew it would be a series of random shapes, circles and squares. It helped him process his thoughts. She didn't rush him.

The pen bounced back on to the table. He nudged it to point at her, channelling renewed positivity. Marcus was nothing if not 'can do'.

'Right, let's rethink this. I wanted you to ride shotgun on my company sale,' he paused for emphasis. 'The purchaser is Mitch Goodridge.'

'How can he afford...?'

'He's – never mind. You said to be quick, I'll explain if we find a way forward. I think this is workable. The guys at Westons have effectively signed off on the accounts. They've worked through the contract and overseen the due-dil with Mitch's team. The contract is a standard one used by Mitch's US pay-masters. It's non-negotiable. My say was reduced to 'yes' or 'no'. The acquisition formula is based on last year's perform-ance. The final sign-off comes in the New Year. For the next six months I must run the company without staff hearing about the sale, keep my costs low and not chase any business that I know Mitch is lining up.

'What I'm thinking, is that while the business is merely treading water, you could do my accounts far cheaper than Westons.'

'But not as well. I'm rusty.'

'Lindi-i,' he sang out the final 'i', 'you'll be brilliant. You know what? I can also throw in a rented home for you and Ash, if you want, in lieu of some wages. You've got six – let's say seven – months of work to get the deal finalised and meanwhile you'll be living rent-free.'

'Go on, I'll have some questions at the end.'

'I can also use your factoring experience. There'll never be a better time for me to chase down bad debt. I know some local businesses of a size to use your services. I'll recommend you but it's down to you to be cheap and sharp enough to convert them from there.'

'It sounds attractive, Marcus, especially the home. Do you have a figure in mind on salary?'

'I'll need to work one out, building in the rent-free option. I can add a small bonus relating to the final company sale cheque.'

'When would you need me to start?'

'Next month?'

'And the property?'

'I'll mail you over the particulars but come and have a look at it. Bring Ash. It's quaint. I'll show you round.'

'Which leaves just one thing,' she said. This is where it all falls apart, she thought.

Marcus waited, smirking disconcertingly. It worked.

'What?' she asked.

'I know your "one thing"s; is it honest and above board?'

'Is it? You know I won't sign off on anything shady. You seeking me out like this smells wrong.'

'It's all kosher, Lindi. If you say yes, I'll explain why I'm nervous about Westons' involvement.'

'Mail me the monthly salary and a formal offer. I'll answer you by return.'

Driving away from the meeting, Lindi couldn't believe how opportune this was. She liked Marcus, she understood his business and his industry. She'd enjoy living in Arlston. She knew there was a good school for Ash there.

But, she was also determined. She was going to get to the bottom of whatever it was Marcus thought he couldn't hide from Westons but could keep secret from her.

His parting shot as they rose was, 'So where's Ayan?'

Long story, she thought.

** 2003 **

Ammi had phoned the day after Lindi's pregnancy confession to Ayan. Lindi knew he would have phoned his mother the moment they parted. Had Ayan told Lindi that he wanted to stay involved and take on the baby, she would have insisted that he first spoke to his family. Her young life was on hold pending uncertainty and upheaval. She was desperate not to add to that.

Thus far she had only met Ammi twice, the second time when she came over from Karachi to see Ayan before Christmas. She had been joined on the trip by her youngest child,

Fawad. Ayan's lean and handsome brother was studying in the US. They'd had a meal out together. That had been fun. Lindi knew this call was business.

'Ayan called me, Lindi. I hope you won't mind. He told me of the situation the two of you are in.' Ammi got straight to the point. 'Do you love my son?'

'No.'

'So, what is your relationship?'

'Untested. We're good together, but up until now, it's been too easy. There's been no friction between us. A child will bring stress. It'll change Ayan's life beyond anything he can imagine.'

'Of course, but his life should include more responsibility.'

'Ammi, may I be honest?'

'You always are, Lindi.'

'This has come too soon. Given time, Ayan and I may have decided to move in together, fallen in love, wanted to commit to each other. We haven't had that time. If I use this baby to push Ayan into a closer relationship, now, it will end in failure. If you do; same result.'

'I think you know Ayan, Lindi. He isn't complicated. Do you think you might grow to love him?'

'I don't know. It's possible.'

'I come from a very different culture. You are already far closer to Ayan now, than I was to his father when we married. We learnt to get on. We became a strong team. We made a good family.'

'A wonderful family.'

'You are right. I can't advise Ayan in this. This is his decision – and yours. I think it will end up being yours.'

It was.

The wedding was hurried and discreet. Lindi's mum came down from Yorkshire. She had met Ayan once before and found him charming. A handful of Lindi's girlfriends came down to Surrey – Ayan paid for them to be put up in the hotel – but the wedding was a Pakistani affair.

Ayan's siblings arrived from various parts of the world, including the two sisters Lindi had not previously met. Various aunts travelled over with Ammi. Also attending was Malik Rahmen, the owner of the paint corporation that had bought out the business owned by Ayan's father. He was also Ayan's employer, although you would never have known it from watching them together. Mr Rahmen treated Ayan more like a favoured nephew. Lindi noticed the businessman was attentive around Ammi.

Mr Rahmen sought Lindi out after the ceremony. 'You must be a special young lady,' he said. Given the circumstances, the comment could be taken several ways.

'Mrs Khan and her family are making me feel like one,' she said. 'They've all been wonderful to me – and to my mum.'

'I live next door to them in Karachi,' said Mr Rahmen. 'I have watched most of them growing up. Naasira and Rahana perhaps a little less. Mrs Khan is a fine mother and a smart business-woman. She negotiated such a tough deal with me when I wanted to buy the family's paint factory, I gave her a position in my company.'

'I didn't know. But I'm not surprised.'

'I don't make her attend meetings, but I get her input on every big decision. Ayan's father was a sharp businessman too. Soon, I hope, Ayan will take more of an interest in business affairs.'

Lindi bought time with a sip of water, working out what Mr Rahmen expected from this conversation.

'I don't know Rahana or Tahira well,' she said, 'but, from what I hear, all Ayan's siblings are doing well in their careers or studies. In Britain we would say they are driven, very focussed on what they want to achieve.'

Mr Rahmen didn't move to agree. Lindi guessed Ammi had told him why this marriage was a rushed affair. She was uncomfortably conscious that she was a stranger, a foreigner, a non-Muslim and (probably more significantly) someone who had yet to prove herself in the world. She had no achievements; not in academia, business or home-making. She was the first person to have married into a family that, she realised, Mr Rahmen felt vicariously responsible for.

'Ayan has yet to reveal that side of his character,' she waited.

This time he nodded. 'Perhaps because of the timing of his father's death.'

'I'm not sure that's what Ammi, Mrs Khan, believes. I have not married Ayan to push him into things he does not want to do...'

'But...'

'I want to make my contribution to this family. Yes, I want to make Ayan happy, and I have been brought up to believe that you are happiest when you are achieving things and fulfilling your potential. Ayan's family love him, I want them to be even prouder of him.'

Mr Rahmen fell silent. Lindi noticed Ammi observing the exchange from a distance.

'I don't think we can be allies, Lindi,' he said at last, 'but I do think we want the same thing. I will keep my distance but observe with interest.'

'I'm not sure I see Ayan's future in paint, though.'

'No, not at first.'

9 SHONA

Thursday morning May 23 2019

After a better night's sleep, fuelled by anxiety exhaustion, I arranged to meet Helen and Harry for a much-needed hug at his school gates. It was much-needed by me, Harry gave the impression it was the last thing he needed. I had brought his phone but gave it to Helen. He scowled.

Helen and I hit Tesco. I ran my eyes over newspaper front pages. Several had a small mention of an '*Arrest in The Doll Killer case*', as a teaser linking to more inside. Only the Mail had the story – a side column – on the front page. I bought the Mail. Helen bought the Guardian. We had coffee.

Helen adjusted her glasses and looked askance at my Mail. Don't judge me I thought.

'What's the Doll Killer story?' She pointed to the column.

'*Man helping police in Doll Killer inquiry,*' read the headline. The story was by-lined '*Victor Dobson*', aka 'Vicious Doberman' as I remembered him from the conversation in my lounge yesterday.

I scanned his story quickly before I responded to Helen. It said that a man had been arrested in Benedicts bar in our village yesterday lunchtime and questioned by detectives regarding the two headless murders. Then it recapped the facts I had gone through on the Internet the night before.

DCI Hossein was quoted as saying: '*It came to our attention that the man arrested may have had information relating to the bruise discovered on the woman found murdered near Whittlesey. A new witness came forward to draw our attention to this suspect. She was able to identify the distinctive imprint of the bruise. We can reveal that the murdered woman's bruise was probably inflicted by a piece of jewellery in the shape of a St Martin's Cross. The original cross is found on the Isle of Iona, off Scotland's West Coast, and is reproduced as pendants and other jewellery.*

'*Now we need the public's help. If you know a woman...*' a list of identifying features.

I was seething and threw the paper down before the end of the column. Having labelled me 'unreliable', Hossein was now milking my story to put his three-month-old case back in the limelight. He had done nothing to allay suspicions away from Toke either. It was immoral. Neither of us had been named, but everyone who knew us would know. Oh god what would they assume?

Helen was scrutinising me over her glasses. 'It affects me that way, too,' she said. 'I haven't bought it for years.'

'It's not the Daily Mail,' I said, 'it's this story.' I pushed the paper towards her.

'Helen,' I said, as she read, 'I don't want to alarm you, and please don't tell Harry, but the woman in that story, who helped the police yesterday, was me.'

'Who was the man?' had she put one and one together and made it add up to the beast with that same number of backs? Helen was more likely to condemn me on my choice of reading material than my sexual morals, but this was the shape of things to come.

Helen departed, saying she'd see me when I dropped off Harry.

I had a pulsating 'to do' list. I started to make inroads into it with a call to Lotte's office.

'Huntingdon Precision Limited, how can we help you today?' The intended sentiment of the words splashed helplessly before drowning beneath the deeply uninterested delivery.

'Could I speak to Lotte, please?'

'Mrs Hadleigh isn't with us today.' I heard a sigh. 'Do you need me to take a message?'

'Can you tell me where she is please and when she'll be back at her desk.'

'Mrs Hadleigh's on a sales trip in the north all this week. She won't be back in the office 'til Monday.'

Bugger! Had Lotte mentioned a trip? 'Has she called in? Has anybody there spoken to her this week?'

'Is there anything I can help you with?'

'Please, this is a personal call. I'm Shona, a really good friend of Lotte's. She's not answering her phone. I just need to know someone's spoken to her.'

'I can't give out that information.' I was getting nowhere, 'For God's sake, Penelope (no final 'e' – oops). I'm not planning industrial sabotage. Are you sure she's OK? Let me speak to Lenecia?'

'No! We don't encourage personal calls. If you're such a good friend I suggest you call her mobile.' And with that the colleague described by Lotte as having 'a face like a wet weekend', clicked off.

Thwarted, I decided to hunt down Shouty. I had no contact details for him. Boy knew him better than I did. Shouty and Lotte had split up before she and I became friends.

Shouty was besties with Toke and Hugo Burrell. Esther and I referred to them as the Three Musketeers. I wasn't sure which of them was Porthos, Athos or Aramaflip, but I was pretty clear that the fourth member of their group – Webby, the village butcher – was D'Artagnan. The other three were all products of upper-middle class stockbroker-ish rural wealth.

Shouty and Toke had built successful businesses out of their sense of entitlement and trust-funded inheritance. Hugo had married a smart and savvy career woman. That left Webby, who had been allowed to join their club – despite being only of lowly (but hearty) butchering stock – possibly because they needed a fourth for bridge.

All four were in their 40s. They had been fixtures at village events. That had changed when Shouty's marriage to Lotte ended and he decamped to entrepreneurial Cambridge.

Toke was our village's most eligible bachelor, well-off despite having oodles of leisure time. A regular in Benedicts – the village's trendy bar – he had a quip for any conversation. Blond, but marking out some silver-fox territory, Toke didn't do long-term girlfriends but rarely came up short in the 'plus one' department. He lived alone in a former farmhouse with plenty of outbuildings, three miles north of the village. It wasn't ostentatiously large or fancy but did boast a well-maintained tennis court. While I had enjoyed a good nose when driving past, I'd never visited.

Hugo was the cheekiest kid in the class, only he had never grown up. He was smiley, sporty, still hunky in a curly-headed, roughly shaven way and, beneath his laddish humour, smart – octopus smart. Hugo and Esther's youngest, Aileen, was the same age as Harry and they were best friends before primary school asserted its gender stereotyping.

House husband Hugo was the darling of the village crèche club. He had previous with daughter Caitlyn, so he bolstered me through the toddler and nursery years with coffee-mornings, soft-toy puppet shows, Winnie-the-Pooh sing-a-longs and marble-run installations that CERN would have struggled to replicate.

Hugo also doubled as Toke's support act. The two would prop up the drinks table at any village occasion, sharing malts and cheeky asides, while Hugo's wife, Esther, spread bonhomie effortlessly and her hands helplessly when anyone pointed towards her husband.

Like Toke and Hugo, Shouty was a strong tennis player, but played in Cambridge. An investor and start-up accelerator, he had put money into Boy's businesses at some point, but no longer held a financial interest. I think he and Boy still talked through business ideas, but Boy didn't mix work and home.

I was now close friends with Shouty's ex-wife, but Lotte and he moved in different circles. Whenever Shouty came to watch Ollie play footy, he'd wave but invariably had a phone cemented to one ear.

What about D'Artagnan? I'll come to Webby shortly. I didn't get anywhere Googling 'Shouty' but 'Scott Hadleigh' proved more successful. I found one such specimen on LinkedIn, in Cambridge and he was an investor, bullseye!

Gone Puss probably had a stronger LinkedIn profile than I did. I mistrusted its Masonic overtones and worried that it encouraged you to spend too much time begging people you had only met once by a watercooler two decades ago to confirm that you had even a smidgeon of professional acumen.

LinkedIn seemed like a home for the professionally incontinent. Still, given my escalating concern for his ex-wife, I sidelined my misgivings and sent a contact message.

'Shouty,' I typed, 'please contact me urgently as I'm worried about Lotte, and my cephalopod-feeding skills needed endorsing'. I left my number.

Two embryonic and malformed Scott Hadleigh profiles had been started on Facebook. I attempted to befriend both.

I unearthed the 'Bizzies' card I'd been given at Linbourn police station, entered Sergeant de Clerc's phone number into my contacts and hit call.

'Hello Miss Patterson.' He answered with the fervour of someone being told it was spam for dinner.

'Sergeant, I'm sorry to bother you again. Thank you for giving me your number and getting my phone back to me.'

'The Linbourn PD tries to deliver on its promises.' He said without even a hint of humour. This was going about as well as my conversation with 'Ms Wet Weekend'.

'I really wouldn't phone, if I didn't feel it was necessary. I appreciated you and PC Jo listening to me yesterday and taking my assault seriously.'

'I thought it was the right call at the time,' he said, leaving me to fill in his unspoken, how stupid was I?

'I hope you didn't get into trouble.'

'You said you had a concern.'

'Two. They're probably nothing.'

A barely audible laugh escaped. 'I really don't think I should be the judge of that, Miss Patterson.'

'Call me Shona, please.'

'That would go against my training.'

'I could call you "Ant" ...' No response. 'Or Sarge, if you prefer? How about Sarge – Ant?'

What the hell was I doing joking with a spiky-haired law enforcement officer when I ought to be reporting the possible murder – or worse – of my close friend?

'Just your concerns please, Miss Patterson.'

'Yes, sorry, they are serious – to me at least. DCI Hossein said he thought you'd tracked down my friend, Charlotte Hadleigh. I can't get hold of her and I'm starting to get concerned.'

'This is the friend you went to the party with? I think you gave us an address and mobile number?'

'Yes.'

'Yes, we did try to track her down. PC Angus called her mobile and left a message I believe. We wanted her to corroborate your story, as much as she was able, also to give us details of the Uber driver she used. The murder team asked us to check these out.'

'So, you didn't get through?'

'She may have come back to PC Angus, but we've stopped actively chasing either her or the driver, as word came down, from on high,' i.e. Derbyshire Constabulary's sex-god, 'that they'd spoken to you and the anonymous texter –'

'Mr Toakley,' I helped.

'I don't think we ever had his name. We were told to stand down. I understood DCI Hossein had gone through things with you in, er... more detail,' Sarge was carefully picking out words from a box labelled 'Milk Tray IEDs' that Hossein had left for him. 'I believe there was a rational explanation for your bruise and text.'

'He thought I was exaggerating things and over-reacting to get attention,' I blurted. 'That I'm neurotic fantasist and borderline delusional.'

'Reading between the lines...' Sarge started. I knew he would be too much of a gentleman to agree, 'Yes.'

Oh!

'If my help was so rubbish,' resurgent anger flooded into my phone and doubtless welled out at the other end all over Sarge's uniform, 'why is it plastered across the Daily Mail's front page this morning? Why has Toke not been exonerated? Everyone in my village now knows it was him. People will assume he's linked to the murders.'

'Above my pay grade, I'm afraid.' Sarge had a ready-made escape hatch. 'Are there specific reasons why you are concerned about your friend?'

I told him. To his credit he didn't interrupt with possible (probable) explanations. Lotte hadn't made it home by Sunday lunchtime. She wasn't answering her phone to me or PC Angus, which was so unlike her. Her office had her down as 'up north' and Wet Weekend wouldn't say if she'd been in touch with them. And, last night, when I'd finally got through on her mobile, there was a disturbing silence, before it clicked off.

'Wet Weekend...?'

'A jobsworth at Lotte's office.'

'Your friend is angry that you abandoned her the other night?'

'Of course she is. And she's a very busy lady. But, Ant, trust me, Lotte gets the screaming fantods if her phone's switched off for more than a recharge cycle.'

'We really can't put more resource on this, Miss Patterson.'

'Jaywalkers?' I guessed, unfairly.

This took a moment to percolate through, before, '...and sometimes worse. Give me her office phone number.'

I did.

'How do I avoid Wet Weekend?' He had been listening beneath his spiky barnet.

'Ask to speak to Lenecia, or, I dunno, the head of engineering.'

'Anything else?'

'Yes, I think I was followed home last night.' I quickly re-capped the angry scene at the lab's front door, offered more de-tail on the car stalking me to the garage, then waiting for me to come out, and finished with Esther's concerns about the bash-ful car, without lights on, parked up close to my house.

'I know the garage you waited in for that car to pass,' said Sarge. 'There's a turn-off just before it. Goes to Hollow Hill Farm.'

I could picture it, he was right. 'Stupid name for a hill,' I said, but conceded, 'the car could have turned up there.' Only I knew it hadn't.

'You've had a tough week, Miss Patterson. Anyone's imagin-ation would be working overtime after that series of events. You wouldn't have noticed this car in normal circumstances. I have to be elsewhere shortly. I'm going to make a call to Mrs Hadleigh's office to put both our minds at rest.'

'Good.'

'I'll let you know if I discover anything. Call me if your texter contacts you in a threatening manner and I'll speak with him.'

'Thank you so much.'

We clicked off. As witness protection schemes went, this sounded pretty low budget, but Sarge had handled me well. I'd meant to ask if DS Grant would continue with the checks on Toke's alibi but Sarge probably wouldn't know.

I picked up the Daily Mail again. The story referenced an in-side page and I turned to it. There was a picture of the real St Martin's Cross in front of Iona Abbey – all four metres plus of it – with the five bosses showing. The bosses hadn't been in quite that position on the two bruises. They were placed closer to the centre of the cross – jewellers had to concertina it together to get the effect – however, there was just enough of an indica-tion of the four external bosses that you could see them, *if* you knew what it was you were looking at. Unlike DCI Hossein's murder team, *I* had known.

I read on from Hossein's quotes down the rest of Doberman's article: '*DCI Hossein believes the dolls found by the murdered women are key to their identification. The South Derby woman was found with a Barbie doll beside her – a model dating from around 1990 – while the Whittlesey woman had a Becca Blue Eyes doll first manufactured in Mexico eight years earlier, but widely available in Europe until the early 1990s.*'

I read it again. *I* had owned a Becca Blue Eyes doll when growing up. The coincidences were stacking up, but the article said that the doll was 'widely available'. Plus, I was confident it wasn't my doll, because I knew where my doll was, safely locked away in the box room in Dad's old cottage.

I flicked through mobile contacts. Yes, there was the number. I hadn't called it for three years. I called now.

'Stanton and Keynes, Property Agents. Robert Keynes speaking. How can I help you this fine morning?' Similar words to Wet Weekend's but delivered with bounce and purpose.

'Robert,' I started, 'I don't know if you remember –'

'Shona,' he said, 'I'd recognise your lovely Scottish burr anywhere. Shona... Patterson! How the hell are you?'

'Great,' I lied. 'I assume you know that Boy and I...?'

'Yes, we saw Boy regularly until a few months ago. We were all so sorry to hear about you two splitting up. Anyway, enough of that; you're better off without him, I'm sure. What can we do for you?'

'If you're in the office, I'd like to pop in. I'm in Arlston now.'

'Wonderful. Should I put the kettle on?' He should. I drove the short distance from Tesco to the agent's office and parked close by.

Boy had six properties he either used or let out, plus two business premises. It meant Robert worked closely with Boy in ensuring the houses were let and tenants behaving. While Boy and I were together, I was actively involved in the management of the properties and I had dealt with Robert then.

He greeted me by the door with a 'Wow!' and twirled me around warmly. 'Shona, I always thought you were too good for him; and look at you now.'

I thanked him. I'd forgotten that the last time he'd seen me I was near on two stone heavier.

'Now I'm even more pleased that you've not been murdered.'

'...Yet,' I added a cryptic note.

'Sounds like it's all kicked-off in your village? It was on the news last night; headless people in ditches and what not. Hardly the kind of stuff we letting agents want to hear.'

'I'm sure you'd find a way to put a positive spin on it.'

'Phew! That's going to be a toughie.'

'Oh, I don't know, "unusual water feature", maybe, or "adjacent to well-known pools – as seen on TV".'

'Haha. "Property unexpectedly on the market",' Robert joined in. 'Or "No onward chain".'

'Not just the prices slashed,' I added. That was enough.

Six years ago, I'd effectively taken over the lease, on behalf of my Dad, for one of Boy's two cottages in the village. The other cottage was the one Boy had since signed over to me, where Harry and I now lived. Back then, Dad had been taken ill, so I persuaded him down from Glasgow and we rented out the smaller of Boy's houses to him. It was on the outskirts of the village. It meant I could keep an eye on Dad, help with hospital visits and some shopping, while Harry could get to know his Granda. Dad had died four years ago; a year before Boy and I had split up.

I had still been involved in managing the rentals when we let the house to a couple of young commuters after Dad died. I knew that they had now moved out. I didn't know who was currently in Dad's old home. It wasn't anything to do with me any more and it was way off my usual beat.

I asked Robert about Boy's village rental, Dell End Cottage. He reported that it was probably empty, but he hadn't been asked to let it since the commuting couple had left.

'We still run everything else for Boy,' he said. 'Well, not your home, obviously, now Boy's signed it over, but the flats in Welwyn and the semi here. I assume we'll be taking on the village property again soon. Boy said as much, before he vamoosed to the wilds of South America.'

'It's unlike Boy to leave things empty,' I said, ignoring the painful exceptions of a) my life and b) my bed.

'He rented it to a work colleague soon after the couple left, but we weren't involved. Boy said he'd handle it himself as it was only a short-term let.'

'Do you know anything about it?' I was pushing at the boundaries of what he should tell me, but he thought Boy and I were still on good terms.

We were 95% of the time. We had to be, to keep Harry's world even halfway-functioning as he shuttled between the two of us. Children extended relationships beyond their natural death. Ours had resurrected into a kind of zombie existence with awkward shambling between our respective homes. We picked hungrily at each other's brains to ensure our son's school, play and sport requirements were met... and that Candi wasn't!

Robert answered cautiously. 'I only know it was a woman from odd things Boy let slip in meetings when we were discussing other properties. I know she moved out shortly after he left for points west. I mailed Boy to say, did he want us to take it back on, give it the once over and get it back on the market? He said he'd sort it out on his return. Shona, I must ask, why the interest? Do you have someone in mind for it?'

'No Rob, sorry, just my curiosity getting the better of me. The real reason I came is that, when my Dad died, we threw a whole load of his memorabilia – ornaments, keep-sakes and stuff – into storage in the cottage, the box room that was too small to be a bedroom. It was a rush job because you'd just landed the... oh god... Tillotsons was it?'

'They weren't married, but who is these days? He was Des Tillotson and I can't remember her name. I remember we wrote the lease up excluding the box room, just left it locked.'

'It's just that I want to get one or two of Dad's things. I guess it'll be easier if it's empty.'

'Well, it's only empty as far as I know.' Robert threw his hands up, 'Hell, empty or not, you have a right to go and get your Dad's stuff. It's nothing to do with me for the moment.'

'Except that I need to borrow a set of keys.'

'You'll have to sign for them and I want them back by, say... what? Monday?'

'That's plenty of time. Och, Robert Keynes, you're a wee star,' I rolled my RRRs at him. 'Be careful or you'll start giving letting agents a good name.'

'No chance of that, Shona, dear.' He rummaged around; I signed a form and he produced a set of keys.

'Promise me you won't do anything in that property that is going to get either of us in trouble,' he cautioned.

'I won't! And I can check it over for headless people while I'm there.'

'Before I hand these keys over, say something else in Scottish for me.'

'Stop yer bickering brattle yer wee glaikit bampot,' I said putting my hand out. I'd no idea what it meant but it seemed to hit the spot.

'Pwhoo-ah! Still sends me,' Robert produced an exaggerated shiver, dropping the keys into my hand. 'That sounded really dirty.'

'Well, I'd never be able to say it to you in English,' I said, truthfully.

I instinctively checked his fourth finger... oh, just as I thought, never mind.

❊ ❊ ❊

I drove back to the village and made my way to Boy's rental. As I was passing the Hart's Haunt pub, my phone went. I pulled into its car park and stared at the number – unknown. I nervously clicked it through, but didn't speak.

'Shona? ...you there?' It was Lotte.

'Oh, Lotte, I'm so glad to hear your voice.'

'I was in two minds about phoning, you thoughtless bitch,' there wasn't any real venom in her voice, 'only Penelop said you sounded desperate.'

Another woman's voice laughed in the background. 'No change there, then.'

'And, as you may have gathered,' Lotte went on, 'Lenecia sends her best. She's so far north of the Watford Gap that she keeps getting nose-bleeds. The only cure seems to be bingeing on Danish pastries.'

There was more background laughter.

'I'm so sorry I left you in the lurch at the party. I'll tell you all about it when you get back,' an elephantine sigh ripped through me.

'I have an inkling. Ollie tells me you're up to your neck in headless murders.'

'How on earth does he know?'

'You're all over his social media. You're trending, darling. You do know kids message each other these days, don't you, Sho? Ollie's got a phone. Talking of which, have you dropped mine off yet?'

'What?'

'My phone, it's with my purse. Don't tell me you haven't got them.'

'I didn't realise I had them.'

'Gods save us, Shona; it's in your shoulder sack thing. You were looking after it for me at the party.'

'Oh no, Lotte. I thought you'd taken it back. I left you so stranded. No wonder you weren't answering my calls.'

'Sho, you nincompoop! I've had to borrow a work phone.' Lotte started hooting with laughter. I heard her rasp to Lenecia, 'Sho's been calling her own sack!'

'I'll find it and drop it off with Ollie today.' I'd look, but I was sure I'd struggle to find it. 'Did you stay over at Shouty's?'

'Long story, Sho. Let's catch up when I'm back. Gotta go; Lenecia's making eyes at my pastry. You stay safe, now.'

'I will.'

She clicked off. Flower of Scotland blossomed on the phone. It was a text from Sarge. 'Can't call MTG. Ms Hadleigh IS OK. Wanted u to know asap. Sgt de C.'

Sometimes it's hard to know what to feel. On the one hand I was quite encouraged that my best chum wasn't lying head-less in a fenland ditch; on the other, the CID file labelled, 'Shona Patterson, delusional neurotic', had just got a smidge thicker. My plans for a career in the constabulary were in tat-ters. I swore myself off policemen.

'Thnx Ant, sorry for panicking.' I texted back. If only Lotte had phoned an hour ago?

I grabbed my keys and walked to Boy's rental. It looked un-occupied. I knocked on the door. No twitching curtains, no sound beyond the gargling birds whose nests were in the tips of some endlessly tall trees at the termination of the tiny road, nothing.

I was about to try the lock, when I heard a warble: 'Yoo-hoo, Shona, is that you?'

I turned and saw the neighbour from across the road, whose name I couldn't remember.

'Yes, hello, Mrs...'

'You look different.' She wasn't coming out of her front gar-den, just hollering from her gate, competing with the belliger-ent birds.

Yes, I thought, believing you're being targeted by cleaver-wielding serial killers can have that effect. 'I've put on weight,' I shouted back, jokingly.

'Oh, never mind dear, you don't look too podgy. We're none of us getting any younger.' Well, I'd asked for that, but she had the grace to look slightly mystified. 'The woman who lived there has left, if that's who you're after.'

'No, I'm not; just going through some of Dad's stuff.'

Then, as an after-thought, 'when did she go?'

'End of February-ish. She wasn't there that long.'

'Anyway, I'd better pop in.' I slotted the key home and made my escape with, 'Good to see you again.'

Her phrase, 'end of February-ish' had not escaped my notice.

The inside of the house didn't feel as though anyone was living there, but it didn't feel three months empty either. It smelt of cleaning chemicals too strongly for one thing. I scouted through the rooms. There were tins and packets in the kitchen cupboards, but nothing perishable in the fridge. Two coffee mugs lurked unwashed, but with evidence of a rudimentary rinsing in the kitchen sink. They may have been there three months, who could tell?

There was cutlery and a few plates in the drawers and cupboards. It had the feel of a spectacularly badly provisioned holiday let. I heard a car turn into the road and then reverse out again. Usually, I wouldn't have been remotely aware of that. It was an indication of how wired my senses were. It set the birds off again, bitching over the disturbance.

Unease permeated any thought of going upstairs, but it was why I was here. I waited listening at the bottom of the stairs. Two spiders lurked either side of the hall corridor. They vibrated in their webs, assessing me through eight pairs of suspicious eyes.

I crept up the steps and opened the master bedroom. The drawers there were half full of women's clothing: tops, underwear, trousers. The wardrobe contained a few dresses and business suits, although half the hangers were missing. This woman had either left in a hurry or hadn't planned to leave at all.

I glanced out of the window. There were no silver cars to be seen; the street was empty apart from my car and a small van driving off beyond the turning. Mrs What's-her-name had returned to her house.

The bathroom door was open. Its tiny bolt had been broken, wrenched open, by someone forcing it from outside. That was scary.

A tiny part of me wondered if I'd see a severed head and hands in the bath. It was clear and clean.

The box-room door was locked. I shuffled keys and unlocked it. It gaped open. I flicked on the light as the room's tiny window was shaded by the tall trees.

It was a midden. Items of clothing had been tossed into the room; mostly women's as far as I could see, much of it still clung to the hangers it had hung on in the wardrobe. A case, I didn't recognise, was on one side of the room. It was locked. All of this rammel belonged to Boy's work colleague, presumably. Why hadn't she taken it with her? How had it got in here, if only Boy and his agent had a key to this room?

I left the questions unanswered. I knew what I was looking for – it squatted beneath the tenant's debris – Dad's chest of memorabilia; stupid things, random things that belonged to Mum, Martin and me. The chest was cheap and cheerful, the stuff inside it was worthless to anyone but me. Boy and I had carried it in here before we had re-let the rental after Dad's death. I had been in no state to work through it then, and I'd had 100 more pressing things to sort out since.

I opened it up and saw things were missing. I started sorting through its contents. I saw my brother Martin's crappy wooden train set and other abandoned childhood toys. I had grabbed a handful in the past and infiltrated them into Harry's collection. There were some Xmas tree decorations Mum had made when I was seven or so. I couldn't find what I was looking for. There should have been a large cardboard box with more sentimental items in it. These would have included Mum's small jewellery box and more personal toys. It wasn't there. I upended the crate.

The pile wasn't that big, and I sorted through it. Several shoeboxes of old slides, thankfully Sellotape-d up. There were albums of pictures of Martin and me as youngsters that I should take back home with me. Dad's old pipe, which had contributed to his early death, was there; as was his guitar.

There was Mum's old sewing box, some dressing up clobber, a handful of Dad's work files, a few items of Mum's clothing. I went through all of it, but it was full only of tacky and unfashionable stuff, charity shop fodder. Mum's only decent jewellery, the stuff that had come from her side of the family (including a few pieces which had been handed down a generation or three) would have been in the jewellery box.

I cursed. The two things I wanted to check on were in the missing cardboard box. Someone had borrowed some of the chest's contents. Among the items missing were my mum's surviving Celtic jewellery – rings, necklaces and pendants – and my old Becca Blue Eyes doll.

The birds' warning cries from outside became a call to leave. I turned on my heel and ran. I didn't pick up the boxes of prints and slides I'd put by the door. I didn't lock the box-room. I leapt downstairs and out into the tiny front garden, shutting and locking the door behind me. I felt as if someone had ransacked my childhood and possibly used it for some vile purpose.

I sat for a moment in the car, my mind tripping over half-discarded memories. Mum had owned a chunky St Martin's Cross ring. She may have had another on a pendant. I was pretty sure that Dad had kept my childhood doll in the box along with a few soft bedroom toys. I'd berated him about the things he'd chosen to bring down with him from Glasgow, and that had been one of them. Had he left the toys for the house clearance jobbie?

I executed (or rather massacred) a three-point turn on the narrow road, before heading back the way I had come. No-one was counting my excess points. The van had gone.

I drove towards home, stopping outside Webb's the Butchers and jumping out. The butchers had two customers, a young mother I didn't know, and an elderly but well-turned-out woman who I was on nodding terms with. Conversation dried up as I entered. I said a breezy hello to both women. The older woman couldn't keep from gawping at me.

Webby was D'Artagnan to the village Musketeers, despite never having attended the right Musketeer school. He had inherited the village butchers and was serving behind the counter. On entering, I merited a tight smile and an indulgent shake of the head. He handed over a pack of meaty goodness to the young mother and turned to me while he prodded the till. 'I leave you alone for five minutes...'

'Well for god's sake, Webby, make sure you never leave me for ten.'

'I take it you're on nights this week?'

'Those lab fish don't experiment on themselves.'

'You should probably stay in Cambridge,' he said, sending the young mum on her way. 'I need a word.'

'Is there anyone in the back room?'

'Yeah, Mother's there, doing the accounts.'

'I thought you had someone –'

'Didn't work out,' he said. 'Let's chat here.' He led the way to the other counter. We'd still be overheard if the listener was attentive.

'Tell me,' I said.

'You probably know already, but keep your head down. I hear Toke is absolutely fuming.'

'I don't blame him,' I said. 'That police inspector has hung him out to dry.'

'Show us your bruise then.'

Webby had been my best chum in the village for a long period. A couple of years after we first moved in, Webby's unsuitable flaky girlfriend and he split up. I was Webby's go-to gal, back then. I provided coffee and a supportive ear when he had foundered on the rocks of online dating. The favour was returned when I was finding Boy's long work absences eroding my patience and self-esteem. Webby was usually on hand when unexpected crevasses appeared in my overlapping work and parenting schedules. We had been close... that was pre-Candi.

Webb's was a three-generation meat and deli business that had diversified to survive and competed with the Arlston supermarkets by dint of distance, charm, quality produce and even better-quality gossip. On the face of it, Webby served the village its meat with a ready smile, knowhow and confidence; perfectly at home in the role he was born to and groomed for. Scratch below the surface though, and the nerves were front and centre.

When Webby despaired of finding a new girlfriend, Boy and I extended dinner invitations (Webby provided the cheese course), encouraging him through some challenging date choices before an unlikely marriage. We welcomed the second Mrs Webb – a fellow tennis club player – into the village. And then our mutual support guarantee had run out. Our friendship fragmented and distanced after Boy got together with Candi. Like so many others, the Webbs felt caught up in my war.

Three years on, Candi, who had never previously managed any relationship with a man, as far as I knew, now had one with my former life partner. She was a frequent weekend visitor to the 'Big House' that Harry still thought of as home – even though he and I had moved back into the village.

The arrival of Candi into our barely functioning ecosystem forced friends to pick sides. The easiest side was the one that didn't involve tip-toeing around my resentment at Boy's new entanglement, or Boy's awkwardness at introducing Candi to former mutual friends. The easiest side didn't involve either of us. The Webbs chose it.

I still bought Webby's sausages, quiches and cheeses; just a whole lot less of them.

I showed him my bruise.

Webby was a good judge of meat. 'It's faded,' he said.

'So people keep telling me.'

'You know Toke made it back to Benedicts last night.'

'Really, at what time?' I asked.

Benedicts had been refurbished three years ago. It closed its doors as the Fur and Feather pub and emerged from the construction hoardings eight months later as a bar. The rebranding was finessed with a minimalist script sign and matching interior. Half its rear car-park had been consumed by a tacky orangery housing a massive table to showcase its mind-blowing (potentially literally) gin-brand collection. Lotte joked it was less a gin palace and more a gin gazebo. We re-christened it Bendy-dicks and refused to drink anywhere else.

Webby supplied the bar's kitchen with meat so was in close touch with Margaux, the manageress. He was also a good friend of Toke's, so had a bone to pick with me – typical butcher!

'Toke made his entrance not long before closing time, according to Margaux,' said Webby. 'She felt she had to stay open after time to give Toke his day in court, so to speak. You didn't come out of it well.'

'I don't deserve to.'

'Margaux said Toke got a half-hearted cheer on entering and a few die-hards stuck around to have a drink with him. Margaux finally kicked them out some time after midnight.'

That meant there was no way Toke could have followed me back from work last night.

'However,' Webby's voice lowered, 'the reason I wanted to see you, is the other thing Margaux told me. Apparently, the place was heaving last night – unusual on a Wednesday – benefitting from its new TV notoriety, I imagine. For most of the clientele, though, Toke's arrival was horribly awkward. People only know rumours and goss. But, they know it's you, they know it's Toke and they know it involves bruises and battered women. Margaux said 90% of the bar settled up within ten minutes.'

'Ouch!' I said, 'that's probably not fair.' Other butcher customers had arrived now, and were openly listening to our discussion, so I pointed to a quiche in his deli-counter.

'Margaux realises that. Innocent until proven... etc. but now you've fingered him as a suspect. It's in the papers. She says she'll have to ask Toke to stay away until the dust settles. The poor man was only round here only two evenings ago. If Toke is innocent... You've got to put it right, Shona.'

Oh crivens!

10 LINDI

August 2018

'It's the middle of nowhere. I can't believe the quiet. We could die here and no-one would ever notice.'

They were in the pinched garden of Marcus's cottage, on the outskirts of the sought-after village of Hartsdell. The stub of a road had one other building; a chalet-style bungalow on the other side of the cul-de-sac, slightly off-set from the empty rental they were viewing.

Tree-covered banks crowded up behind the cottage hemming it in so much that the strip of garden was set to one side.

'Something's visiting this cottage.' Ash gestured to a twisted slide of dark mud that slipped down from the bank between two of the glossy bushes. 'Something big.'

The banks behind and to the side of the cottage climbed at a 30-degree angle. Slender trees gave way to established ash specimens towards the top of the hill. It would soon be midday, but the sun had only just clambered over the tallest of them.

'It's rent-free for the first six months.' Lindi sat on the single-flag patio between pots of wayward herbs, many thriving on neglect. 'And it comes with a job that may help get me back into the kind of work I should be doing. It's what, ten minutes from the school we saw in Arlston; less from Marcus's offices.'

'I see you're already sold on it,' Ash's speculative kick caught a low shrub.

'I'm about to lose my job, Ash. You need a new school. We have to move. This is better than I expected.'

'It's a long way from Luton.'

Exactly, thought Lindi.

Ash knew he was no longer welcome at his current school but wanted to stay in Luton. Lindi wanted out. She knew – without asking – that all the reasons he wanted to stay, corresponded to her list of why she wanted to leave.

Her only reservation about accepting Marcus's job was the conviction that he had an angle he wasn't revealing. Everything else on offer would have been high on her wish-list over the last year, had she dared to dream.

'We could search for a flat in Arlston or Letchworth, but I won't be able to afford anything this good.'

'You'll be working for him again.' Ash meant Marcus, who had met them outside the small cottage and let them in.

He awaited their decision in the local pub, 'It's The Hart's Haunt, just around the corner. I'll make myself scarce while you two talk it through.'

'Only for six months or so. Do you have anything against Marcus?'

'Never met him before today, but I remember those late nights, from when we were in Hitchin.'

'It's going to be a lot less pressured this time, Ash,' Lindi promised, 'but the package is still good – especially if we move in here.'

'I hate it,' he said, 'but I'll hate anything around here.'

❋ ❋ ❋

'Looks like you have two new tenants,' said Lindi as they joined Marcus in the gloomy old-fashioned pub bar.

'Wonderful.' Marcus's wave took in the dingy surroundings, 'So, welcome to your new local. What do you reckon Ash?'

'It's crap.' Ash took a sip of his water. A couple of rough-hewn locals hogged the bar stools. 'But I suppose it's authentic crap. It feels like it belongs here.'

Marcus raised an eyebrow to Lindi, and then laughed. 'I can't argue with any of that. I certainly wouldn't recommend their Beef Carpaccio.'

Ash looked blank. The joke fell flat. Marcus had at least avoided asking Ash about school, girlfriends or football. All of which tended to be the first thing adults reached for and all of which made Ash determinedly mono-syllabic.

'The sign outside is the best thing about it,' Lindi fanned the conversation. The pub's scruffy car-park was fronted by a tall free-standing inn sign. A striking white stag's head stared out from it through two chillingly absent eyes. Dark countryside framed the pub's namesake.

'The Winter Hart,' Marcus said. 'Now he's a local character you don't want to get on the wrong side of.'

'Go on.'

'He's the reason Hartsdell is here,' Marcus leaned in. 'The village is named after him. The story goes that two huntsmen were tracking a white hart. They found him sipping from a crystal-clear spring. They decided it was a perfect spot for a settlement. It didn't turn out well for the Hart though.'

'And does he haunt it?' asked Ash.

'My son says so, but we've never seen him. We get fallow deer on the hills. I've spotted a few pale sandy specimens, mainly hinds, but never a white stag. There's plenty on the Winter Hart in the library here, and the art gallery. You should check them out. Tell you what, Ash, if you spot it, let me know and I'll cook you and your mum up some venison steak.'

Marcus went to settle up before they left. He came back with a card. The barmaid had scribbled the owner's details on it. He handed it to Lindi. 'Hester here reckons the landlord could be interested in help with his books. If you're cheap, she says. Apparently, he's as tight as a ferret's fanny, according to those two at the bar. I promised her you were cheap.'

Lindi spluttered. 'Thanks! Good to get my reputation established right on my doorstep.' She was grateful, though. Marcus's relentless go-getter optimism was the opposite of her 'what could go wrong here' default setting. It was why they had been a good business team, they came at things from different ends and balanced each other out.

On the way home, she and Ash stopped off at the little library. Their old Hitchin tickets were valid, so they borrowed some books on Hartsdell. A drive around the village included a stop at an old chapel behind a neglected car-park. Its sign read 'Hartsdell Old Chapel Gallery'. It was shut and didn't advertise opening times. There was a magnificent church, St Cecilia's, and the village hub was marinated in history. It was, Lindi reminded herself, 'a long way from Luton'.

She had accepted Marcus's offer, which included seven months' rent free at the cottage and the option of staying on if she picked up enough other clients. Tomorrow she would hand her notice in to Dafiyah. It would be a relief all round.

* * *

Lindi went in to see Dafiyah first thing. She apologised for having had such a disrupted spell, thanked her boss for her understanding but added that she knew she would fail her probation. She didn't want to put Dafiyah in the position of having to sack her, so was resigning.

'How is Ash doing now?' Dafiyah asked. Lindi hadn't expected her boss to remember Ash's name.

'They've kicked him out of school,' Lindi said. 'He's trying out being Muslim. It was sparked by the programme they've put him on. He's hoovering up information, understands the politics better than I do. His knowledge makes the school nervous, but I don't think he's radicalised.'

'None of us really know, Lindi,' said Dafiyah. 'There are so many ways for people's views to be shaped these days. The world is packed with injustice and horror, pick any side and you'll find 100 reasons to be aggrieved.'

'Let me know when it's best for me to go,' said Lindi.

'Leave when it most helps you and your son. That's what's important.' They agreed two weeks.

'You set a terrible example to the rest of the team,' said Dafiyah. 'If you don't mind I'm going to tell them I kicked you out.'

Lindi laughed. 'Makes sense. I'll tell them you were a real bitch in here.'

'Do it,' Dafiyah smiled. 'But just so you know, you were good at this. I'd have kept you on.'

'Thanks, that's important to me.'

'No, what's important is that you stay close to your son. Don't let him go.'

'I won't. Not ever'

** 2004 **

Ayan would later joke that nappies forced him into his first real job. Ashal arrived a little earlier than expected. They agreed the name together. Ayan told Lindi it meant 'most bright'.

He revelled in fatherhood, receiving more attention and visits from his family. It came with a hardening of Ammi's resolve that his 'boy-in-the-city' lifestyle should end. It did, causing Lindi to gently probe, 'Not missing nights out with arrogant ex-Oxbridge wasters?'

'I'm happy being a dad. It suits me.'

'I warned it would be a sea-change in your world.'

'My nightlife was never as glamorous as you pretend, Lindi.'

'But having one gave you a focus and a rhythm.'

'Alright, out with it. You've been spending too much time listening to Ammi and Naasira. Let's hear what they want of me.'

'They haven't changed their views. I just wondered if you're more amenable to them, now. You're a super dad but you shouldn't just be that.'

'I'll get a real job if you want me to.'

'I want you to have challenges, to test yourself. I know you'll be more capable than you joke you'll be.'

'I do think about it, Lindi, but it's hard to know where to start. I've no idea what I'd be good at.'

'Can I help?'

'Please.'

'If it's hard to decide what you'll be good at, let's approach it from completely the other way around.'

'You're being clever,' Ayan laughed. 'You've lost me.'

'As you once famously said, "leave it with me."'

Lindi called Ammi and won an email address for Malik Rahmen.

'Do you want me to speak to him?'

'Thank you, Ammi. I know he'd do anything you ask, but I feel it's important I do this.'

Her mail was returned with a date and time for a phone call. She sent Ayan out beforehand.

Mr Rahmen was intrigued but busy.

'Ayan is ready for a challenge,' she told him. 'He's trying to work out what he could do. I think we should come at it a different way. I wondered if you have contacts in London business circles. Companies that might give him a start.'

'You have to give me more than that, Lindi. If I'm going to request a favour I need to know Ayan won't let me down. He'll be representing me.'

'I think sales,' said Lindi. 'Ayan is charming and smart. He starts at the bottom; no special treatment and I'll do the groundwork with him to ensure he prepares properly. It doesn't have to be a career. It's about planting his business seed and seeing what develops.'

'I have absolutely no ideas,' Mr Rahmen said, 'but I'll try to help. Let me talk to some people here. The best I can do is get Ayan an interview. After that it's down to you two.'

A week later an email came from Mr Rahmen. It was sent to Lindi – not CC-ed to Ayan. It contained a date, a business name and a contact. The position was 'car sales executive'.

Lindi wondered how to sell it to Ayan. Her research came up with a posh car brand's flagship central London showroom. She tapped on a 'vacancies' link and read the bullet points. Top of the list were: 'motor industry experience' and 'proven sales track record'.

Ayan owned a moderately smart, sporty, rarely used car. He grabbed cabs round London and was as far removed from a 'petrol-head' as it was possible to imagine. Ayan's CV wouldn't get him within a day's drive of this job and yet he already had an interview.

Before she spoke to Ayan, Lindi wrote down his points of difference against what, she imagined, would be a long list of car-industry execs. He did have something to offer; he was the brand's archetypal customer. He had the status, wardrobe, sense of entitlement and charm to move among them as equals. It wasn't enough to get the job.

But he had something none of the other candidates would have. It was proved by his invite to the interview – he had contacts. Everything else could be taught but, if you didn't have it, Aran's advantage was all impossible to add to your CV.

At this end of the market, she decided, it wasn't about knowing the number of cylinders, it was about cachet. By the time she mentioned the interview to Ayan, she had an answer for every objection.

11 SHONA

Thursday afternoon May 23 2019

I bought a slice of hi-cal quiche from Webby. It only increased my feelings of guilt. Back in my cottage I found my shoulder bag from Saturday night and poured the contents on to Harry's bed. I didn't bother hunting through the pile. It was clear neither Lotte's purse, nor phone, were there. I called her on her temporary number.

'Lotte, I don't have your phone or purse. I suspect they were stolen on Saturday night,' I said. 'I was attacked at the party…'

'Oh no, you poor sausage. Was this Toke?'

'You've heard then? No; Toke's only guilty of sending stupid texts. I think I was drugged. The attacker was disturbed before any harm was done, but when I came to, my bag's contents were everywhere. Because I thought you'd taken the purse out earlier I didn't miss it.'

'It was still in there, Sho. You'll have to report the missing phone to the police, so I can claim for it. I'll mail through its details shortly.'

'Any plastic?'

'No, I didn't have any cards with me, thank god. The purse contained £85-odd cash and I dropped some earrings in your bag, but don't worry about that. Be a dear and get a crime number for me will you?' After a deep breath I called Sergeant de Clerc. I had no pride left to swallow and kept things very formal – no 'Sarge' taunts or 'Ant'-ics.

He listened, but quickly pointed me to Cambridge police's online report service.

'One more thing,' I said.

'Quickly please.'

'I had a Becca Blue Eyes doll.'

'*That* was stolen too?' I detected major exasperation and disbelief now. He would be cursing the day he had ever given me his 'bizzies' card.

'No, maybe, I don't know. It's the same type of doll they found beside that body with a bruise.'

'Oh right, I see. So this is nothing to do with Saturday night.'

'No, the murder.'

'It's not my case, Miss Patterson. Do you want me to pass this on to DCI Hossein?'

This had huge potential to add to my 'fantasist' credentials. I could just imagine the inspector demanding, 'Is this your scarlet harlot again, de Clerc!?' I decided I couldn't put him through it.

'No better not. It's just the coincidences seem a bit extraordinary. I felt someone ought to know.'

'Thanks for thinking of me, Miss Patterson. Are we done?'

We were. I duly reported the phone theft to the hard-working Cambridge Police web-servers. While I had the laptop open, I Googled information on the 'Whittlesey murder doll'. A report leapt out at me, '*Gruesome find on Doll Killer's victim.*' I clicked.

'*The Doll Killer's sick sense of humour was revealed when police reported that the mutilated doll found beside the second victim had also been given a "bruise", writes Chief Crime Correspondent Steve Shelby.*

'*In yet another macabre twist, the doll (a Becca Blue Eyes model) found beside the serial killer's second victim was not only left headless and handless – in a parody of the murdered woman – it also had a "bruise" 'tattooed' on its left arm.*

'*It seems the cold-hearted killer found time to doodle on the doll in the same place and in the same design as he inflicted on the mutilated corpse.*'

The article dated from March 2nd, four days after the body had been found. The report helpfully showed two pictures side by side. One was the close-up of the cross bruise on the victim's arm and the other was of a tiny doll's arm.

I didn't gasp. I didn't scream; I just stared and determined I was going mad. When I'd been seven – maybe eight – and Martin a year older, Mum had taken us to the West Coast of Scotland. We'd immersed ourselves in Mum's Clan MacInnes roots. For a sunny fortnight we were little Somerleds, lording it over the Isles. Much was made of the cross on Iona, with which Martin shared a name and I think Mum's St Martin's Cross ring dated from that trip.

On our return to Glasgow, we invented new tartans for Clan MacInnes, coloured in little crests and decorated everything with Celtic designs. Had the Bonnie Prince turned up on the Firth of Clyde that summer, Martin and I would have been first in line, plastic claymores brandished aloft.

During this frenzy of Highlander birth-right, Martin had 'tattooed' my old doll with his version of the St Martin Cross. It was little more than a series of tiny blue biro lines and dots and I'd forgotten all about it – until that moment when I stared at it once more, replicated fuzzily on the computer screen in front of me.

Steve Shelby had regurgitated the basic facts yet again and embellished them with the inevitable quotes from the all-pervading DCI Bloody Hossein... '"*The killer has taken a psychotic pleasure in re-crafting two murdered women with doll doppelgangers, right down to the duplication of the bruise on the second woman's arm,*" said Hossein. "*These two dolls, a 90s Barbie [found by the first victim near Derby] and now a 1980s Becca Blue Eyes, could be vital clues in identifying the killer. We are convinced that in each case the doll was owned by the murdered woman.*"'

A fog of unreality sallied from the screen to engulf me. I felt as if the torso floating in the stagnant ditch water must be the real me, and these last three months had all been some illicit reincarnation, during which I'd discovered where I'd left my head and hands and was still pretending to live out my old life.

The report was again from the Peterborough paper. I recognised the name of the correspondent. I clicked on a link to his email. 'Mr Shelby,' I typed, 'I have recently become involved in the Whittlesey murder investigation. Would you be interested in an exclusive? Please call asap.'

Was I imagining things or were there too many coincidences for me to ignore? I opened a new document on my laptop. I wrote:

Mysteries

1. Who is the dead woman?
2. Who attacked me in Cambridge?
3. Why bruise me to look like the murder victim? Coincidence or daring?
4. Why take Lotte's phone? – it was there!
5. Is my attack a connection to the murderer?
6. Who followed me home Wednesday night? If anyone!
7. How did my doll get in the death ditch?
8. WHO? Is the woman in cottage!?
9. Have cops checked on Toke's business activities yet
10. Is DCI Hossein married?

That was more than enough mysteries and I could sense my mind was starting to wander. I tried a new headline:

My Connections to Victim

1. St Martins Cross – part of my family history
2. Identical bruise
3. Same type of doll!! Missing from cottage!
4. Mum's missing jewellery? Including RING!
5. Anonymous Text? – not according to Hoss-pants.
6. I fit victim profile! – says Ant.

Set down it came across as lightweight, unless you believed totally – as I did – that the bruise and doll were the same. So, forgetting the murder for a moment, I concentrated on my attacker:

<u>Who knew I would be at the party?</u>
   1. Toke – police say he has alibi
   2. Shouty
   3. Hugo – how?! (told by Shouty or Toke)
   4. Lotte
   5. Webby? (told by Shouty or Toke?)

None of this was insightful but I felt I'd reclaimed some control. Something occurred to me. Webby had said Toke was round his on Tuesday night. I wondered at what time.

Quiched-up, I wandered back to the butchers. Thursday afternoons were quiet and Webbs was devoid of customers. It was also devoid of Webby. I asked his sous-butcher, who said he was out visiting a local farmer. He added that Kotryna was in the back-office if I wanted to see her. He shouted out, 'Kotty, someone to see you.'

In TV Musketeer adaptations D'Artagnan scores the best-looking girl. Our village wasn't the kind to mess with dramatic tradition. The second Mrs Webb was Kotryna, a leggy Lithuanian blonde. We used to play doubles together. As a tennis player, she had an iffy serve and a tame forehand, but good all-round court coverage. She retrieved with the same defensive mind-set that kept the Russians from re-invading her country.

I, by contrast, inflicted offence any time opponents offered anything in reach of my forehand, hammering the white lines and unwary spectators. After Boy left me I was thumping that ball with Serena Williams' intensity and woe betide any umpires that crossed me.

Despite my on-court prowess, Kotryna had asked for a change of partner. I was serving up too much vitriol. I wanted to rant about Boy taking up with Candi; Kotryna didn't want to listen. Her Eastern European perspective was, 'worse things occur in the Baltic. Man leaves for younger woman, happens all the time. Take a paracetamol, get over it, move on'.

At first sight the Webbs made an unlikely couple: Webby was well into his 40s, Kotryna was in her early 30s; Webby was quiet and self-effacing, Kotryna was forceful and direct; Webby ran an old-fashioned family meat-emporium, Kotryna was a self-employed beauty and health consultant who plied her trade in her customers' homes and was in demand over a wide area.

Five years on from their wedding, though, it was easy to see how good they were for each other. Webby was utterly smitten. He had slimmed down and the confidence of having the best-looking wife at any dinner-party had made him more out-going. Kotryna was embedded in the heart of a posh village. She enjoyed tennis, numerous holidays, the independence of her own business, a holiday home in the south of France, and a network of friends and neighbours.

She was chewing on paperwork when I entered the snug office. She glanced up brightly and her face fell when she saw it was me. Normally, we tried to pretend we were still friends. Before Boy departed we had been close – Lotte close. Inevitably our new cooler relationship had grown stilted and awkward. Today it felt abnormally icy, perhaps because she had a long-standing friendship with Toke. He had introduced her to her husband.

'Sho,' she sat back in her chair, 'what do you want?' She could be disturbingly abrupt. Her clipped accent reinforced the curtness.

'I spoke to Webby earlier – '

'He's out.'

'I know. I had a question you can probably help with.' Her stare wasn't encouraging. 'He told me Toke was here on Tuesday night. Toke and I are in a situation with the police. I just wondered what time Toke was with you on Tuesday.'

'I can't help you.' She returned to her paperwork.

'It may sound trivial, Kotryna, but it's really important to me. You know Toke was arrested yesterday. I either need to clear him or...' Or what? I hadn't thought this through. 'I may be in danger.'

'If, you are in danger, Sho, and that would not surprise me,' Kotryna raised her head and made flicking gestures at me with her pen, 'go to the police. Make them understand. Don't bring your danger to us. Don't involve me. Don't you dare involve Webby again. In anything!'

I stared in dazed surprise. My expression was likely similar to one of my more zonked zebra fish after an aquarium drug test. Kotryna's head was down again, pen wantonly ticking at her paperwork. I had already turned to leave when three more words were directed at my back.

'Shona,' she hissed, 'I know.'

I ran out.

Two questions flared in my head: what did she know, and did I even want to know? As I ran back down to my place, hurt swelling my tear-ducts, I saw Esther loading her car. She shook her head at my patently fragile state, 'Shona, how're you doing now?'

'Not well,' I admitted. 'Thanks for being there for me last night. I don't think I'd have made it into my house without you.'

'You were lucky Hugo was out.' She grinned. 'He's such a wuss. You'd have ended up sleeping at ours.'

I sighed, 'Now you've been so nice to me, I'll have to give up all my plans of having an affair with your husband.'

Esther waved her hand dismissively, 'No, you go right ahead, all my sisters slept with him after all.'

Strange but nearly true: Esther came from a family of six girls and all but one of them had slept with near-neighbour Hugo before Esther (the second youngest) had married him. It seemed no-one was remotely embarrassed about the fact.

'I thought he forgot one of them.'

'Typical man never completes anything he starts.' Esther was mining familiar territory. 'He neglected to sleep with Judith, sister number four. She says she's fine about it, but deep down you know she's hurt and mystified. Hugo says he would happily put it right, but you can't repair these things after the event.'

I laughed. It always made me laugh.

'Moving on, did you do anything about being followed?'

'I did report the car to the police. They're not buying it.'

'Really, I thought you were their star witness according to the morning papers. Not that they're naming you or giving you any credit. Oh, I Googled your Police Inspector. You're right; he's far too hunky.'

'Hossein hasn't named Toke or me,' I said. 'The trouble is everyone knows who it is. Everyone now assumes Toke attacked me and is involved in the murders.'

'That's down to the police, surely.'

'Is it? I feel responsible. I keep feeling I over-reacted.'

'Don't. I keep thinking about that car. How it was so determined not to drive past me.'

'Hugo's at work I guess,' I said. The Burrells shared work and childcare duties. Esther was the bread-winner and did Monday to Wednesday. Hugo's work was more casual, shifts in London, Thursday to Saturday, sometimes days, sometimes nights and not every week.

'Yes, he should be back tonight, if his golfing buddies aren't still around, why? Do I need to put him on night patrol, watching out for your return from work?'

'No,' I laughed, 'I'm going to leave lots of lights on and load up the car with a hammer or sharp garden implements.'

'The thought that you'll be roaming the village after midnight wielding a scythe, means I'll certainly be sleeping easier in my bed.'

'Esther, can I ask, how did you know I was at that awful party on Saturday night?'

'Hugo told me. He thought it was a great joke, wondering

how Cambridge would cope with you and Lotte masked up, scantily clad and on the pull.'

'How did Hugo know?'

'Shona, where is this going?'

'Sorry, Esther, because the police didn't believe me, I'm obsessing over every detail. I'm trying to convince myself I'm not inventing it all.'

'Hugo was in London on Saturday night, at his desk. Is that what you need?'

'Of course, I wasn't suggesting...'

'I'll ask him to let you know how he knew but then we're all going to drop the subject.'

'Yes, I will.'

'You say the police have already wrongly cast suspicion on one man. They don't need any more help from you starting conjecture about another.'

'I wouldn't, you know that.'

'Glad we're clear.' Esther turned away. She had a hard edge. She had fought off four and a half sisters to land Hugo, she wasn't going to put up with me bad-mouthing him.

'On another matter,' I shouted at her retreating back. 'Did you ever run into the woman who recently rented Boy's cottage down the south end of the village?'

'Yeah, I liked her. She did some work for Webby.'

∗ ∗ ∗

At 3.15pm I joined the queue of cars outside Harry's school. First it was the mums ogling me. I scanned for friendly faces, so I could hide my unease in conversation, but most village children came and went by school bus. I had to bear my new notoriety alone. An alert must have put out on the local Mumsnet pod: 'Murderer bruises local mum.' It was probably vying for 'Discussion of the Day' alongside, 'My 6-year-old wants to laser off his tats.'

Groups of mums snuck together. Glances slithered over to where I stood trying to develop an unmerited interested in my shoes.

If the mums were intrigued but discreet, the children were agog. I'd never liked holidaying in places where you go out to find the local attraction and discover you're it. This was that feeling. The Year 9s-and-up squeaked in awe, stopped and pointed at 'murder woman' as they trooped out of the school gates. The Year 8s-and-below kept their distance and ran to their mums.

I had no idea how any of them recognised me. My Facebook picture was so dated and touched up it made me look like Cameron Diaz in her heyday. I started to wonder what form my Facebook tributes might take when I was inevitably murdered: 'A great mum, a mould-breaking youth soccer coach, kind to cephalopods.' I hoped my mistreatment of zebra fish embryos in gene research would be glossed over.

I felt a tug on my sleeve. Harry stood beside me beaming up, 'Hey Mum.' He wasn't quite ready to hold my hand, but his closeness suggested a turn-around in my 'cool-mom' status.

'Have you been arrested?' he asked, with undue chirpiness. He seemed to be basking in borrowed celeb glow.

'Not yet.'

'Everyone at school says you're involved with murders.'

'Just one murder,' I played things down modestly. 'The first one was nothing to do with me.'

We reached the car. I resisted the temptation to wave to my new followers. Harry belted up. 'Mr Bandini asked if I needed to talk to anyone about things at home.'

'Right.' Was the Mafia taking an interest now?

'I said, "Yes", and asked if he could tell me why you were in the news. He said he couldn't.'

'I'm not surprised.' Finally, Harry had found a subject (other than biology) where his mum knew more than his teachers.

'Some third years came up to talk to me about you – even girls.' This was news.

Since Harry and Aileen had gone their separate ways aged six-ish, Harry had given girls a wide berth. As far as I knew he was still in love with Paul Pogba but maybe things were changing.

'The police were searching for you at school yesterday.'

'I know. I spoke to them in the afternoon.'

'This is to do with your bruise, Mum, isn't it?' We were queuing for the A1.

'It looked a bit like a dead woman's bruise, but the police say it's not connected, so nothing for you to worry over,' I explained badly.

'Hugo said it looked very cross,' said Harry.

'Like a cross, perhaps. You heard him talking about it?'

'He and Toke were laughing about it. Hugo said you'd got it at your party thing. That's why I asked to see it.'

I filed this away. 'I wouldn't mention any of this if you speak to Dad, though, eh.'

I caught Helen's arm as I dropped Harry off. 'Helen, he knows about the newspaper story,' I said. She didn't look surprised. 'He's got a lot of homework; try to keep him off the internet.'

* * *

Back at home, I put in a call to Dieter. He was the Head of I.T. at Boy's company and, effectively, second-in-command. We hadn't met often. Boy filed work and home in separate cabinets. He answered, we exchanged a few awkward thoughts on Boy's sabbatical. Dieter said he'd seen something or other about it on Boy's Facebook page. Really, I hadn't looked at Boy's Facebook page for years. As far as I knew he didn't have a personal account. I thought he only used Facebook as a business tool.

'Anyway Dieter, the reason for my call, was to ask about Boy's recent employee. The one he took on last summer and rented my dad's old cottage in the village to.'

'What's her name?'

'That's it, I don't know much about her. She's left it in a mess and the rental agents don't know if she's coming back. Is she still with you?'

'No. We weren't taking people on last year, Shona. Whoever it was, she didn't work here. You'll have to ask Boy.'

She was turning into a real mystery woman. I had an idea and called up my Cambridge-based labs supply company. I ordered them to deliver some material to my office before end of play that afternoon.

I put a torch in the car and put a couple of house-lights on for when I came back. I thought about adding a hefty wrench or garden fork to my armoury but couldn't come up with anything that, if whipped out of my belt in a crisis, wouldn't reduce both my assailant – and me – to hysterical laughter.

Just as I was about to leave for work the phone went. It was DCI Hossein. I caught myself playing with a curl of hair as I listened to his heady voice.

'Miss Patterson, I've been informed you think you were followed home last night.'

'Sergeant de Clerc thought there were other possible explanations,' I said.

'So I understand. And that you were also harangued at work?'

'I was on my rounds at the time, but the security guard told me that an angry man in a saloon car demanded to see me.'

'A pale saloon car similar to the one Mr Toakley drives?'

'The guard didn't let him in. Since I didn't see anything myself, it's hard to be sure.'

'Mr Toakley was released from Cambridge's Police Department's interview rooms and dropped by his car just before 7pm. Would that coincide with the man's visit?'

I'd heard the phone go around 7.50pm, but he'd had to track my office down. I said, 'Yes, but I don't want to get Mr Toakley into yet more trouble now we know he's innocent.'

'That's hardly your call, Miss Patterson. If a car did follow you back from your office, as you thought, could that have been Mr Toakley's car, a silver Jaguar XJ saloon?'

I explained that my friend thought a car was waiting outside my cottage, and that she thought it may have been dark-coloured but couldn't be sure as it had driven off when she clocked it. I added that witnesses placed Toke in the pub until late, so he couldn't have followed me from the office.

'He could have been establishing an alibi and then following you from closer to home.' Golly, police minds work very deviously and suspiciously... and quickly!

'That's possible.' I heard Hossein talking with someone else at his end.

'Inspector Hossein? Did you check Mr Toakley's alibi for Saturday night?' It sounded like he was relaying the question. A moment later I had been switched to speaker and DS Grant's less cultured voice came on. I guessed his all-revealing notebook was probably in play.

'His alibi checked out,' he said. 'We weren't really chasing it as we'd agreed that Toakley's connection to our case was unlikely. Anyway, a Mr... Martinaitis, confirmed this morning that he'd had a business meeting with Toakley at the relevant time last Saturday.'

'So, you believe Mr Toakley isn't involved.'

'It seems to clear him of involvement in the attack you reported to us, yes, Miss Patterson.' DS Grant was choosing his words carefully.

'Then shouldn't you clear his name in the media?' I suggested. 'People, here, assume he's beaten me up and is involved in your murders.'

Hossein came back on this. 'We've never used either of your names in the media. We didn't release them. We certainly didn't say anyone had beaten you up.'

'But you arrested Toke in broad daylight in a very public place, where he is well known –'

'Acting on a tip-off *you* gave us.'

'Your arresting officers let slip that you had ordered his arrest,' I recalled what DS Grant had said about how the village journalist had been tipped off about the inspector's interest. 'And you and a squad car were parked outside my house, after the arrest. People put two and two together.'

'They usually do. I can't be held responsible if they come up with five.'

'But –'

'I can't clear his name without releasing it to the public. I don't intend to do that.'

'Everyone here thinks Toke's involved.' My Celtic blood was up, and I was ready to fight against the tyranny of Sassenach injustice and oppression. 'It's hardly fair.'

'Then I suggest you put them right.'

'Did Sergeant de Clerc mention that I owned a Becca Blue Eyes doll?'

'Ye-es,' he said in a way that caused me to imagine him rolling his luscious dark eyes at DS Grant.

'Isn't that a coincidence too far?' I snapped into the phone, a tad aggressively.

'You don't get it, do you, Miss Patterson?' God, but he had a seductive growl. 'Firstly, these dolls weren't common, but they were widely available. Secondly, the dolls left at the scene were almost certainly opportunistically picked up from the vicinity of the murdered women at the time of their deaths.' His voice was rising now. 'Thirdly, why would the killer attack you and draw attention to the fact that he had given you the same bruise as on the dead woman? It would only implicate him in the murder.'

Was that a good point? I didn't have time to consider it, as DCI Hossein played his trump card. 'The killer is not targeting people based on their choice of doll; he's murdering flesh and blood women. This doll didn't belong to you, Miss Patterson, it belonged to the poor woman we pulled from a ditch.'

'I just –'

'You had a bruise; a faded bruise, that you didn't take a picture of. Only you know what it represented when it was vivid. It isn't evidence of anything. No-one is trying to murder you.'

'I have to go to work,' I said meekly. I had basically lost the argument because I wasn't dead. That hardly seemed fair.

'Yes, thanks for your help.'

In what?

12 LINDI

September 2018

'He's already sold out his own company – two years ago – to an extraordinarily acquisitive US player. Their strategy is to buy market share over here, and quickly. Mitch made me an offer and I thought, you know what, the time is right. He's buying my company now and others will follow.'

Marcus had arrived at the cottage mid-morning with a laptop, a bundle of files and two still warm coffees, snatched from somewhere en route. Ash was in his second day at the new school and Marcus had asked Lindi to wait for him at the Hartsdell cottage. He explained that, with the sale still under the radar, he didn't want to have to explain her presence at his offices. She would work from the modest dining room.

'And Mitch Goodridge is the CEO?' asked Lindi. Mitch had been one of Marcus's rivals when she had last worked with him six years ago. Their two companies were a similar size, with similar tech solutions. They ended up pitching against each other for medium-size contracts – neither had enough clout to go after big contracts. It sounded like Mitch and his US buyers were changing that.

'Mitch is the man. His hands are tied of course, but in the UK he's boss. That is until he misses forecast or screws anything up. At which point some Stanford alumni will be sent over to royally kick his butt and take over. I don't envy him; he spends his entire time in conference calls with guys in Delaware.'

'And what about you, after the sale goes through?' Lindi couldn't imagine Marcus not running his business.

'In theory, I'm tied to the new company for 18 months, but you know how these things usually pan out. They wanted to attach post-sale performance bonuses to it. I said I wasn't interested.'

'We'd best get on.' Lindi was all too conscious that she was in this man's debt and wanted to start repaying it with work.

'There are three parts to your role, Lindi,' said Marcus. Her dinner table lay submerged under A4 printouts. 'You need to prepare the monthly accounts for the company from the start of my financial year in July, until the sale. That won't be before January but, hopefully, not long after. It's all on the laptop I've given you and what small paper trail we have these days, is in this pile.' His fingers drummed on it.

'Who do I go to with queries? I'm bound to have questions.'

'That would be me,' Marcus tapped his chest. 'I don't want you going to the office, or Westons, for obvious reasons. Whatever we sign off will have to be filed with Mitch to this timetable.'

A sheet passed to her as he continued. 'His people come back to me with any concerns; I bring them to you. Fact is, they won't care. The company sale multiples are based on the previous financial year, not this one. Plus they know I'm running the company at half speed over these six months.'

'Your timetable says July should be done by now,' Lindi pointed to the sheet.

'Westons' accountants have done 90% of it. Mitch isn't sweating it. But let's get it signed off in the first week or two. After that we really need to play catch-up and get ahead of the timetable. I want us reporting December within 14 days of month end.'

Lindi's second task was to go after outstanding debtors. The third was to write up the accounts for the final contract. Although, he added, apart from finalising the bad debt, last year's accounts were already cleared by Westons.

Lindi shook her head. 'Marcus, you know this isn't worth what you're forking out for me. You could have found independent accountants; given your bad debt to a small factoring company and rented out your cottage for £2K a month. You'd have been far better off.'

'I want a second pair of eyes I can trust.' A serious stare over his glasses pitched into a laugh. 'Who am I kidding? Truth is I'm going to take Mitch's Yanks to the cleaners. I want someone to share that moment with.'

'Take them to the cleaners, within the rules.' Lindi hid her serious reminder with a bob of her head. Marcus thought rules were things that applied to other people.

'Lindi, don't be such a wuss. The Yanks are based in Delaware for crissakes. They're far bigger pirates than me.'

Marcus would take Mitch to the cleaners, she felt sure. Not for one moment did she believe he was going to share how he was doing it with her.

* * *

'Rashid' was a name that continued to come up in the cottage. Lindi only knew he was a Luton schoolboy from the year below Ash. The two hadn't been close before the final month of Ash's GCSE year but bonds had been forged by the fateful Religious Education debate.

Ash never gave much away but neither did he lie. If a text came in when they were together and Lindi asked who it was from, he'd tell her. 'Rashid' was the answer more than any of the friends that Lindi had met. One reason for the increased calls with Rashid came attached to another name, 'Zainab'. She turned out to be Rashid's cousin. Ash told Lindi that Zainab's family also lived in Luton.

Zainab didn't call or text, but her name cropped up in discussions with Rashid. When Lindi probed, Ash coyly admitted that he and Zainab were close Facebook friends.

'How close?' Lindi teased.

'Don't start going all ridiculous, Mum, we've never even met.'

'What have you got in common then?'

'Not a lot. I just admire her that's all. She doing a lot of stuff with her life,' he said.

'How old is she?' was the next question that occurred to Lindi. 'Dunno 18-or-19 I think.'

'So, what do you admire about her?'

'She's just brave and principled. The rest of us talk about stuff, Zainab gets stuck in.'

And that was all she could get out of him.

Lindi felt things were getting back on track. A girl's influence, even older, even on Facebook, was likely to be a good thing, she reasoned. There hadn't been girls in his life before. Ash's involvement with the 'free-range anti-radicals' (as he referred to the counter-terrorism agency), had scaled down since the move.

Lindi knew he was still on their radar – he had to check-in from time-to-time – but their interest had lessened. As she'd suspected, the longer it took a programme co-ordinator to drive out to you, or the more difficult it was to get you to a specific programme module, the less of a national threat you became. Most systems fall apart when they butted up against life's practicalities.

Hartsdell brought mother and son closer together. It was a less busy time in both their lives and the first month in the new cottage coincided with a glorious late summer. They started exploring their new surroundings on Hartsdell's network of footpaths.

The village was bigger than they'd realised. Backroads and alleyways led to new discoveries. Picturesque and historic homes revealed themselves around each corner. A greater draw was the tangle of woodland bordering the cottage's tiny unkempt garden. The lawn was hemmed in by a stretch of be-leaguered hedge that had given up trying to keep the wild at bay.

The animal trail Ash had discovered ran through the bound-ary and up a steep bank of shaded ash and spindly hawthorn. Out of sight of the cottage it linked to a footpath following a winding gulley cut by a dribbling ditch.

A turn downhill plunged them back into another amputated limb of Hartsdell. Uphill led them through, and beyond, the trees to a heaving vastness of manicured farmland. Here, the bare shoulders of the Chilterns, rose from tightly wooded val-leys. Small copses crested them. Footpaths ran everywhere, between and across the fields; remnants, Ash said, from a time when agriculture ruled the economy and farm workers tramped from villages to their labours.

Ash's revision-honed mind was topped-up by a froth of Hartsdell history. His trawl of the library netted books on Hartsdell's past and Ash consumed anything about the Win-ter Hart. He started walking to see if white deer still lingered among the chalky hills.

Lindi was captivated more by the flora. After their first ramble up and over the ridge, she borrowed a book on wild flowers. Strips of them edged the paths and huddled against the tightly-shorn hedgerows. Cue-chalk blue cushions of sca-bious, low creeping bindweed peppered with pink saucers and rose-purple stars of wild mallow were most common. Occa-sional corners of fields were still bloodied by poppies drifting above the short-stemmed wheat.

She hoarded ancient names: lords and ladies, daffadowndilly, venus-naval, Queen Anne's Lace and lady-smocks. For every romanticised heroine she unearthed a corresponding villain: devil's parsley, dead-men's bells, and adders' root.

The fields they'd assumed to be flat tilted plains rising to blunted ridge-tops, were anything but. Deceptive undulations and secret hollows loitered in every field. It was by one of these, on their third excursion, that Lindi felt Ash catch her arm. She instinctively stilled. He pointed into a dip opening up in their view across a freshly-harvested field.

Lindi could only make out dusty stubble, and then she saw them, a close group of dusky brown bodies, half of them sitting, half standing and all staring tensely back. Ash dropped to his haunches, and she did the same. The deer raised heads and ceased feeding. They stared, ears twitching, but none bolted.

'How many?' wondered Lindi, 'ten or twelve?'

'There's more than you think,' said Ash. It became their catchphrase whenever they saw the deer. Sure enough, one deer trotted a few paces away leading others, which Lindi hadn't been aware of, to totter to their feet. A group she had taken to be three, revealed six as they broke up and nudged away. More skittered past their colleagues, and the herd became a chorus line of animals gently waltzing towards the far hedge before melding into it and melting away.

'I made it 21,' said Ash. 'Fallow, I think; like the Winter Hart.' None of the deer had been obvious stags or white but a couple were a pale sandy colour. Lindi supposed it had been triggered by Marcus's challenge to spot a white stag in return for a venison supper, but Ash regularly roamed out, returning with reports on herds he'd seen scattering over the chalk.

'Still pursuing venison steaks?' she asked after he trailed home from an afternoon amble.

'The legend just appeals,' said Ash. 'The Hart's a medieval quandary. Half the legends hail it as a hero who led the hunters to the spring, so founding the village. The other half view it a bogeyman, a visitation of plague and death, a wandering curse.'

'Why does that appeal?' Lindi laughed. 'Remind you of someone?'

'I dunno, Zainab maybe?'

** 2009 **

'I need to speak to Ayan, Lindi,' Ammi's voice kept breaking. The line was poor but Lindi was sure she could hear the strong-willed woman sobbing. 'It's very urgent.'

'I'll get him.' Lindi called out. 'Ayan, it's Ammi and it sounds important. I'll come up.' To Ammi she said, 'He's in the bath. I'm taking the phone. Can you tell me as we go?'

'It's Naasira; she's been involved in an attack. They've stabbed her.'

They had been in the Hitchin house for nearly three years. Ayan commuted into work, although he kept the flat in London. He wasn't the most natural salesman the car company had employed, but some business acumen had started to kick in. He was bringing organisational and marketing ideas to the dealership. He had even, quite independently of Lindi or Mr Rahmen, won some small UK action for Mr Rahmen's paint corporation.

Ashal was now Ash, easily among the brightest in primary school. Lindi helped with homework and Ayan read to him when he returned from work. They had tried for more children but been unsuccessful. Instead, Lindi had trained as a book-keeper, starting her course as soon as Ash began nursery.

Lindi's life was running along a track that her 16-year-old self would have desperately kicked against. She was content, but the gentle tapestry of her life included a thread she was watching closely. It wasn't yet loose but, if she kept worrying at it the way she was, that would change. She could barely remember Connor, yet every so often she'd glance at Ash and see something in him that would make her think of her occasional bed-mate from uni.

She kept telling herself it was paranoia, but in her head the small possibility that Ash wasn't Ayan's son weighed more than all the evidence that he was. He had Ayan's hair, his laugh was rarer than Ayan's but similar. He needed pushing the way Lindi pushed Ayan. Ash wasn't sporty; Connor had obsessed over football, she remembered. There was no evidence that he wouldn't end up looking like his dad, but nothing yet to suggest he would.

If Lindi watched Ash, she also watched Ayan watching Ash.

Nothing hinted that her husband wondered whether Ash wasn't his son. He loved the boy fiercely. The only thing to justify her fretting was that Ash had Lindi's pale northern England complexion. And, even then, Ammi and the rest of her children were all paler than Ayan.

'Ammi, here's Ayan.' Her husband was struggling with a towel. Lindi didn't wait. She whipped it from him, thrust the phone into his hand and whispered, 'Naasira's been hurt'.

As soon as the call was over, Lindi sat Ayan down with a coffee. He gave her the details. Two men had been waiting for Naasira close to her office in the Clifton business area of Karachi. One had stabbed her twice and the other had punched her with his fists. As passers-by rushed up, the pair leapt on a moped and escaped. Nothing had been stolen. The attack was thought to be political and cultural.

Several prominent Pakistani women had been active recently in highlighting the high number of girls and women knifed, raped and attacked weekly in the country. It had been a problem for years, but a recent burst of stabbings in Karachi, including several teenage girls, put it on the front pages. Naasira had been particularly vocal in calling the Government and police to account for not doing more to find the assailants and protect the women of the city.

Ammi said the police were behaving as if Naasira brought it on herself by criticising the authorities and the misogynistic culture of men in her country. The police response was to attack the media for giving the assaults, and the protests they sparked, too much coverage.

'They are using this assault on Naasira to argue that women should keep quiet about the barbaric way their sex is treated in my country,' Ayan said.

'Silence is an overrated virtue,' said Lindi.

'The appalling truth is that the men saying this likely believe it. It's shaming.'

Ammi said the doctors counselled that Naasira would survive but that her wounds were serious. It was too soon to say if there would be any lasting injury, but she would be scarred for life.

'I have to go,' Ayan said.

'Of course,' said Lindi, 'Ammi and Naasira need you.'

'They are both a lot tougher than me,' said Ayan, 'but I was supposed to be head of the family. Even though I abdicated that role, I should be there. It is a sad fact, but the police and authorities will take more notice of me than they will of Ammi.'

'Speak to Mr Rahmen while you are there,' said Lindi. 'He'll help you make a stink about this and get people to take notice.'

13 SHONA

Thursday evening May 23 2019

Why, I wondered, as I rumbled through the aquaria dispensing fishy goodies from my trolley, had DCI Hossein phoned. Was he seeking more ammo from me to keep the public's eye on the case at Toke's expense? A wild notion came to me – I must have either seen it on the telly or read it in a book – but don't ruggedly handsome maverick detectives always set up a strong, (usually) attractive woman as bait, promising to keep her safe when the deranged axe-murderer finally reveals himself and homes in on her?

I ran it past Gone Puss, but his arm gestures suggested he'd spotted a few flaws in my theory.

My phone warbled, and I answered.

'And you are... Shona Peterson, I take it?' said a frayed male voice.

'Patterson,' I was wary. 'Who am I talking to?'

'Patterson, that's it (three weak coughs). I understand you have an exclusive for me. My pen is at your disposal, Ms Patterson.'

I went momentarily blank, before it came to me. 'You're the criminal guy?' I was expecting a thrusting and forceful voice, baying above a pack of barking newshounds, hunting down answers. This one had barely limped out of the kennel before needing a kip.

A wheezy throat-clearance came down my phone, which morphed into a gargled chuckle. 'That's not how I usually introduce myself.'

'The crime correspondent,' I corrected, and then added, 'chief.'

'Yes, I also turn out for am-drams, court cases, occasional council meetings and Posh home matches. How, exactly, are you involved in this Whittlesey murder?'

'Have you seen the papers today?'

'Yes, it's an occupational hazard. I take it you're the St Martin's Cross woman?'

'That's right.'

'I thought it was a bit of a non-story.' He coughed again, 'having said that, you did make our front page.'

'Let me guess: "Doll Killer's grisly cross clue on headless victim?" perhaps.'

'Uncanny, almost word for word.'

'I want to do a deal with you,' I said.

'Ahh, we don't pay members of the public for stories,' he chuckled hoarsely. 'We barely pay reporters for stories, these days, Miss Peterson.'

'Patterson. I don't want money,' I said, 'I'd like to swap information with you.'

'I can't see a problem with that. They assure me I'm an information hub. Can I ask why?'

I told him that the man, who had been arrested and let go on Wednesday, was innocent. That the police investigation had shown he wasn't responsible but that everyone who knew the man still thought he was involved in some way. His innocence needed to be made public.

'Ms Pet... Shona, I'm going to call you, Shona,' he said. 'Firstly, I guessed he wasn't the murderer because... they let him go. Also, your village isn't in our catchment area and this isn't an exciting enough story. Tell me how you're involved.'

'I had a very similar bruise to the Whittlesey victim. This

man saw it and texted me to say it was the same as on the murdered woman.'

Was he even listening to me? I heard snuffling and shuffling noises before, 'And was it?'

'Yes, it was on the same spot on my arm. I recognised my bruise as being made by a piece of jewellery in the shape of one of the Iona crosses. I told the police. They hadn't made that connection.'

'But they assumed that the murderer must have given you the same bruise. So that made your man a suspect?'

'Except that he didn't give me the bruise.'

'I see. Who did?'

'We don't know.'

'You were thumped hard enough by a piece of Gaelic jewellery for the shape to be visible in the resulting bruise and you don't know who did it?'

I didn't like where this was going. 'It's complicated.'

'Let me get this straight. It was in the exact same spot, it was made in the same way as the murder victim – a way that hadn't been put into the public domain – and using what sounds like the exact same piece of jewellery? That's got to be the murderer, surely.'

The coughing had stopped, and the tired hack had been replaced by something energised.

'It seems not,' I squeaked.

'Hossein didn't believe you.' Steve Shelby was sharper than his battered voice.

My hesitation confirmed this.

'Can I ask where you were when you received the bruise?'

'That's not important.'

'Were you in Peterborough or the surrounding area?'

'No.'

'Do you honestly believe, Shona, that there's a connection between you and the murder?'

Did I? I hadn't been so sure, but this guy was the chief crime correspondent and he'd made some telling points.

'Before I answer that, let's talk about your information.'

'OK, you know we put all our stuff in a newspaper, don't you?'

'Are you going to answer my questions?'

'I am.'

'Where did the victim come from, have they said?'

'No. She's unidentified obviously, but they'll have a good idea of the area.'

'Isotopes?' I guessed.

A lazy whistle: 'Smart girl. Yes, they've done something they call "stable isotope analysis". It narrows down the area where the victim lives and works. They haven't released it, so I assume it's not definitive. However, I know someone... I could try to find out.'

'What do you know about the dolls?'

'Only what I've put in the papers.'

'You keep reporting it as a "serial killer". I think you asked Hossein a question about that.'

'Got me, Shona. It seems I *do* have more information than is in the paper. I'm wary about giving it to you until I understand what you're doing here.'

'DCI Hossein has arrested my... er...friend and he's taking a lot of flak. Hossein hasn't released the man's name, but it was a very public arrest and everyone in the village knows who it is.'

'Mr Toakley.'

'How did you know?'

'Word went around. A local reporter had it and was pitching the story. The police told us we couldn't use the name.'

'Hossein is using the two of us to draw attention back on to the case,' I said.

'Yes,' said Shelby, 'and he's very good at it. He exploits us, the media, to reach out to the public. Do you notice how he never refers to them as "victims"?'

'You use the word "victim" all the time.'

'It's bloody hard to avoid it when you're writing up a murder. Hossein, though, studiously shuns it. They are always "women". He goes out of his way not to dehumanise them.

It's part of his strategy to engage the public. You asked about whether the police think it's a serial killer. I'm not going to answer that but, given that Hossein is all about maximising publicity, if you were him, would you correct the press from referring to it as a "serial killer"?'

'No,' I said. 'He'll get better headlines and more public interest if we all believe a serial killer is on the prowl.'

'You said it, not me. Shona, I'm going to have to go if I'm going to write up your story. Can I call you back on this number if I have any more questions?'

'What story?'

'The "Shona Peterson: marked by the Doll Killer!" story.'

'What!? You can't do that. That's not why I spoke to you.'

'Oh sorry, did you put in your email that this was off the record?'

He knew full well I hadn't. 'Of course, I didn't. I thought I had to say if I was going "on the record".'

'That's not how it works.'

'Look Steve, I'm in deep enough here, already. If I am involved –'

'Are you? You said you'd tell me.'

'Off the record,' I stressed, 'yes, I'm pretty sure there is a connection.'

'But Hossein says not.'

I was desperate and that is the only excuse for what came out of my mouth next. 'I think I know who the woman killed in Whittlesey was. That's the real reason I'm talking to you. I need to be sure before I go to Hossein. If you don't print the story yet, and I'm right, I'll give you the victim's name first. You'd have the scoop before anyone else.'

'That sounds like all jam tomorrow. I want a story that's going to sell the next edition.'

'You said yourself that, if my bruise was the same, the murderer had to be stalking me. The bruise was the same.'

'And if the victim is the woman you think, then the killer must be someone you know.'

'I guess, but I don't know for sure. I only know it's not Toke.'

'You're playing a dangerous game, Shona. I tell you what we'll do. I'm going to write a story for tomorrow, which doesn't name you, which does explain why Mr Toakley was arrested but exonerates him.'

'You need to keep me out of it.'

'I can't. I need "a source". A witness must tell me Mr Toakley's name otherwise I can't use it. I also need that source to say categorically that he's innocent. The police aren't saying that. I won't name you, but Hossein will obviously know it was you and he's not going to be happy.'

That also applies to the killer, I thought.

'Are you sure you don't have a Peterborough connection for this?'

'Mr Toakley has business interests up your way,' I remembered.

'That helps.'

'Are you a stringy for Vicious Doberman?' I asked, half recalling what DS Grant said yesterday.

'I now have no idea what you are talking about.'

'Sorry, me neither. Can you get it into the national papers too?'

'Yes, after we've stolen a lead, I'll ensure it's picked up. Other questions will almost certainly occur to me. What time can I call you 'til?'

We agreed we'd stay in touch. I felt, not the first time, that I'd been played.

Why had I said that I knew the victim of the second murder? If it was the mystery woman Boy had installed in his rental, then Boy was surely the most likely suspect. For all his faults, he was still Harry's dad; someone I had lived with and mostly loved for nearly 16 years. I couldn't imagine Boy chopping the head off anyone – alive or dead, except...

Except that Boy could handle a meat cleaver. He had gone on one of Webby's butchery courses a few years back.

He'd claimed it was a culinary thing. Boy rarely cooked, only when we were entertaining. He'd casually wander in from the office, later than promised. A kitchen full of hungry guests would watch him toss lentils in pans, roasts in ovens, sprinkle wine lavishly and send singed meat fumes tornado-ing towards the smoke detector. Conversations caught fire around his relaxed bustle and culinary renown was achieved without a recipe in sight.

I'd met Boy on a holiday with mutual family members. My brother Martin married someone who knew someone, who was married to Boy's sister. They were on a group holiday when I crashed for a couple of days. Boy arrived unannounced on a whim and a bike with only one pair of underpants.

He was from Welwyn Garden City, I lived in Glasgow, he was walking out with some filly, and I had just broken up with some dork. The improbability of us ever getting together still makes my head spin.

Boy was 38 and I was 23 – did I mention the 15-year age-gap? No, well that was because no-one ever did, it wasn't obvious or important. When I first set eyes on him, I didn't think, 'wow, he's old enough to be my uncle.' I just thought 'wow!' Quickly followed by 'and he's only got one pair of underpants... and they're in the wash! It must be fate.'

I was just the right side (wrong in many outfits) of full-figured. He was fit. We made each other laugh. I got on well with his friends, and those bits of his extensive family I met. I moved south to be closer. I moved in. We both moved out and into the village. Boy's ethic was work hard, play hard. We enjoyed a wide circle of existing chums, to which we added village friends. We entertained a lot, went out more, holidayed relentlessly.

I waited patiently for Boy to pop the question. Time was on my side. Friends dropped heavy hints. We both put on weight. Boy said if I got down to nine stone, he'd marry me. I tried but our lifestyle was against me. I cut back on snacks, lowered my wine consumption, played more tennis. but it was beyond me. I was too desperate, too anxious. With the benefit of hindsight, the target was well chosen. It wasn't that I'd have been seriously malnourished at nine stone, but I would have been a shape I had never been in my life.

One morning I woke up alone. Boy had got in late. He'd fallen asleep downstairs. Alone in bed I reflected that my life (and, more to the point, Boy's) was slipping away. Soon we might not be able to have children together. I panicked. I didn't consult, I gambled and in one way it worked, Harry arrived.

Harry was a great kid. Boy, when not at work, was a cool dad. Thanks to nursery and a safety net of village friends, I could still work. I enjoyed being a mum, and we were well off. We left Harry's 'Happy Home' and moved into 'Big House' outside the village, without selling the cottage we'd been living in. Inevitably, we entertained less, we didn't go out so much, holidays became a very different proposition. Life revolved around Harry. I cultivated other new parents at the expense of old friends.

Boy still worked hard, but only Harry was playing hard.

We'd separated three years ago, on date-night. If your relationship needs 'date-night' it's probably too late.

'Enough!' I had told Boy over a meal out, downing cutlery.

'Sho?'

'Leave if you're that miserable,' I said. He did; the next day.

If Boy had been having an affair, then at least one of us would have been happy. Instead, his demonstrable dissatisfaction, even embarrassment, at being my partner made us both miserable. My confidence evaporated. My weight was up. I drank too much, too often. I over-compensated for being depressed by being loud.

Boy's put-downs were habit, not cruelty, but they ceased to be funny. Maybe, I just stopped being assured enough to laugh them off. I thought I'd be better off alone. I was wrong, but I had made my ridiculous ultimatum and spurred him into action. Since I had initiated the split I could hardly blame Boy for it. It would be like being angry at him for something he'd done in one of my dreams. Our rich and varied social circle had tried to be there for both of us. Harry made endless plans to bring us back together.

Leave if you're that miserable.

And we know how that ended.

Six months after the split, I discovered Boy had started a relationship with the youngest of our extended circle, Candi. She was a friend of a friend. She rarely turned up at events and didn't have a boyfriend. An up-for-it sort, if quiet-ish. She wasn't trim – the same shape I'd been when Boy and I first met – or fashionable. She was 21 years younger than Boy.

For 33 years – Candi would whine, to anyone bored enough to ask – she'd failed to generate a meaningful sexual liaison. However, within three to four months of Boy being back on the single peg, she had surreptitiously slipped him off, slipped him on (or was that in) and got a relationship on the cheap. It was my second-hand relationship, which I'd stupidly thought was worn out. She didn't move in, she kept her home just outside Huntingdon and didn't crowd Boy at all.

'Smart girl', as Steve Shelby would have noted.

Before they got together, Harry and I had moved out of Big House and back to the village, back to Happy Home, which Boy still owned. He had begun the relationship with Candi secretly. No-one told me. I was utterly livid – unreasonably so, after all Boy was a free-agent, but being rational isn't usually part of the process. Lines were drawn, sides were taken, long-term friendships stumbled and stalled.

Harry was nine then. We both loved him, but he had utterly changed our lives, as kids do. Boy hadn't been in on my sneaky plan to make him a dad. I had gambled a lot on my son – it had cost me dear.

News of Candi's arrival triggered two reactions: I poured myself into the dating market, and, ironically, I lost weight – pounds, then stones, without consciously trying. I hadn't coped well emotionally with Boy and Candi's pairing-up, but he was still a necessary part of mine and Harry's life. He was essentially not a murdering kind of guy, of that I was pretty sure.

But he had been on a butchery course... I went on online and rechecked that first BBC report on the body being found. I was right; it was on Wednesday the 27th of February. I knew Boy had left on a flight for Buenos Aires on Saturday 23rd of February. He was probably already being kitted out with poncho, gaucho hat and whip when this woman had been killed. Phew!

To be super-sure, I texted him: 'Hi, Boy, how goes it? Lassoed any tuco-tucos yet?' It was a test. I knew they only existed in Patagonia.

I threw myself into work. Half an hour later my phone went – Boy.

I left it a few burbles before picking up. For some needy reason I wanted him to think I was up to Gone Puss's armpits in important cephalopod initiatives.

'Hey, Boy, is this the "I'm running out of underpants" call?' I said lightly.

'Sho, I know you're at work, but I had to phone. What the hell are you up to?' He sounded suitably faint, familiarly distant.

'Aquaria mainly.'

'I've been Skyping,' he said. 'Harry and Helen are worried sick.' That seemed like an exaggeration even allowing for 11,000km of Skype connection.

'They were fine when I left them.'

'They showed me a newspaper story. How did you get mixed up in a murder investigation?'

'Good question. I've got a bruise that's very similar, identical actually, to one on a murder victim.'

'So I hear. Just having a bruise seems a bit of a stretch to link you to a murder.'

'It's Toke's fault.'

'Toke!? What's he got to do with anything? Did he bruise you?'

'No. He texted me anonymously about my bruise being like the victim's.'

'He...what?' Boy spluttered.

'I know. He's such an airhead. He doesn't think.' I was finding Boy's concern touching.

'Sho, why don't you and Harry go away for a while?'

'Don't be ridiculous. Harry's at school; I've got work. I know you and Toke don't get on, but he's fine. The police have decided I'm over-reacting, so...'

'Be careful, I mean it. I couldn't cope if anything happened to you. Promise me you'll keep your head down.'

'Yup.' When was the last time he'd shown this much concern for me? Probably not since Harry was born. This was all too cosy. Time for: 'How's Candi?'

'What? How do you mean?' Straight onto the defensive.

'Harry said she's there with you.'

'Harry said?'

'Oh, for goodness sake, Boy, if you don't want to tell me she's on your, "I was just want some time alone" super Sabbatical with you, fine.'

'I really don't see what concern it is of yours, Sho.'

'I don't see why it's such a big secret. I only mentioned it because Harry asked me, after you spoke last week.'

'Never mind Candi.'

'I don't *mind* Candi. I just don't understand why you'd lie to your son about your big adventure not including your new... partner – if it, in fact, does.' The 'p' word had come to me reluctantly. Others had been considered.

'It doesn't, OK. Why is this such a big deal?'

'Because you keep saying you want Harry to meet her.'

I'd refused to give my permission for Harry to be introduced to Candi. It sounded childish, even petty, but Harry still hoped his mum and dad might get back together and I'd initially refused to believe that Candi would last. I didn't want Harry exposed to a revolving door of loose women skipping in and out of the bedrooms of his former home. No, all right, it was pettiness masquerading as bad logic and born out of bitterness that Candi was now as important in Boy's life as –

'Harry should have met her.' He sounded sad more than

angry. 'You wonder why I don't talk to you about Candi; it's because any mention of her screws you up. It screws us up.'

He'd hung up. I was still none the wiser about tuco-tucos. I logged on to Facebook. It had been ages since I'd found time to do anything with it. I'd never used it much and now used other messaging and photo apps instead. There was a bunch of posts from people I didn't know, mainly random groups I'd joined in my brief flirtation with the medium. My page needed a serious overhaul. If any prospective dates checked me out here, they'd assume I'd died – worse, that I'd died and was still in a relationship.

I clicked on the relationship status drop-down menu. Nothing seemed to fit. 'Single' sounded like I was a left-on-the shelf 41-year-old spinster. Neither was I 'divorced', 'widowed' or strictly-speaking 'separated'. Posting 'it's complicated' was surely instant death to any would-be date aspirations.

I'd read that Facebook now recognised 71 different gender designations. A google search confirmed it. I could be 'pan-gender', 'inter-sex', 'CIS-gender'. I wondered if I was a 'big-ender' until, a second later, it occurred to me it meant 'bi-gender' but with the hyphen left out. Sadly neither 'post-sexual' nor 'CIS-tercian nun' were options so I couldn't be accurate or funny. I went for 'Other'. Keep everyone guessing.

I found and clicked a Facebook page that Boy must have started to post up his Patagonia ramblings. Boy's IT guy, Dieter, was right: there was an irregular sprinkling of posts and some pictures of exotic scenery with 'off here tomorrow' type comments before it all petered out.

I gained some pathetic pleasure to see he had very few friends. From Boy's page I clicked on to Candi Egan. She described herself with the tagline 'I (heart) peanut butter: and that's OK! Yay!' Hunting for evidence of her whereabouts wasn't tricky. There was a fence-load of posts with pictures of holiday brochure porn. No hog-nosed skunks were immediately visible, but I knew that this, too, was magnificent Patagonia, yay! And there was Candi photographed (badly) in a stupid hat and sun-glasses, which I recognised from a group skiing holiday years ago. She intruded frumpily in front of a spectacular backdrop of snowy mountains. 'Cerro Catedral – check it OUT!'

Patagonia agreed with her. She looked better than when Boy had started going out with her. I knew she was supposedly slimmer. How come he hadn't worked that magic on me? Maybe she'd Photo-shopped the picture.

I Googled 'Cerro Catedral' but I'd already remembered some-one mentioning it. It was a famous tourist destination close to the Chilean border. Case proved, your honour.

I'd half a mind to phone Boy back, but decided I was bigger than that. If I hadn't been at work I'd have trawled through Candi's Facebook posts looking for instaguff featuring Boy, but I'd have to be bigger than that too. And, it would be a long trawl as (unlike Boy's ungrazed Facebook efforts) Candi's posts attracted a coterie of likes, emojis, comments and discourse: 'looking good Cand', or, 'I'm so jealous right now'.

I refused to let this last message define me. After all, I was front page news and in daily contact with the hunkiest cop on The Force. He'd probably call me again tomorrow.

Probably after he'd read the Peterborough Evening whatever.

14 LINDI

October 2019

'So, has Ash seen any Winter Hart candidates yet?' asked Marcus.

'Not yet, but not for want of trying. We've seen two white hinds in one of the herds to the south, but all the white stags are studiously avoiding us'

'I'd better cook you both up some venison, anyhow.' Marcus grinned, 'I'd no idea he was going to take it so seriously. Thought he'd be a townie.'

'As Ash keeps reminding me, "we're a long way from Luton." Let's leave the venison supper until the nights draw in. It's good for him to have time away from screens and phone signals.'

Marcus eased some papers from a slim briefcase. 'This is the acquisition contract for the company. It was finalised in July and based on last year's finances, which Westons have all but signed-off.'

'All but..?'

'Just waiting for you to shake down my bad debtors. Luckily the big one I was sweating on, was paid off in full two months ago, but there's still £240,000-odd to chase. That's just the stuff owing from last financial year. Only that is relevant to my sales earn out.'

'That's what, 7% of billings? Sounds very different from last time I was working with you.' Lindi was surprised; the company was usually running at double-figure bad debt six years ago.

'Thought you'd be impressed,' Marcus said. 'There's nothing like a mega payout to concentrate your mind.'

'Seems not. I take it I can go in hard: threats, lawyers' letters, burn their credit ratings?' Lindi had to ask. Chasing debts in any service industry was usually a compromise with fault on both sides meaning they met in the middle and continued to trade. Go in too hard and bad relations compromised future contracts; the customer took their business elsewhere.

'Take what ye can...' Marcus affected a pirate accent.

'Give nothing back.' Lindi remembered her line.

'Too right. As far as I'm concerned none of it is repeat custom. But all dosh must be in my bank account by December 31st, or it gets written down by Mitch's accountants.'

'Which impacts the purchase price?' Lindi was flicking through the contract.

'Big time. In fact, if you bring it in under 6% there's a £30K bonus in it for you.'

Lindi whistled. 'They must be over-paying for your business.' She sensed he was keen to tell someone.

'It's all in the contract,' Marcus indicated the papers. 'The Yanks work to a strict acquisition formula – multiples of revenue or profit, based on your last full year's trading.'

'Minus any uncollected debt,' guessed Lindi.

'Well, you can hardly blame them for that. Plus, I'm a gnat's away,' he pinched a thumb and forefinger in front of her, 'from a profit margin trigger that increases my pay-out exponentially.'

'I see.' Lindi now knew what rocks to look under for Marcus's scam.

❋ ❋ ❋

Lindi had persuaded Jimmy, the landlord of The Hart's Haunt, to let her have a 'free go' at his books. She popped in to pick them up. They were in a predictable mess. She sorted them out and returned one afternoon to talk him through the results. The pub was struggling – hardly a surprise to anyone – but Lindi was clear where it was going wrong and had some ideas.

Perching on a bar-stool she waited for Jimmy to find her some time. A handful of customers whiled away the afternoon. The two rustic regulars took an interest. 'You're in Boy Compton's cottage, right?' said one.

'You mean *Marcus* Compton,' Lindi needed clarification.

'He's always been "Boy" in the village.'

They were farm labourers, they said. It was an on-off job through the year. They worked for several farms in the area.

Lindi listened, then told them about the walks she and Ash regularly took over the fields they ploughed.

'I've seen you pair up on the Chalk.'

'Probably, my son has a bet on with someone in the village. He's been challenged to spot a white stag.'

'You'll be hunting The Hart, then.'

'That's the idea,' laughed Lindi. 'What do you reckon our chances are?'

'Everyone's chances will be better if you don't see it.' A new customer, older and probably retired, walked over, nestling his pint into the conversation.

'How do you mean?' she asked.

'The Winter Hart carries a curse,' continued the newcomer. 'If you see him, that's bad enough, but if he sees you...'

All three regulars tutted theatrically, heads shook.

'All manner of grief descends on you,' a farmworker added.

'And on the village,' the retiree emphasised. 'Plague?' wondered Lindi.

'Not so much. Crops, livestock, maybe the weather will turn something cruel.'

'There'll be a death – an awful harrowing one.'

'Now you're worrying me,' said Lindi, adopting their mock-calamitous tone. 'Would Ash or I be in the firing line?'

'Most like.'

'Death would be a blessing,' said the retiree. 'The village would turn on you if it was known you'd awoken the Winter Hart.'

'I'll warn my son,' Lindi promised.

'S'fer the best.'

'So, when was the last time anyone saw The Hart?'

'There's been a few pie-balds but no pure white bucks seen in my time,' said one of the farm-workers. 'Or if there have been, folk have kept quiet about it.'

'The Winter Hart only haunts Hartsdell and its immediate surroundings. That means the old Parish boundaries I'd say,' said the older man. 'I heard tell it was sighted before both World Wars, up on Chalk Knoll, by the old hill fort that was.'

'Ash and I walk there.'

'I've seen herds of over 50; Chiltern brown fallows, not the spotty chestnuts. One or two may be whites; some will be a sandy colour. There's a black variation at the other end of the Chilterns. Statistics would suggest there must be white stags around, but they shy away from Hartsdell.'

'And vice versa, I reckon,' said the farm-worker. 'They never shoot a white, mind.'

'Bad luck?' asked Lindi.

The man chuckled. 'No, love, the whites are easy to spot, means that their herds are more likely to be seen, so they can be shot.'

'That's part of their curse,' the retiree withdrew his pint.

✳ ✳ ✳

Lindi entertained Ash with the conversation after school. She felt the discussion had been half in jest but detected an underlying edge. The farm-workers both sounded as if they'd prefer to let sleeping harbingers of doom lie. Lindi detected the older man's longing for a sighting of The Hart.

'He's out there,' said Ash.

Conversation continued over dinner. Lindi put out a few feelers. 'How's things with Rashid and Zainab?'

'Why the sudden interest?' Ash was immediately guarded.

'Because I'm your mum. It's my job to take an interest.'

Ash couldn't hide his suspicion. 'Only, I just found out today, Zainab's pregnant.'

'Oh, didn't you say she was 19? That's early.' The same age Lindi had been, she remembered. 'Is she married?'

'Yes, but her husband's badly wounded, she says.'

'Wounded? Where is she?'

'Northern Syria.'

'Oh my god, Ash. I thought you said she was in Luton.'

'I said her family comes from Luton. She left two years ago. She went to help in Syria.'

'Help who, Ash?'

'Muslims.'

'Is she part of Isis?'

'Not originally. She left to join the Free Syrian movement.'

Cutlery fell from Lindi's hands. 'She is with Isis isn't she? Her family must be frantic. Was she coerced out there? Ash, is she trying to recruit you?'

'Mum, you need to calm down. She's not recruiting anyone. She's married to a guy from Islamic State, yes. And yes, her parents are seriously upset, but she's 19, it's her choice. She saw all the trouble over there and wanted to help.'

'These people have committed all kinds of unspeakable atrocities. This is the girl you admire?'

'It's war. There are terrible atrocities on all sides. Assad's used chemical weapons. I admire the fact that she's a girl from a housing estate in Luton who's taken brave choices. Doesn't mean I want to do what she's doing, or to be with her.'

Lindi's hands began a staccato dance in front of her. 'You can't do this Ash. What if Mr Norton or the Prevent people got to hear of it?'

'They'd go bat-shit crazy, I know. All their prejudices would burst out, like pus. The fact is, even you know more about what's going on in Syria than they do. Zainab is my way to form a balanced view of one of the biggest issues facing the world right now.'

'Promise me, Ash. This stops now.'

'Or what? You'll report me to the school; to Norton; to the police?'

'Only as a last resort. Ash, you're playing with fire.'

'No, Mum, I'm just chatting to a friend on Facebook; a girl who needs friends at the moment, who can't talk to her family, who's going through all kinds of hell because of what she believes in. I'm not going to desert her – what the –?'

There was a crashing sound from outside. Lindi imagined anti-terrorism police banging on the cottage door. Ash leapt up and ran out to the lounge at the back. Lindi half-wondered if he'd come to the same conclusion and was making an escape.

He wasn't.

'Can't see anything out there,' he said on his return. 'I think that was one of your herb pots going over.'

'What could have caused that?'

'Something big and white with pointy antlers.'

** 2011 **

'How are things?' The Skype connection was erratic. When Ash wasn't involved, she and Ayan usually phoned each other. 'More importantly, how's Naasira?'

Ayan had been out in Karachi for six months with only two trips back to the UK.

'At home still, but not fit to go out. She won't be returning to work, that's obvious.'

'I assume they're no closer to finding her attackers?'

'That boat has long since sailed,' Aran snorted. 'I'm not sure they ever looked. A trial would've reminded everyone of the police's poor record.'

'Where does this leave you, Ayan? I know you have to support your family there, but Ash and I need you home.'

'It's knocked all our confidence,' replied Ayan. 'I told you Fawad's gone back to the States, but I suspect Rahana and Tahira see it as a betrayal of their elder sister to return to normal life. Naasira was – I mean, she is – their idol.'

'And Ammi?' 'Ammi is too busy stressing over Naasira to be family head any more. She's had an idea, though: she wants you and Ash to come and visit us. You are part of this family and they all want to show you Karachi. It would also mean we could spend time together. It's going to be several months before I can return.'

'What about your work, Ayan?'

'I've told them. They say they will keep a place for me but it's right that they are no longer paying me.' Ayan paused and Lindi waited. 'I'm doing some things for Mr Rahmen – just to keep my hand in.'

She had already guessed. Karachi, the family and their old business were always likely to reclaim a part of Ayan's life given the chance. Naasira's injury had been that chance. If she and Ash went out there, they would be pressed to stay and remake their life in Karachi. Naasira's attack was reason enough for her to be nervous about that, but there was something else. She couldn't rid herself of the thought that over there, Ayan could make it very hard for her and Ash to leave. Hard as it was to reconcile this with the man she married, the thought wouldn't go away.

'It's not a good time, Ayan. My book-keeping is just taking off. I've this new client in Arlston whose business is flying. You'd like the owner; he's nearly as laid back as you are.'

Ayan laughed. 'Like I used to be before you took me in hand, you mean.'

'Plus, Ash is doing so well at school. My mum's back's getting worse and she's going to take early retirement. Can we talk about it when you're next back?'

'That's just it, Lindi, it'll be a while. I'm undertaking a lot of work to the house, here, to make it fit for Naasira's new circumstances.'

It was typical of the conversations she and Ayan would have. Lindi was especially concerned that Ash would not come back from any trip out there. It seemed Ayan (or perhaps Ammi) had another card to play. Mr Rahmen sent her an email asking if she would take over the UK accounts for his small but growing paint business there.

Lindi suspected it was a ruse to get her involved, so she'd have a role waiting for her, if (and when?) she was persuaded to join Ayan in Pakistan. Nevertheless, she agreed, and the company immediately became her biggest client.

It was largely picking up business as extensions of contracts with existing clients in other parts of the world. It didn't market and Ayan and Lindi had outsourced servicing and distribution to a third-party while he was back in Pakistan. All of which meant Lindi was its only UK employee and effectively her own client. It began to grow faster.

15 SHONA

Thursday night May 23 2019

I had one last job to do on Facebook. I didn't trust Steve Shelby, so I decided to 'control the narrative', as I've heard PR people say. I located the village's Facebook page. It looked nearly as out of date as mine. The second from top post was, 'Five knitwear patterns baby Royals would kill for,' as selected by the village sewing circle, Stitch n' Bitch. It dated from the last Royal sprogging.

Stitch n' Bitch never got around to much actual sewing. Along with most village clubs it was just an excuse for *a wee swally*. Lotte believed they should all be renamed 'wine club' with an optional 'h'. A friend who survived three club nights – not unscathed – claimed it was a bit like Fight Club, except that the first rule of Stitch n' Bitch was *everyone* snitched.

The results of a quiz-evening fundraiser for the Friends of St Cecilia's was top post. Thankfully, it didn't mention that my Soccer Moms team had finished last, even being beaten by The Prosecco Girls – hard to imagine a fluffier flock of airheads, but they were enthusiastic champions of their product.

It would be worth posting anything just to knock that item off the top. I entered: -

'Everyone should know that Chester Toakley (Toke) ISN'T involved in the murder of the headless woman in Whittlesey. Police

released him last night and confirmed he was innocent. It was all a misunderstanding.'

I'd have preferred to post anonymously but it wasn't an option.

Chief Crime Correspondent Shelby sent me some banal texted background questions.

As I answered them, a thought came. Could the mystery woman in the rental have been Candi? Perhaps she'd given up her cottage and moved in. It would explain why Boy had dealt with the tenancy himself and why his colleague Dieter had known nothing about her.

It was possible, but surely, she would have just moved into Big House with Boy, and anyway, wouldn't Esther have said?

While I did my lab work, two of Shelby's comments clamoured for attention: 'That's got to be the murderer, surely;' and 'the killer must be someone you know.'

I went back on to Facebook and added to my last post: - *'There is still a man attacking women in the Hartsdell and West Cambridge area – so be careful. I only know it's not Toke.'*

If it was that obvious to Shelby, why hadn't Hossein seen it?

OK, Shelby was a chief crime correspondent but, while Hossein and I hadn't exactly hit it off, nothing about him suggested he was incompetent – in fact the reverse was true, and I could tell Shelby rated him.

It came down to their reading of me: Shelby believed me when I said my bruise was identical, Hossein didn't. He said I'd exaggerated the two bruises' similarity to get attention.

Who was the better judge of my character?

Worryingly, Shelby only had a phone call (with a woman he assumed rational) to draw his evaluation from; Hossein had actually met me. This insight could explain my whole online dating history: I scrubbed up well at the end of an app or peeping sweetly out of an online dating profile but when we met, they saw through me – discerning the mad bitter neurotic behind the sociable sporty exterior.

Back to work: lab experiment forms were filled in, notes on

zebra fish's shoacial lives written up at top speed. My mobile bleeped up an alert for one of my messaging apps.

It was from Lotte: 'Still at work huh?'

'Yep, 'til 12. Why?' I flipped the conversation back. It occurred to me that zebra fish were cut out (and frequently cut up) for lab work specifically because they are outwardly social and patently transparent. Did that remind me of anyone? Yes, and I was in lab work.

'Wanna hook up later?'

'Too-oo knacked. You're back then?'

'How about tomorrow?'

My finger froze on my phone screen. Ice crept along it, skated up my arm and sluiced through to my stupid dull-witted brain. A message from Lotte's phone, but it wasn't Lotte. In the micro-eternity that followed this realisation, Shelby's warning about my assailant being the killer, about me knowing him, rang all too hauntingly true.

Break off! Block him!

It was the natural reaction...

Or get mad! Give him both barrels.

That could be briefly satisfying. Or... I glanced over at Gone Puss, hunting down some unsuspecting morsel of shrimp crud in his tank. What would he do? He'd ambush his prey, rip off its claws and turn it into lunch!

So... reinvent the scenario (as I think I once learned on a poorly-cast Future Leaders course). Change the rules, so I become the hunter and he becomes the prey. It would be gratifying on two counts:

1. getting my own back on the man who branded me 'Sucker' and

2. making DCI Dani (smarmy-pants) Hossein eat his words, preferably with a side helping of shrimp crud.

It was no contest. It was going to take guile.

'Who are you?' I messaged. This would be my first 'honey trap'; well second, if you counted Boy.

'Your friend from Sat obvs.' This guy was brazen.

'You stole this phone.' I reminded him.

'Sorry, I'll return when we meet.'

'And £80!'

'Gone but I'll buy drinks.'

'You spiked my last drink.' I typed. It was good to get these things out in the open early on in relationships, according to dating guides I'd read.

'Not me but u were woozy.'

'I passed out!'

'Yeh but u were into me 'til then.' He added an emoji that I sickeningly realised was a long tongue.

Yeuck!! I hunted for a retching emoji. Did one exist? If this was sexting, I was struggling to see its attractions.

'Was I?!'

'O yeah!' More racy emojis that I didn't dare investigate.

'Remind me.' Most of me didn't want to know but one mortified segment of my mind was insisting: you must, you really must.

'When we meet.'

'Meet?'

'Tomorrow?'

'Somewhere public.'

'Pub.'

'5pm?'

'8pm?'

'At work,' I typed,

'5pm to 6.30 is OK, otherwise, no.'

'5pm @ The Mill.' Big touristy and busy, that would do.

'How will I know u?' I didn't want to appear too eager.

'I know u!' he messaged ominously.

'No promises.' I turned my phone off. I was mentally exhausted.

I wondered if I should bring the police into my trap. I had to. The noxious creature I'd been messaging was at very least a phone-nicking, woman-graffiti-ing bastard. Right now, I was half convinced he was a killer.

I heard shambling steps coming through the aquarium room beyond mine. They turned into Leroy. He wandered up to my desk, said his 'Hey Shona' before pressing himself close to the glass of Gone Puss's tank.

I returned to my work and thoughts.

After a while Leroy asked, 'He in there?'

'Yeah. I saw him moments ago.' The tank showed no signs of life, but octopuses excelled at hiding. They were camouflage experts and could squeeze into impossible corners.

'I can't see him.' Hold up. Here was Leroy awake enough for a conversation. What had brought this on?

'Are you hiding in here?' I asked. 'Is Angry Guy out front?'

'Nah, all quiet tonight.' He sounded disappointed. 'Perhaps he's got out.'

'Angry Guy?'

'Nah,' he finally prised his eyes away from the tank. 'The octopussy. Don't they escape a lot?'

'Who have you been talking to?' I asked, surprised he was showing an interest in anything beyond his fags, his course notes and inventing new ways to get both feet higher than his head while keeping his eyes closed.

'What? No-one.' He picked up my coffee mug and turned it round to scrutinise the text on it. 'Biologist: D.N.A.', it read, and in smaller script, 'Do Not Antagonise.'

'Heed the mug, Leroy.'

He put it down gently. 'So, do they?'

'Yes,' I relented, 'they're ninja escapers. If our soldiers in the Stalags had octopus skills, The Great Escape would have been a very short film.'

'Yeah,' he breathed, not even pretending that he'd understood a word I'd said. "I can't even see a tentacle.'

Lotte's first rule: never miss a chance to show off. 'They don't have tentacles,' I said. 'They have limbs, strictly speaking six arms and two legs.'

'Nah,' this was Leroy at his most obstreperous, 'I've seen their suckers.'

'To be a tentacle it can *only* have suckers at the end of the limb; octopuses have them all the way along.'

'Anyhow, this one's gone. Can they breathe out of water?'

'Yes, for a surprisingly long time. And they can slither around.'

'Do they cost a lot?'

'It's just calamari, Leroy,' I wanted him gone. I wanted my semi-comatose security guard back. This version was plain distracting. 'Why the sudden interest?'

'N'reason. Ain't you worried he's not there?'

'I'll check later,' I said. 'Leroy, what are you doing before your night shift tomorrow?' It could be a back-up plan, for when DCI Hossein refused to mobilise his SWAT team.

'Revising. Exams next week. Why?'

'Nothing.' It had been a rubbish idea. Leroy would probably have nodded off in the middle of disarming the killer. 'I'm going to be in a little bit later, tomorrow, maybe seven-ish.'

'OK cool.' He transferred his interest to the bobtail squid tank. The adorable cuttle-fish relatives waved their tiny tentacles at him. 'How long do these little guys live?'

'Not long.' Male cephalopods usually stagger off to die after mating, neatly sidestepping all those child-care arguments and toilet-training. See, smart. Female cephalopods stopped eating after giving birth. I had experienced the opposite effect.

I sent Leroy back to his desk in case Angry Guy turned up.

On a mad impulse I sent Boy a text. 'Did you put Candi up at your village cottage this autumn?'

It would be past 7 o'clock in the evening in Patagonia. I didn't like the idea of Boy and Candi chinking their glasses of subtly nuanced Argentinian Malbec together and giggling at my text – more evidence of my inability to move on – but I had to check. If it had indeed been Candi in the house, and not a murdered woman, I was heading for another nose-dive in my investigator credibility ratings.

My phone went, Steve Shelby. 'I'm calling it a night,' he said, 'story's done.' It sounded like he was too.

'Can I see it?'

'No, Shona. We're on the same side but I can't do that. I've got these three rules, see: one, claim everything on expenses; two, reveal my sources only if offered drink; and three –.' He broke off coughing and came back retching. 'Three, never let an interviewee see anything until it's in print. It leads to less threats.'

'Fewer.' I corrected.

'What?'

'Fewer threats.'

'Who's the wordsmith here?'

'I'm starting to wonder,' I said. 'I've put a lot of trust in you, Steve.'

'I know, and because of that I have a morsel of information I'm going to give you. It may aid your identification of your mystery woman as the victim.'

'Right.'

'You have to promise me that it goes no further. Hossein will rip up my NUJ pass if he finds out I've told you.'

'I promise.' Just at this moment my promise to DCI Hossein never to talk to the press came back to me. Oh well, too late now.

'As you'll have gathered, this hasn't been released by the police, but the second victim had a tattoo. Did your woman have a tattoo?'

'Not that I'm aware of,' I played for time. 'Where and what was it?'

'They don't know. That's why they're not saying.'

'How can they not know?'

'This'll sound weird but it's not on the corpse. They assume it must have been on her hands or face, or neck.'

I was puzzled, but then I remembered a science article I'd half digested. 'Was it in her blood?' I asked.

'Something like that,' coughed Shelby. 'Apparently, if you've had a tattoo it will show in your lymph nodes, even if the limb has been amputated; even if they've been lasered off.'

'Traces of the ink's toxins I imagine.' I processed what he said. 'Why wouldn't they release that? How come they told you, of all people?'

A hacking noise, which I now recognised as Shelby laughing and dying in equal measure. 'They wouldn't have done; only some 12-year-old digital news reporter – Buzzfoetal, I think it was – asked the question. Hossein didn't want to say yes or no, but he couldn't admit to not knowing about the technique, either.'

'Bad for his DCI Cool image,' I suggested.

'Hossein thought not knowing the where and what of the tattoo would be less of a help to identification and more of a distraction. At least he came clean. He treats us like grown-ups.'

'But the public don't know?'

'No. Which brings me to the serial killer aspect we spoke about...'

'Go on.'

'This is only me reading between the lines, picking up on bits n pieces.'

'I'm still interested.'

'Good. I think there are some small discrepancies between the two murders. Enough to make Hossein keep an open mind on whether it's the same killer. Although, when I asked if it could be a copycat killer, he said, "no, there was a definitive connection". There's something – no idea what – that hasn't been made public, something a copycat couldn't know. They often hold one thing back.'

'Mr Shelby, Steve...' I started... and stopped.

'I don't have the answer to what you're about to ask.'

'I haven't asked it yet.'

'I can tell from your tone. It's going to be something ethically harrowing.'

'Children are knifed in our cities every week. How come this case gets so much police attention?'

'Rarity. A 15-year-old knifed by his best friend after school's out, rates um… four column inches on page seven. There was what, 40,000 knife crimes in England and Wales last year. But a mysterious naked woman with no head and a mutilated doll for company, whoo… that's a whole different ball-game. That'll shift papers. It's a case on which police careers are made… or broken.' 'Mr Shelby, I think your social conscience just peeked out of my hand-set.'

'Don't have one. Can't afford it. Local newspapers are haemorrhaging readers faster than our schoolkids are knifing each other. I need all the spine-chilling, grisly, unfathomably bizarre murders I can get.'

'You're painting Hossein as a puppet, dancing in the media glare.'

'Far from it, but this case will make or break him.'

'If it is my woman lying on that pathologist's table, I don't have the first idea of a motive.'

My admission made him pause. 'That's not really our concern, Shona. Fact is, the police don't get too hung up on motive anyhow. They want means, opportunity and hard forensic evidence. But that's their job; ours is just to point them in the right direction.'

'Had the dead woman given birth?' I asked.

'Dunno.'

'They'd know if she'd had a child.'

'I'll check.' Shelby signed off with, 'You'll be in our first online edition tomorrow. Stay in touch.'

Before leaving I picked up the special delivery of 'luminol', that I'd ordered from the lab supply company and grabbed a piece of kit from one of the storerooms.

Leroy's feet were arranged in their usual formation above the front desk when I came to leave. 'How did that World Cup octopus do it?' he asked as I walked up. 'I mean foretelling those match results and getting 'em right?'

'They're not that smart,' I laughed. 'They can't see into the future. Obviously, the Germans had showed it lots of video footage before the tournament.'

'Kind of like a form guide, yeah?'

'Though most of those games were only over one leg.'

I raised my hands and gave him my 'I can't say any more without breaching my Octoscience Guild code' look.

He nodded. He knew I'd already told him as much as I safely could. At the front door, Leroy peered elaborately in both directions even though only his van and my car were in the car-park.

'Good to go.' He seemed to be enjoying this.

I ducked low and ran, reaching my car without incident.

As I turned out of the lab car-park, I saw the silver saloon. I think I had been half-expecting it. It idled in the larger car-park opposite. Under the dim car-park lights my senses, super-fuelled by adrenaline, divined a figure in the driving seat. He was waiting for me to leave. Here we go again, I thought. The saloon flashed its headlights to confirm my suspicion.

I sped off with eyes on my rear-view mirror. The car didn't make a move to follow me initially, but I still floored the accelerator as soon as I hit the road leading off the lab area. A red light halted my get-away. Just as it turned green, I saw headlights turn carefully, surreptitiously, out of the road I had left. I shot away.

There was more traffic around tonight. I was being followed again, this time, possibly, by a man whose anger had been given another 24 hours to marinate in the injustice of his incarceration. As I approached the train crossing, I saw red lights flashing. The crossing arm was descending. I couldn't countenance slowing down, let alone stopping. Instead, I sharply turned on to a side road. I knew it meandered westwards a couple of miles to another large village and then some smaller ones. It was out of my way and involved slow winding rural lanes, deserted at this time of night. This was exactly the kind of inane option a plucky, but doomed, starlet would take when an axe murderer was on her tail.

A plan formed. There was a small opening that I knew led onto a disused quarry. I once brought Harry up here butterfly-spotting years ago.

It was just 75 yards past a tight bend and hidden from any pursuit. I swerved into the space cut between the high hedging and snapped off my lights. The track was a pot-holed tarmac road leading into the wasteland site. It quickly turned into a patch of compacted chalk covered in scrub with occasional dark shapes, which I remembered were bushes, many of them buddleia. I cut the engine 50 metres in. My car came to a halt on the rougher ground and I steered it behind a clump of bushes and, rather stupidly, ducked down again in the seat.

Silence.

I thought back to the visit here with Harry. It had been sunny, I remembered, windless, a few clouds maybe, warm. He'd hated it, I remembered. I'd had to drag him out of the car.

'No, mum. What is this place?'

'A butterfly sanctuary.'

'I want to go home.'

'Let's have a look while we're here. There's a big lake down there.'

'Take me home. I don't want to.'

I picked him up, stroked his hair. 'There's nothing to worry about.'

'There is.'

'It's quite safe. We might see some creatures.' I walked over the low chain, towards the quarry. There wasn't a butterfly in sight.

'Mum, don't!'

'Look, there's the lake, see.'

His eyes were scrunched tight. The drowned quarry spread deep before us. A leaden strip refusing to reflect the sky, untouched by wind. A sour reek of rot came from nowhere. On the breathless afternoon, the reeds started up a raspy chatter.

'What's that?'

'Just reeds.'

He opened his eyes and I hunched him round to see the quarry lake. A dark bird shrieked past us low into the bushes.

Its shrill warnings scudded after. Harry screamed and started kicking at me.

His response affected me, and I started to walk back up the incline. He was yelling and keening and stretching out his arms to the car. I half-tripped. My foot had caught on a child's small broken dusty shoe. I started running, reached the car, threw my screaming son into his car seat.

'Go, mummy, go, go.'

I'd driven out three times the speed I'd come in. Within two minutes Harry was playing with some toy, smiling and singing a song about a blackbird. My nerves were knotted like a sack of seething snakes.

It was the same now. I wound down the window. The reeds jabbered their warning. A fetid scent crept from the unseen quarry.

Had I heard a vehicle pass by earlier. This was the second night I'd ducked off the road to hide. I listened, compressed back against my seat, praying no-one was creeping up on me disguised as a buddleia and wondering if this breached any of the terms of my insurance. Dark shapes that may have been bushes inched closer to the car. I could stand it no longer. My ignition whined as I twisted too hard. The car groaned at the impossibly tight circle demanded of it and I shot back out onto the B-road.

I convinced myself I could see Toke's car's beams lighting up the lane in the distance behind me as I retraced my route back to the main road.

Rather than approach the village over the chalk ridge again, I turned off the dual carriageway at the same spot as the previous night. This time I kept going. I would be arriving at my cottage from the opposite direction. I'd be able to sneak up behind any car parked in the spot Esther had mentioned. I would be a few minutes ahead of Toke if he had followed me down the slow village lanes. Before I turned on to my road, I switched off my main-beams.

My low running lights offered just enough illumination to

see twenty metres ahead. I didn't need them to know that the shadow on the road opposite my cottage was a car. It was parked up against the paddock where no-one ever parked. It made it hard for me to swing around the 180° into my drive – impossible from this direction.

I was driving slowly, and my brakes brought me to an instant stop 25 metres from the dark shape. I turned off the ignition and running lights to wait. There were no street lights in our road but, as my eyes acclimatised to the darkness, I could make out a shadow leaning back on the car's side.

I couldn't see who it was. I would have said it was Toke, if I wasn't so convinced he'd been following me from Cambridge and was still mired in twisting rural byroads. The dark figure turned to study me. My options were: -

1) park up and confront whoever it was;

2) drive up not too close and talk to him with the engine running and the option of high-tailing it if I sensed aggression;

3) or I could do a three – OK, seven – point turn and head back the way I had come.

While I dithered, the shape lifted away from the car and started towards me. He was in the centre of the road. I reached for my ignition. I couldn't go forward without running him over, there was no time for my seven-point turn, and I didn't trust myself to reverse fast under pressure down windy village roads.

The shadow was halfway towards me. I hit central locking, my indecision sliding into panic. Then a third car rounded the road behind me. Its lights were off, but its tyres scrabbled on the tarmac as it braked. I heard it and saw it in my mirror, ominously glinting despite the low light. I was surrounded.

A Mexican stand-off. The shadow ahead of me stopped, everything stilled. Eventually the shadow turned, marched back to his car, slipped in and drove away, up the road. His internal light flared briefly when he got in. I couldn't identify him, but it was a man.

I had no idea what was going on but felt a ridiculous surge of relief. I lurched forward, spun and parked up on my drive, scattering gravel. Grabbing keys, I hurtled through the gate and dashed to my door. Fingers and keys were on different wavelengths but, as the security light grudgingly acknowledged my presence, I managed to twist the right one home and threw myself inside, slamming my door and collapsing back against it.

When my heart settled, and my mad panting stopped, I listened. I couldn't hear steps outside. My head dropped down and then I saw something beneath my feet. It was a sheet of A4 paper folded in half to get it through the letterbox.

I opened it and read the typed message: '*I don't know what the hell you think you are doing. But STOP!*'

16 LINDI

November 2018

Marcus's work didn't keep Lindi occupied, so she started seeking out other local businesses on his list of possible clients.

First up was The Old Chapel Gallery that she and Ash had spotted on their first trawl into the village centre. She walked through several small twitchels, as she'd learnt to call narrow back alleyways in Yorkshire. She emerged by the Chapel, set back from the road by a crumbling concrete apron. There was parking for several cars and some ancient wooden garaging behind. Little suggested it was open and only a sign stating the gallery's name even hinted that it was a business. But the web said otherwise and gave the proprietress as a Mrs Brett-Reynolds. Sure enough, she sold art but, judging from the dark fusty works haunting the website, Lindi doubted she sold much.

A brittle leafless tree speckled with pairs of amber berries was the only plant in the front yard. It gave a good impression of being dead. The double doors were closed but Lindi, armed with the business hours from the website, pushed anyway.

They opened on to a small foyer. Before a second set of glazed doors, a dated diorama was displayed at eye level. Contained within its cube of glass was a dusty set of puppet figures arranged in a circus ring.

The trapeze artist clung by her finger-tips to a twisted bar. Below her a dwarfish clown furtively opened the lion's cage. A top-hatted ring-master disrobed an obese woman. A harlequin juggler armed himself with five murderous blades. A second male clown, dressed perversely in moth-eaten ballerina garb, tottered on two stilts that dangled from his tattered skirts.

'Welcoming,' muttered Lindi, pushing open the secondary doors to enter the gloomy interior beyond.

A raucous burst of ringing blared out to announce her intrusion into the gallery's sanctum. The double height room was square and not over-large. An easel faced the door displaying a dark-hued canvas. On it, two startled and ragged crows launched themselves into the dusk. Examining the canvas, Lindi saw a mutilated scarecrow head below them. Pecked eyes and a lopsidedly hanging jaw etched terror on his features. A background of tortured trees completed the grim canvas.

It was a raw but affecting work. Only the immature signature suggested any lack of competence. 'A. Reynolds', it read. 'Something Wicked' aptly titled the piece.

The door swung closed behind her triggering a repeat of the jangling bells. There was no welcome or any responding indication of life. The room returned to its disturbing silence.

To either side were sparsely-populated art print racks. A press of heavy-framed mournful paintings covered one wall. Through glass doors Lindi glimpsed a prodigious desk dominating a second unlit room. A final set of double doors stood opposite it, below an ornate staircase.

Lindi was beneath it when she heard a door above her open and a creak on the stairs. A woman's voice, resonant and clear, sung down. 'Hello, are you finding what you came for?'

'Hello,' said Lindi, 'I was just admiring what you have on show.'

A slim elderly woman turned the stair. Shoulder-length hair

hung straight to a slight curl and swam through silver to cream. Her lips were a stab of crimson. She was neatly attired in black; waistcoat and short tailored jacket over wide trousers. It was hard to guess her age but Lindi suspected her straight posture and modish wardrobe concealed an 80-something. She was as clear-eyed and glossy as a spring rook.

'Good, good, have you visited before?'

Lindi confessed she hadn't. She was new to Hartsdell, and really wasn't in a position to buy art. She didn't add 'at these prices'.

'Such a pity,' said the woman. 'Well you are, nonetheless, in a position to appreciate what's in front of you and I don't charge for just admiring. Can I interest you in a coffee?'

'Only if you have time?'

'My dear, all I have is time, and some very fine Columbian beans.'

Lindi wandered through the two rooms. Every spare inch of wall was covered in pictures, many by 'A. Reynolds' and most offering dark or disturbing visions. Lindi roughly calculated the average price in her head and the number of images on display.

Over coffee, she admitted her reason for visiting and asked who did the woman's accounts.

'There's not enough business for it to qualify as "accounts". I keep a rough check on sales and stock.' Mrs Brett-Reynolds pointed to a small, once high-end, lap-top on the heavy desk. 'I only set up the gallery originally to display my former husband's work.'

'Mr Reynolds,' Lindi guessed. The woman nodded. 'He's no longer with you?'

'Oh, Angus is no longer upon this physical plane. He died over 40 years ago.'

'Sorry to hear that. Could I look at your accounts from a business viewpoint? I'm happy to have a go for free to see if I can suggest anything. If it turns out my ideas are a help, and you start to make money as a result, we could then work out a fee.'

'Don't waste your time.' Mrs Brett-Reynolds was abrupt but not impolite. 'I don't sell much. Angus ceased to be collectable from an early age. Probably from the time he married me, come to think of it,' she said. The line sounded well-worn and wasn't followed by a smile.

'Was he local?'

'Hartsdell born and very well bred. He was reckoned a prodigious talent when a boy, but he lost his muse, poor man.'

'You weren't his muse, I take it,' Lindi kept the conversation flowing.

'Thankfully not, dear, given his penchant for the macabre. That's his muse over there.' She pointed to a series of three oil paintings featuring an eerie and moody white stag.

Armed with a few more Winter Hart tales – Evelyn Brett-Reynolds was an authority – and permission to study the accounts, Lindi walked home. She would research some business models. She had a few ideas to reinvigorate the gallery.

❋ ❋ ❋

Lindi had been working Marcus's bad debt ledger for a month and could provide him with an accurate estimate of what monies would – and wouldn't – arrive. 6% was the target and she would beat it. Entering the estimate into the simple spreadsheet worked out the final value of Marcus's companies under the terms of the sale.

Marcus picked up her call and took it into his office.

'How much are the Americans expecting to pay for the business?' she asked.

'If they base their estimate on the average of my last three trading years, that's a tad under £3m revenue a year. The revenue multiple is 1.2-times so £3.5m.'

'Marcus,' she swallowed, 'that's not what it's going to be.'

'I know. So does Mitch. He's seen the billings are slightly up, he knows costs are down and he's warned the Yanks I'll be into the profit clauses.'

The acquisition contract moved into a profit multiple if Marcus's bottom line was over a 12% margin. It rewarded Marcus for cutting cost, saving the US company from having to downsize so much when they took over. The more Marcus tackled the pain of reducing staffing, the less they had to do.

The better the profit margin, the more the multiplier increased. The contract stipulated ten times profits for a 12% margin; eleven times profits for a 15% margin, and so on.

'So what does Mitch think now?' she asked.

'I don't know. If I was him, I'd be expecting bad debts to come in at 12% - it's been a good industry average over the years. That would still leave me better than 15% profit margin and he'd be paying just over £5m.'

'In fact, £5.4 million,' said Lindi, who had every eventuality a key-touch away on her spreadsheet.

'I've done my sums too,' laughed Marcus. 'Mitch's expecting between five maybe six million sterling.'

'Except we know we won't have anything like 12% bad debts. I've got an estimate for you.'

'Go on...' Lindi could almost hear Marcus rubbing his hands with glee.

'No promises, but I'll be disappointed if I don't get you in at 6% or just under.'

'Tell me then. What does your spreadsheet say?'

'Marcus, I know you've done these sums 100 times over already.'

'I just want to hear you say it, Lindi.'

'They'll be paying you a shade over £10 million.'

'Ah-harrh! Take all ye can.'

'Are they really going to wear that?'

'What choice do they have? It's their contract after all. They signed it. These are their standard buy-out criteria. They didn't reckon on your ninja bad-debt chasing skills. Lindi Mills, it's bonus time.'

'That's just it, Marcus, I've done very little. You'd already got

95% of this sorted since...' she consulted her register, 'since that big cheque came in, mid-August.'

'Wooh-wooh!' Was the only sound she heard from the phone.

She laughed. She believed it was honestly earned too. Her checks had shown no evidence of any fraud. She was genuinely pleased that his years of hard work would pay off so handsomely.

** 2013 **

Ayan had only made it back to Hitchin once in the last year. He was working his way up Mr Rahmen's corporation, coordinating Naasira's many medical appointments and pursuing the authorities for compensation. Not so much for Naasira, he said, but for all victims of the many brutal attacks on young women in Karachi. He was almost unrecognisable from the close-to 30-year-old wastrel she had married ten years before.

Over the last 18 months, he had become less insistent that Lindi visited Karachi. He started to accept that his life was in Pakistan and that she was determined hers never would be.

They still Skyped and phoned. Her long-distance interest in his intriguing family hadn't diminished. But their chats were often about the business that Mr Rahmen's paint company was doing, in the UK, where Lindi was successfully nurturing it.

Ayan was especially attentive with Ash. The father and son relationship still blossomed, in spite of, or possibly because of, the enforced separation. They used social networks between the Skype sessions.

Ash often suggested holidays in Karachi for them both, or just him. Ayan may have sparked the interest but Ash genuinely wanted to visit the country. He was curious about the big family mansion over there, loved Ammi and felt close to his father.

Rahana called to say she was in London with a new husband in tow. Could she come up to Hitchin. Lindi reversed the arrangement and travelled to London to see Rahana.

The husband made himself scarce and the two women

visited the V&A. Coffee fuelled discussions about Ash, Naa-sira's slow recovery and about Ammi's struggle to come to terms with the attack. Rahana was full of Ayan's success in the paint business.

Finally, Rahana brought up the subject they had both known was the real purpose of her visit.

'You and Ash must come and visit us in Karachi. I know a dreadful thing happened to Naasira, but you can't judge a whole city on one tragedy. Come for a holiday and if you like it there, well, anything is possible.'

'Rahana, if I may speak plainly,' Lindi downed her coffee. 'Ash and I both miss Ayan. We want him back. I have come to realise, though, that Ayan's future is in Karachi, and perhaps it always was. Ash's life, and mine, is here. That was the plan Ayan and I set out, when we married. We didn't change that. Circumstances have intervened.'

'We adapt to what life throws at us, Lindi. Yes, we love you, Ayan respects you, too, for all you did to wake him up to his re-sponsibilities. And yes, we want you to come over, fall in love with our lifestyle there, and remake your life with us. If not for you, for Ash, a boy must be with his father.'

'That's kind, Rahana, but it's not that simple. You have ral-lied around Naasira, in her misfortune, but I have a mum here. She's not well. She won't be around for much longer. Mum only has a daughter and a grandson here. If Ammi was alone and ser-iously ill, I know none of you would desert her.'

Rahana sighed. To her credit, she knew when she was beaten.

The more pressure built, the more conscious Lindi was that she was depriving father and son of each others' company. Their bond, she convinced herself, meant that if Ash visited, he would make his life in Pakistan.

Ironically, Lindi was spending most of her time managing the paint company's business in the UK. She did the accounts, managed the servicing and distribution suppliers, spoke to key clients, and engaged a marketing company.

All other book-keeping accounts, bar one, had been dropped.

She enjoyed working with Marcus Compton and his small but thriving internet company. Marcus was a handful. He kept trying to sneak things past her in accounts. The bad habits she thought she had weaned him off kept resurfacing. They disagreed but arguments were resolved through humour and by Marcus ultimately relenting and submitting to Lindi's principles.

He started these mock feuds, she thought, to entertain himself and as an office joke for other staff. While he deferred to her on accounts and to his IT head on all things tech, his word was law in all other respects.

Using his 'Pirate Code' analogy, Marcus ran a tight ship. The young staff were given responsibility and instruction. If they screwed up, they were out; if they did well, they left anyway – for better salaries in the myriad of industries and service companies that required similar skills, but the company survived and grew.

Marcus was a lot older than his staff, but he had the most energy. His voice and laughter were loudest, he worked the longest hours. The IT team clocked long hours too, but in the building next door. The admin and marketing office usually saw Marcus and Lindi, working late, alone, tying up the next business pitch.

Lindi most admired that Marcus kept his business and personal life separate. Lindi knew he had a long-term partner but had only met her twice fleetingly. He had a young son but she had never heard his name. Marcus could surely have indulged in office romances, but it wasn't his style.

As for her, she would never make a phone call to Ayan, saying she had met or slept with someone new, without first receiving a call from him, saying their relationship was over.

One day, she sought Marcus out.

'You need to sack me,' she said.

'What's on the charge sheet, choccy biscuits bought with petty cash?'

'You've outgrown me. My qualifications aren't going to impress the larger clients you need to go after. Before they sign a deal, they'll check you over and expect to see accounts filed by a company they know.'

'I've employed accountancy firms before, all highly qualified, lots of letters after their names, none of them had your common sense. You're even picking up some of my business acumen, Lindi.'

'But', she said, 'big accountancy firms do have contacts and impressive reputations. You've reached a size where you need both. I've got a paint company to run anyway.'

'OK, who are you recommending?'

'Westons', she said, 'I've set up a meeting.'

She left his business and his life.

17 SHONA

Friday morning May 24 2019

Another night of double-checking locks and closing curtains ensued. Intruders would face Harry's most pointy, squeaky and awkward toys lying in not-so-deep cover behind all entry points to the cottage. The warning 'stop' note hung in the shadows of my mind. Someone's toes had been trodden on.

Before 7am I gave up on sleep, stumbled out of bed and lurched towards the curtains. My scream was cut short, subsiding into a series of murderous curses. A Lego piece clung tenaciously to the underside of my foot. I blundered into several other traps, before coffee made me sufficiently alert to avoid them.

Next, I updated the rough notes I'd started the previous afternoon. To 'Mysteries' I added:

10.   Who left the note warning me off? - Toke?
11.   Who was outside my house last night? Murderer?
12.   ...and who was in the car that scared him off?
13.   Did Toke send text (incriminating himself?).
Toke never calls me Sho – always Shona!
14.   ...or did someone else send it – Hugo? – as a joke?
15.   Did woman in cottage have a tattoo?

16.   Will phone stealing attacker keep our date tomorrow?
17.   And why did Hoss-Pants phone me yesterday.
Succumbing to my raw magnetism?

Under my 'Connections to Victim' I could only come with one more – but it was a corker!

7.   Shelby says my attacker must be the killer!
How else would they know about the St Martin's Cross?
It wasn't in the public domain.

Feeling I was growing more confused, rather than less, I went to my car. Staring across to where the shadowy man had parked, I noticed something pale in the road: a tissue maybe? I returned to my kitchen for a plastic food bag. I picked up the item– a grubby hanky – without touching it and sealed the bag. The hanky was well used. There was also some faint brown staining on it. Blood? – well, possibly.

I drove over to the school to meet Helen and Harry.

They parked up shortly after me. Harry looked impressed that I was still alive. Hell, I was impressed I was still alive. The threatening note and Shelby's conviction that I'd shared a bed – briefly and, admittedly, while comatose – with a murderer, meant I felt less of a fraud.

Plus, I'd successfully honey-trapped a sex attacker. I was living up to my billing and no longer fazed by the lingering unease of other mums and pupils.

'She still here, then,' their looks said. 'I give her to the end of the week – tops!'

I chatted with Harry and Helen. 'You Skyped Dad I hear.'

'No, we spoke on the phone.'

'When he called, I'm sure he said he'd been told in a Skype.'

'We tried,' said Harry, 'but couldn't get through.'

'We were supposed to Skype,' said Helen, 'but we had a long phone chat instead didn't we, Harry?'

'You weren't supposed to tell him about my bruise,' I teased

Harry.

'I didn't!' said Harry with all the indignation an 11-year-old can muster.

I was getting confused. Hadn't Boy said they'd shown him the newspaper picture?

Helen backed Harry up. 'We said we were worried about you, that's all.'

'Oh?'

'We talked football. I told Dad about our defeat on Sunday. He thinks you shouldn't have played me at the back.'

This would have been hurtful criticism from anyone else, but Boy knew nothing about football and couldn't tell a sweeper from a *Libero*. Though, I'm not sure Gary Neville can either.

'Do you ever look at Dad's Facebook page?' I asked Harry.

'Mum, you always say, "I'm too young for Facebook yet".'

Fair point.

I told Helen I needed to go to work early that evening. Was she available to pick Harry up and run him back to hers? She said she was. I told them both that I would have time to come and say 'hi' before dashing off to work. I'd check they had met up OK.

On the way back to the village, I stopped for a paper. Two texts and two missed calls jostled for attention. The first text was from Boy answering my, 'did Candi move into the village?' text.

'No! She didn't. Drop it!' it read. Hmm stroppage! That text hadn't been there when I checked earlier. Boy must have sent it in the last 20 minutes. And that would make it about 5am in Argentina. Why was he up so early? Shouldn't he be cuddled up with Candi?

The second text and both missed calls were from DCI Hossein; oh-oh. 'Call me when you get this. Urgent!' read the text. No smiley emoticons.

I didn't. I switched the phone off and drove home.

Before I phoned anyone, I needed another coffee, and a check on the Peterborough Evening Thingie's first online edition.

And there I was; the second headline on their home screen. *'New woman marked for death by Doll Killer.'* I clicked and read: *'The mystery of the woman founded beheaded at Whittlesey in February deepened further when another woman was attacked and left with a St Martin's Cross bruise last weekend.*

'The woman, who has asked not to be named, was unable to identify her attacker. She was given an "identical bruise" on the same part of the upper left arm as the murder victim. "I recognised my bruise as having been made by a piece of jewellery in the shape of the [famous] Iona cross," she exclusively told our Chief Crime Correspondent, Steve Shelby.

'The witness was at pains to point out that the suspect subsequently arrested by police, was not the culprit. The arrested man, Mr Chester Toakley from North Hertfordshire, was innocent she said. "Mr Toakley saw my bruise and texted me to say it was the same as on the murdered woman, that's all. He was right; it was the same."

'She reported the text and the bruise to police and was subsequently interviewed by Detective Chief Inspector Dani Hossein, who's leading the investigation into the two murdered women in Whittlesey and Derby. Although Mr Toakley's name wasn't originally released by the police, it was a very public arrest and many people in the area knew it was Mr Toakley and that his arrest was linked to the murders.

'"People naturally assumed he was involved in the murders," the bruise victim told this paper. "Mr Toakley wasn't officially cleared, so he's taking a lot of flak." However, police yesterday told the witness that Mr Toakley wasn't involved, and they released him a few hours later.

'The question remains whether this woman has had a horrifically close encounter with a serial killer, was marked for death and is lucky to still be alive.

'DCI Hossein refused to comment on the story.'

I tentatively picked up the phone, dialled and prepared for an encounter with an angry DCI.

'Miss Patterson,' Hossein answered with put-on weariness, 'I thought we had a deal.'

'We did,' I was reduced to a squeak.

'Then why did you break your promise to me and speak to the newspapers?'

'I had to. I wanted to clear Mr Toakley's name. He's been banned from the village pub.'

'You felt Mr Toakley's ability to choose a drinking establishment was more important than catching a man who's murdering women.'

'Of course not,' I responded with a bit more spirit, 'but you were doing nothing to clear an innocent man. I had to. Seems to me I did more good than harm.'

'You are not leading this investigation, Miss Patterson. You are not privy to our information. You can't possibly know if you are doing harm or not.'

'Well if he's innoce – '

'The big picture is that I need public information. I know what media buttons to push. If our well of information runs dry as a result of your interference...'

'I just got fed up with you treating me like a bloody button!' I hung up. Moments later I realised I'd forgotten to ask him to send a policeman to help me catch his murderer at The Mill this evening. Even for a murder investigation beginner like me that seemed a pretty basic error.

Rather than swallow my pride I called Sarge. There was a standard Linbourn police department voicemail: 'Leave a message'.

I left: 'Sarge, I've arranged to meet the phone thief-cum-murderer at 5pm in Cambridge tonight. Any chance you could be there as back-up?'

It ought to rate a call back at least.

I poured a coffee and grabbed what I needed for my trip to the cottage. The phone burbled and I answered.

'Miss Patterson,' it was a DCI, not a Sergeant. 'Have you taken a moment to cool down?' He was plain infuriating.

'I'm calm.'

'Let's try again, then. One in four homicides is left unsolved in the UK. I ask you to accept that in this information age, the media is a key part of the things I must manage as part of any murder investigation.'

'Yes.'

'I require that you stop commenting in the press. When the national media inevitably find out who you are and contact you, to follow up on the story Shelby has printed, please don't respond. Don't add to my problems. Do you agree?'

'Yes.'

'I need you to stop any involvement in my investigation, starting now. You are not part of it. These murders weren't committed to raise your social media profile.'

'Too late,' I snapped into the phone, 'I've already posted on the village Facebook page about Toke's innocence.'

'You wh–' he'd either exploded or expired at the other end. I heard him ask Grant to check the Hartsdell Facebook page.

'And I am part of this whether you like it or not.'

'Trust me,' he sounded snarly, 'I don't!'

'Steve Shelby is convinced whoever attacked me must be the murderer. Shelby says, "How else would anyone know about the St Martin's Cross?" They couldn't, could they?'

'Shelby is –'

'A chief crime reporter,' I stressed the 'chief'. 'He's seen the pattern of events and realises it can't be coincidence. I've made notes on all my connections to this case. They're very convincing.'

'Right, send them.'

'What?'

'Send them now.' He gave me an email address – Grant's unfortunately. Muttering about me doing all their work, I attached and despatched the document, while he continued.

'I'll get someone here to review your notes. If you convince us, trust me, we'll be back down there in an instant. Now back off,' he roared, 'and leave it to us!'

'Er...' I said.

There followed a long silence. 'Did you just say "er", Miss Patterson?' he asked, dangerously softly. He sounded dazed.

'Have you got time for a couple of things?'

'No.' A sigh.

'It's just that I found a note in my door on my return from work last night. It said: "I don't know what the hell you think you are doing. But STOP!"'

'That was probably me,' he said.

OMG jokes now! I wasn't in the mood. 'It may have been delivered by a man I saw, who was waiting for me on my return.' I went on to explain the circumstances involving the following car.

He asked a few questions before adding: 'And the other thing?' I heard Grant laughing in the background and realised he was probably reacting to the notes I'd sent through. What was so funny?

'I've arranged to meet your murderer in the pub,' I said.

He gave a kind of cough of shock. I heard him murmuring something uncomplimentary to Grant. 'You do understand the expression "back off"?' he said to me.

'Usually.' I explained about the phone messages and my honey trap. There was more background laughing and rustling of paper at the far end of the phone. Oh no no NO! I remembered I'd made some references about DCI Hossein in my notes.

Grant came on the phone. 'I've read your notes, Miss Patterson,' he said, unable to subdue the smirk in his voice. 'Remind me who "Shouty" is.'

I resisted the temptation to say 'DCI Hossein', and told him it was Scott Hadleigh, Lotte's ex.

'And who's the woman in the cottage?'

'I'm finding out,' I said.

'Is there a concrete reason to believe she may be involved?'

'N-not exactly concrete, no.' I stumbled. I needed to be sure if Boy's tenant (and by inevitable deduction, Boy) was involved, before I started dragging him into this.

'Your Facebook posting...' said Grant. 'It's caused a... situation, Miss Patterson.'

'How? No-one reads the village Facebook.'

'"*There is still a man attacking women in the Hartsdell and Cambridge area,*"' he quoted. 'Our Crimestoppers line has been inundated with calls all morning. All people in and around Hartsdell, we didn't understand why. People have reported their husbands, aggressive ex-partners, dodgy neighbours, anyone with a moped. At this rate we'll be investigating half the males in south Cambs and north Herts for the next five years.'

'Oh, I'm so sorry. I didn't think...'

'No, you didn't. Please tell me you don't have a Twitter account.'

'I don't. I didn't mean to cause a great stramash.'

'I have no idea what that is. DCI Hoss-pants would like another word.'

Oh double expletive! I found my knuckles in my mouth and bit them hard. I'd forgotten the Hoss-pants reference.

Hossein came back on. 'We've taken on board *everything* in your exhaustive and vividly descriptive notes,' he said. 'I'll have someone quickly follow up on a few things at this end. However, here's what I think is going on: it is likely Toakley is trying to talk to you. That likelihood answers many of your points here. Leave us to deal with that. Beyond that, there is one fundamental fact that Shelby is basing his conclusions on, that we aren't convinced by.'

'What's that?'

'That you had the same bruise as the murdered woman: we don't buy that. I think you may or may not meet someone who stole your friend's phone this evening, but... it won't be my murderer.'

'You're so sure?'

'Yes. Call Cambridge CID, mention my name. Do NOT tell them it's connected to the Doll Killer or the Whittlesey murder. See if they can spare any manpower to meet you before your appointment. If they can't, you have nothing to gain from entering that pub. Do I make myself clear?'

'Yes.'

'Don't go in there alone, Shona.'

I was so taken aback at him calling me 'Shona', I agreed I wouldn't. He gave me a name and a number. We hung up.

I called the Cambridge CID man's number and left a message as a voice requested. I did include DCI Hossein's name. I clicked on the village Facebook site to view the devastation. Only a handful had 'liked' my post, but 55 people had commented on it. 'WTF – is Toke involved in the Doll Killer murders?!' someone called Nile had typed.

'Thought Toke was a harmless eccentric who told rubbish jokes. Who knew?!' Charlie Jessop's post had prompted a line of shocked emojis.

'Who is Toke? What are cops doing 'bout it?' Zina Payne offered.

'My ex, Lee Douglas, is probs the attacker. He was mean to my cat, Sparkle.' And so it went on.

'This story's online too,' Muna had attached a link, 'feel free to share.' 18 people had.

Her link took me to a national paper website, which had lifted Shelby's story.

I clicked back to find the Timeline had updated.

'Ignore Shona Patterson,' the top post now read. 'Her head's halfway up her Scottish A@!*.' This post had come from Fidel Castrol. I didn't bother clicking through to look at his profile. I was pretty sure he had nothing to do with Cuba (or petroleum!) This wasn't the result I'd hoped for. My post had exposed a certain social media naivety.

I had an unrelated notification. Shouty had been in touch and left his phone number. Too late. I saved it for future Lotte disappearances.

I clicked off. I had been unfairly cast adrift from the village I'd thrown myself into for 15 years. I was a woman, living alone with an 11-year-old, and people, who knew me well enough to know I was Scottish, hated me. Within two nights I had become a pariah. I wished I'd never mentioned my bruise.

I had to buy some things for Helen. Visiting our little village stores, I picked up a basket. The well-turned-out older woman from Webby's was in the shop. Again, she stared at me before a slight shake of her head. I turned into canned food. Although we didn't speak, it affected me. Someone in this village was warning me off, I remembered. Another was slagging me off. People were waiting for me. A man followed me home. Why would anyone go to the trouble, unless he was a killer? He knew where I lived. He knew where I'd be and when. He always seemed to kn...

Of course, it hit me, he'd be tracking my phone. While I lay unconscious, he had stolen Lotte's phone, but he'd had access to mine. A GPS location app took moments to load. That's how he stayed on my trail. I'd investigated how these things worked. They claimed to be for keeping tabs on your kids, but that didn't fool anyone. Could they listen in to my calls too?

I wallowed in vulnerability. It could be anyone – well any man – in the village. No, what had Grant said, 'half the men in south Cambs and north Herts'? He could be in the shop now, pretending to buy kitchen towels.

I stalled completely next to the Cornflakes. This wasn't the best aisle in which to succumb to a serial killer – the headline writers wouldn't be able to help themselves. My closeness to comfort foods fed old paranoias. I was ready to batter any passing male with a box of Captain Crunch. My murder musings were briefly interrupted by a BOGOF on Harry's favourite cereal.

My phone rang, and I nearly dropped my basket. It was Cambridge CID. I handed the basket to the till girl and snuck outside, so no-one would overhear as I explained how I came to have a stalker date thingy this afternoon. CID listened and then said he wasn't hopeful. It was a Friday night in Cambridge. They had a festival on, manpower was short and when it came down to it this was only a phone theft. He repeated Hossein's warning about not going ahead with my rendezvous. My honey trap was alarmingly short of Bizzie-bees.

Another call came through instantly, from a newspaper reporter. I said, 'no comment' and hung up. Another call followed moments later. Then, just as I was about to use the phone, another came in. I switched my phone off. Leaving my basket in the store I drove to Arlston. 50 minutes later I returned with a new acquisition, two pre-paid phones – like all smart people engulfed in clandestine investigations, I now had a 'burner'.

As I drove down my road, I passed Hugo, outside his house. He waved me down.

I parked up and got out as he marched down the street towards me. 'Have you got a moment, Sho'? I want a word.'

'Yes,' I said, catching an edge to his voice.

'Good, because I'd really like to know what in fuck is going on?' He was visibly trembling.

'What, I'm...?'

'I've just had some tart from Peterborough Police calling me asking about my movements last Saturday night and how I knew about the party you and Lotte were going to.'

'Sorry, Hugo, I'd no idea they'd do that. Look, don't worry about it. I think it's just routine.'

'It seems to be part of your routine these days. It's not part of mine. Esther warned me you were pointing fingers and to keep my head down. I don't need to be a suspect in a sodding murder investigation.'

'It's not like that.' I had only ever seen Hugo's amiable jocular side. I was rendered almost speechless.

'Now I've got to find alibis for Saturday. They're asking if I followed you home the last two nights. This WPC said you suggested I'd tampered with Toke's phone! I mean, what the fuck!? Why would you suggest that?'

Because, I thought, Toke never calls me 'Sho'. Because I can't imagine Toke has the remotest idea what an emoji is. And if he has an alibi for last Saturday, the person who did inflict my bruise might have borrowed his phone on Tuesday to implicate him while remaining anonymous.

'I didn't!' or... did I, in my stupid notes? I should have checked them before I pressed 'send'.

'You've got Toke dangling on a piece of wire, every time he hopes it's about to die down, you twang it again to set him dancing to your fucked-up tune.' His hands sprang up and for a moment I thought... I don't know what I thought, but I flinched.

'I really didn't mean –'

'It's not enough that you've ruined Toke's reputation... Esther's apoplectic. Christ, we've looked after Harry more times than I can count; Caitlyn too. We've been there for you when Boy upped and sodded off for some younger skirt. I understand why he went now!'

He had worked himself into a state, but that was uncalled for.

'Hugo!' It came out more loudly than I'd intended but he'd wounded me. It acted like a verbal slap.

'What?'

'You're over-reacting. I didn't intentionally pitch Toke into this. I know he didn't attack me now and I'm trying to put it right. I know he has an alibi for Saturday.'

'He does?'

'Someone told the cops that Toke was with him on business near Ely.'

'Right?' Hugo was momentarily knocked off kilter. 'Then why was he arrested?'

'Because of the text I received about my bruise on Tuesday night. The police spoke to you about it, the other day, didn't they?'

'Yeah, they showed me a picture of some bruise. I told them it was nothing like yours.'

'What the fuck, Hugo?'

'Well, it just didn't. Yours was smaller for starters.'

'Whatever. Look, just tell the police you were with your golf mates and they'll back off.'

'It's not that easy, Shona. You have no idea what you've kicked off!' he turned and walked back. I looked up and saw Esther in their doorway. She was watching us tight-lipped.

Back home I checked Facebook. The libellous comments outnumbered any 'likes', they proliferated, emojis rampant.

'The cops should talk to Brian Dicken at Camworth, he's got a shotgun.' Veganlassy had been overdosing on the walnut risotto.

'Never mind murdered people, Dicken shoots foxes.' Madbutt was living up to his (or her) handle.

'Dicken definitely, and that Troy O'Neill's got a temper on him.'

'Toke ISN'T innocent! The Cops should ask him about Big Mart in Derby.' This came from Hartsmuch, who may have had it in for a shopping centre for all I knew.

'Haven't they caught that f**!!## yet?' Kirsty Hawkins could have been referring to Toke, Big Mart, Brian Dicken or The Doll Killer.

What had I kicked off?

18 LINDI

December 2018

Webbs the Butchers accounts had been submitted by Gloria Webb for three decades. She was mum to William – the current butcher – and widow of Bertram, William's predecessor.

Gloria's books were meticulous. They deviated not a penny from the bank accounts she based them on. But she didn't use spreadsheets and wasn't abreast of modern accountancy practises. When her son suggested she step aside to allow Boy's book-keeper to take over the finances, Gloria enthusiastically accepted.

At the first meeting Lindi saw tax savings and benefits missed by the one-man accountancy practice Webbs used in Arlston to oversee (rubberstamp) Gloria's efforts. That alone covered Lindi's annual fees.

Webby (as his regulars knew him) and his meat emporium-cum-delicatessen were perfectly attuned to village needs. The butchers complemented the limited shop, reliant on basics forgotten during the weekly supermarket trip; the Hartsdell bakery and a few assorted eateries.

Lindi admired the prowess on show. Webbs delivered on its promise of quality produce and traditional fare. Customers were served on a first name basis. One morning a week Lindi worked in its small back-office. Webby asked to be taken through the accounts in person. Gloria told Lindi he had rarely shown any interest when she'd managed the books. Lindi viewed it as a key business responsibility stepping down a generation.

She generated simple spreadsheets, so Webby could quantify his produce against profit margins. Lindi showed how figures could be put to work to predict business through the year. Here, he could make better use of sale-or-return terms for example. She didn't overdo it – Webbs had survived three generations without budgeting.

The butcher's wife, Kotryna, was in the meat presentation business too. She ran a thriving one-woman beauty treatment and make-up service. Fiercely independent from her husband, she wouldn't countenance Lindi taking over her books. Kotryna was the perfect advert for her services with an athletic build, blonde locks and Slavic cheek-bones. She topped her natural assets off with an Eastern European work ethic that saw her in clients' homes late into the evening.

How the marriage worked wasn't clear to Lindi. The couple worked different shift patterns, almost different time zones, but – as she knew from experience – unlikely relationships sometimes clicked. Webby was smitten and keen to show off his fashionable, slim wife. Kotryna gave every impression of being content and attentive around her husband.

Lindi's spreadsheet flagged-up one regular supplier, Lone Marsh Holdings, that received a regular monthly pay-out without offering any visible goods or services. Lindi's check revealed it was a property company but offered no clues as to where the money went.

She asked Gloria, who shrugged. It had been an ever-present in the accounts for several years. Webby approved it. Referred to Webby, Lindi enquired about Lone Marsh.

He was unusually off-hand with her: 'Nothing for you to worry about.' And later, 'It's a prominent local farming family out Huntingdon way. They tip me off about herds, farmers worth talking to.'

If that was the best he could come up with, Lindi knew it was suspect, but she didn't press further.

Her company search revealed a property portfolio that wasn't easily pigeon-holed. The properties weren't in rural areas. They weren't retail, office or industrial. They were in residential areas in cities – Derby, Nottingham and Peterborough – and the company kept a low profile. It had no website, minimal accounts information and only one active director, a Mr Chester Make-peace Toakley.

* * *

Through the winter, Ash continued his walks in the rolling fields above the village. After one, he entered the cottage triumphantly holding his phone aloft. Its screen showed a field. It expanded under his fingers to reveal a Chiltern fallow – a stag, a pure white.

'Show Marcus,' she told him. They texted the evidence that the village's founder had returned – not just sighted but caught on screen. Marcus, now switching off from work, texted back a promise to, 'buy the biggest venison steaks in Webbs. I'll be over one night to cook up a storm.'

Lindi was pushing the marketing for both The Hart's Haunt and The Old Chapel Gallery. Did Marcus know anyone who could help with social media campaigns? He had 'just the woman' and would introduce them.

A call alerted them to Marcus's impending arrival one night. His bag of provender included three extravagant venison steaks and a bottle of champagne. He cooked, chatted, quaffed and coped, with laid-back charm, when the cottage's limited kitchen threw challenges his way. If imminent disaster threatened, Marcus waded in wielding tongs or shaking pans at crucial moments. Lindi never once imagined the steaks would be anything but perfect. It was the same magic he worked on his business.

Buoyed by triumphing in Marcus's challenge and emboldened by a glass of champagne, Ash didn't spiral into silence. He offered opinions on headline issues. He took the knife off Lindi and chopped veg.

With the plates emptied of all but abandoned cutlery and scrapings of jus, Marcus conjured two wedges of Webbs cheese and a stick of French bread from his bag. Soon after, Ash was excused to his bedroom for whatever homework or Facebook tasks awaited him. Lindi and Marcus perched on bar-stools the barely touched cheese and coffee between them.

'Judging from Webby's reports and your pub and gallery marketing plans, I'm guessing the book-keeping business is up and running,' said Marcus. 'I'm anticipating full-time tenants for my cottage.'

'I hope so.'

'Paying a proper market rate.'

'Of course. I only have six clients, though, and need to double that.'

'You'll have a £30K bonus to tide you over,' he reminded her.

'You're far too generous. I've hardly done anything to earn it.'

'You've shared in my big moment and made it that bit bigger.'

'I've enjoyed it,' said Lindi. 'And you earned it for all those years of long hours you put in.'

'We both put in,' he reminded. 'Back in the day, we were a good team.'

It was becoming too self-congratulatory. Lindi wondered where it would lead. 'I want to say something and then ask you a question.'

'I'm intrigued.'

'You have rescued me, Marcus Compton. Ash and I were both drifting off-course in Luton. You came, sought me out – I can't think why – reminded me that I have some business skills and acumen. You created a place where I could apply them. No idea how I'll repay you.'

'No need. You were always an under-exploited talent. I

should never have let you leave in 2014 – you kept me focussed. We'll do something together when I get back from
Patagonia.'

'What the hell will you do in Patagonia?'

'Nothing – that's the plan. Six months of cycling around,
with one change of clothes, no thought of where I'll be next
and no demands. It's my sabbatical to myself.'

'Sounds like purgatory. Are you going on your own?'

'Still trying to decide on that.'

'That brings me to my question. What happened to you and
Shona?'

'We started making each other miserable,' Marcus played
with the cheese. 'My fault more than Shona's. I worked hard,
then Harry came along, but I didn't slow down. We love him
to death but, ancient as I was, I still wasn't ready to be a dad.
Our lives ran to Harry's clock. I loved playing with him, reading to him, spending time with him, when work allowed, but
I wanted things to continue as before: holidays, dinner parties, dropping everything to go somewhere. Of course, they
couldn't.' The cheese plate was pushed away.

'Sho did all the school clubs, PTS-stuff, parental networking.
She shouldered too much of the parenting burden. We spent
less time with just us – even as a threesome – less time treating ourselves. I turned Shona from someone who was funny,
someone everyone loved, into a woman without confidence,
who grated on people.'

'You didn't mean to.'

'I wonder. I'd always teased her about her weight. She just
laughed and had a go back. Post-Harry it stopped being funny
– hurtful probably – I didn't notice. The irony being that now
she's way slimmer.'

'Children are about changing plans. They reinvent your
dreams,' said Lindi.

'True. I was too childish to factor that in. No-one had an
affair. We weren't arguing especially, we were just noisily miserable. We would have continued like that, only, one night,

Sho said, and I quote: "Boy, if you're that miserable, leave."'

'I'd forgotten she called you "Boy".'

'Everyone calls me "Boy", my mates, my family. I only use Marcus at work. Boy didn't seem to set the right tone for an aspiring businessman somehow.'

'So, you left.'

'It was a wake-up call. I went before I over-thought it. It's not made me happy exactly. Shona regrets the split, but I know we were sleepwalking into friction and misery. I'll always have a soft spot for her, but she hates me now. We're at it like Tom and Jerry, any time there's something to sort out.'

'And your current partner?'

'Girlfriend. You're going to meet her. She's a social network and online whizz. I'm sure Candi'll give you good advice on starting some low-cost campaigns.'

Had there been 'a moment?' Lindi wondered later. A moment, before she'd ruined it with her question. The evening ended shortly after.

She'd lost touch with the world of dates and romance – and men – so much so that she had no idea if she and Marcus were attracted to each other. She decided not – it would be out of character for them both.

❉ ❉ ❉

'"Gallery of the Macabre"; that's the working title,' Lindi said.

Candi adjusted the laptop screen. 'Love the stag,' Candi flicked through the pictures. 'That's the notorious Hart, I take it.'

They were in Harty Fare, the thriving cafe on the village's main street. Its 'low-cal wifi' fed several small screens in the Saturday morning bustle. Marcus (or 'Boy' – Lindi now thought of him by his village persona) had arrived with Candi. He bought the first round of coffees, said 'hi' to a smart pair of 40-something men at the next table and vamoosed. Harry had to be at a playmate's house.

Initially, Candi was cautious, suspicious of Lindi's relationship with Boy, but as soon as they moved on to business, she switched-on.

'I've cherry-picked details from larger paintings,' admitted Lindi. 'Subjects where the painter's skill shines out. Angus Reynolds was a local and he was obsessed by the Hart.'

'It shows, there's something demonic about it. He's also responsible for the crows, I take it?'

Lindi nodded. 'Detail from another series. It's a van Gogh thing, an artist painting a handful of subjects again and again, variations on topics that obsessed him. Hard to know what demons made it on to the canvas and what stayed in his head.'

'And all these crazy little fairy critters, how do they come into it?' Candi pushed her glasses up into short dark auburn-tinted hair.

'According to his widow, Angus had dreams where the Hart ruled some fae kingdom. Hence all the Arthur Rackham creatures. His subject matter ceased to be fashionable and he couldn't move his style or talent to more modern subjects. He became increasingly withdrawn. The dreams took over and won out.'

'The curse of The Hart,' Candi added a faux quaver. 'It drove him mad.'

'I don't know about mad. Severe depression followed by an early death. Evelyn says his best work was before his mid-20s. I think some groups and markets will go for his macabre visions now. His backgrounds are sombre, but we're reworking them as prints focussing on the foreground subjects. Evelyn's having all the paintings in the gallery reframed for modern tastes.'

'Sombre works with the Goth crowd,' Candi's business intuition chimed in.

Lindi's vision for the gallery meant finding and marketing to new audiences. She was focussing on three: Hartsdell, Arlston and its surrounds; a wider online market obsessing over dark art; and selling rights to supernatural ebook authors wanting cover art striking enough to pull in a readership.

Boy's hyperbole-strewn introduction depicted Candi as a social marketing wolf hunting down Millennials for an up-and-coming brand in Peterborough. Facebook and Google ads hummed to her tune. Candi glowed with shy pride.

When she discussed the campaign, her voice wired with certainty. Every suggestion for the marketing seemed obvious to Lindi – little more than simple common sense. It sounded like child's-play because Candi breathed the process. She'd been there, done it and it worked.

It also sounded cheap. 'Spend peanuts on ads until the percentage hitting "buy" pays for the marketing,' said Candi. 'The people I'll put you in touch with will A-B test seven bells out of it.'

The projects absorbed them, but when Boy's apocryphal 20 minutes had turned into 30, Lindi reverted to small-talk.

'How do you get on with Harry?'

'I never see him. Shona's being a real bitch about it. She tells Boy that it's too soon – it's been three years, mind! She hates me and is determined our relationship won't last.'

'Time will help her over that.'

'No, it won't. She blames me for dating Boy, even though he'd already left her by then. She expects everyone else's lives to be put on hold until she gets a new man.'

'That's just human nature,' said Lindi.

'No, frankly, it's unnatural. Shona's warped by her unwillingness to accept Boy's moved on. She can't get a man because people feel the bitterness seeping out.'

Feeding off her outburst, Candi asked about Lindi's involvement in Boy's business. It ended with a pointed: 'But why you? He had proper accountants.'

'I've asked that same question. It's nothing to do with my talent. He just needed someone cheap who was free for a few months. I qualified on both counts.'

'So, just up until the sale,' Candi was conspiratorial, showing she and Boy didn't keep secrets from each other – not even business ones.

Lindi laughed, 'The truth: he just wanted someone to help him add up all the zeroes.'

'And then, Patagonia.'

'You're going with him?'

'Well it is a lot of time off work,' said Candi. She toyed with her wrists. Lindi noticed the evasive 'tell'. Two tattoos ran across the junction between her wrists and hands. On her left it read 'empower' with a feminist symbol 'o'. On the right 'be with me'. The tattoos were simple black script, matching in everything except sentiment. Lindi guessed they had been created at different times. She suspected that one of them pre-dated Boy and wondered which.

'Boy is prone to mad ideas,' said Candi. 'I'm still deciding whether to go...'

'I would,' jumped in Lindi surprising herself.

Candi stared.

At that moment Lindi found her attention straying beyond Candi to the pair of men Boy had spoken to earlier. They were deep into an argument. Their voices were low, but one was moving to get up, leave the table, end the discussion. The other, a bearded man, caught his companion's wrist, yanking it back onto the table. Lindi caught some expletives in her lip-reading of his hissed entreaties. The leaver smiled, infuriatingly indifferent. He wrenched his wrist free, threw a £10 note down, laughed and ruffled his companion's hair in a final humiliation before leaving.

Lindi saw the departing man pass Boy in the street. The two exchanged words. She couldn't determine if it was friendship or business. Boy strode back into the Harty Fare. 'Marketing campaigns on track?' he asked the two women. They both said 'yes.'

Boy span around to the bearded man, now standing in readiness to leave. They shook hands before Boy brayed, 'C'mon, Scott, man-hug.'

The embrace was an attempt to tease him out of his mood. Boy man-handled the stranger to Lindi's table, sat him down on the fourth chair and leant on his shoulders. 'This is Scott, Lindi, more commonly known as "Shouty"; god knows why, he's the most even-tempered man you'll meet today.'

* * *

'Chester Makepeace Toakley', Lindi's mild interest tripped over the name. She was setting out a schedule of clients for Boy's business against monies received. This was the previous year's revenues. It was a task she expected to take only moments, but now it had her full attention. One receipt in the schedule stood out, a cheque for £522,000, paid in full by Peak Location Services Ltd. The cheque had been banked in early August relating to an invoice for a Peak District holiday locations online service. It was banked before Lindi had taken over.

Out of idle curiosity, Lindi had searched it out on Companies House. It had one named director, Toakley. She would have moved straight onto the next client except that name triggered a warning siren. Mr Toakley was fresh in her mind from his appearance in the Webbs' accounts. The company, she saw, had only been incorporated this year. There was almost no supporting information.

The contracted work was a fairly typical example of Boy's company's skill-set: booking systems, directional maps, attractions, suggested itineraries, searches every which way. The kind of thing his company did better than almost anybody, the kind of online service that local tourist boards or holiday cottage companies could buy off the peg, re-skin and fill with data. It used many of Boy's core software modules.

He had proudly showed it off when updating her on his business. Compared to similar sites it was faster, better populated, more intuitive and more flexible. She could imagine herself using it to research and book Peak District holidays. Boy said it had been delivered to Peak Location fully populated and functional, but they hadn't yet launched it.

Lindi entered 'Peak Location' into Google and found it trading as 'PLS'. A website linked to 15 'heritage 5-star' hotels spread across the Peak District and wandering into Leicestershire, Nottinghamshire and Northamptonshire. Sure enough you could book into these hotels online; everything was as it should be. It was a natural business diversification.

At Companies House, Peak Location Services Ltd had the same registered address as Mr Toakley's Lone Marsh Holdings Ltd. A quick trawl through the internet didn't unearth any more contact details for Toakley. She wrote him a quick letter explaining that she was doing the accounts for Boy's companies and asking if Mr Toakley would contact her. She addressed it to the registered office, printed it out on the same letterheaded stationery she sent to Boy's debtors and posted it that afternoon.

* * *

'Mum, I have to ask you something.' Ash and Lindi were up on the chalk ridge, crunching through morning frost. 'It's important. I need you to focus and not fuss.'

'I'll try.'

'I've checked this out on the interweb but it doesn't help. I think this is a more instinctual thing. It's about problems in pregnancy.'

'This is Zainab?' Lindi guessed.

'It's a pregnant girl, who can't access medical help, thinks she has problems and is scared.'

'Ash,' Lindi stopped and waited until her son had turned to face her. 'If you are still in contact with her, and she's with terrorists, the police are going to lock you away. Let her family help.'

'Her family has disowned her, Mum. As far as they are concerned, they have no daughter. I'm not turning my back on her.'

'You need –'

'No listen, you don't understand. Whatever we think of Isis, Zainab went to Syria to help when people, her people, Muslims – my people I guess – were getting gassed and bombed.

'I only know her through Facebook, but we've bonded. Rashid says that since she was little, she has always tried to do the right thing, no matter what. She's caught up in events and she's in a bad place –'

'You said she married an Isis fighter. That's not "caught up with events" – that's picking sides.'

'She was with the Syrian opposition. That's the side the West supports, remember. Where she was, in Raqqa, Isis took over the Free Syrian forces. You don't get a choice –'

Lindi put up her hand to stop him. 'I know you know far more about the politics of this than I do, Ash. Maybe Zainab is genuine and went to Syria with the best motivations but that isn't the issue. Contact with her now could derail your life – that's the point.'

They walked on in silence. Lindi could almost hear Ash running through arguments in his head, deciding which to pick. Eventually he spoke up.

'You remember when the Government people first got on my case?'

'Yes.'

'... and they took me to talk to Imam Ghalib at the mosque.'

'I regret it to this day.'

'No, he was fine. He said, don't judge Islam by what is happening in Iraq and Syria, that the West and Russia had set up those states to fail, filling them with a volatile mix of different sects and tribes. He said the plan was to ensure they spent so much time fighting each other they had no time to fight anyone else. We left them to it. Only when oil and Israel arrived did anyone notice the region and only after 9-11 did the West and Russia get involved again.' They had renewed walking and Lindi let Ash have his say.

'The Imam said if I had awoken to Islam, which I hadn't by the way, I couldn't trust newspapers, the BBC, or the web, because they all only offered two visions of Islam. It's either extremism, which exists but is far from one simplistic movement as the Western press suggests. Or they offer multi-culturist Islam. He said that only exists in liberal western imaginations.'

'That hardly sounds a useful way to address children flagged up as possible extremists,' Lindi said.

'Well, it was helpful. It was the only time I thought anyone on that programme was telling me what they thought, and not what they'd regurgitated from a pamphlet. Anyway, Ghalib said I had to find people and talk to them, if I wanted to understand Islam. Then form my opinions.'

'I doubt he meant talk to people in Isis.'

'There's no point only taking in the views you want to believe.'

'What does Zainab tell you to believe?'

'That over 14 million people are displaced from Iraq and Syria, there are currently eight wars in progress involving Muslim countries and the West has no answers.'

Lindi touched her son's arm. 'You can't solve this, Ash.'

'No, I know' he turned to her, 'but I can advise a young pregnant girl about whether her symptoms are serious or not.'

'Not if it involves communicating with a member of Isis on Facebook. They'll be monitoring you both, surely.'

'Maybe, but we use Surespot, anyhow.'

'What's that?' Lindi's alarm was escalating with each new admission.

'A phone chat messenger with end-to-end encryption. Governments can't monitor it.'

'Christ, Ash, you are behaving like a terrorist. This has to stop.'

'So once again the West fails to help. You should get together with Norton.' He spun round and retraced his steps in silent fury.

'Either you stop it, Ash, or I will,' Lindi's desperation pursued him.

✳ ✳ ✳

The Hartsdell Xmas Fayre overflowed from the new village hall, built with lottery money. Next to the cricket pitch, it doubled as the players' changing-room. Inside 20 trestle-table stalls offered food, drink, tat and taste in equal measure.

A jaded winter sun topped the lime trees at one end of a sports field and slanted in through the hall doors. Lindi paid £5 to join the throng inside, to view and sample the produce. The entry price included a beverage and a slice of home-made cake. Ash, still angered by the previous day's conversation, had turned down her suggestion of a walk to the Fayre. Lindi sat on the fringes of the coffee-shop space, conscious she knew nobody in the hall. She was still an outsider.

'Free botox with every purchase,' boomed a raven-haired woman at a nearby stall, encouraging a group of village mums to sample her wares.

'Keep Hartsdell's wee laddies on the fields and off the streets,' shouted her fellow stall-holder. The stall was decorated in vertical yellow and black stripes and someone had painstakingly written out 'Hartsdell Hornets Youth Football' on an accompanying sheet.

'Hand-picked gourmet treats that we guarantee will make your Christmas hamper the talk of Bendy-Dicks,' the second woman continued. She held up a rag-topped home-made jar and pretended to read: 'Wrap your lips around our award-winning Balsamic Pickled Nuts?'

'And unlike your husband's…' her companion chimed in, 'our nuts have aphrodisiac qualities.'

'Lotte's personally tested 14 jars.'

'Just one walnut from each, mind,' Lotte assured the crowd. 'They all worked. I didn't even need a wall.'

Good humour radiated from the stall. It was the busiest in the room.

It took Lindi a moment to place the second woman on the stall. It was a slim-line Shona, Boy's former partner. Lindi had only seen her twice before, across crowded party functions many years ago. She seemed far from the bitter and warped woman Candi had described.

Lindi was pondering whether any of her clients could make use of the Fayre next year, when a man loomed over her table.

'Ms Lindi Mills, I believe.' It didn't seem to be a question.

'Yes.' Lindi found herself talking to the man who had left the Harty Fare cafe after the argument with Shouty on the next table.

'I'm Ches Toakley,' he held out his hand, 'but everyone around here calls me, Toke.'

Lindi rose and shook the proffered hand. This was the man she'd written to, the man who'd paid off that huge account to Boy's company. His handshake was limp, his blue eyes low-lidded, his voice soft but his demeanour confident. He was smart but not over-dressed for the occasion. He indicated the spare chair, 'May I?'

She nodded without knowing if it was the right thing to do, 'Please.'

'You're ridge woman.'

'What?'

'I've driven past you a couple of times, striding out over the footpaths towards Camworth.' He sat. 'Once with your boy.'

'I go walking up there when I need to think things through.'

'Ah, too much thinking; that explains the letter I received from you. You're working on Boy's accounts, as I understand it.'

'Yes. How did you know who I was?'

'I live just outside Hartsdell. It's my parish and not a particularly big one. One quick question revealed that you not only work with Boy, you also live in his cottage,' he smiled.

Lindi couldn't work out if he was implying anything improper. She decided not. 'But you wouldn't know what I looked like.'

'Hugo did,' he indicated a man standing nearby and laughing at the banter around Shona's stall. The man turned, sensing he was being talked about. He gave a cheeky wink. Lindi had seen him a few times at Webbs. He was more than just a customer at the butchers, he was Webby's friend.

'Hugo texted me to say you were here.'

'Oh, OK. I didn't need to see you personally,' said Lindi. 'I just had a couple of questions about your account. I can't discuss them here. I don't have the details with me.'

'No, I just wanted to meet you and say "hello". I'm happy to discuss my business dealings with Boy. I have some questions I'd like to raise about it too. Perhaps we could meet up with your details and swap notes on the deal.'

Linda said, 'I won't be able to help you. I have a duty to my client, to Boy, to keep his business dealings confidential.'

'I quite understand. Then, why didn't you talk to Boy about my account, if I may ask?'

'He's not always around.' It sounded stupid and Mr Toakley's sideways smile suggested exactly that.

'Ms Mills, I won't ask you to divulge anything improper. Let's meet up early in the New Year. I'll try to answer your questions and you need only answer questions you're comfortable with, ones that relate just to my business dealings with your client. Is that fair?'

* * *

'Could I speak to Mr Norton from the anti-radicalisation programme please?'

'Norton speaking,' came the brusque response from her phone.

'Hello, Mr Norton. I don't know if you remember me. I'm Ash Khan's mum; we met a few times when your agency took an interest in Ash. His school misrepresented his activities to you in my view, but anyway...'

'Yes, I remember Ash, very bright boy. How's he doing? You've moved from Luton, haven't you?'

'Yes, we're in a village outside Arlston. Ash is in a new school and doing well. As you know, he's not actually Muslim and definitely isn't radicalised, but there is one thing I'd like your advice on...'

* * *

Webbs the Butchers Xmas party was the night before Xmas eve, at Benedicts bar a few doors down from the butchers. Bar manager Margaux was a customer of Webbs. She had reserved their table in a sought-after alcove, slightly out of the hubbub and heave of the main bar.

They were only eight. Apart from Webby and Lindi, his wife Kotryna attended, dressed and made up as an impossibly aspirational advert for her beauty business. Webby's mother, Gloria, came, as did his full-time butcher plus two part-timers and an occasional delivery man.

The wine flowed, lubricating the conversation, initially prompted by eating their own produce. Soon, the five men were discussing football. Lindi knew Webby made sure he knew just enough to join in the mock-teasing with his colleagues. Gloria, stately at the far end of the table, closest to the raucous bar, had her duty smile on. It left Kotryna and Lindi together, deepest into the alcove. Kotryna questioned her about Ash and Ayan. She pushed hardest about what Lindi did for Boy and their working arrangements. In return, Kotryna offered nothing about life before Webby.

Kotryna leaned across to Lindi, 'What do you think of Webby?' she spoke close to Lindi's ear.

'He's good at what he does. It's a tough business, especially these days, and he's made it a success.'

'I mean as a man.'

'I like him. He's considerate, makes time for people, customers appreciate that, and he's open to new ideas.'

'He's fit too,' Kotryna confided. 'Good-looking, yes, slim. I keep him on a taut leash. No cakes for Webby. He's in good shape.'

Later, Kotryna followed Lindi into the ladies. Inside the therapist waited until another woman left, almost shooing her out of the door. She moved uncomfortably close to Lindi, while they washed hands. 'You should sleep with Webby,' she said.

Lindi had been expecting something – it wasn't this.

'He's a fine man. You're a discreet lady, I can tell,' said Kotryna. 'I know he likes you. You must be lonely here. It would be good for both of you.'

'Kotryna, Webby's not going to look at anyone else when he's got you. You're the most glamorous woman in the village. He's not interested in me.'

'You're wrong. Webby and I have...' the words eluded her. 'There's a saying for it. It's an arrangement that doesn't include sex.'

'You don't –'

'At all.'

Lindi had stumbled into a minefield. 'A marriage of convenience, I think you mean. Kotryna, I really don't need to know about Webby's personal life. I'm just his book-keeper. That's all I'll ever be.' She found the door.

'Think about what I said. You'd have my blessing. We could find more work for you too. You could help with my business.'

Lindi left shortly afterwards. Webby's goodbye, she felt, had a puppyish quality about it.

As she crossed the dark street, she heard her name, a man trotted after her. It was Toke's friend, Hugo. 'Book-keeping,' he said breathlessly, as Lindi shone her tiny torch on his drunkeness.

'What about it?'

'Webby recommended your services. We're interested.' He pushed a card at her.

Lindi turned it over but couldn't read it without taking her torch from Hugo. 'What is it you do, exactly?'

'I've written my mobile number on the back,' he said. 'Give me a bell in the New Year, let's catch up and see if we can work together.' He turned and lurched back to the lights billowing from the bar.

2014

'Why don't you both come to us.' Ayan's jerky Skype image did its best to defuse his suggestion of the 5,000 miles it entailed. 'We'd love you to share Christmas with us. We usually have chicken curry for lunch. I know you'll enjoy that.'

'Can we, mum?' Ash was agog – curry for Xmas. Lindi's mother had died earlier in the year. She'd run out of excuses.

'Maybe,' she told him before returning to Ayan. 'Let's look into the practicalities; work is still busy.' They both knew she meant no.

Ayan had come over for a few days for Lindi's mother's funeral. It was his only visit of 2014. Lindi had surprised him by insisting that they'd slept together. It had been awkward and only confirmed that the spark of their relationship had been lost in the intervening years.

It was rare now that she got involved in Ash's regular Skype sessions with his dad. Ash pleaded that they visit Karachi every school holiday. Lindi couldn't countenance a trip to Pakistan. She no longer heard from the rest of his family.

'I'm worried Ash'll want to stay over there with you,' she'd confessed to Ayan, unwilling to invent more lies that it was mere inconvenience.

'If that happens, you know you're both welcome.'

'I do, Ayan, but my life is here, and I can't live it without Ash. You've got a whole family there; I've only got Ash.'

'It's wrong to keep a son from his father, Lindi.' It was Ayan's perennial refrain. Lindi was fed up of hearing it.

After the funeral he returned, and she reached for the specimen taken during Ayan's deep-phase sleep. Swabs from Ash and herself were added and the online DNA testing kit was mailed off. Her guilt at purchasing it dissolving in her certainty that she should have done one before. She paid extra for a fast service.

The results, waiting on the web site, confirmed what she had known – probably from his birth – Ash wasn't Ayan's son. He must be Connor's child. Lindi didn't know what had happened to Connor and had no intention of finding out. She wouldn't tell Ash, but she sent Ayan an email with the password to her DNA website account, so he could see the result for himself. She then called him to break the news personally before he had a chance to view it.

Before he consumed too much energy and invested more time on Ash, she said, she'd wanted him to know. They wouldn't be coming over to Pakistan for...

Ayan had hung up.

19 SHONA

Friday afternoon May 24 2019

I parked outside Dell End Cottage but instead of going in, I went across the road to talk to Mrs Whatsit about the woman who had lived there.

Ding-dong.

'Shona, back again, so lovely to see you. Come and say hello to Henry. He doesn't get many visitors. Would you like a tea? Don't mind Buffy, she gets over-excited. Down Buffy, leave Shona's trousers in one piece. She won't bite.'

But she will do everything else she can to make me feel awkward. I removed Buffy's nose from my crotch for the third time and followed my host into a small overly snug living room. Henry was sat in a tall armchair, secure in his dufferage. His vantage point was ideal for both the telly and the cottage opposite.

'I won't stop thanks,' I said. 'I just thought I'd pop in and say "hi" this time. Last time I was in such a rush.'

Mrs Oojamaflip showed me to a chair so low I had to look over my knees at everyone but at least she tucked Buffy between her legs and clamped her there. I imagined a wistful look passed through Henry's eyes at the sight.

'Are you and Mr Compton' (she meant Boy) 'going to let the cottage again soon? We've so missed people being there. Des

Tillotson was such a lovely man and so was Francesca, wasn't she, Henry? You remember Francesca, Henry, don't you?'

'Nice legs.' It seemed she had left an impression on him.

'Boy's away at the moment,' I said. 'We'll rent it out again as soon as he's back.'

'And we liked having your dad there as well, didn't we Henry?'

Silence. Dad's legs hadn't cut the mustard.

'I wanted to talk to you about the most recent lady,' I said. 'She's left some of her stuff in the house and I need to get it back to her before we can rent it out again.'

I was taking advantage of their loneliness, I knew, but this was a murder investigation after all. If they thought answering my awkward questions might speed up the cottage being rented again, it would help.

'Lindi, you mean?' she said. I had a name and thankfully it wasn't 'Candi'.

'Yes, I didn't know her,' I said. 'Boy dealt with it.'

'Ooh we know. He was always over here with her... during the day,' she added quickly in case I'd got the wrong impression. Too late!

'I think she was working for him. That's it. He said she was doing his accounts. She was there with her son, Ash, wasn't it Henry?'

'Bad sort,' said Henry, 'mixed up with those Muslims.' Buffy barked in bigoted agreement.

'What's that?'

'Muslims!' asserted Henry, 'bombers.'

'I'm so sorry,' I said in astonishment, 'I'd no idea.'

'I'm sure you didn't know, Shona,' said Mrs Whassa-name, 'but there was quite a to-do. Police cars, visits, government people. We were watching when he was arrested.'

'Oh my god, what happened?'

'Five police cars came to take him; early it was, before Henry's breakfast. Then a day or so later, they let him go. He was back for a short while and then he disappeared.'

'Went and joined Al Qaeda,' Henry was livening up. Even Mrs Tillotson's legs never put on a show as good as this. It had passed me by though. If this woman was involved with Al Qaeda or Isis, it could explain how she and my doll had ended up headless in a fenland ditch. It was almost an Isis trademark.

'Lindi seemed a nice lady, though, a bit quiet, maybe, but a hard worker; she had jobs everywhere in the village.'

'Where did she work?' I asked. How had I missed this woman?

'In the pub, the Hart, down the road; at Webby's too, I think. Oh, and she did quite a bit with Evelyn.'

'Evelyn?'

'In the Old Chapel Gallery. Mrs... ooh my computer's gone on search, bear with me... Mrs Brett-Reynolds. There may have been others.'

'You said she left in late February, I think.'

'In February certainly. Yes, it was quite dramatic. A lot of cars and people coming and going through the night before she and Mr Compton left.'

'Cars?'

'Yes, at least three, wasn't it Henry? This is usually such a quiet road you see, we notice.'

'And she definitely left with Boy, er... Mr Compton?'

'Ooh, I'm not really sure about that, but I remember seeing his car driving away and we didn't see Lindi again after that. We thought she might have come and said goodbye.'

'Can you remember the exact date?'

'Oh gosh. No, dear. Is that important?'

'Buffy's vet day,' announced Henry, surprising everyone. Even Buffy turned to stare. 'Oh, he's right,' confirmed Mrs Whatsit, and jumped up to fetch a calendar. Buffy and I awaited developments. 'It was a Thursday. Buffy had been in the vets for a few days and we collected her on the morning of the 21st of Feb. It was that night.'

'That's really helpful. So that was the last time you saw Lindi?'

'Yes.'

'Can you remember Lindi's surname? I've got to track her down, you see.'

She pondered, glanced at Henry, thought better of it and shook her head, 'No, sorry, Shona, I don't think we were ever told. Evelyn will know. She's good with names.'

I wasn't. I thanked them both, said goodbye to Buffy and left. I wished now I'd spoken to her more yesterday. I slowed at the gate: 'What colour was Lindi's hair?'

'Now you've got me. Light brown, I think.'

'I don't suppose you saw if she had any tattoos.'

'I'm not sure I'd notice, dear, but she didn't seem the type. You should put it in the tenants' conditions. We want the right sort.'

I returned to my car boot to collect the bits and pieces I'd brought from the lab last night. There was a powerful portable ultra-violet light, which we used in the lab for shining on zebrafish after we've pumped them full of transgenic material. The luminol spray, wasn't used in the lab. I'd ordered it in for this investigation. I unlocked Dell End and carried my SOCO (scene of crime officer) stuff in a largish cardboard box. Once inside I donned a set of disposable clean-room overalls from a pack of such things I kept at home for rare visits to another company facility in north London. They came in useful in domestic situations too.

TV detective stories involve SOCOs flashing UV light around to reveal blood or spraying chemicals over everything – usually both. I was searching for blood but (unlike TV execs) I knew UV light wouldn't help as blood doesn't fluoresce under UV. However, it can be made to glow when you apply certain chemicals, luminol being the one I had read up on, which seemed best for these conditions.

I had a whole cottage (plus a small garage) to cover, though, and no idea where the crime scene might be, with an each-way bet on the bathroom. I was hoping that the UV light might pick up on other things that would help pinpoint where to concentrate my hunt.

Donning lab gloves I moved to the bottom of the stairs. I listened again. The two spiders still skulked there, webs empty, either side of the corridor. Slightly skinnier, they sized each-other up. Was he a future lover or just lunch? A quandary reminiscent of most of my recent dates.

I climbed the stairs and started with the UV.

I drew curtains to make it gloomy. UV shows up several bodily fluids, these include saliva and urine as they absorb the UV and then re-emit it. Dead bodies leak all-sorts.

However, in bedrooms and bathrooms I was going to see a lot of this stuff anyway and I wasn't expert enough to draw many conclusions. I did spray plenty of luminol in the bathroom as I expected it to be the prime area for body hackage. I crawled inside the cardboard box as I'd read luminol performed better in low-light. Nothing – phew!

However, in the kitchen, the UV picked up something near the centre on the floor, beside the mock-granite quartz-composite worktop Boy and I had installed. There was a small pool of radiance plus a few random drops. I guessed saliva – a pool of drool? I sprayed the luminol and crawled inside my box. There was splatter and a few smudges of glow. My guess would be blood droplets that someone had cleaned up but not well enough to fool the luminol.

I tried again on the cupboards and the nearby area of worktop – bingo, there was another scuff of stuff. Blood on a kitchen worktop... could be evidence of cold-blooded murder, or maybe they'd just had liver for tea. Being a SOCO wasn't as cut and dried as it looked on TV.

I started emptying the bins out on the floor. This isn't recommended SOCO procedure, but I was in a hurry. There wasn't much in them. A crumpled ball of kitchen towel, exhibiting a dried brown smear, hid behind the bin. A similarly stained tissue had escaped under an empty wine rack. Crivens! Both excited luminol interest.

I popped the them into a plastic food bag I had brought along. That would do for now. I tidied up to make it look as if I had never been there and removed my sterile lab gear.

Before I left, I used Robert Keynes' keys to open the garage. It seemed a likely spot to hide murder implements, but all I found was a pale green car. I made a note of its make, model and registration. I assumed it must belong to Lindi. Who else could it belong to?

Mrs Whatsit was busy in her garden when I reloaded my car. She watched me carry my evidence kit back, which, I suspected, was the real reason she had grabbed her trowel.

I waved. 'What kind of car did Lindi drive?' I shouted as I walked over. 'Oh, I don't know, I'm afraid,' she said. 'I'm useless with cars. That was Henry's area, not mine. It was a silvery green one, that's all I remember.'

'And there were no ambulances called when she left in February?'

'Lord no, dear, we'd have noticed anything like that – even at night. There were a lot of police cars in January, mind, when they came for her son.'

January ran a bell. I remembered Lotte mentioning someone at the village being suspected of terrorism, but I was obsessed with lawyers and preventing Boy going to Patagonia at the time. I thanked Mrs W. and drove off.

I went about 200m and pulled into the Hart's Haunt pub car park. It was lunchtime and ten other vehicles were parked there. I entered, sat on a bar-stool and ordered a sparkling water. The barmaid served me a winning smile and asked if I wanted a menu. I told her I probably wasn't eating today, but I'd look for a future occasion. She handed it over and went back to chatting to two rugged regulars at the bar, who seemed to have commandeered all the bar-snacks.

There were several spooky prints of the pub's Hart for sale on the walls and a small selection of postcards featuring him in a display case on the bar. It had been years since I had been in here, I realised. The gentrification was subtle, but it was happening.

'This place has changed for the better,' I said when I caught the barmaid's eye. I waved the menu, 'And this looks really interesting. I'll be back.'

I meant it. I was pleasantly surprised by the menu. It was new, tastefully designed and the small number of dishes catered for both the rustic creatures hogging the bar and for Lotte's and my more pretentious palettes. To be honest, we cared less about what we ate and more about what (and where) we were seen to eat. Maybe this place was trending on something. I could make a comment about it on the village Facebook page – I didn't want to get labelled as a murder-only postee.

'Good to hear' said the barmaid. 'We've had a bit of a makeover. Pass the word around.'

'You're off your patch, aren't you, love?' said one of the lords of the bar-snacks.

'I was in Dell End Cottage,' I said. 'Looking into what happened to our tenant there. Lindi, did you know her? And I'll take a wee crispie off ya' by the way?'

He laughed and passed them along the bar. Sometimes 'doing Scottish' worked for me. I hutched up the bar, so I was in their conversational orbit.

'She did some work for Jimmy, the landlord here,' said the barmaid. 'Did the books, shamed him into a bit of repainting here and there, sorted out the website, suggested some changes to the menu...'

'...then buggered off just as soon as she'd ruined it,' said the burlier of the regulars.

'She didn't ruin it, Wayne,' the barmaid said, staunch in her defence. 'Our takings are up. She got Jimmy some great deals with craft beer suppliers. And we're finally doing decent business at the weekends.'

'Beer's gone off in't it Wayne?' said the other regular. 'There's eleven bloody gins, I ask you! And Jimmy reckons he wants us to smarten up if we come here in the evenings. S'not right.'

'He's joking,' laughed the barmaid uncertainly.

'So, what happened to Lindi. As far as we know she's disappeared, leaving a lot of stuff in the house that we need to get back to her.'

'Her lad!' said Wayne, stretching and scratching at his arm-pits in one less-than-decorous flourish. 'He had some Muslim in 'im. Went off the rails. Fu... disappeared off to join Isis, they reckon.'

'No!' I was shocked.

'We told her, didn't we Wayne?' said his mate.

'You'll back me up here, Hester. We said, if you go hunting for the Hart, no good'll come of it. Curse is a curse.'

'How'd her son get into Isis then?' I asked.

'Dad was a Paki, I heard,' said Wayne. 'Nothing against Muslims but they just get too riled up over religion sometimes. Look at Syria, Iraq and the rest. They're all at each other's throats. And Blair wades in, bloody idiot! Any ten-year-old with a history book could have told him how it always ends up for us out there.'

'Social media doesn't help,' added Hester. 'Lindi told me Ash was messaging a girl from Luton, who was involved somehow. It's hard to keep tabs on what your kids are doing on screen nowadays.'

'Tell me about it,' I agreed. 'Was she in here often, then?'

'A few times. Mainly to talk things through with Jimmy.'

'She had your fellow in tow, a coupl'a times.' Wayne's mate couldn't resist the dig. Hester glared but he continued, 'You and Compton still together?'

I didn't bother answering. I figured he knew.

'Cos when she ran off,' Wayne pulled the crisps back into his ambit, 'we wondered if she was pregnant.'

✳ ✳ ✳

My next call was Webbs. On the way I fired off an immature text to Shelby at the paper.

'Was the vic pregnant?'

Webby's and my eyes met briefly before he whisked them back to the customer he was serving. I'd seen him look more charming. A break in customer traffic gave him time to pull me into the backroom. Thankfully Kotryna wasn't there on this occasion. His mum was sorting out some shelves just outside, though, and would be ear-wigging.

'You are screwing this village over,' was his hissed opener. 'Everyone's talking about you, your comments on the Facebook page. I've had the press calling – as, I suspect, have Benedicts and other local businesses. Some police woman phoned wanting to know if I have an alibi for last Saturday and if I knew you were going to be at that perv party in Cambridge?'

I wondered what Webby's mum made of that indiscretion.

'You knew, then?' I could see it in his face.

'Yes, I knew you were there. Toke and Hugo were laughing about it. And, of course, I don't have an alibi. Kotryna was up somewhere near Sandy at a client's make-over evening. I'm strongly of the impression that I'm now a suspect in your attack. Thanks for that Sho. When Kotty discovers I'm suspected – and she will – I'll get the silent treatment for days.'

I spread my hands. 'It's escalating faster than I ever imagined. I'll tell them you didn't attack me, though.'

'Please don't. This is out of control and so are you. I want distance between us. Hugo just texted – it was all effing and blinding about you! I tried to call to warn you.'

'I know. Hugo's savaged me once already. About my phone; I've leaving it off. I'm being followed. My mobile's probably being tracked.' I pulled out one of the cheap phones I'd bought in Arlston and popped one into his trouser pocket. I reduced my voice to a whisper. 'When that goes, it'll be me. And it'll be an emergency. You can choose whether or not you answer.'

He moved to pull the phone back out. 'I don't bloody want it,' he whispered. 'I can't be involv –'

I stayed his hand. 'There's no-one else I can turn to, Webby, really. You need to do this.'

We both fell silent, undeniably guilty as his mum's head

glanced into the room to see what we were doing. Her eyes roamed meaningfully over me, flicked to her son and moved unsubtly towards the shop-front. Finally, she went back to re-arranging things on her shelves.

'Two questions then I'm gone,' I spoke loudly so his mum didn't have to strain to hear. I was news – notorious, morbidly riveting news. People would want to listen in.

'Be quick.'

'Did Lindi someone work for you?'

'Lindi Mills. She took over the books briefly in the autumn. Did a good job too, but I had to let her go. Mum's back on the case. Why?'

Lindi Mills, I knew that name. 'Why did you let her go?'

'Her son; he was involved with Muslim extremists. You must have heard, surely. Call me old fashioned but I don't need to be around that.'

'When did she leave?'

'My employ? January. When did she leave Hartsdell? No idea.'

'Did she have a tattoo?'

'How the hell would I know?'

'It would have been on her hands or her face.'

'No then, she didn't!'

'Was she involved with Boy?'

'So that's what this is about. I should've known.' He stepped back, shaking his head. 'Don't drag me in, Sho. That's not even your business. Boy put in a word with me to try her book-keeping out. All I know. Forget about her. She's hardly your biggest problem.'

'Oh, what is?'

'Right now, you are!'

Webby's mum reappeared, 'It's filling up out there.'

Webby nodded. She didn't move.

I swallowed down his last comment and went on. 'You said Toke was with you last Tuesday evening. That's when he sent me the text. Who else was with you then?'

'For Christ sake, Sho!' he moved to the door; pushing his mum back towards the shop.

'I need to know.' I grabbed his sleeve.

'Toke, me, Hugo and Shouty were playing bridge; From 7.30-to-11.30-ish. Kotty was working upstairs but had laid on a spread for us. Are we done?'

'Yes. Keep the phone on. It's charged and has one preset number – mine.'

I walked the 100 metres up the road to the Old Chapel Gallery. Unusually it had its door open. It normally gave every impression of being closed. A sign outside was newly printed with opening times and, my god, a web address. Two posh cars were in its car-park, now adorned with box balls in sage-green containers. Evelyn Brett-Reynolds was making one last go of it.

I stepped into the foyer. I'd not been in here for years but remembered the weird circus tableau. Someone had taken a much-needed duster to the gruesome puppets inside and a new sign said, 'Welcome to the Old Chapel Gallery – step into the macabre.'

I did.

There were two middle-aged couples inside, plus an attentive Evelyn, understatedly immaculate in a long black skirt, creamy blouse and elaborate gold necklace. I remembered her now. In fact, I'd seen her in the shop that morning and at Webby's yesterday. Perhaps she was my stalker! She stared at me again, in surprise this time, but quickly reverted to a professional smile and turned back to one pair of customers. They were discussing a mid-sized painting on the wall. After a moment the woman won the argument and the man reached into his pocket.

Evelyn took the picture off the wall and they all went through to her desk. I had a prowl around. Most of the heavy oak-framed darkly depressing pictures that I associated with the gallery were gone. There were three fashionably mounted pictures of Hartsdell village's founder, staring hauntingly at me with the same eerily pale eyes that adorned the sign of the pub. This explained where the pub postcards had originated from.

I still had time before I needed to get to Harry's school to check Helen had made it. Then off I would trot to my murderer appointment. I hoped it wouldn't be the last time Harry would see me alive. I assumed Evelyn was going to be a while and, feeling safe in the gallery, I switched my phone back on. I called Boy.

'Shona,' he answered warily.

'Truce,' I said. 'I want to talk to you about Lindi Mills.'

'Why? What about her?' Still wary but at least he hadn't asked, 'who?'

'You know I'm mixed up in this unidentified murdered woman case?'

'What, still?'

'Well, I can't track down your former book-keeper...' (I'd placed her now; she had run Boy's books, six-or-so years ago) '...cum recent tenant. She seems to have gone missing around the date of the murder.'

'What the hell are you playing at, Shona?' He sounded convincingly mystified.

'I need to find out if you know why she left the village in such a hurry.'

'Who says she did?'

'Everyone.'

'I heard her son got mixed up with some extremists.'

'You heard? Was this when she was doing your accounts?'

'Shona, you really need *not* to be doing this.'

'Why?'

'It sounds dangerous, for one thing. Just keep your head down. Let the police do their job.'

'They don't think I'm involved. Won't believe I had *exactly* the same bruise that they found on this dead woman. They're wrong and I'm out to prove it.'

'Look, I can't understand what it's to do with you, but... but, *if* you're right about there being something connecting you to the murder of this woman, that's all the more reason not to draw the killer's attention to you.'

Oops, a bit late for that!

'Plus you've got to think about Harry. I don't want our son put in harm's way.'

'He's not. You know he's at Helen's. If it *is* Lindi...'

'It's not Lindi! She's not dead. I can guarantee that.'

'How?'

'Alright, she *was* doing some accounts work for me either side of Xmas,' he said, 'but I've spoken to her since the murder.'

'When? When was the murder?'

'I don't know. I've been in Patagonia for three months. I've no idea what's going on or what you've stirred up.' Boy was lying. I could tell because 15 years is a long time to live with someone. He didn't do it often, and he wasn't practised at it.

'So, you can categorically assure me, I'm wasting my time with Lindi? She's not dead?'

Evelyn was walking past, and her mouth dropped. I gave her a smiley shrug.

'Categorically!'

'Good, in that case what happened to my old doll and my mum's jewellery bits? It was in a cardboard box in dad's chest at Bell End' (it was our jokey nick-name for the cottage).

'Why?' I'd expected him to ask, 'what?'

'Because I checked the cottage, and they're gone – like Lindi?'

'What were you doing round my rental? How did you get in?'

'Doors into the back garden.' I found I could lie effortlessly when required and I didn't want to get Robert into trouble. 'I hid a key under a pot when Dad was living there, for emergencies.'

'Shit, Shona, that's secure! Lock it and get those keys to Robert Keynes.'

'You're avoiding my question. You remember my doll.'

'The scary one with the blue eyes, yes, and your pathetic bear with no stuffing left.'

I'd forgotten about poor Threadbear Ted. He would have

been in that same box. Perhaps he was being saved ready for my murder. A disturbingly vivid image came to mind of my beheaded body rotating gently below a dank mist in a reedy pool. Spinning next to me was Threadbear Ted, a proud Scottish heirloom, abandoned by his primary carer, then ending up headless and paw-less in a Sassenach ditch.

'I thought I'd taken the cardboard box, which contained your mum's jewellery, out,' said Boy. '

And?'

'I gave it to you.'

'No, you didn't.'

'In that case it's still in the box room, I'll look when I'm back.'

'It's definitely not there. There's been a complete stramash in that room.'

'Why are we even talking about this? We must have chucked it, then, when the Tillotsons moved in.'

'No, that's when we put it in the box-room. Some of Mum's stuff is still there but the good jewellery – the hand-me-down stuff – is missing.'

'You sure you don't have it?'

'No. I think it's missing for a reason, I thi –'

'Actually, I do remember bringing the box with the Scottish jewellery and stuff home. I thought I gave it to you but if you haven't got it, it'll still be in Big House.' I wasn't the only one who could lie effortlessly.

'Why are you lying about this?' And, then I knew. 'You've let Candi borrow them.'

'Don't be ridiculous. You've lost me, Sho? In fact, what does it matter if Candi did borrow them? She'll have put them back.' There was a sudden catch in Boy's voice. It went quiet, something had occurred to him. Had he put his hand over the receiver?

'What did Candi just say about it?' I asked. 'Has she got them?'

'She's not here, Shona.'

'Fine. Then, how come Candi's enjoying Patagonia so much?'

'Don't start on that again.'

'Only, she seems to be having a fine old time there from posts on her Facebook page.'

'Her Facebook page?' utter bemusement.

'Fact is, I'd say, comparing your two Facebook pages, Candi's having an even more obviously stupendous time stravaiging around Patagonia than you are.'

'Now you have totally lost me.'

'Stravaiging, it's Scottish, it means –'

'I know what stravaiging means. I don't do Facebook.'

'Well, that's a lie for starters. Don't tell me you don't check out each other's right-on Facebook pages; that you don't coorie down together each night in the gloaming to decide what piccies and posts you're going to put up to make us all so bloody jealous. It's pathetic, Boy, it really is.' I hung up.

Evelyn's second couple of gallery-goers were staring at me as if I was a piece of impromptu performance art.

'My Ex', I mouthed. They hastily returned their interest to a picture with a pair of murderously evil crows that probably wouldn't have seemed out of place wheeling around my head. Had I been loud? I switched my phone back off. There were messages. I ignored them.

The first couple departed with a diligently-wrapped picture under one arm and Evelyn Brett-Reynolds strode towards me.

'Evelyn', she reintroduced herself briskly. 'What can I do for you, Shona?'

'Can you spare a minute to talk to me about Lindi Mills?'

'As long as you understand, my customers come first.' She turned to the remaining couple. 'Don't hesitate to interrupt if you want to ask anything.'

They assured her they wouldn't and that that were just browsing. I knew they'd keep their distance until after the disquieting Scottish lady was gone.

'What about Lindi?' Evelyn spun back to me.

'I understand she did some accounts work for you.'

'She did, and I recommend her services.'

'But she's not working for you now?'

'No, she left the village.'

'When was that?'

'February.'

'Has she been in touch since?'

'No, she set things up so I can manage the business on my own.'

Evelyn's answers were crisp, instant and to the point. Why did I think she was hiding something? Ah, because she hadn't asked why I was asking. 'Did she tell you she'd be leaving?'

'No, but I thought she might go.'

'Oh, why?'

'After her son left. I think he missed Luton.'

'Because of the extremists?'

'You'll find I don't gossip, Shona, and I don't meddle.' There was a clear message for me in that sentence. 'How do things stand between you and Mr Toakley?'

'Badly,' I admitted. 'Seems like Lindi did a good job promoting your business.'

'Lindi saw an angle I'd missed and had the contacts and knowledge to exploit it. She also reignited the enthusiasm I'd lost and helped me set things up very quickly and without fuss, despite...'

'Please go on.'

'No, like I said, I don't gossip.'

'Can I leave a number, in case she gets in touch?'

'She may not,' said Evelyn. 'I'm not expecting her to.'

'If she does, please let her know I urgently need to speak to her.'

'What about?'

'We may have...' how could I even start to phrase this? '...some experiences in common. Really, I just want to know she's OK.'

I wrote a mobile number on the back of one of the gallery's cards. Neither of us looked hopeful.

'Is she...' Evelyn's rethought her question. 'Do you think something's happened to her?'

❉ ❉ ❉

I went back to my cottage to change into something that could double as murder vigilante date/work attire and drove over to Arlston and parked up, waiting for Harry's school to break-up.

I recapped what I'd learned from Dell End. Lindi Mills had not left there according to the tenancy agreement terms: i.e. she hadn't given notice, packed up her stuff or taken her car.

At best, she had left in a hurry – in a panic? – and not returned. Maybe she had suffered some injury in the cottage and Boy (probably) had run her to a hospital... and she hadn't needed her car since? Frankly, none of that stacked up.

At worst, Lindi Mills had been killed, her body mutilated and left in a ditch with my beheaded doll for company. If it was my doll, then surely my mum's St Martin's Cross ring had been used to bruise her – both of which may have been at Lindi's rental.

Why bruise the victim post-mortem?

I face-palmed as the realisation came to me. Hossein assumed the doll had been 'bruised' to resemble the victim, but he was wrong. If the Becca Blue Eyes doll was mine, the victim had been bruised to resemble Becca. She was thumped with mum's ring to match Martin's old biro 'tattoo' on my doll. That opened a whole new rabbit hole.

Lindi hadn't been chopped-up at Dell End. The absence of substantial blood or bodily fluids was telling. People underestimate how tough human bodies are. Household knives and kitchen implements are no match for our bones and tendons. She could have been killed in the cottage, during the Friday night ruckus, but the nosy neighbours would surely have seen her carried to a car.

If it was Lindi's body, and my doll and ring, then Boy must be involved. I could understand why he'd lie about Candi being in Patagonia – he knew that Candi just being anywhere on the planet riled me (even now!) – but why would he be shifty about his accountant being taken to hospital?

If the blood on the tissues I'd bagged, and put in my glove compartment, matched the DNA of the murder victim, Boy was the blindingly obvious suspect. But he was also Harry's dad and what kind of situation would provoke anyone to start killing and mutilating women?

I felt pig-headedly angry with Boy for taking up with Candi, but I had loved him for a lot longer than I'd hated him. The Boy I knew, was squeamish. I was the one who dealt with anything involving death (mainly mice, Harry's errant tortoise or kamikaze birds) or bodily fluids (mainly Harry's) around the house. I couldn't imagine Boy taking a cleaver to anyone – let alone his accountant!

Hell, of course, cleavers! I called Webby on our new burners, intrigued to see if he'd pick up. He did, but after a delay, which, I suspected, involved him relocating to a safe haven.

'You there,' he said tentatively. I don't think Webby had much experience of burner culture.

'When Boy did your butchery course,' I asked, 'I assume it involved modules on cleavers.'

There was a shaky silence. 'It's hard to do any serious butchery without a cleaver.'

'Webby, for God's sake; the whole point of these phones is that no-one can listen in or track us.'

'Maybe at your end.'

'Was Toke on that course too?'

'I know where you're going with this, but I ran a course a year for four years, almost exclusively attended by Hartsdell and Camworth men – that's almost 40 people who I taught how to use a cleaver.'

'Including Hugo and Shouty?'

'Yes, they were on the same course with Toke and Boy, now drop it. Haven't you alienated enough people already?'

That was true, 'Yes'.

'One thing you should know: I'm meeting Toke for a drink in Cambridge tonight. He's desperate for an old-fashioned boys' night out. Says that some WPC called about his business associates. They're trying to track someone down. Toke thinks it could compromise a key business account. Guess who he blames for that?'

'What are his business dealings?'

'Property mainly.'

'That sounds harmless. I've told the cops it wasn't him.'

'No-one listens, Sho. It's out there, you can't unsay it. Anyway, Toke wanted to hit Benedicts and fingers-up to the village. We said, no way. Hugo badly needs a Friday loosener. He's in the doghouse thanks to you. I'm driving him to Cambridge to meet up with Shouty and Toke for a beer.'

'Or three?'

'Or six! Toke's driving down from a meeting near Ely to join us at 7pm and he's talking about getting hammered and us getting a cab back. Keep your head down.'

'Webby, do me a favour, stay sober.'

'What now?'

'I've been followed home the last two nights. Everything's kicking off. I may need you at the cottage.'

'Couldn't be worse timing, Sho.'

'Don't go for this drink.'

'I've got to at least drive Hugo there. OK, I won't tarry.'

So, the case against Boy now included a Webbs the Butchers diploma in 'cleavage' and it wasn't Candi's because she didn't have one! Ouch, that sounded bitchy.

*   *   *

'I've seen the bruise, Mum. It's all over the Internet.' Harry and I were chatting, waiting for Helen. She'd called to say she had underestimated the traffic going north on the A1.

'How is it you're allowed all over the Internet?'

'Mum, everybody at school's seen it. It would be weird if I hadn't.'

'You know not to listen to what people say don't you? It's just a silly bruise.'

'They say it's a St Martin's Cross; like the earrings we bought Ollie's mum from Scotland.'

'Gosh yes.'

Harry and I had bought them in a gift shop on a trip to Oban, two years ago. Lotte had been of inestimable help when I was piecing together the shards of my life, post-Boy. She and Ollie kept Harry entertained for me, while I re-organised work schedules, sorted out post-school activities and mentally re-evaluated. As a kind of life-rekindling statement, I'd taken Harry up to the land of his ancestors and we'd trolled around ticking off lochs – but unfortunately no lairds. I'd encouraged Harry to connect with his Scottish heritage, so when he came to choose a gift for Lotte as thanks for her help, he'd chosen the earrings in the shape of the cross from the famous isle.

'Will the police catch the murderer?'

'It's tricky, Harry.' I saw Helen park up and waved. 'They need to find the name of the murdered woman to help their investigation. Did Dad ever introduce you to his accountant, Lindi, who lived in Granda's old cottage?'

'Nah.'

'You never met Candi either did you?' '

I wanted to. You told Dad it wasn't the right time yet. Why?'

'Nothing, it's OK.' I gave Harry such a hug he started writhing to escape. I gave Helen a hug too. 'You both take care. I'll pick you up tomorrow morning, Harry.'

I hoped that would prove true, but only if I survived a round of drinks with a possible murderer.

20 LINDI

January 2019

The New Year arrived with Boy declaring himself, 'Demob crazy'.

Papers loitered in lawyers' in-trays waiting to be ratified. The US company just had to sign off on the final year figures – primarily the bad debt ledger Lindi had sent through. She imagined Mitch would be busy justifying why they were shelling out £10 million – over-double what he would originally have estimated. However, it was the firm's standard contract. It was signed, and they had no way out. Mentally, Boy was already in Patagonia. He finalised his plans for the end of February. Lindi had a bonus coming.

The Old Chapel Gallery website was designed and being tested by Candi's freelance marketeers. The small team published, reviewed, tweaked and republished at a rapid rate. Lindi knew that Boy had got Candi to lean on them.

A-B testing would go on until the site hit the requisite percentage of its audience clicking 'buy'. Lindi had calculated the point at which the gallery started earning.

Decorators had invaded The Hart's Haunt during the post New Year lull. 'Fifty Shades of Grey,' joked barmaid Hester as she and Lindi watched panelled woodwork and walls transform. 'It matches the subject matter of the bar conversations I get.'

Webbs was pleased with Lindi's input into the business. William was considering her proposal for a stall selling 'gourmet burgers' at next year's Christmas Fayre.

Her clients were happy, but Lindi was troubled. She felt the Hart's cursed breath on her neck. It was sniffing out her two darkest secrets.

Firstly, she dreaded the forthcoming meeting with Chester Toakley. Her concern was that Toke would reveal something shady about the work Boy had undertaken for Peak Location Services Ltd.

On the face of it, things added up. The hotel websites showed PLS was a genuine and prosperous business. The work done by Boy's company was cutting edge. The payment matched the headline details of the contract Lindi had tracked down. Companies House showed Toakley was the registered owner. The most telling fact was that the account had been paid in full – companies don't pay out half a million pounds unless they are entirely satisfied.

Lindi's suspicions were only on simmer because the hotel chain was a big operation. It didn't make sense that it would have only one named director and present such minimal information. She wanted to shelve her concerns; if she found out anything untoward it would derail Boy's deal.

Her second secret was that she had 'shopped' Ash to the government's anti-radicalisation agency. She wanted help regarding his contact with Zainab in whichever Arab State she was hiding. Lindi had expected the agency's Mr Norton to come and speak to them. Her fear was that Ash would be summoned to the agency's offices in Luton. He would be back on their radar with a more severe black mark against his name. Instead of which, Mr Norton had been understanding, accepted her explanations and asked her not to tell Ash about their discussions. Let him first consult with colleagues.

That was a week before Christmas, since when... nothing. Lindi had resisted the temptation to follow up. Ash no longer spoke to her about Zainab or Isis or Islam and left the room if she probed. The rest of their relationship had returned to normal.

* * *

The meeting with Chester Toakley took place in the cafe, Harty Fare. It was a wintry morning. A light frost edged the roofs of houses and cars. Linda took her laptop and a printed list of questions.

Toakley was at a table with a newspaper when she entered. He had brought neither documents nor briefcase. A dated phone lay on his paper. He rose to greet her and helped her shrug off her coat.

'Mr Toakley –' Lindi started.

'I'm sorry,' his soft voice was at odds with the confidence of his demeanour, 'but we can't continue this meeting, until you call me "Toke".'

'Is that your "village" name like, Marcus is called "Boy" in Hartsdell?'

'It's my everything name, Mrs Mills.'

'Lindi.'

'Thank you, that will make everything run smoother.' The young waitress hovered. He ordered coffees. 'This place is my unofficial office. It's much nicer than my real one. I only need a phone and coffee.'

Lindi started on her agenda, but Toke held up a hand. 'Why don't I just explain the business arrangement between my company and Boy's. It's not complicated. Then you can ask any supplementary questions and I'll answer them if I can.'

'That's kind.'

'In return, Lindi, I'd like to know a few things. Why was Boy so insistent about this being a one-off payment and the timing of it as regards his financial year end? It seemed an unusual request and got me wondering.'

'Mr... Toke, as I've said, I can't reveal my clients' business dealings, they're confidential.'

'Yet you expect me to reveal mine.'

'Let's do this a different way. I'll tell you what I know – information you're already privy to. If I get anything wrong and you can put me right, please do.'

'Fine.'

'You run Peak Location and are it's only named director. You contracted Boy's company to create a digital holiday destinations service, relating to the Peak District. It will link to cottages, hotels, campsites, etc., plus tourist services and locations, restaurants, activities, attractions, tours and so on.'

'Very well summed up,' said Toke.

Not 'Yes', Lindi noted.

'Boy demonstrated the site to me. When operational, it'll create a joined-up search and social media experience for anyone planning to visit the area. You're providing a new service to existing holiday cottage owners and creating a chain of other accommodation outlets to sit alongside your hotels.'

'I couldn't have put it better.'

'But you haven't yet launched the site to holiday makers or accommodation owners.'

'Not yet.'

'Are you entirely happy with the work done and the service it provides?'

'Boy's team have done a great job. You've seen it – it's faster and more intuitive than anything out there.'

'It's pioneering. That's what they do.'

'Makes other providers look tired in comparison. Which is why Mitch Goodridge and his US paymasters are willing to pay millions for Boy's operation.'

Lindi floundered. 'I can't comment.' She had confirmed his speculation.

Toke sat back. A moment thickened before he smiled, 'Not even if I buy cake?'

Her breathy laugh relieved the tension.

Toke clamped his hands together. 'Oh dear, I didn't mean for us to fall out, my lovely. Give me your list of questions, Lindi. I'll answer those I can.'

She passed over her paper. 'Thanks, I must sign off Boy's companies' accounts for the last financial year. I'm legally responsible for ensuring it adds up and there's no fraud. I can't just take Boy's word for it. This is me investigating.'

'Thorough as well as enchanting. My accountants barely glance at anything I send them.' Toke ran his eye down her list.

'Who set up the contract?' he read from it. 'When is the new business due to launch? Why was the company only incorporated this year when Boy's been working on this for 14 months? Why wasn't payment phased against delivery targets?' He laughed. 'There's a lot here.'

He tucked the paper into his jacket pocket. 'I'll have to get back to you on some of these. Let's meet up in a few days. I'll have answers for you.'

Lindi didn't believe him. Neither did she believe this man ran a 15-strong 5-star heritage hotel chain. It confirmed her suspicion that Toke was the middle man in Boy's deal. He came across as a harmless, slightly hapless charmer, just posh enough to be well-connected. They finished their drinks and shook hands.

'One last thing,' Lindi held on. 'What is it your Lone Marsh Holdings company does for Webbs the Butchers?'

Toke was momentarily off guard. She held his ice-blue eyes, saw anger flash, puzzlement and finally understanding.

'Oh Lordy,' he shook his head, 'you do Webby's books too.'

* * *

The next morning Webby pitched up outside Lindi's door. He held a bottle of wine and a Webbs Christmas hamper. 'Because you weren't in over Christmas, I didn't get a chance to give you your hamper.'

Encouraged by Lindi, Ash had gone to see a film in Cambridge with two new friends, so she was alone in the cottage. 'Really, you didn't have to Webby. I'm only hired help.'

He didn't pass it over to her, so, reluctantly, she opened the door wider. He carried it into the compact kitchen. He glanced around with an expert eye. 'First time I've been in here. Boy's done a good job.'

'Yes, I'm lucky to be allowed to stay here.'

'Where are your glasses?' He was unfoiling a bottle of sparkling wine, pulled from the hamper.

'Webby, it's barely 11 o'clock. I'm not drinking fizz at this time. I'd thought you'd be working today. Who's looking after the shop?'

'Please, Lindi, I understand Kotryna had words with you at the Christmas party. I need to explain, and I can't begin to do that without a glass of something.'

'It's not necessary, we'd all been drinking. Christmas parties are famous for this kind of thing. There's nothing to explain.'

There was a controlled pop. A trickle of fizz escaped Webby's thumb as he held the bottle over the sink. Lindi sighed and selected her smallest glasses from a cupboard. 'Only a splash.'

He poured. They moved to comfy chairs in the cold lounge. Lindi perched on the armchair, Webby dropped into the sofa. He made awkward small-talk about the Christmas party evening and the state of his workforce the following day. Lindi clenched her glass tightly, barely sipped and waited.

Eventually it came. 'I know Kotryna propositioned you on my behalf.'

'I didn't take her seriously.'

'Let me explain, anyway. Kotty's my second wife. When I found myself single again, I dated and broke up with several girlfriends... actually, most broke up with me. I wasn't having any luck dating women. Then someone, a mutual friend, introduced me to Kotty. I met her. I couldn't believe she'd be interested in anyone like me. Let's face it; she should be going out with a movie-star.'

'She's breath-taking.' Kotryna was certainly blonde and slim, immaculately groomed.

'Exactly. My friend asked if I was interested. I said "definitely". We'd only met once, had some drinks and a meal. We'd got on well. Kotty can be very accommodating and considerate. It wasn't just her looks. She wasn't brash. She asked lots of questions about me, the village, the business; genuinely interested. She was also fragile, a little broken somehow.' He poured himself another glass.

Lindi declined a refill. 'Webby, you don't have to share this with me, honestly.'

'It's good to talk to someone about it. I have to say, Boy knows nothing about this, even though I was close to him and Shona when Kotty and I first met.'

'I won't tell anyone.'

'The way it worked – this is going to sound weird – was like an arranged marriage. Our friend explained that Kotty was in trouble. She'd lost her way and wanted to start again somewhere new. I said great. We went out again. I introduced her to friends. She can be effervescent when called upon. They loved her.

'The friend said Kotty was interested in marrying me but there were two problems: she had to buy herself out of a financial commitment; and she was done with sex. The latter gave me pause, I can tell you. I spoke to her. Kotty wouldn't go into detail, but said she'd had such bad experiences with sex – being abused, I guess – she was traumatised by it. She would love me as her husband emotionally, but not physically.'

'It was good of you to take it further, Webby, knowing that.'

'At the time I just wanted company, someone to share stuff with. I wasn't having sex anyhow. Stupidly, I convinced myself it wasn't important.'

'Sounds like me. Nothing and no-one since Ayan left.'

'I wondered if you and Boy...?' Webby gestured around the

cottage.

'Goodness no, he's taken. Can I ask, did you agree to pay off her debts, too?'

'Yes, my friend organised it all. I came to an arrangement with her creditors, through him.'

'It's Toke isn't it? That's what you're paying off to Lone Marsh Holdings each month.'

'Bloody hell!' Webby's drink sploshed. Lindi knew this had flown further than he'd intended. 'You can't tell anyone. Lindi, you mustn't.'

'I know.'

'Shi-it. Don't even mention this to Boy. The only person I've ever told was Sho. She was my confidante back then.' His glass banged down on the coffee table. It wobbled. 'I suppose you're filling that role now.'

'Your secret's safe with me, Webby, but we have a *professional* relationship. I'm not confidante material.'

'I don't regret being with Kotty for an instant, but I still have physical needs.' He hadn't caught her warning note. Without the glass, his hands danced. 'Kotty understands that. She knows I find you attractive. That's why she said those things at Christmas. We both think we can trust you. We could also offer you more work.'

The Hart's breath coiled into the room. Lindi inhaled its forbidding chill. 'I'm flattered, Webby.'

There was no way to undo this conversation. 'I'm flattered that you feel you can trust me.'

No way back to what had been. 'But what you're asking me to do is have clandestine sex with you in return for money.'

Things would change. 'That's not who I am.'

Utterly. Inevitably.

'It's not what I am.'

* * *

Boy had stopped coming around. Had Toke said something, she wondered. She called him for an update.

'Snowed at work?' she asked.

'Hardly,' he said, 'I'm sorting out an exchange of legal letters with Shona's solicitors.'

'What?'

'She's determined to sabotage my sabbatical. Her solicitors are making a case that's it's an abdication of my parental responsibilities. Which it is, of course,' he admitted. 'But I've spoken to Harry, he's cool and I'm planning a big-bugger holiday with him when I get back in the summer.'

'Is Shona OK with Harry meeting Candi, now?'

'Far from it, but Harry wants to meet her. He has to really, because, nevermind…' He changed tack, 'It's been three years for heaven's sake. Shona's being petty – she knows it. My lawyers assure me she's just kite-flying; she's brow-beaten her solicitor into sending the letter, but legally it won't wash as long as I provide extra support for Harry, which I would do anyway.'

'So, Patagonia is still a goer, then?'

'Yeah. I don't think it can be six months, though. When I'm back I'll be planning what to do next. Candi's got some ideas. Whatever it is, I want you involved, Lindi.'

❉ ❉ ❉

There were five police cars. They arrived, blue lights flashing and with kerb-flattening urgency just after 7am on a wet weekday morning. Lindi was already up and gaping out of the window. The lead car gave a gratuitous blare of siren on arrival. Ash was getting dressed.

On the list of Lindi's fears, this was second top, headed only by Ash disappearing and calling a week later from a Turkish border. She hollered to Ash to get dressed and rushed to open the front door in case the police burst in. A horde of black jackets and helmets rampaged past her into the cottage. There seemed more of them than it could accommodate.

One policewoman stayed at the door with Lindi, preventing her from moving. After a moment she heard them shouting at Ash from the top of the stairs.

The cottage reverberated with the clamour of their search. Lindi, Ash, their computers and phones, school bags and briefcases were finally bundled into a car. Her two elderly neighbours watched aghast from their front gate. The procession sped away, Ash and Lindi in separate cars.

Lindi didn't need to ask, she knew what this was about. She did protest that she had volunteered the information about Ash being in contact with a girl in Syria before Christmas. No-one had been interested. They were co-operating, she said. It was a complete over-reaction, she said.

No-one was interested.

She and Ash were kept apart at the Police Station. It was hours before she was interviewed. They had been given a lawyer. His advice was to answer 'no comment' to everything.

'But neither of us has done anything,' she protested. 'We'll just sound guilty.'

He shrugged. 'I'm here at your request. Do you want to listen to my advice or not?'

'You won't believe what we've found on your son's communication devices,' said the interviewing officers.

She braced herself for the worst.

'He's in constant contact with members of Isis.'

'Members?' her need for clarification earned a glare from her solicitor.

'He was communicating with a dangerous Isis warlord and his family.'

'You mean Zainab?'

'You knew?' The police officer shook her head. 'What kind of mother are you?'

'The kind that informed you about this weeks ago, in case it was a problem.'

'Your son is a Muslim extremist, potentially facing a charge of conspiracy to commit acts of terror inspired by Isis. And you want to know if that's a problem?'

Lindi turned in horror to her solicitor. 'My client would prefer not to comment,' he said.

It went on until nobody's heart was still in it. The police left her alone for her thoughts to chafe for hours. Eventually she was allowed to see Ash. She would be sent home. He was staying in.

He shrugged off her flustered hug, recoiled from her need.

'Ash please.'

'See what you've done?' he said.

'What I've done? This is what I was so afraid of, Ash. I knew they'd be tracking you; that they'd haul us in for questioning.'

He gave an ugly laugh, 'That's hardly what's important here. Zainab's dead. Because of us.'

'How?' Lindi couldn't process this latest shock. 'How's she dead? How's it our fault?'

'You tipped them off. They traced my contact in some way. The police say that her husband was taken out by an American Hellfire missile last night. Since they were targeting her phone, it's pretty certain Zainab was with him.'

'Oh no, Ash.'

'She was pregnant, mum. How's that make you feel?'

The police insisted she abandon Ash in the cell. It was a miracle she'd been able to.

Boy was waiting on a seat in the police-station's reception. He had driven there to pick them up. She had no idea how he'd known or how long he'd been waiting. Lindi collapsed into him. Tears burst against his neck. All her remaining courage bled away into his collar.

Back at the police station early next day, Lindi brought a change of clothes and toiletries. After a wait she was allowed to take them in to Ash herself. He was tired, slumped over but still defiant.

'They've found stuff on your phone and laptop, Ash. They're saying you're a Muslim extremist.'

'That's ridiculous. I suppose you buy that. Is that what you told them? Is that why Zainab's dead.'

'No, but I know you were researching Muslim conflicts.'

'I was doing what their stupid programme told me to do. Find things out for myself. That's not a crime. I'm allowed to research my Muslim culture.'

'Ash, for God's sake, you're not a Muslim. Tell them.'

'Of course I'm a Muslim. My name's Khan. My dad's a Pakistani from Karachi. It didn't used to be a thing. Now it is.'

'Alright, Ash, I want you to listen. This is something I never dreamt I would tell you. I need to, now.' Lindi stole three panicky breaths. Ash feigned disinterest, shaking his head against her gravitas.

'Ayan isn't your birth father. He's your dad in every other way, and a good one in most of them. I didn't know when we married, or when I had you. I've found out since. Another man I was seeing at that time, he's your biological father.'

'Pathetic, mum. You'll say anything. Just lies. I don't believe you.'

'You must. I can prove it. I had a DNA test after your... Ayan's last visit. I didn't intend telling you – not ever – but you don't have any Pakistani blood, no Muslim heritage. You have to stop pretending you do before all this gets even worse.'

2015

Ammi called early in the New Year. Lindi hadn't had any direct contact from Ayan since he had hung up on her. He'd sent a Christmas card and a cheque for Ash, no more or less generous than in previous years. Ash still Skyped him but less often. Even Ash had realised that Ayan would no longer be a significant part of their lives.

'Lindi, we are disappointed in all that has happened,' Ammi told her.

'I'm sorry we've reached this situation too, Ammi,' replied Lindi, 'but I didn't sign up for Pakistan when I married Ayan. If things had been different, he would still be here with us in the

UK.'

'If Naasira hadn't been attacked, you mean.'

'I understand Ayan has done what he feels he must. I don't feel any bitterness towards him.'

'And yet you have taken this DNA test. You've waved its results in his face.'

'I was trying –'

'He knew. Ayan knew Ash was not his biological son. I think he had always known from your boy's earliest days. It didn't mean he was ever less of a father to Ash. It didn't mean he didn't love him. You know he was desperate to keep you all together as a family. He wanted you to be part of our family – a family that loved you both and would have loved you more.

'A DNA test didn't destroy that gift, Lindi, you did. You could have been part of a warm vibrant family. Instead, you are there on your own. You are closing all the doors of your life. I think you will end up very alone.'

The letter from Mr Rahmen came through the following week. It thanked her for her work on his business but informed her that it was time for the company to set up properly in the UK with full-time staff. There was a reasonable redundancy and notice payment. It would not keep them in their current circumstances for very long.

Lindi sold up, sent Ayan a cheque for his share of the house and looked around for somewhere she could afford with a good chance of employment. She didn't know anyone in Luton. It was the obvious choice.

January 2019

Ash was allowed home at the end of the day. There were no charges. He refused to talk in the car. He had no interest in the DNA proof. He wouldn't look at it if she showed him.

'It doesn't prove anything,' he told her. 'DNA's easy to manipulate. It depends on who's providing the samples and what they want the outcome to be.'

Lindi had poured everything – 16 years of love, life and energy – into her relationship with her son. He represented almost the entirety of her world. It was draining away before her eyes.

She had lost Ash before he disappeared. His school had agreed that it would be best if he took time off while all sides considered their options. Lindi didn't know if they had been told of his detention officially or unofficially, but they knew. Word had churned through the village. The Arlston paper wrote a short, legally straight-jacketed piece. A boy in the Arlston area, who couldn't be named, had been questioned by police about contact with extremists. It hadn't made the front page, but even so.

Ash waited until Lindi left for a meeting and then he went. He left in the same way as he had spent every moment since his return from the police station. He went without a word.

Lindi reported his disappearance to the police. Heads shook. Forms filled and filed. Motions were gone through. 'We knew it,' they didn't say, 'a wrong 'un and now he's going to turn up on some Middle Eastern border or in a Home Counties market town with a bomb strapped to his chest.'

It was, Lindi understood, a half-hearted hunt for a terrorist suspect. It wasn't a search for a missing schoolboy.

Lindi had run out of answers; out of options, ideas, energy. What was it Ammi had said? 'You will die alone.'

21 SHONA

Friday evening May 24 2019

Harry's words fizzed disconcertingly in my head as I drove away. A nagging pill dropped into my glass of certainties. Bubbles of impending humiliation effervesced as I reached home. All my conviction about the bruise and what it signified hinged on what I'd find in the jetsam on Harry's bed.

At stake was my assertion that my assault in Cambridge was connected to the murder. The evidence on Harry's duvet could prove Hossein right.

It could prove me, horribly, humiliatingly wrong.

On the one hand that meant, not being marked for murder – good! On the other, the ignominy of having to acknowledge Hossein's superior murder investigation skills – horrendous! I had to know.

I slewed the car to a halt and raced inside and upstairs. In Harry's room, I smeared the contents of my bag across his bed. I had up-ended it yesterday when hunting for Lotte's phone. This examination was more thorough. And there it was: an earring. Only one, its twin must have been left languishing in the room where I was attacked; perhaps my attacker had seized it for a trophy.

Harry and I had bought the earrings for Lotte in Scotland.

Each was a simplified St Martin's Cross. She must have placed them in my 'sack' at the party. The earring was smaller than my mother's ring or pendant had been. It was – I felt sickeningly certain – smaller than the bruise inflicted on the murdered woman. I no longer felt sure that the bruise I'd had on my arm was the same size as the victim's bruise. Hugo had said he thought it was smaller.

Hossein was vindicated. The murders weren't anything to do with me. I would have to tell the police, I supposed, admit my mistake to Shelby, post up an apology on the village Facebook site. All enthusiasm for confronting my attacker, even in a crowded pub, evaporated with the discovery. He wasn't even a serial killer, only an opportunist creep. Lotte's earring had escaped my bag and he'd punched my arm with it in frustration at being disturbed by other party-goers.

Good upsides: it meant Harry's dad wasn't a murderer; it meant that Lindi was walking around somewhere, albeit carless and minus a lot of clothes. A bloody tissue or two and a missing doll seemed scant evidence of foul play.

Firstly, no one had chopped up any bodies in Boy's cottage. Yes, you could clean this stuff up, but no-one would have done that good a job; not in the madness that followed a murder; not when dealing with a cumbersome mutilated body leaking fluids everywhere.

Secondly, Lindi had disappeared from Hartsdell on Thursday 21st of February and the body only turned up on Wednesday 27th Feb which was nearly a week away from being a noteworthy coincidence. Lindi had undergone a horrendous ordeal with her son. The village gossips were carping. She'd lost work from Webby and the pub. There may have been issues with Islamic extremists too – she wasn't short of reasons to leave Hartsdell urgently.

From Boy's point of view, you couldn't murder your accountant when they were in the Home Counties and you were in Patagonia – not even if they'd screwed up your tax returns!

Thirdly, no-one had seen a tattoo on Lindi's head or hands.

The victim had had a tattoo.

Fourthly, I would soon run out of fingers, Boy had confessed (admittedly under duress) that he'd taken the box, with the doll and ring in it, out of Dell End Cottage.

What had I been thinking? I slumped back on the bed, wallowing in the detritus of that fateful party. Delusional, harebrained, naïve, needy, what had Hossein said: 'I'd exaggerated the facts to get myself some attention?'

Of course he didn't believe me. Of course Boy didn't want me back. Of course my former friends deserted and despaired of me. I made a mental list of the people I'd exasperated, people I'd screwed over and who would never believe in me again. People whose friendships I'd burned away because of earrings I didn't know were in my bag. People I had to say sorry to:

1. Boy,
2. Toke,
3. Hossein and Grant,
4 Hugo and Esther (oh god),
5. Webby and Kotryna,
6. Shelby,
7. Lotte,
8. Evelyn Brett-Reynolds – maybe – who knew?
9. Gone Puss,
10. Fidel Castrol (insightful village troll),
11. Ant...

A final name dawned on me. I added it to the list:
12. Me

I'd incinerated what was left of my old reputation, wasted money on burner phones – I wasn't being tracked and traced – who'd bother?

I dabbed with a tissue from the pack on the bed. My small cottage felt vast and empty. It echoed with the lovely life I'd had and thrown away with five ill-starred words: 'If you're that miserable, leave.'

I had Harry, I had friends, I had soccer, and work I reminded myself. But hadn't Lindi had her son, her work, presumably an ex-husband somewhere, neighbours. She had gone, and no-one had missed her.

Who should I apologise to first?

Reluctantly, I released my phone from my handbag and switched it on. It went haywire. Flower of Scotland had never sounded so depressing. I scrolled through a cluster of messages and missed calls. There was one (creepily) from Lotte's phone, two from Boy (both marked 'urgent'), two from Sergeant de Clerc, and others (many unknown). Nothing from Grant and Hossein. I had been half-expecting a clairvoyant, 'see I told you so, Miss Patterson, now escort yourself the hell out of my murder investigation,' text from the DCI.

Feeding my depression, I clicked on the text from Lotte's phone first.

'Mill at 5. No need to dress up.'

What did that mean? Cheeky beggar! Was he alluding to the fact that he'd already seen me half-naked on a bed at the party?

Well, at least he still believed in me. He thought I'd turn up. I decided I had – at the very least – to find out who my attacker was. And get Lotte's phone back, I reminded myself.

I had on a summery mid-length dress. It wouldn't look out of place among a touristy crowd at The Mill. It would dodge shrimp debris under a lab-coat at work.

I returned Boy's call. He answered immediately, 'Shona, thanks for getting back.'

'It said "urgent".'

'I needed you to know. I've no idea what's going on, but that Facebook page is a hoax.'

'Right, a hoax?'

'It's not mine. It's identity theft.'

'Boy... I really don't have time for these games. It's not important to me any more.'

'Well, it's important to me. It's bollocks. Half the places it mentions, I've never been to. The only Facebook presence I've got; the only one I've ever had, is about the business –'

'OK, Boy, whatever, I've got to go.'

'This one only has posts dating back two and a half months. It was started up when I went to Patagonia. I think I know who's –'

'Boy, enough! I have a date with a murde… well, a sexual predator, at any rate. I've got to go.'

This only made Boy more agitated. I hadn't thought it through.

'Shona, what the hell are you talking about?'

'I've got a 5 o'clock at The Mill in Cambridge with the person who attacked me last Saturday. If I don't leave in the next five minutes, I'll be late.'

'I don't und… is this a police thing? Is it entrapment?'

'Nope it's Sho-trapment; just me and my mystery admirer.'

'You can't be serious? Why would you even think about doing this? Don't go, I for – ' I clicked off. And called Sarge quickly before Boy could hit redial.

'Miss Patterson,' Sarge answered with unusual alacrity, 'are you about to do something stupid?'

'Yes.' I confessed immediately; god these cops were good.

'Inspector Hossein called. He said you were going to do something reckless. I've got to tell you not to.' Sarge was business-like despite the absurdity of his words. In the light of my discovery that I had totally misled a major murder inquiry, this now seemed a further misuse of scarce police resources.

I really ought to tell him about the earring discovery. It meant my attacker wasn't marking me for murder after all. He was just marking me – maybe as his property. It could be a nostalgic conversation topic for any future investigations Sarge and I ran together.

'You've told me, thanks.' I said, locking my door and heading to the car. In a bag I carried implements to be used in extreme circumstances – e.g. needing to brain the guy in the pub.

'I must stress that meeting this man – even if we don't believe him to be a murderer – is foolhardy, possibly dangerous and pointless.' Sarge had been well-briefed by Hossein.

'Noted.'

'Are you going ahead anyway, against police advice, only...'

'Yes,' I said. 'He's got my friend's phone.'

'...only it has been made clear to me that DCI Hossein considers me responsible for you,' finished Sarge. Ah bless.

'I'm far too much trouble for any one policeman,' I said. 'I absolve you of your responsibility, Sarge. I don't want any sudden outbreaks of jaywalking in Linbourn on my conscience.'

'I'm off duty,' he continued, ignoring my lame attempt at levity. 'Do you still want back-up?'

'Yes,' I sobbed, 'please.'

'You know the small car-park off West Street?'

'Uh-huh.'

'It empties before 5pm. I'll meet you there at 4.50.'

'I'm leaving now,' I said. 'Thanks, Sarge.'

'Miss Patterson, I'll be off duty and off my patch. Strictly speaking I can arrest people, but I'm not going to. I'm only there to stop you getting hurt.'

'I know,' I sniffed loudly. 'If you're off duty, can I call you "Ant"?'

'Not in front of other people, Miss Patterson.'

I made better time than I expected into Cambridge as I was going against the flow of shoppers and flexi-timers. I parked up just after time. Ant was there in plain clothes, jeans and a weirdly on-trend casual jacket that didn't holler: 'C-O-P!'

He had kept a parking spot for me.

Our small-talk extended to: 'Did you find your doll?'

'Not yet, it seems my ex-partner let his new girlfriend borrow it.'

Ant gave me a long look, 'That sounds really perv –'

'It was in a box with some of my mum's jewellery,' I explained inadequately. 'Boy didn't know it was there when he lent her the jewellery stuff. Becca Blue Eyes is not the kind of doll to get involved in any obscure sex acts.'

'Agalmatophilia.'

'How could you know?'

'Cop-thing.' He spread his hands and smiled. 'Not big in Linbourn, though.'

'Nor do I think my Becca doll was involved in DCI Hossein's murder. In truth, Ant, I don't think I was either.'

'Well, I'm here now, so...' He waved me towards The Mill.

'Yes, I'm so grateful.'

Ant was keen to impress me with his undercover training. 'I'll go in the pub first, order a drink and stay at the bar. You come in three minutes later and sit where I can easily see you. If you recognise anyone in the bar, don't approach them, or acknowledge them,' he warned. 'Or hit them,' he added.

'I won't.'

'We are going to leave your phone on and I will listen in with this.' He indicated a small ear-bud. 'I'll also be recording the conversation on my phone. We need them to make themselves known to you and make some reference to your interaction at the party.' I was thankful he hadn't said, 'orgy'.

'Ideally, we want them to show you the phone they stole. If they do, say something like "that's the phone you stole from me". If I hear that I may come over and make myself known. If I feel he is likely to incriminate himself more, I'll wait. Don't look at me, don't play with your phone, I suggest we leave it in your open handbag. Understood?'

'Yes, how long do we wait if no-one comes?'

'Leave that to me. I'll keep scanning the room and see if anyone is showing you too much interest. If you see someone there you recognise, who you think may have been at the party, let's agree a sign so that you can let me know.'

'I'll cross my legs,' I said. They looked shapely below my summer dress and for some mad reason I wanted Ant to have an excuse to keep staring at... woah, concentrate Sho.

'That's good. I'm going in now.'

'Suppose someone jumps me with a cleaver?'

'We cops have a nose for danger. This location doesn't scream cleavers to me.'

I wanted to synchronise watches, but Ant thought exact timing wasn't a mission-critical factor. 'You going to be OK?'

I nodded, 'Can you get some crisps in? I missed lunch and stakeouts alwa – '

'You need to be serious, Miss Patterson.'

'I will. Thanks for doing this, Ant.'

He left me, turned the corner and walked to the busy pub. I followed roughly three unsynchronised minutes later and made my way to the bar area we'd agreed on. A round table with two spindly wooden chairs and two stools was vacant. It was at the far end from where Ant stood at a crowded bar, but he could clearly see me. On a sunny May evening much of the youthful clientele were outside by the River Cam. I ensured my handbag was open and studied the people at the bar. No face leapt out at me. There were plenty of areas of the pub that I couldn't see. My assailant could be hidden. They could just as easily be mask-less in plain sight.

After two minutes a man in a tee-shirt came over and loitered beside me. 'Waiting for anyone?' His beery breath pitched up straight after the question. I was. He shrugged and returned to the bar, where his friend grinned an 'I told you so'.

After five minutes a man raced in from another bar area, looking out of breath. He spotted me and my jaw dropped open in recognition. He was smartly casual in a tailored open-necked shirt, in his 40s with sandy short-cropped hair, a sporty physique and a beard that hadn't been there last time I'd seen him. He recognised me too but immediately pretended he hadn't. He joined the squeeze at the bar.

Shouty!? After a moment I remembered to cross my legs. A sideways glance at Ant showed that he had already taken in the situation without any help from my pert knees.

This felt weird. It was obvious that Shouty had been looking for me, found me, recognised me and realised that I'd seen him. Now he was ignoring me. Was he just checking that I was really unaccompanied? Shouty was surely too refined to attack women at parties, and why would he have stolen his ex-wife's phone – unless as a joke. I had a momentary fear that this whole thing had been staged by Hugo and Shouty as an elaborate prank at my expense, which had got unforgivably out of hand.

I was still puzzling over this when a drink was placed on the table in front of me. A bottle of low-alcohol lager also bumped down, followed by Lotte's phone.

I followed the arm up to the man at its end, 'You!' I said.

'Gin with Mediterranean tonic,' he replied.

'I'm driving,' I replied automatically. 'I'm at work after this.'

'Me too. I'm sorry I stole your phone,' said our Saturday night Uber driver, Brandon.

'It's not m –' I started, forgetting my line.

'I know now that it's Lotte's,' he interrupted. 'I didn't know that at the time. It just seemed that taking the phone was a good excuse for keeping in touch. I wasn't thinking clearly.'

'What about Lotte's purse and money?'

'I dropped the purse on the way out of the room. I didn't check whether it had money in it. Like I said, I wasn't thinking.' He seemed genuinely abashed and wouldn't meet my eye. He reminded me of one of the Hartsdell Under-12s who'd just missed a vital penalty.

'You have no idea of the fucking grief and heartache you've caused,' I said loudly enough for a few heads to turn. My initial shock was rapidly maturing into anger. What had Ant said about not hitting him?

Bran's head dropped lower, and his eyes roamed the table. Shouty was moving towards us but I shook my head as a message to him to keep back. I also saw Ant grab his shoulder.

'I should have called you straight away and come clean.' Bran's eyes were locked on his glass. 'But next morning I felt so stupid and nervous. That other guy was frankly a bit threatening.'

'Other guy!?' My worst fears yawned before me. I remembered Ant summarising my Saturday night at the swingers' party, saying, '...persuaded upstairs by a man or men...' And now Ant was here recording all the sordid details of my potential threesome on his mobile.

'Sorry I got a bit cryptic on the phone,' said Bran. 'I wanted to meet, partly, to remind you of the events of that evening – you were in such a state – you probably can't remember anything.'

'That was because you drugged me,' I hissed, loudly, close to my open handbag.

'Wasn't me,' he insisted. 'Must have been the devil.'

'Oh yeah, course it was. And you attacked me when I was unconscious, stripped me, took advantage.'

Bran raised his head. I think he meant to look me in in the eye, but his gaze snagged on my breasts. We were both grateful.

'No,' he said, 'I didn't. Do you want to hear what happened or not?'

'Excuse me! I was there.' Then I remembered I was supposed to be recording his confession. 'Go on, enlighten me.'

'You and Lotte were obviously out for a good night. I thought we'd connected, so I bought the cheapest cossie I could find.'

'You were Asda Man.'

'Tescos, but yeah, I was Zorro,' Bran smiled shyly. 'By the time I got back to the party, Lotte was taken, and you were legless. Some guy in a horned devil costume was latched on to you. He kept trying to manoeuvre you away from me, but I stuck at it. Eventually he suggested we all find a room together. You seemed to have no objections, but we had to half-carry you upstairs.

'In the bedroom horny guy suggested I go get more wine. I did, but when I got back he'd wedged something against the door. I couldn't get in.'

'Shit.'

'I waited outside at first, then I made a racket, then I started trying to force it. Eventually he came to the door and threatened to break my legs. I said I just wanted to see you were OK. After an argument, he said to give him two minutes, then I could have you. Like an idiot I waited but, after five minutes, I finally pushed my way in.'

'Go on.' I didn't know whether to believe him or not.

'The devil left. He was livid, told me I'd ruined everyone's evening, told me he'd be waiting for me outside. He sounded serious. Even in the costume he looked tall and fit. You were barely conscious, half-dressed, mask over your head. Stuff from your bag was all over the bed. I panicked. You seemed to be coming around. I grabbed your... I mean, Lotte's phone, and legged it.'

'Can you prove any of it?'

'No, course not. A cop left a message. This is why I wasn't sure about meeting up.'

Bran had gone quiet. I flicked eyes to Ant, who was already coming towards us. He pulled a stool away from the table and sat down. A firm hand clasped Bran's shoulder as he tried to stand and pull away. Ant flashed some police ID at him and asked if he'd answer some questions.

Bran just swore. He looked betrayed.

Ant turned to me. 'Shall we invite your other friend to join us?'

I nodded and beckoned Shouty over. He arrived with a half of something and I did the introductions, using Ant's 'Sergeant de Clerc' alias.

Ant showed his phone to Bran and informed him he'd already been recorded confessing to stealing a phone and might be facing a charge unless he cooperated fully. He asked for Bran's full name and address and noted it down.

Shouty had to follow suit. Ant asked what he was doing here?

Shouty told us Boy had called him up and begged him to get to The Mill. He was there to keep an eye on me in case I got out of my depth.

I nodded to Ant. It sounded plausible, likely even.

'How long between you dropping off Miss Patterson and seeing her at the party?' Ant asked Bran.

'Fifty minutes, maybe an hour.'

'Did you think that Miss Patterson was unusually drunk, given the time that had elapsed?'

'She wasn't slurring or anything, just woozy.'

'Describe the man in the devil costume.'

'I can't, he had this latex mask on. I took photos.' He reached for Lotte's phone. 'May I?'

Ant told him to go ahead. Pictures flipped up. They were taken from across a crowded room and I couldn't see that they'd be any help identifying the attacker. I was wrong.

'That's the devil,' said Bran. The rest of us crowded round the phone screen. The figure he pointed out was in three pictures. In two, the man had his back to us, but now I remembered the red costume, the grotesque crimson latex mask, the pointy ears and pointier white teeth. The horns resembled a cow's. Piggy eyes peeked out from the mask. They would be ingrained in my nightmares forever.

He wore a plain black polo-neck underneath. In all three pictures he was talking to another costumed man. He had a gingery-brown beard and wore a Venetian festival mask in black, white and gold.

'These two were ganging up on me,' said Bran.

'Er...' stuttered Shouty, 'that's me, in the harlequin mask.'

Ant scratched his spiky hair. 'You were at the party, Mr Hadleigh?'

'Yes, I invited my ex-wife, Lotte, and she invited Shona.' Shouty looked sheepish.

'And did you make yourself known to Miss Patterson?'

'I only chatted to her briefly. And no, I didn't make myself known to her. It wasn't that kind of party – or rather it was, if you see what I mean.'

'Do you know the man in the devil mask?'

'It's a Mr Toakley. He lives near Shona's village.'

I wouldn't have recognised the devil as Toke, but it could have been anyone.

'Why haven't you mentioned this before?' asked Ant. 'Were you aware that Miss Patterson was attacked in a bedroom at the party you indirectly invited her to?'

'Only when I spoke to Boy 25 minutes ago.' Shouty turned to

me. 'I'm really sorry Shona.'

'Surely Lotte would have told you.'

'No!' he said, 'she most certainly wouldn't. Lotte and I drunk-
enly hooked up that evening and then unhooked in spectacular fashion next day. We're not currently speaking, exactly.'

'Are you and Mr Toakley good friends?' Ant leaned in. Shouty
developed new interest in his beard. Carefully, he answered,
'Yes, I suppose, in that we go way back. We were involved
in business together when I was living in Hartsdell. We play
sports together from time to time.'

'Like on Tuesday, at Webby's,' I said.

'Yep, bridge evening.'

I pictured Hugo, Toke and Shouty at village events I'd seen
them at, many over the years. As thick as thieves, giggling and
joking like naughty adolescents. 'You want me to believe that
you invited Toke to that party, told him I'd be coming, invited
him to try it on with me, and he didn't tell you what went on
afterwards?' My voice was rising above nearby conversations.
People were staring.

Ant put a precautionary hand on my arm. 'Answer the question please, Mr Hadleigh.'

'I asked immediately after you both went upstairs, but he
said...' Shouty rummaged in his rubbish beard, but the words
he found there weren't helpful – or pleasant. 'He told me you
were all over him, Shona. You couldn't get enough, but he said
he changed his mind in the bedroom. He said he didn't fancy
it.'

'Bastard,' my comment incorporated Toke and Shouty. 'Toke
showed DCI Hossein a text from you, saying, "I'd be up for it."
Why the hell would you do that?'

'Who's DCI Hossein? Look, I really need to know what's going
on here.'

'DCI Hossein is investigating this case and you'll need to give
a statement to him in due course. For now, you need to answer
the question, Mr Hadleigh.'

'Because, as Shona well knows, Toke has been obsessed with

her for years. They went on a date after Boy... er departed the scene. You blew Toke out, as I understand it, Shona, after spending the whole evening talking about Boy. He's had an itch for you ever since. It's been an open secret he's wanted to get...' Shouty stumbled.

'Get even?' I suggested. 'Get his hands on me? Get rid of me!'

'Get back with you, I was going to say,' said Shouty. 'How would Toke get rid of you?'

'DCI Hossein is investigating a murder.' It came out more accusatory then I'd intended.

Bran visibly started.

'Whose?' Shouty's glance swirled around the table. 'That's mad! Toke certainly has his faults, a nasty streak, even, but he's not remotely capable of murder. Shona, you know that.'

'Oh really! He drugs and attacks women. Lies to the police. He said he was nowhere near that party. He even phoned in an alibi,' I was ranting.

'He was there, definitely. I bought him the devil costume. I saw him put it on.' Shouty responded angrily. A circle was enlarging around us as people moved away.

'That's enough!' decided Ant with calm authority. 'We're almost done here, Mr Hadleigh. Thanks for your co-operation. My colleagues will almost certainly want a full statement from you, but for now, please just take us through what you observed happen to Miss Patterson during the party.'

He did, and it backed up what Bran had told me, in every detail.

As our meeting ended, I took a moment to thank Bran for sticking by me when Toke turned ugly, and not taking advantage when I was unconscious. I later realised I'd never know whether that was true.

'Have you also been following me home, Bran, in your car?'

'Of course not.' Then, he added, 'I did wait outside your office after my shift last night. I flashed you as you left. It was after midnight, so I didn't follow you.'

I told him I hoped he'd understand if we didn't stay in touch.

The implied intimacy of his anonymous tongue emojis were too icky to get past.

My anger towards Shouty meant any thanks for responding to Boy's SOS so promptly would have to wait. I'd find it hard to forgive him for watching me stagger upstairs, clearly the worse for wear, with Toke and another man.

Ant reminded Shouty that the police would formally need to take his statement and to repeat nothing from this meeting until then.

Back at our cars, Ant told me that Bran wouldn't be prosecuted based on what he had heard. Shouty hadn't committed a crime. And because two witnesses said I'd gone willingly to the bedroom with Toke, he probably didn't have a case to answer either.

It was a pass thing. He'd made a pass at me. I'd passed out, he'd passed on the opportunity to get my tights down. Ant would pass his information on to his superiors.

At the least, he said, the police should have double-checked Toke's alibi. 'These things can fall off the to-do list as soon as someone ceases to be a suspect. Other leads become the priority.'

I felt doubly ridiculous as I had gone public to protest Toke's innocence. Against that, I had flushed my attacker out into the open. Ant said he'd try to keep me up to date with developments. I had the impression my 'honey trap' had excited him more than jaywalking duties.

This was my chance to tell Ant about the earring. I could admit the suspicions I'd reported were by-products of coincidence, not murder. Toke had come across Lotte's earring, punched me with it and then been stupid enough to send the jokey text.

Instead of coming clean, I asked: 'Why would Toke send that text when it just linked him to an attack he'd committed and potentially to a murder?'

'Happens all the time,' Ant said. 'You'd be amazed how many criminals do something mad and unnecessary to draw attention to themselves when they ought to keep their heads down. It's some psychological need to have their cunning recognised I think. Murderers want their crime headlining in the papers.'

'DCI Hossein doesn't think my attack and the murder are connected,' I said, without adding: and, annoyingly, he's right.

'He should know. It's a weird coincidence that Mr Toakley had some Iona cross jewellery with him though.'

I swallowed and changed the subject.

'It's probably nothing,' I said, 'but someone, a man, was waiting for me outside my cottage late last night.'

'Who?'

'Too dark to describe either the man or their car, I'm afraid. There was a note warning me off posted in my letterbox too. I imagine the man left it. I did tell Hossein.'

'OK, good.'

'But I didn't tell him that I found a handkerchief next morning where the man had been waiting. He'd probably dropped it. I er... bagged it.'

'You what?'

'I put it in a plastic bag without touching it.'

'You should be a SOCO. I'm not sure a man waiting in a road warrants DNA analysis though.'

'There was a faint dark-brown stain on it. It could be blood.'

'Even so. The murder was committed three months ago. A murderer would have washed it out long ago.'

'How often does your missus wash your hankies, Ant?'

'She doesn't, Miss Patterson. Firstly, we're no longer together, secondly, I use tissues.' He coloured slightly, I couldn't imagine why; were these two facts related?

'Trust me, men's hankies hang around unwashed in trouser pockets for ages. I know.'

Ant and I parted more like friends than cop and witness. It was the camaraderie of the stakeout possibly helped by Ant's admission that he was single.

I got back in my car, switched on my phone and texted Boy a thank you for sending Shouty to my rescue. I reported that I was safe.

A list of missed calls congregated on my phone. Nothing from Webby. I still had an hour before the 7pm start time I'd given Leroy.

I called Lotte's temporary number.

'Sho, hey, where's you?'

'Cambridge, I'm on nights.'

'You're there early, aren't you?'

'I had a meet.'

'Mm-hmm. Who with?'

'Doesn't matter.'

'Humour me.'

'Why? I only called to say I've got your phone back.'

'Who from, this tacky attacker of yours?'

'Yes, well no, it's complicated.'

'Sounds it.'

'What's wrong, Lotte? I thought you'd be pleased.'

'Why have you befriended Shouty on Facebook?'

'Is that what this is about?'

'Oh... maybe. Shouty and I... As you just said, "it's complicated". He's not involved in your attacky thing, is he, darling?'

'No,' I lied, 'I just need more Facebook chums.'

'Why? You planning to rival Kim Kardashian?'

'Hardly, anyway, all her followers are bots.'

It took a moment before Lotte groaned, then laughed.

We arranged to catch-up. I wouldn't tell her about Shouty's role in my attack.

I hit Steve Shelby's number. The reporter had called twice. I had to tell him that my 'murder victim' timeline didn't fit, even if I kept schtum about the earring.

'Shelby,' he coughed.

'It's Shona,' I said.

'Ah yes, Miss Peterson.'

'Patterson.' I wondered why I'd ever worried about this guy putting my name in his paper.

'As you like. In answer to your pithy text, no, she wasn't pregnant. Was your girl pregnant?'

'Probably not.' I felt ridiculous. I'd so fallen for a stupid wind-up. Why had I been so ready to believe Boy had made Lindi pregnant? I knew why. Because just the thought that Boy might become a dad again was an angry dark wave I doubted I could survive.

'Right. DCI Hossein's attack dog has been giving me a hard time about talking to you.'

'Oh, I'm sorry.' I supposed he meant DS Grant.

'Can't be helped. However, it does mean I'm "*persona non*" at their press conferences until they forget I'm important. This, in turn, means I've decided to tell you some more stuff I shouldn't.'

'Before you do...'

'Call it my small futile gesture on behalf of press freed –' he rumbled on.

'Mr Shelby!' I used my football coach voice; the one that helped order vigilante parents back off the pitch after unfathomable refereeing decisions. 'First, I need to tell you something.'

'You were saying.'

'I owe you an apology. I don't think my possible victim's timeline fits with your murdered woman.'

'Bugger. I take it she's no longer missing.'

'She *is* still missing,' I said, 'but there may be other reasons for that. My investigations have shown that not only did she leave the village nearly a week before the murder but my most likely murderer suspect was out of the country by that time.'

'I see. That's a damn pity.'

'Not for her!' I pointed out. 'I've traced her last evening in Hartsdell to the Thursday 21st of February, when it seems she was involved in some kind of ruckus and vanished. My murder suspect left on the 23rd, so he was on the other side of the Atlantic by the date of the killing.' I didn't say he was my ex-partner.

'What date *exactly*,' I could almost hear Shelby's mental arithmetic, 'do you have for the murder, Miss Peterson?'

'The police told me the 27th February I think. Wasn't that also in your report?'

'The body was *found* on the 27th. But the woman had been lying dead in that ditch for many days. Police estimate between five and six days.'

'Oh god!' I slumped back in the car seat.

'If your lady went missing after a disturbance on Thursday 21st that puts her bang on the money.'

'Oh god!'

'Your murder suspect was still in the UK then. Before he fled across the Atlantic.'

'Oh god!' Now I was doing the maths: Lindi disappeared from Boy's cottage on the 21st. Boy had been there with her. He left the country within a day or two of the murder. My recent hard-won police expertise told me this new timeline looked bad.

'There's something else you need to know,' Shelby said. 'Remember we spoke about stable isotope analysis? The police analyse teeth, or in this case, bones and hair, to determine the concentration of certain isotopes in a victim's body. It enables them to narrow down where she was in the months before her death. Remember, you didn't hear this from me. The isotopes say she spent those months in the west-Cambs, north-Herts area. You need to tell the good inspector about your woman.'

'Oh god.'

'Can I quote you on that?'

'What?'

'Focus, Miss Peterson. Ignore the suspect for now; I assume he's gone to ground in Venezuela –'

'Why Venezuela?'

'No extradition treaty with the UK.'

'Oh, but he's in Patagonia.'

'That's what he wants you to think.'

'Oh god.'

'Much as I'd love to print this as an exclusive, we don't know for sure it's your woman. The police would be able to run DNA immediately. If it is her, it would be irresponsible for me to print before they have a chance to hunt your man down, so I want you to do two things for me.'

'What.' I was still dazed.

'You are going to tell Hossein about your woman first thing tomorrow. But now, tonight, I want you to write down *everything* about how you worked back from your attack to this woman. Our story will be about how you tracked down the Doll Killer in three days, when the police failed to do so in three months.'

'Our story...?'

'Do it, Miss Peterson. Do it while it's still fresh in your mind. You'll need to do it for the police, anyhow. Just the salient points plus any thoughts and emotions for now. I'll help you turn it into a serialisation in due course. The weekend papers will pay for this and I know a true crime publisher who will definitely want the rights.'

'Let me think.'

You've got all night. Final thought from me: the police are almost certain that the Doll Killer's first victim is a sex worker from the Normanton area of Derby, probably East European. I don't know if there was anything dubious about your friend's profession...'

'Yes, she was an accountant.' I hung up.

Shelby made it sound so blindingly obvious. My doll and my mum's jewellery must have been in Lindi's cottage after all. Lindi disappeared on the exact date the police had pencilled-in. Boy had vamoosed a little earlier than I expected to Patag... to Venezuela!? Was that possible?

Could Boy have fabricated a Facebook trip posting about a place he wasn't in? Hell yes, I was pretty sure I could do that and Boy ran an I.T. company.

A book cover flashed into my imagination: '*The Serial Killer who Fathered my Child*' by Shona Peterson.

22 LINDI

February 2019

Ash had taken a bus to Arlston. The police confirmed what Lindi had already guessed when they eventually reported back. From there, they had placed him at the Arlston train station. After that the trail went cold. He'd paid cash. They couldn't say if he'd gone down to London, up to Peterborough or further north. The police weren't hopeful or helpful. They asked about his Muslim contacts. In a daze Lindi could only think of Imam Ghalib at the mosque in Luton. The police suspected that Ash had gone to ground. They'd let her know when he turned up (in whatever terrorist cell).

She waited by her mobile. It rarely rang.

When it did it was Toke of all people. 'Lindi, it's a bad time I realise.'

'I know we said we'd meet, Mr Toakley, but I don't think there's any point. I can't help you. I've passed the financial information on alr –'

'I know mine and Boy's affairs are the last thing on your mind now, Lindi. I'm calling about Ashal. I want to help you. I know your son is missing. I have a business associate. He's good at tracking people down. I told him about your lad. He thinks he can help.'

'How do you know about Ash?'

'The Hartsdell grapevine is a supremely efficient ecosystem.'

'The police are doing all they can, Mr Toakley.' It was a gross exaggeration.

'I'm sure, but Ash has dropped off the grid; you know, out of the world the police understand and operate in. My associate works in more covert circles, talks to people the police won't.'

'I can't afford to pay anyo – '

'No payment required, Lindi. I just want to help.'

'Alright, that's kind.'

'You'll need to get me Ash's social media info, Facebook, whatever, as a start point.'

She agreed she would see Toke and his associate in Lone Marsh Holdings' offices in Peterborough. She didn't believe his friend would find Ash, but it was the only offer of help she'd had.

Time was her enemy, and there was more of it. Her work for Boy was done. Jimmy, the landlord of the Hart's Haunt called to say they would progress her project from here-on. The actual words didn't form part of the call, but the message was clear, 'stay away, you're bad for business right now.'

Word had diffused around Hartsdell: a terrorist living down by the Haunt had been arrested. Those that knew her wouldn't want to any more. Luckily, they weren't many. She couldn't bring herself to call Evelyn in the gallery. She didn't want her favourite client placed in an embarrassing situation.

Boy was attentive. He called daily, offered meals she wouldn't eat, company she didn't want. She put him off. He couldn't give her what she needed – her son back. It was painful seeing him not knowing what to say or do. She had no use for his unfounded optimism. The contrived gusto with which Boy attacked life and business, was entirely inappropriate to this crisis. He wanted to be there for her. He didn't know how to be.

Lindi tried calling Ayan but was told curtly by one of his sisters – she couldn't determine which – that he was out of the country and out of contact. She wasn't asked if she wanted to leave a message. She didn't have one to leave.

After two days, Lindi pieced herself together enough to get busy, to distract herself. She looked up a PLS hotel online, spoke to a receptionist and got a phone number for the company finance team. She introduced herself as working in Marcus Compton's company's accounts: she wanted to talk about a recent invoice for £522,000. After two minutes on hold a new voice came on.

'Ms Mills, is that right? I'm Daniel Andrews finance director at PLS. I'm not sure we've talked before, but I have spoken to your MD, Marcus Compton – several times. Our position hasn't changed.'

'I'm new here and have to write a report on this, Mr Andrews. Can you just take a minute to reprise me of your position regarding this invoice?'

'Simple. We won't be paying it.'

But you did, thought Lindi. She continued, 'Can you quickly remind me why.'

'Because this deal was thrashed out between your Mr Compton, an intermediary – '

'That would be Mr Toakley?'

'Yes, not a businessman we will have any future dealings with, I have to say. Compton and Toakley dealt solely with our most inexperienced director – a member of the owner's family – and persuaded him that this diversification would be a sensible expansion of our business. In signing off on this deal, our director acted beyond his authority. He did not seek the required board approval for his actions.'

'So, you are not diversifying into holiday cottages or planning to use the products and services our company supplied.'

'Regrettably not. I am prepared to accept that Mr Compton acted in good faith, but he placed too much confidence in Mr Toakley, and he did not undertake proper checks with us, regarding our intentions and approval of this strategy. Believe me, we have reviewed this at length at our end. We are advised that any legal action to recover the debt would founder on Toakley's role in all this, which was shady, to say the least. Your company did not do its due diligence. I thought Mr Compton now accepted this.'

'Possibly so, but I still have to write up a report. As you'll appreciate, it's a big sum.'

'Yes, I understand. Is there anything else?'

'Can you remind me of this director's responsibilities at Peak Location.'

The FD cleared his throat. 'Well, Mr Brindle's brief was New Business.'

That covered a multitude of sins, thought Lindi. 'And did he have any business relationship with Mr Toakley, perhaps regarding property?'

'Not any more.'

Lindi thanked him, put down the phone and began to piece together what had happened. She thought she knew.

* * *

The police still had Ash's and Lindi's mobiles and laptops. All her experience of social media came from business. She knew enough to set up a fake Facebook account. She did it in the village library, under the pseudonym, Hartsmuch. She trawled through Ash's screed of news. It was busy. She didn't recognise any of his old friends' names. Neither could she find any direct evidence of extremism. He had joined groups that posted about the Government targeting and labelling Muslims.

* * *

The day before her meeting with Toke and his associate in Peterborough, Lindi dropped into Webbs. The butcher nodded coolly at her. A jerk of his head meant 'wait in the backroom'. He wanted her out of his shop, away from his customers.

Lindi found Kotryna in the back office. The woman looked up. 'Things are not going so well since we had our little talk.'

'I've lost my son.'

'Yes, and Webby still smarts that you turned him down.'

'I'm sorry.'

'Don't be. I understand. He tells me that you know about Toke too. That you guessed.'

'I don't know details. And, I don't want to, Kotryna. I've come to warn Webby I'm seeing Toke tomorrow.'

'Why?'

'He's invited me to Peterborough, to his offices. Says a friend of his can help find Ash.'

'Don't go. He can't. Toke helped me once, but I still don't trust him. You mustn't.'

'Helped how?'

'Pulled me out from a bear trap, saved my life I think. A friend of mine was not so lucky. She didn't have a Toke. The bear got her.'

'I have to take any chance to save my son.'

'Listen, Toke is a good man who enjoys being a naughty man too much. He's a friend *only* when it works for him. I used to think he was too much in love with money. He's not. It's control he loves. Toke has power over us, Webby and me.'

'Your hush money?'

'He'll find a way to get power over you. That is why he asks you to Peterborough.' Kotryna got up and, as Webby came through the door, she moved towards it. 'Webby has things he must say to you.' She left and closed the door.

'Mum's taking over the accounts again,' said Webby. 'Thanks for your help but we don't need you any more.'

Lindi was half expecting this but was stung by his callousness. In two conversations Webby had gone from pleadingly desirous to plainly dismissive.

'This is because I won't sleep with you?' She bit back more loudly than she'd meant to.

'Pipe down! No, nor is it your terrorist son, though, that would surely be enough.'

'Ash is not a terrorist.'

'Oh? The police seem to think differently.'

'What then?'

'You've screwed me over with Toke. I told you things in confidence. He knows you know.'

'That comes from a conversation I had with Toke before you told me anything. It dates from when you were still lying to me about the payments.'

'Just get out.' He loomed over her.

She tilted her head up, 'Just so you know, your cheap secrets will still be safe with me.'

'Get your meat from elsewhere,' he shouted at her as she left the room.

A muttering queue of customers were stared into silence as she strode back through the shop.

❈ ❈ ❈

She parked the car in a 'residents only' box, leaving the permit Toke had sent her displayed in the windscreen. The long road was on the margins of Peterborough city centre, a mix of light industrial and retail, fading into rundown residential. The address she had was towards the residential end, terraced houses freckled with Asian food stores.

The sleet that had buffeted her car all the way up the A1 lessened in town but Lindi fastened her winter coat as she left her car. The registered address for Lone Marsh Holdings coincided with The Horizon Hotel, where two large Victorian townhouses had been merged, painted the same shade of cream and united by a single entrance.

Lindi trotted up the short set of steps and pushed open the swing doors. A thickset 40-something woman was coming across the lobby towards the exit and Lindi held the door for her. Tousled blonde hair parted over a broad forehead; the woman's puffy eyes drifted blankly over Lindi, without noticing her. She wasn't dressed for the weather, a knee-length skirt above black boots and a thin jacket open over a glitzy blue blouse.

A small older Asian woman watched Lindi approach the lobby desk. Lindi asked if she was in the right place for Lone Marsh Holdings and the woman shook her head slightly.

'Mr Toakley?' got a better response. Lindi was led past the stale reek of small bar/cafe where two women were chatting over coffee, and through a dark-brown door. The first door beyond that was open but the woman knocked on it.

'Come in,' said Toke from inside the room. 'Lindi, my lovely, you're early; no matter. What would you like to drink?'

Lindi asked for a coffee and Toke nodded at the woman, who disappeared. She hadn't said a word.

'Welcome to Lone Marsh Holdings HQ,' said Toke, as if it was a plush West End agency. 'My colleague will be here shortly. He's driving across from Derby.'

The office was large but sparse: a heavy leather-topped desk, phone, filing cabinet, small round meeting table with three cheap chairs. Lindi had already noted the three locks on the sturdy door.

'Do you own the hotel?' asked Lindi.

'And the house next door and the two guest-houses beyond that. I own them but they're all rented out. I don't run the hotel, but Tandy lets me keep an office here.'

Lindi couldn't tell whether 'Tandy' was a surname or a Christian name, a man or a woman.

'I don't spend a lot of time here – for obvious reasons,' Toke gestured at the surroundings. 'Please, take a seat.'

'How do you know your business associate?' asked Lindi. 'Does he have a name?'

'Not one I'm going to give you. As I said on the phone, he works on the margins of society and it's only that, which gives me any confidence he can find Ashal.'

'Ash,' said Lindi automatically.

'Call him "Mart". He uses properties I own in Derby, a hotel, some houses.'

'Similar to these here?'

'That hotel is more upmarket than The Horizon,' Toke smiled, 'Not that that's saying much.'

'Like Peak Locations, er... PLS?'

'Catering for a different end of the market.' Toke chuckled this time.

'Mainly lonely single males?'

'You'd be surprised but yes, I think you've gleaned the nature of our primary market sector.'

The coffee arrived in a brown cup and saucer, quickly followed by large short-haired man in an expensive but plain winter jacket. He seemed surprised to find Lindi there already but put out a meaty hand. He was tall broad-chested and somewhere between muscular and fat. Lindi estimated his age at early-40s.

'Lindi, this is Mart,' said Toke. 'Mart; Lindi Mills. Would you give us a moment please, Lindi, so I can bring Mart up to speed? He has already put out some feelers, so he'll tell you where he is with Ash when you come back in.'

Lindi took her coffee and departed. She drifted to the bar where the two women watched with limited interest as she took a seat at a table.

'Alright, love,' said one, an emaciated blonde with impressive false eyelashes and an unhealthy pallor.

Her friend was a younger Asian girl, in a big sheepskin coat, thin legs shrouded in black tights poking out beneath. 'You working?' she asked.

'I'm here to see Mr Toakley...'

The blonde woman nodded, 'Toke.'

'...and Mart,' said Lindi.

The two women shook their heads.

'Big man, short hair, from Derby.' Lindi used her hands to suggest his girth.

The two shared a glance. The Asian girl grimaced. The blonde raised her eyebrows to her friend.

'Do either of you know a woman called Kotryna?' asked Lindi. They shook their heads. 'Is she from around here?'

'Lithuanian, I think,' said Lindi.

'More likely to be Derby, love' said the blonde.

'There's a lot of Eastern Europeans there, Poles, girls from the Baltics. Is she your friend?'

Lindi thought about her relationship with Kotryna for a moment before answering. 'Yes, I think she's looking out for me.'

'We all need someone to do that,' the Asian girl nodded.

'Steer clear of Derby,' said the blonde. 'A girl was killed there a few months ago. She was from one of them Baltic States.'

Her younger friend kicked her under the table.

'What?!' exclaimed the blonde, staring at her friend, who twitched her head to the lobby and mouthed something.

Lindi lip-read, 'He's here; in Toke's office.'

'Forget I said anything,' the blonde looked back at Lindi. 'Just rumours and bollocks in this business, innit.'

There were steps from across the lobby. Toke poked his head around the door to the bar, 'We're all set,' he said.

Toke had put a chair for Lindi on his side of the desk.

'Can I call you Lindi,' asked Mart in slightly accented English. He continued without waiting for an answer. 'I want to be clear with you. If Ash is with friends, I'm probably not going to be able to find him. If he's alone and looks for help in the Muslim and Pakistani community, I have a better chance.'

'He's not with friends.'

'Family?'

'None in the UK.'

'OK, here's what I've got. He's 16. He's been in contact with ISIS and been questioned by police about that. His father's Pakistani. Ash was groomed and activated in Luton by members of Zainab Qumar's family – '

'I'm not sure that's true,' Lindi said, surprised by her new hesitancy to deny Ash's involvement in extremism.

'You'd be the last to know,' said Mart. 'Which mosque was he with?'

'He's never attended a mosque,' said Lindi with more certainty, 'but he did know Imam Ghalib from one of the Luton mosques. I told the police.'

Toke broke in, glancing to Mart, 'Is that significant?'

'I'll check. I don't know much about the Muslim radical world myself, but I do work with a lot of well-connected men from the Pakistani community. They've been good at chasing their people down. If this Imam is actively recruiting for ISIS, they'll know and if he did recruit Ash, my guess is Ash will be in contact with him.'

'He can't have,' said Lindi. 'This Imam works with the Government's anti-radicalisation teams.'

Mart spread his big meaty hands out. 'And your point is?'

Lindi sighed helplessly.

'We need to move quickly. Ash has been interviewed by the police. If serious extremists suspect he's told the police anything, Ash will be in trouble.'

'You mean they might hurt him?'

'Or worse. I don't want to be alarmist, though. Few Muslim terror groups are potent and well trained, far more are enthusiastic amateurs who are in love with the ideology but end up doing nothing or doing something shit. Ash is more likely to be involved with these amateur dabblers. I don't imagine they would kill him.'

'Oh Christ. What do we do now?'

'I will need to knock some heads and – how do you say it – grease some palms,' he circled his fingers in the palm of a hand.

'I can't afford to pay –' started Lindi.

'So I hear, but Toke will help with that. As I understand it, you have some information you can give him in return.'

There it was. Kotryna had been right. Toke was unembarrassed by his associate's bluntness. 'We can chat about that after,' he said.

Mart shrugged and nodded. 'I have already put some feelies –

is that right? – out. I know your son took a train to London last Wednesday. Do you want me to pursue him there?'

I don't want anyone like you within a million miles of my son, thought Lindi, but it sounded like he would get results faster than the police. She hesitated.

'Mart, could you give us a moment?' asked Toke.

The big man got up. 'I'll go talk to the girls,' he said.

'The girls in your cafe won't thank me for that,' said Lindi, when she and Toke sat alone.

Toke dismissed the suggestion. 'They're used to him. And, they don't work for him, not directly.'

'They thought I was one of them,' said Lindi.

'They've recognised something. There's an air of desperation hanging around you these days, Lindi. They smell it on you. You're a woman who's about to do all kinds of things you wouldn't ever have imagined.'

'Like use Mart to find my son?'

'He's very effective,' said Toke. 'He gets things done.'

'It's how he gets things done, I'm worried about.'

'He's clever, but he's also street smart. In his business...' Toke left Lindi to fill in the obvious. 'He'll threaten people, call in favours. If Ash is in an extremist safe-house or cell, and Mart fishes him out, they'll give him up. It may not be what Ash wants, but you're his mum. At the very least you need to know he's safe. Do you care how that's done?'

'Probably not?'

'Let me tell you about the Peak Location deal. You'll see that you don't need to protect Boy.'

'You don't have to. I think I've worked it out. There are two companies, and, anyway, I've passed the accounts through, now.'

'Good. Boy and I set up Peak Location *Services* Ltd, but Peak Location *Solutions*, trading as PLS, is a company in the hotel business, based in Derby. I ran into one of their directors at a hotel supplier freebie.'

'Their New Business Director, Carlton Brindle.'

'Very good, Lindi, I can see why Boy employs you. Yes, well, Carl explained some of his thoughts to me about how he wanted to expand and diversify their business online. It sounded perfect for Boy's company, so I introduced the two of them, and negotiated a small, but agreeable, finder's fee for myself from Boy, payable when the deal completed. I attended a couple of early meetings but largely left them to it.'

'Yes, I see.' Lindi saw that the 'small' finder's fee would have been many thousands of pounds.

'Boy and I haven't done business before, so I wanted to ensure my fee was honoured. I insisted that I sat in the middle of the deal, so to speak. PLS paid me and I paid Boy, after taking my cut.'

That didn't ring true, thought Lindi. 'But why did you set up a company with an almost identical name to the established company you were working with?'

'Carl suggested that himself, when it came time to pay. I suspect he was organising a small slice of side action for himself.'

'He was on the take, you mean. He had put through a bigger bill than Boy was charging to his own company and was defrauding them for the difference,' Lindi had worked out Toke's role for herself but this new element didn't surprise her.

'Defraud is too strong, Lindi,' Toke said. 'Carl's dad owns the company. I imagine it was just a way of the family massaging better profits out of it.'

'Defrauding the taxman, then?'

'You're an accountant. Your profession largely exists to do exactly that, remember,' said Toke. 'Don't get all holier-than-thou, my lovely. The key point is that Boy knew I was on a cut and there's nothing wrong with that. He didn't know about the Brindles' own arrangements, and I suggest we preserve his innocence.'

'So what do you want from me?'

'I know Boy is selling up to Mitch Goodridge's company. I don't know the particulars. I just need to know what part my deal played in that acquisition.'

Because you think there is more going on than you know and you want to blackmail Boy into paying you more. Lindi filled in some blanks herself.

'Are you blackmailing the Webbs?'

'Lord no, but I do keep some secrets for Webby and Kotryna. Secrets you've compromised.'

'You're taking money from them because you know Kotryna is a former call girl.'

'Is that what Webby's told you?'

'I worked it out.'

'So smart; so wrong!' Toke clapped his hands. 'I paid good money to buy Kotryna out of a world she should never have gotten into. She was at the top end of the market. Clients paid a lot for her attention. The people around her weren't going to just let her go.'

'She couldn't go home to Lithuania?'

'Not without a beating, disfigurement, maybe worse. Someone saw it was going to end badly. They asked me for ideas. I spoke to her. She told me that if forced to continue she'd kill herself. I negotiated her out. Now she has just one punter to satisfy, Webby, so she's happier. And Webby is no longer spending a fortune sleeping his way through all the call girls of the East Midlands.'

'Webby was using prostitutes?'

'And I thought you'd worked it all out, Lindi.' Toke's waving finger admonished her. 'Did you think he'd met Kotryna at the hunt ball?'

'He said you'd introduced them.'

'Ah, so you believed I was keeping secrets for Kotryna...' Toke giggled. 'Dear me no, it's my good friend Webby's reputation that I'm protecting.'

'I won't tell.'

'Strangely, I know that. Of course, your son's future isn't riding on Webby's customers' sensibilities. What can you tell me about Boy's deal?'

'Only that your involvement doesn't have a specific role in

the wider deal,' she lied. 'Beyond that I can't give you any detail. I keep clients' information confidential.'

'You're lying, Lindi. I suspect it's the one thing you are shit at. It's the first time I've been disappointed in you.'

'I don't betray business confidentialities.'

'On your son's life?' The change in the atmosphere was instant.

'What are you threatening?' Lindi felt cold fear wash through her.

'I don't threaten people, Lindi. Do you want time to think about it?'

'I can't do what you're asking.'

'Then we'd better tell my colleague he's wasted his time.' Toke rose and stepped to the door. Lindi moved to stand. 'Stay please. He's driven a long way to help you. You owe him an explanation.'

No, thought Lindi, she didn't. She continued fastening her coat. The door opened and Toke's associate stepped into the room. He was alone. He closed the door behind him. The same man but different: bigger, faster, colder.

'So, lady, you don't want my services.' His voice matched Lindi's fear.

'No, I'm sorry. Toke hadn't properly explained the deal. I can't give him what he wants.'

'To me, it doesn't sound like he asks so much.' He picked up a stapler from the desk, flipped it open.

'Too much for me.'

'You value some vague business principle more than your son?' He hammered the open stapler into the desk. A slither of silver threaded the leather top.

Lindi couldn't stop herself jumping. 'I've got to go. I've another appointment.'

'Bullshit.' The stapler provided an exclamation mark. Lindi recoiled.

'I've already started tracking your son.' Staple.

'I'm going to find Ash whether or not you want me to.' Staple.

'Please don't.'

'Have a talk with him.' Staple.

'You can't...' but he probably could. He probably would, without thinking twice. He was between her and the door. She'd have to push past.

'There are people I know...' Staple.

Lindi moved to pass him by the wall. A thick arm stopped her.

'Sharia Muslims, Islamic hardliners who work in the UK but want a Sharia state.'

A staple broke against the wall by Lindi's head. She flinched.

'If I tell them that Ash is informing on Imams who support their cause... well, at the very least they'd take his hand off.'

Lindi had no words. Her imagination was mired in horror.

'...maybe his head, too.'

'I must go.' She ducked his arm, reached for the door. Twisted it open.

'I don't think so, *chiulpedra*, not 'til you give Toke the information he wants.' He spun her round to face him. Forced her back against the door.

'I...'

'Maybe I underestimate my Sharia friends.' The stapler rested on her forehead. 'They'll probably take his head off *and* both hands. You read the papers, lady?'

Lindi pushed to escape. He held her effortlessly. A staple fired into the door by her ear. Her scream started and stopped. His after-shave assaulted her, but he didn't. He let her open it.

'Think about it. I don't take "no" for an answer. Be seeing you.' Sing-song belligerence pursued her into the lobby.

Toke was standing, drinking coffee in the lobby. He smiled, raised his mug to her, '*I* don't make threats, Lindi...'

❋ ❋ ❋

Numbed in mind and body, Lindi, opened the door to Boy's

cottage and locked it behind her. Her phone was ringing. She picked up but didn't speak.

'Lindi, is that you?' It was Boy. 'I've been trying your mobile.'

'I've been driving,' she said.

'Looking for Ash?'

'In a way, yes.'

'I was worried. You sound so low. Are you OK? Do you want me to come 'round?'

'Only if you have time,' she struggled not to sob. It was getting to be a new habit.

'I'll make time.' He hung up.

He was with her 25 minutes later with a carrier bag of impromptu lunch items, sourced from Webbs. Lindi was slumped in a sofa, watching the clock, because she didn't want to do anything and she daren't think anything.

She opened the door after checking it was Boy. He took-in her puffy eyes, running eye-liner and broken lifeless expression. He dropped the bag, put both arms around her and tried to hug some hope back into her. She didn't mention Toke, his brutish associate, or the false hopes and persistent fears they had awoken.

Boy had learnt not to try to jolly her out of her depression. He didn't offer his worthless expectation that Ash would come home. Instead he held her close as a shared secret and stilled her trembling and sobbing with his proximity.

Eventually Lindi pulled away and asked what was in the bag. He sat her on an old-fashioned wooden bar stool and concocted lunch. She watched, forehead in one palm, shoulder length sandy hair matted in strands against her cheeks and trapped beneath the collar of her business shirt. Boy gambled a hand between her hair and the back of her neck, to release her hair. His hand brushed her neck on the hairline.

'What's this?' he asked.

'All that's left of my teenage self's embarrassing recipe for life,' she said without moving her head. 'A dish I never found the ingredients for.'

Boy lifted her hair up and she lowered her head, so he could see the back of her neck. The scar tissue wasn't apparent to the eye.

'A tattoo? What was it? What did it portray?'

'Do you know Hokusai's Great Wave?' Lindi laughed, 'Well my tattoo said, "Make a splash". I had it done when I was 19. Three mates from Uni and me, we all got one.'

'Why get rid of it?'

'Because it was a depressing lie. It supposedly embodied my determination to attack life, go everywhere, do everything, never compromise.' Lindi coughed up a laugh, 'It was doomed from the start. The tattoo was tiny and butted against my hairline. Why? Cos my mum would have killed me if she'd ever seen it. Some rebel, huh?'

Boy kissed the scar. 'None of us achieve our 19-year-old dreams, Lindi. Or, if we do, then they weren't ambitious enough.'

'You're off to cycle round Patagonia,' she reminded him.

'I'd never heard of Patagonia, when I was 19.'

'What was your dream at 19?'

'That I'd stop being so shy.'

She smiled, lifted her head and shook her hair back over the scar. 'You're probably the least shy person I know.'

'My point exactly. My dream was never ambitious enough. Anyhow, all my bravado is an act.'

'I funnelled all my dreams into Ash,' said Lindi. 'Look how that turned out.'

'I'm not leaving for Patagonia until we track him down,' he said.

'Oh Boy. You know I'll never hold you to that.'

'When was the last time you'd cried before Ash was arrested?' he returned to his food prep.

'Can't remember. Never as an adult. I was always in control… I thought.'

'Tears are one way of "Making a splash". A small start. It suggests you're losing control of something.'

Boy left, at her insistence after their meal. Lindi curled up in the lounge, going through every misstep with Ash, everything she could have done differently, each tiny miscalculation that added up to the sum of her failure.

A noise intruded, something moving in the back garden. Lindi squeezed herself up tighter. Through closed eyes she imagined shadowy men on her patio, saw the Winter Hart picking its way through untended pots to breathe its curse at her door.

❋ ❋ ❋

Next morning the phone went. It was Evelyn. 'Lindi, I need help with this campaign thing. You're supposed to be my advisor.'

'Evelyn, you probably haven't heard –'

'About Ash, of course I've heard. What are you doing about it?'

'There's nothing much I can do. The police aren't helpful. Yesterday, I looked into hiring someone to track him down. That only made things unimaginably worse.'

'So, what are you doing at home?'

'Feeling useless, miserable and very scared.'

'Could you do those things, drink my coffee and help me talk to the printers?'

'You don't want me around like this, Evelyn.'

'No I bloody don't. I want my campaign manager back on full throttle. Still, however miserable you are, I need you here and I'm paying you to help.'

'If you're sure.'

'Well, I have consulted with my insurers. If you do blow up the gallery, I'm covered – but only as long as you don't tell me you're going to do it first. You wouldn't do that would you, dear?'

'I definitely wouldn't tell you beforehand,' Lindi promised.

'That's sorted then. The coffee is on.' The line went dead.

✳ ✳ ✳

The following day her mobile went. The voice was faint. It was Ayan, 'Hey Lindi, Rahana said you'd called.'

'Oh Ayan, thanks so much for getting back, I've got news, it's not –'

'I have news too, Lindi. There's someone here to speak to you. After that we must both apologise to you.'

'Hey, mum,' another voice came on the line.

'Oh, Ash, you have no idea...'

'I know I've put you through hell. I'm really sorry. We couldn't tell you until I was here. In case you tried to stop me.'

'I would have too. But you're 16, Ash, you can go anywhere, do anything.'

'Dad got money to me. He came over to the UK and met me. We have just arrived in Karachi.'

'You always wanted to go. Make the most of it.'

'Yeah, it's crazy here. There are armed guards when we go out, Ammi's got servants. The streets are just mad, total chaos. My feet have hardly touched Pakistani soil, yet, but I want to take it all in. You don't mind if I stay a while?'

'As long as you're healthy and happy... and guarded. I think it's a really good idea.'

'You sound different.'

'I am. I don't know what's changed yet. Let's hope it's for the better.'

'Certainly sounds like it. Love you. Here's Dad.'

Ayan came on. 'I want to apologise too, Lindi. He called me last week. Turned out he just wanted to spend some time with his father.'

Lindi wasn't searching for any irony or stressing of the last word. She didn't hear any.

'Smart kid. He's better off there with you at the moment,

Ayan. There's fewer Islamic issues in Pakistan.'

'Yes, I've heard it all. Ammi and all his aunts are already spoiling him rotten. His uncle wants to beat him at all the latest games. You can imagine.'

'It's going to be so different for him. It'll do him the world of good. Please send them all my love.'

'I don't need to. They know.'

Lindi found tears streaming down her cheeks. Again. 'Oh, Ayan, I've been so stupid.'

'They know that too, of course.'

She laughed through her tears. 'I'm different, Ash says. Let's hope it means I'll be smarter in future.'

'You were always the smart one, Lindi. Give Ash and me some time together, then come out for a holiday, if you can.'

She said she had to wrap up one important deal. She phoned Evelyn with the news. Then she called Boy. He told her his deal had gone through a few days ago but he didn't want to say until Ash had been found.

'You're free to go to Patagonia after all.'

'I'm packing spare underpants as we speak. When's Ash coming home?'

'Not for a few months I hope. He needs to spend time with his dad and his family there. Actually, he's far better off out there, for now.'

'Look, I'm going to organise a party for a few friends to celebrate and say goodbye for six months. You up for it?'

'I'm up for everything from now on.'

'That sounds different.'

'So I hear.'

* * *

Lindi drove to the police station. The officers who had previously interviewed her weren't there, but she sat down with a PC. She told him that Ash wasn't missing any more, he'd turned up with his father in Karachi. The PC just nodded. Further proof that the boy was on the path to terrorism. He said he'd ensure that the search was called off. His tone convinced Lindi that there had never been one on. She suspected that Ash would be picked up on an airport watch-list when he returned to the UK.

There was something else, she said. She had spoken to two men in Peterborough, who claimed they could help in finding Ash, through Islamic contacts. She didn't know if they could or not. One was involved in the sex trade. He had threatened her when she declined to use his services.

The PC strongly advised against meeting with anyone on that basis. It was good that she had seen sense.

He asked if the man had physically attacked her. She said not. Were there witnesses? No.

Was there a record of these threats? No, she hadn't recorded them.

Did she want to press charges?

She had never been given his name. He was Eastern European.

Could the police trace him through the address she was visiting?

No, he came from Derby; she thought he might run a hotel there. The second man, a Mr Chester Toakley, had set up the meeting. He'd know the man's real name.

Would he reveal it to police? No, not voluntarily.

'How do you want to pursue it?' The way the PC asked the question suggested the answer.

'What do you recommend?'

'Even if you had a name I doubt it would be genuine. He's in a shadowy part of society. He will be hard to track down, even with a good description. If we did apprehend him, you have no witnesses. He didn't physically or sexually assault you...'

'You've made your point,' said Lindi. 'He hinted that he knew about the murder of an Eastern European sex-worker in Derby.'

'How hinted?'

'That he knew of hard-line Islamists who kill or maim people.'

'That doesn't really make sense does it? Why would Muslim extremists kill a sex-worker?'

'You're not interested?'

'There's not enough here. I'm sure you can see that.'

'Can I fill in a report, anyway?'

'It won't change anything.'

'I realise that, but it will mean there's a record. If something happens to me, the police will know that Toakley is behind it.'

The PC sighed, and they filled in some details.

* * *

Lindi checked the internet on her return. She knew a woman had been found headless and handless in the Midlands in the autumn. She found the reports and read several. The woman had been beheaded and had both hands removed. A Barbie doll next to the body was similarly mutilated. She was discovered in a gravel pit five kilometres south of Derby. She was unidentified to this day. There was no mention of her coming from the Baltic States or being a sex-worker.

She unearthed Kotryna's business card and called her.

'Who's this?'

'Kotryna, it's Lindi. Is this convenient?'

'I'm driving, Lindi. I've pulled over. What have you to say?'

'First, Ash has been found. He's in Karachi with his dad.'

'Good, Happy for you.'

'Before I knew that, I met with Toke yesterday. You were right, he was trying to get power over me.'

'Kotty's not so stupid, huh?'

'Smarter than me. There were threats. Something came up about a murder near Derby.'

Silence.

'Is Toke involved with that do you think?'

'Not Toke, no. Toke can be naughty but he's not crazy. However...'

'Please tell me.'

'Toke knows things about this murder, things he shouldn't know, things not in the papers. Toke is close to a shameful world, cruel people. He hears things. He's a man, so he boasts. Who can he boast to about these things he knows? No-one, except Webby and me. Only we know his connection to those people.' Other noises came through the phone.

'Kotryna, I'm so sorry. I've upset you. I shouldn't have called.'

'Now I must redo my make-up before seeing client. This murder is – how you say? – too close for me.'

'He brought a big beast of a man from Derby to the meeting.'

Kotty spoke a Lithuanian word. Probably a swear word. It went quiet.

'This man threatened me and Ash.' Lindi broke the silence. 'He said he'd cut our head and hands off.'

'Stay away from him, Lindi.'

'I intend to.'

'Lindi, don't say anything about this. Don't say you have told me. Where is your son?'

'Pakistan.'

'He's safer there. Lindi, we cannot speak again. Don't contact me.'

* * *

Lindi helped Evelyn with the revamp of the gallery. The website was up. The marketing Candi's contacts had organised, was starting to work its magic. Lindi called Boy's other half to thank her.

'Just brilliant, Candi. Thanks for all your help. If you ever need anyone to do your tax returns...'

'Pleased it's working,' said Candi. 'Boy tells me your expertise has made him a rich man.'

'He's exaggerating,' said Lindi. Boy had, after all, employed her counting on her *lack* of expertise.

'Not about the riches, I hope,' said Candi. 'We can work that capital. We've got massive plans post-Sabbatical: combining our skill sets in the vacation space. Shouty has investors who are up for it.'

'The riches *are* true, but don't tell anyone. It won't be made public. I know there are people in Hartsdell, who would be very jealous.'

'I can think of someone in particular.' Candi didn't need to name-check Shona.

'So are you joining Boy on his cycling tour?'

'Mmm, I think so. I've told all my friends I'm off. I've told them at work. They're gutted, said they'll keep the job open for me obviously, but I probably won't be back. Boy's desperate to share the trip. We can work on our start-up ideas. It's important to him. I think I have to go.'

'Go,' advised Lindi. 'I've recently realised how little I've done with my life. You can't miss this trip. Someone needs to keep Boy from wreaking havoc in Patagonia.'

The call stung Lindi's professional pride. Why had Boy used her? Had he been so sure he could pull the wool over her eyes? She revisited her copy of Boy's sale contract. She knew what had happened. It was a perfect scam – almost perfect. She decided to work out how much it had netted him.

Boy's company had turned over £3.5m in its last financial year. Under the terms of the contract Mitch's company paid a 1.2 multiple of turnover, so £4.2m. That was what Mitch had expected to pay. Normally it would take Boy 12 years to achieve that in profit.

However, if Boy's final profit margin was over 12 %, the contract paid out a multiple of profits. The formula was: -

- over 12% but under 15% = 10 times profits
- over 15% but under 18% = 11 times profits
- over 18% but under 21% = 12 times profits

and then it increased...

- over 21% = 13 times profits
- over 22% = 14 times profits and so on.

Mitch wasn't expecting to pay that, but Lindi saw that the formula made business sense. It gave Mitch latitude to talk up a more exciting figure. It encouraged Boy to take costs out of the business, which meant the US company had less pain to go through after handover.

Mitch was relying on his industry's tendency to run up bad debts to keep the purchase price low. Unpaid or partly paid invoices were a feature of every service business and would eat away at turnover and especially profit, as it came straight off the bottom line.

Including Toke's deal with PLS, Boy had a higher-than-usual turnover. £3.5m was £200K better than anything he'd achieved in the last four years. He was also looking at a good profit, even allowing for the expected bad debt of 10-12%.

His hopes must have plummeted when PLS announced that they didn't recognise the contract as binding and would pay for none of the work. Boy had trusted Toke and Carl Brindle, believing Brindle had approval for the deal. Boy had a contract and he honoured it; he did the work.

But PLS wouldn't pay. Brindle didn't have authority to sign off, they said. Normally a director could make binding decisions on behalf of their company, but Boy should have checked the director had board approval.

When PLS wouldn't pay for the work, he must have been frantic. He could chase them through the courts, but not in time to include the money in Mitch's deal. Any money that wasn't in his bank account by December 31 would be written off. Court action wasn't guaranteed to be successful and could just put legal costs on his bottom line.

Instead of being able to show a financial year-end delivering a sale based on profit multiples, Boy was going to be fixed to 1.2 times turnover – and that turnover would reduce by the contracted £522,000. Lindi calculated the difference. It was huge.

Without that £522,000, Boy's company would be valued at £3.6m. With it he'd be on 14 times £730,000 profits, a £10.2m valuation.

Boy had come up with a plan. He set up a company similar in name to PLS and told Toke he had to be registered as its named director. If Toke didn't play ball he could kiss goodbye to his bonus, possibly tens of thousands.

Boy set up and controlled the new company's bank account. He then paid his company £522,000 out of his personal money, via the shell company.

What could go wrong? Only that his accountants, Westons, could spot Toakley's name and would know of his association with Boy. Once Westons had audited his accounts for the financial year-end and confirmed to Mitch's team that the only thing outstanding was bad debts, Boy acted. He told Westons he was running the company down before the sale and no longer needed their services.

He paid over the £522,000 invoice in August and appointed Lindi in September. Even including the £522,000 he had personally paid out, he would clear close to £10m and nearly three times what he would have got without that deal.

It was a clever scam and it had worked. There were just two flies in the ointment. Lindi spotting and having reason to be suspicious of the name 'Toakley' in the accounts was one. The other was Toke himself. He knew the original deal had gone sour. He would be paid when the company sale came through, so had an incentive to keep quiet, but thought he might blackmail Boy for more if he could just get to the bottom of what had gone on.

Lindi could understand Boy's sense of injustice – he had done the work in good faith to an exemplary standard. Brindle reneging on the deal could not have come at a worse time – but it was still fraud. Boy and Toke would be prosecuted if it came to light, Boy would also lose over £6m.

Who should Lindi tell?

✽ ✽ ✽

She was still wrestling with her conscience when Boy's party came around. Two weeks before she'd have said 'no thanks' but now she was 'making a splash'. She hadn't seen much of Boy since Ash's call. He was clearing his desk, briefing Mitch, and organising things in readiness for six months on the other side of the world. Even allowing for this, he was unusually distracted.

The party was on a Wednesday, the 20th of February, three days before Boy left. It would be held at his big house outside the village. Boy was cooking. He had invited Candi, Shouty, Webby and Kotryna, Toke's friend Hugo plus his wife, Esther, and Lindi. Mitch Goodridge was popping in for a pre-dinner drink. Lindi breathed a sigh of relief that Toke wasn't on the guest list. It would be awkward seeing Webby, but she agreed to go.

The guests had the run of the large house. A log fire blazed in the drawing room. The drinks table drew them to the dining room. If they entered the kitchen, Boy took delight in shooing them out.

Webby was civil but kept his distance. He was there alone. Kotryna was hosting a beauty products party for a client near Huntingdon and had arranged to sleep over there. Lindi guessed why. Candi was closeted with Webby. She was conspicuously drinking water despite not driving, but her blend of nervous laughter and sullen expressions suggested to Lindi that she may have been drinking earlier.

Lindi chatted to Mitch Goodridge about his plans for the merged company. They got on. He explained that he and Boy had been friendly rivals for years. After much encouragement, Lindi gave him her thoughts on his industry. He congratulated her on her debt-chasing skills and laughed that she had cost him a small fortune. They swapped business cards and he said he'd be in touch. Lindi felt compromised. He left before dinner. She wished she'd hated him.

Lindi sat next to Shouty over dinner. He lived in Cambridge, so was staying over at Boy's house. Boy had uncorked the oldest wines in his rack and Shouty was making the most of not driving. They chatted about the only thing they had in common, Boy. Shouty brought up Boy's ex, Shona. He said his ex-wife, Lotte, and Shona were storming the online dating market together with variable success.

Shouty was hoping Lotte could find someone and move on. 'Any time she dates anyone halfway decent, she's on the phone, telling me how and why she ditched them. I've no idea what she wants me to say.'

'That you'll have her back?'

'Maybe. It's hard not to love Lotte, but we weren't good for each other.'

'What about Shona?'

'She'll never get beyond Boy. The closest she's ever dated to a kindred spirit was Toke. He says he wasn't sure if it was a date or an agony aunt session.'

Lindi confessed she and Toke had fallen out in Peterborough.

'Good for you. I hate Toke,' said Shouty. 'He's probably my oldest friend. Gave me the loan that got me started in business. He refuses to let me pay him back. He believed in me when others didn't. I get to use the tennis court and changing rooms at his farm, whether he's there or not. He trusts me with a key to his barns. I beat him at tennis six times out of ten, he beats me at squash more often than not, we always set up on different sides in a bridge foursome.'

'Sounds complicated. How did you meet?'

'Just part of the same group of adolescent friends. With his dad's backing Toke and I started a business, importing furniture. It's still going, in a sordid sort of way, from the barns at his farm, though I wish it wasn't.'

'Why?'

'Long degrading story. Where do you stand on legal highs?'

'I'm a mother of a 16-year-old.'

'Actually, I knew that. OK well, we probably stand together. My son, Ollie, is eleven. Toke started importing legal high compounds from China, hidden in the furniture and selling to contacts he'd made in Peterborough, Nottingham –'

'Sex trade contacts?'

'You know about that huh? I thought only Webby knew.' Shouty scratched at his beard. 'Let's just say the furniture business became a front. I've wanted out for years – two decades actually – Toke won't hear of it.'

'Just resign.'

'If only. My company is set up as a subsidiary of Toakley Hadleigh Investments Ltd. The old bastard's attitude is: we're mates, we started it together, we're in it together, and if we go down, we go down together. If I resigned, he might make waves. Legally he'd cop it as much as me, but we'd both get a slap on the wrists.'

'You would face a ruling against you for unfit conduct,' said Lindi.

'There's fraudulent dealings, certainly, legal highs become "illegal" for a period every time the legislation changes. Plus, Toke is hardly "Mr Rulebook" when complying with The Companies Act.'

'That's why you were arguing in the cafe before Xmas?'

'I'm dealing with blue-chip companies now, big-name investors. He treats it all as a massive joke, of course.'

'So what do you do?'

'Whip his ass at tennis,' Shouty laughed.

＊　＊　＊

Hugo came over later when Lindi was by the drinks table. The two of them were both 'out' of a lively dice game that was taking place before the cheese course.

'You didn't call,' he said.

'I've had a lot going on.'

'So I hear. Can't have been easy. I imagine you lose a lot of friends in that situation.'

'Not the good ones.'

'About that; I'd like to help fill the gap while Boy's away.'

Hugo was leaning half on the wall, half on Lindi. She had put that down to the drink, now she realised it was something else.

'Boy's girlfriend is Candi, remember?' She stepped away.

'Word is Candice has blotted her copy book.' His hand ran an exaggerated semi-circle out from his stomach.

'Candi's pregnant? That's good news surely?'

'Is it? Boy loves Harry to death. He's been a terrific dad.'

'Then…?'

'Boy's life doesn't fit with full-time parenting. Harry's the reason he and Sho split. You didn't know about Candi?'

'Boy didn't say.' Then Lindi wondered if he had, just not in words.

'He's older, perhaps he's more ready now. Candi's been desperate to be a mum since before I met her.' Hugo stroked Lindi's arm. 'Anyway, my offer still stands.'

'Your beautiful and talented wife is just over there,' she pointed at Esther who was laughingly engrossed in the game.

'Esther's OK with a bit of flirting but, beyond that, we'll need to be discreet.'

Lindi walked away, back to the game.

✱ ✱ ✱

Toke turned up uninvited before the cheese course with a bottle of single malt that made Boy whistle when he read the label.

'Had to say goodbye,' Toke explained. His smile to Lindi widened with surprise that she was there. He wouldn't know she had found Ash, she thought, and vowed to keep it that way.

Hugo embraced the newcomer and snatched the Scotch bottle away to the kitchen, returning with glasses, and pouring.

Lindi was talking to Esther as guffaws broke out. Webby, Toke, Shouty and Hugo were standing in front of the fire. 'I nickname them The Four Musketeers,' said Esther looking across. 'I imagine that makes me Milady de Winter.'

'I've never read it,' admitted Lindi, 'but I wouldn't care to be a princess waiting for a rescue.'

'Fat chance,' Esther laughed. 'They're all sweet enough on their own, but banded together I think they're just about capable of anything.'

Toke was confiding something to the others at that moment and Lindi caught some sly glances in her direction. The alcohol meant they weren't as surreptitious as they'd intended.

'Is Candi drinking, do you know?'

'Not that I've seen.' Esther's surmising glance slipped from Lindi to her husband. 'Shit. Hugo's middle name is "indiscreet". Candi's let it slip to Webby, Boy told Shouty a few weeks back. I don't know how it's gone down, mind. The way Candi's been bending Webby's ear all night, suggests not well. I'm hardly surprised, Boy's going to be close to 80 when the child graduates. I definitely wouldn't want be the one to tell Shona. It'll knock her sideways.'

Toke caught Lindi alone. 'Had you just done me one tiny favour, I'd have done my utmost to find your son. I don't think we'd ever work well together, but we could have helped each other.'

'Like you help Shouty?'

'Has he been telling tales? Oh dear. He's so image-conscious now. Shouty wasn't this scrupulous when he needed to build capital quickly and set himself up as a venture thingy.'

'You're blackmailing him, too, aren't you?'

'Lindi dear, you're determined to dress me as your pantomime villain. These friends of ours all get into trouble through their own misdemeanours, then look to me to bail them out, save their reputations – even lives in some cases.

Who do you think Candi'll call when Boy leaves her high and dry?'

'You're wasting your breath.'

'I'm a Good Samaritan, admittedly a business-savvy one. The business deal I brought to Boy's tab –'

'Not again. Give it up.'

His voice fell to a whisper. 'I understand Mitch was in earlier.'

'Yes.' Pay-back time thought Lindi. 'Congratulating me on my talent at hunting down invoices.'

'I hope you didn't feel the need to say anything... unnecessary.'

'Not at the party, but we've arranged to meet up to discuss a business matter.' She found and flashed Mitch's business card.

'Nothing's really changed you know, Lindi. Yes, Ash has surfaced. The only thing that's different: now we know where your boy is.'

She glared. 'That's the last time you threaten me.'

'It's not me you need to worry about. Mart took your refusal of his help personally. He's got some staples with Ash's name on them.'

'I'll make sure you never get paid your cut of that deal.' Lindi walked away to join Candi.

Boy's girlfriend had been detached and distracted all evening. Boy was cook and host, so Candi and Webby had been thrown together. Lindi had seen Candi in two moods: suspiciously uncertain and yearningly enthusiastic. Tonight, she emitted a brittle mixture of both. Webby had been called into the kitchen to sort the cheeseboard he'd provided. Lindi decided not to probe.

'Are you excited? Packed your cycling gear?'

'No, not yet, too busy at work. The pressure's on. You know how it is.' Candi's laugh was sombre. 'One of my campaigns has hit the sweet spot; awesome take-up. There's other stuff to sort out too. I've taken tomorrow off to think it through.'

Lindi hadn't seen Candi drinking but her eyes were shiny, her face patchily rosy. Words tripped out too fast and a little unravelled.

'Sounds like you've earned a break. Are they still keeping your job open?'

'Yes, but I may call in tomorrow. Suggest I delay flying to Argentina until later. A few weeks should crack the campaign.'

'But Boy's booked the flight. It's all set. Two tickets, United flight at 9.30am on the 23rd. He's off on Saturday. He told me.'

Candi stared. 'But..!' She emitted a strangled cry, turned and ran to the kitchen. There were raised voices. The dining room went quiet. Webby emerged but only offered a shake of the head and an expansive shrug. Candi was screaming and ranting. Boy was placating but Lindi could hear the edge to his words.

'Should I try to mediate?' asked Esther.

'First rule of domestic barneys,' said Hugo, 'don't add to the casualty list.'

'It's been coming,' said Webby. 'Candi's been screwed up all night. She reckons Boy's cooled on their relationship. Couldn't have come at a worse time either.'

'No, indeed.' Hugo clearly interpreted this statement as confirmation of his gossip.

'But,' Lindi gasped, 'they're going away in two and-a-bit days.'

'Woo-hoo.' Hugo again, 'Six months to kiss and make-up.'

A disturbingly loud silence broke out in the kitchen. A door slammed. Boy ran into the room, 'Candi's leaving,' he shouted from the door. 'Can someone talk some sense into her? She was drinking earlier. She's in no state.'

'I'll go,' said Hugo.

Esther grabbed his hand. 'Don't add to the casualty list,' she advised.

'I've got it,' sighed Webby. He was the only sober one there.

As he left, the rest of the room looked to Boy. 'Totally my fault,' he said. 'But please don't ask.'

A few minutes later Webby popped his head back into the room and flashed some keys. 'I'm running her back to her home,' he said. 'I'm using her car; she's already puked out there.'

'I owe you, mate,' said Boy. 'I'll pay your cab fare back here.'

Webby would be gone over an hour, Boy said. The party was spent. Esther was on her phone. Five minutes later a cab hauled up outside. Lindi had arranged to share one back with Hugo and Esther. She said her goodbyes to Shouty and Boy.

Leaving the house, she noticed Toke pulling Boy to one side. He jabbered away urgently and aggressively. Lindi guessed the message Toke was imparting: 'Lindi knows and she's going to tell Mitch.' Boy turned white. His eyes flashed to Lindi. She ran to the cab.

* * *

Thursday 21st February was going to be a big day. It came wrapped in mist. Lindi put boots and coat on, left her phone off and set out between shadowed saplings. Deer-tracks bit into the still-copper leaf litter. Reaching the ridge, she emerged from the dewy vapour into cold angled sunlight. To either side of her mist pooled and played in the valleys and gullies, hemming in the trees.

The next conversation with Boy would set her course. She should shop him to Mitch. Her business ethics demanded it; her professional pride craved it, the code she lived life by called for it.

The only argument for staying quiet came down to one thing – Boy. Speaking out would shipwreck his life, negate every-thing he had spent decades working for. He had been there for her when others ducked away. She enjoyed his company, en-vied the way he attacked life, felt content around him. Lindi had loved, liked and admired Ayan. With Boy her attraction was stronger, the connection ran deeper.

They had become close, even before Ash's arrest. Candi's con-viction that Boy was less committed to their relationship, wasn't groundless. But any warmth Boy felt for Lindi couldn't survive the knowledge that she could bring him down. He knew her too well. He would expect her to keep to her business principles. He'd expect her honesty to ruin him.

Lindi side-lined her threats towards Toke. She wouldn't waste her anger on the blackmailer. Boy was the issue she had to wrestle with.

She imagined his messages piling up on her mobile. Sure enough, her phone revealed eight missed calls from Boy.

Texts exhorted Lindi to call. One had been sent from outside her cottage this morning, asking her to open the door. She wondered if he had used his keys.

The texts were frantic. 'Toke says you've upset some Muslim fundamentalists. I'm worried.'

'Where are you?' said the most recent text. 'We NEED to talk – urgently.'

'Not ready.' She sent back, 'I'll text if that changes.'

'Talk to me before I leave,' appeared when next she checked. She knew it meant, 'don't talk to Mitch before I get a chance to plead my case'.

Among all Boy's messages was one from Kotryna. Lindi tapped to call back.

'Lindi,' snapped Kotryna, on answering. 'Did you sleep with Webby?'

'No. Christ, of course not.'

'Oh, I thought… He has slept with someone. Like a feral tom creeping in this morning. He has the smell of her all over him… Oh, never mind. It's not important.' Kotryna hung up.

Lindi left the ridge to follow a footpath arrow signed to Camworth. She diverted off on to another path, a shorter way, she hoped. It plunged down between towering silhouettes of mature beech and oak, their tree-tops vanishing into the mist. Shrouded saplings sprang out to ambush her.

A new text from Boy awaited her: 'Toke thinks you're up on the ridge. Just so u know.' Lindi's pace quickened. On one side of the ridge a straight road split the valley, but it was submerged beneath the white blanket. On the other side, a higher road snaked along, halfway up the chalk. Lindi had seen cars weaving in and out of its misty fringe during the morning.

If Toke had driven along it, he'd possibly have spotted her. Soaking leaves cloaked her path. Sharply defined hoof prints rambled back and forth across it. Lindi wished she'd skirted the wood. It was too easy to imagine the shade of the Hart rearing out at her in this veiled landscape. Every half-seen projection became an antler or a clubbing branch. She ran now, knowing the village lay below her. She half-tripped and caught a scream as some creature barrelled up from right beside her, a whirring clatter of frantic flight, a squall of propelling wings.

Fifty metres on, the shape of a spire loomed above her and she emerged on to deserted village lanes. The Camworth Arms was close, so she treated herself to a sandwich. She called Ash and chatted to him and Ayan. Ammi came on the phone and cajoled her to come and join them, perhaps in a month or two, just for a holiday, maybe a longer stay. The call ended. Lindi knew her life was at a crossroads. The mist lifted before she was halfway back to Hartsdell.

It was evening before she called Boy. 'I'm at the cottage.'

'On my way.'

She watched the road. Two cars turned up. Boy was in the first. The second was a silver saloon. Toke stepped out.

23 SHONA

Friday night May 24 2019

I arrived at the lab 25 minutes earlier than I'd told Leroy. His blue van sulked on its usual hedge-hugging spot. A huge anonymous grey van was the only other car-park occupant.

I pressed the door keypad button for Leroy to buzz me in. Peering inside there was no sign of him. I hunted out my keys and entered. The door clicked and locked behind me.

A burly 30-40-something man I didn't recognise came running through the internal doors. His open brown shirt was an almost perfect colour match for his close-cropped hair. He wiped his hands on a towel. He wasn't pleased to see me.

I stepped back.

'I need some ID, lady,' he said as he slowed and walked towards me.

'Where's Leroy?'

'Night off; he's revising. Said there'd be no-one here until seven.' His east-European accent nuzzled the c's and s's.

I ferreted in my handbag for the lab pass keeping my eyes on him. 'That's near enough.' I flashed the pass.

He threw the small towel towards the reception desk and moved closer. I extended my arm, so the pass was in his face. 'Shona Patterson,' he nodded. 'That checks, you're good to go.'

'Now let's see your ID.'

He lifted a laminated card from a shirt pocket and handed it over. It gave his name as George Stonis, his job as Security Guard, his company as SPS Services and a date of issue as two years ago. I figured I could have knocked one up in an hour. There was a phone number on the back.

'No objection if I call this?'

'That's what it's there for,' he shrugged.

'How come Leroy's card's got his picture on it?'

'Has it?' He knew I was bluffing.

'To do your job properly, you need to stay in sight of the doors.'

'When you gotta go,' he said taking his card back. 'You always this paranoid?'

I walked past him. 'I'm going to be on my rounds now,' I said. 'I'm expecting a visitor. Call my extension when he turns up.'

'Your number on the list?'

'Yes.'

Why had I lied about a visitor? Some defensive mechanism kicking in to make him think he'd have some explaining to do if he was caught cleaving off my head. I'd been over-cautious, but murder enquiries make you twitchy. And he was wearing leather gloves. Do men wear gloves in the loo?

Wet splashes glazed the floor of my room. Perhaps the security guard had been touching up some foxy fish he fancied – he wouldn't have been the first. Or, more likely, my colleagues were running tests on Gone Puss before they left.

I ignored my feeding station and used a side-lab set-up with equipment for extracting and amplifying DNA. I had two pieces of material I was going to test. First the bloodied tissue I'd bagged at Boy's cottage, which I assumed was daubed with Lindi Mills' blood. Hossein may not believe me, but, if I'd already done the DNA work, I assumed he would ask his lab guys to check this DNA against that of the corpse. Why wouldn't he?

The second sample was the handkerchief dropped by the

man waiting at my cottage last night. It was a long shot, but he hadn't visited with good intentions. I wanted to confirm the stain on the hankie was blood and, if so, did it belong to the handkerchief owner? Using the lab's equipment and the new next-gen sequencer, I could do the test in around two and a half hours.

I separated the DNA using cheap silica gel kits. When I'd washed away the contaminants and checked the purity was good enough, my samples were popped into the thermal cycler to amplify the DNA.

It was a routine process and I left it to feed lab specimens. My mind was whizzing faster than the cycler. Was Boy capable of murder? Would I tip-off Hossein about Lindi being the victim if it led him straight to Boy?

Could Boy really be in Venezuela? Had he ever gone to Patagonia? The only evidence I had was gleaned from mobile calls, texts and Skype sessions, showing anonymous indistinguishable hotel rooms. I set no store by the Facebook posts.

But if Toke attacked and bruised me, was that just a bizarre coincidence? Was it Toke or Boy who had killed Lindi? I was mentally scribbling down notes. I'd made a start on Shelby's manuscript.

I called Webby. 'Where are you?'

'Pub, with Toke and Hugo. Shouty's here, though you'd barely know it from all he's said.'

'You drinking?'

'No, you asked me not to.'

'Webby, please leave. It's going to come to a head tonight. I can feel it. Whatever the game is, it's on. Please can you go to the cottage now?'

'Tonight? Really? I've got to drive Hugo home later.'

'Shouty'll do it. I'll call him now. He owes me.'

I phoned a sheepish Shouty, who sullenly agreed to drive Hugo home.

I threw myself into feeding. Later, I broke off from work to put the DNA into the next gen sequencer. This was the expensive bit. And it would leave a computer trail – straight back to me. Would the police recompense my lab for the materials I'd used, if I helped them solve a murder? If not, would Shelby's book royalties cover it?

I began filling my little notebook with all the events since last Saturday, while the sequencer read and assembled DNA from the two samples. It was slowly building up a picture of their genetic code. I'd been in the lab coming up for two hours before my scrambled thoughts worked round to an anomaly. If the smart grey van belonged to the new security guard, that didn't explain the presence of Leroy's scruffy blue van in the far corner of the car-park.

Was Leroy tied up in the gents?

Abandoning my experiments, I hunted around. OK, nothing unusual in the gents according to my limited experience.

I took a deep breath and pushed at the door to the thrumming pump room. It was where I'd dump anyone I wanted out of the way. The light switch location was known only to an inner circle of aquatic engineers. The low blue light of the labs blustered in through the door but quickly scampered back to the threshold, buffeted by the low throb, and cowed by menacing pipe and tank shadows.

Leroy could easily have been bound and gagged somewhere in the darkness, but I wasn't going in there after him. An empty bucket of aquarium water and a dripping net were against the wall inside the door. That made sense of the splashes I'd seen. It suggested I'd disturbed George in the middle of some weird security practices.

I marched to reception. George's feet were splayed up on the desk, instantly doing far more to bolster his security guard credentials than his pass ever had. He glanced up.

'Why is Leroy's blue van here?'

'What blue van?'

'Leroy drives a shabby old van,' I scanned the further reaches of the car-park. It was gone.

'Leroy comes by bike, Princess,' he said.

'The grey van is yours I take it?'

'Why?'

'There was a blue van parked there earlier. It's gone now. Whose was it?'

'No idea. It's gone. You need to calm down. What time is your visitor coming?'

'Visitor?' I started, before recalling my lie. 'Never mind. I've got to make some calls.' I sped back through the doors. If George had come here to murder me, he'd be convinced by now that he'd be doing the world a kindness if he did.

Back at my workstation I texted Shouty. 'Calling u in two mins, go to the loo.'

Then I phoned him. It was 9.15pm, Toke and Hugo should be a few rounds to the good by now.

'This a typical day for you?' Shouty wasn't having a good time, I could tell.

'Pretty much,' I said. 'Webby?'

The doors to the aquarium opened and the guard came in. He saw me on the phone and hesitated. I gave him a questioning stare.

'Later,' he said and left.

'Long gone' Shouty's voice rose over the background bar racket. 'Your ears must be burning. This whole crap night is about you, you know. Toke's livid. Hugo's stirring. I'm so fucking compromised. Do you know what you're doing? Toke's spitting tacks about some Facebook comment. Reckons the police are still investigating him and, as of today, one of his associates. He didn't say anything before Webby left, but he's convinced that Kotryna's helped you to set him up. I can't say anything. It's causing mega friction.'

'Are he and Hugo getting blitzed?'

'Hugo is, but Toke's being cautious. I played the "driver" card, as you demanded.'

'Why is Hugo going for it?'

'He's been caught playing away. It came out earlier today when the police needed his alibi. It included dates when he'd told Esther he was working. He didn't think on his feet fast enough.'

'Hugo? Hugo's been unfaithful to Esther?'

'It may have escaped your notice, Shona, but Hugo will make a pass at most things in a skirt, and anything in a trouser-suit. Ask Lotte.'

Hugo was an infamous flirt, but I'd thought that was as far as it went.

'If Hugo is such a letch, how come he's never tried it on with me?' I didn't know whether to feel thankful or suicidal. I'd have to review my selection of trouser-suits.

Shouty let out a sigh. 'You really don't want to know?'

'Now I have to.'

'O-K. "Too damaged," he says. Reckons every time he's got you both in the mood, you go all maudlin and start banging on about Boy. He says you'd fall to pieces, get too clingy.'

'Well he's...' I couldn't think of anything bad enough. '...mixing his metaphors. Who was he seeing?'

'That's what makes it worse this time; one of Esther's sisters.'

'Oh no, not Judith?'

'No idea. In your shoes, I'd count myself lucky. I'd better get back. This purgatory is going to last another two hours, plus a curry by my reckoning.'

'Shouty,' I felt a mad gratitude, 'you're doing great, thanks. I may still need help.'

'That's an understatement.' He clicked off.

I fed the shy little bobtail squids. They glowed with excitement.

I went back to my experiment. The sequencer matches the DNA to a reference human genome. I had results. Not one, but two identical matches came through. In each sample, one of the genomes was better represented than the other. In my experience that would be from the blood. The other set was more fragmented, probably from the hankie owner and the tissue handler. I made notes:

1) Two sets of DNA were on the hankie I'd found by the road:
-

It was blood on it and it belonged to a female. I called this person 'V' (for victim?)

A second set of DNA on the hankie belonged to a male, 'O' (for owner?)

2) Two sets of DNA were on the tissue I'd found in Dell End kitchen: -

This blood belonged to the same female, 'V'

A second set of DNA on the tissue belonged to the same man, 'O'

The person who had cleaned up after Lindi when she was bleeding – dying? – in Dell End (or Dead End as I was starting to think of it) had been waiting for me outside my cottage. I was too astonished and horrified to be triumphant.

I only had, I reminded myself, evidence (almost certainly not admissible in court) that linked my cottage stalker to an injury at Dell End sustained, presumably, by Lindi. However, the test was repeatable.

If this DNA matched the victim's, all the other coincidences made sense: my missing doll, my mum's vanished ring, Lindi's disappearance, the fracas outside the cottage, the timeline, Boy's depar –

Boy.

Boy would be prime suspect in the murder enquiry. The neighbours said he'd been in the cottage with Lindi on the night of the murder. For a day and a half, a grenade had bounced around in my mind that Boy could be a murderer. This had just shaken the pin loose and there was no way that Harry or I were prepared for that explosion.

I must have some of Boy's DNA somewhere at home, surely. I could test it before I spoke to the police. Only... only if it was Boy's DNA, then it meant he wasn't in Patagonia, or Venezuela, but in Hartsdell, leaving his hankie outside my cottage. He was here, stalking me.

Why would you lie about being on the other side of the world for three months? To put distance between yourself and a murder. I ran through my phone conversations with him. He knew I was investigating Lindi, stirring it up, getting closer. Oh God, suppose he –

My mobile went.

A text opened: 'Get out of there now.' It wasn't from Shouty or Webby. I didn't recognise the number, but its urgency held me. 'No questions. You're in danger. Just get out.'

I had no idea who this was. Could I trust them? If this danger came from the guard, well, I had to get past him to leave. The tranquil low light and calming gurgling of my surroundings was instantly repackaged as a shadowy sinister backdrop. I had my keys out when the landline on my desk rang. I jumped, hesitated then picked it up and gingerly put it to my ear.

'Hey, Shona.'

'Leroy?' Phew! 'You're not tied up in the pump room.'

'Yeah. Er... no, not really!'

'Aren't you revising?'

'Kinda.'

'There's another guard here.'

'George.'

'Yes, you know him?' A wash of relief.

'Kinda.'

'Do you drive a blue van?'

'No, I got a bike.'

'Why have you called, Leroy? It's not a good time.' I pictured the blue van. I'd seen it in Hartsdell yesterday, I realised.

'How much do octopuses cost?'

'Why on –'

'I looked it up online. They say $200.'

'Probably a bit steep for our specimens, why?' I scrutinised Gone Puss's tank. I couldn't see him.

'Because George offered me £500 if I'd let him do my shift tonight.'

'I don't understand.' But I did understand why George felt wrong. I looked at the top of Gone Puss's tank. It was lifted slightly off, like a Tupperware lid letting air in on Harry's sandwiches. If George had left Gone Puss in that bucket, he could be anywhere by now. People didn't realise how capable octopuses were out of water.

'He said he wanted to borrow your octopus.'

'Borrow?!'

'Someone on the internet will pay him two grand to use it in a film, George says.'

'That doesn't sound likely, Leroy.'

'He said they were always escaping. If anyone missed it before he put it back, everyone would think it had got out.'

'Not on my watch.'

'But if you can buy them for £150... It doesn't make sense.'

It did to me. I could hear footsteps approaching.

'Leroy, just call the police. Tell them I'm being attacked by a fake security guard.'

'Nah, Shona,' Leroy giggled. 'He's after the octopus.'

'Do it, Leroy. I'm serious. Do it now.' The door opened. I snapped the phone down.

George sauntered in. 'No visitors so far.'

I picked up my mobile and placed it in my open bag. I got up from my desk but kept it between us.

'It's still early.'

'It's still fucking bullshit *chiulpedra*, that's what it is.' I'd no idea what he'd said but no more 'nice' George, was what it meant.

'What's happened to my octopus?'

'In a bucket.'

'No, he's not. If you put him in there, he had other ideas.'

He shrugged. He wasn't here for Gone Puss. 'Creatures disappear,' his accent tripped over more c's and s's. 'Women too, I hear. Your friend in the village, first her boy, then her.'

'You mean Lindi?' Had this man killed her? Had he disappeared her son?

'Let's talk about you and the unholy shit-storm you're creating.'

'Leroy's calling the police,' I said.

'I don't think so.' He had reached my desk. I stepped back, taking the phone off its stand and dialling. He calmly grabbed its base and hurled it away. Its lead flew out. Dead phone, possibly dead octopus, limited life-span lab lady.

He hitched his backside onto the desk. 'Help me here. I don't know whether you'll respond best to threats or a beating.' He'd picked up my Biologist mug. He read it, amused.

'I don't respond to either.' I struggled to picture Toke or Boy chopping up women – neither seemed the type. This brute would do it. I had the clear impression he was used to doing it. The emanations that had me backing towards the door when I first encountered him were an instinctive reaction to the fetid breath of a predator.

'Wrong answer.' He hurled my mug at the nearest tank. It smashed through and the glass exploded. Gallons of water and all the bobtail squid gushed to the floor. I screamed, ran to the wall.

'Let's talk about your son. Harry. Down Welwyn way tonight, I hear. He's with Helen, right?'

How did he know? 'The police are all over this.'

'Yes. We need them not to be. Toke has an alibi for your fuck-party; me. I've told the police he was with me that night. So, you will stop now. No more stupid Facebook posts. Tell the police you were mistaken. There was no attack. The bruise wasn't the same, it was just a mistake, a mad coincidence. Do you understand?'

My mouth dried up. My bruise *had* been a mad coincidence, but even that admission wilted away. I didn't understand at all. Up until this moment, I had been playing a game, I realised. Find my attacker, link them to the murder, send them to jail, pass Go. It was an intellectual challenge, a plan to prove someone guilty, an infantile attempt to impress an arrogant cop.

My worst fear was having an awkward altercation with Toke

after two pints. This jackal ambushing me in my place of work formed no part of my schemes. I had naively tinkered around with things I didn't have a clue about and awoken a feral monster from a world I didn't know existed.

He turned his stare from dying squid to me. Nothing in his gaze changed. 'No, I see you don't understand.'

He was still perched on the desk, but a long knife had appeared in his hands – his gloved hands. My mind spelt out the ramification of the gloves. He was going to cut me. He would calmly and cruelly damage me until he was sure I would stop my meddling. And I would stop. Because he would do worse to Harry.

I stumbled along the wall. He was heavily built, but spry. I wouldn't get past him. My car keys were in my hand, but I wouldn't get to the door before he was on me. My phone was on, but I wouldn't get to two nines, let alone three.

I reached for the pump room door. There was no lock on it. I'd never keep him out.

'Make me fetch you out of that room, I'll scar you twice as much, twice as deep, as I was going to.' He unhurriedly stepped around the desk.

'Please don't.'

'Afterwards, compare your scars with Kotryna's. Hers are in some private places. She'll tell you to keep your pretty mouth shut. She'll say, better to suffer in silence.'

The door to the pump room nudged open behind me. I stepped back involuntarily.

'No further, lady' he warned.

'I won't, please.' The pump room's throbbing darkness made me more fearful. It would grant more licence to his cruelty. I glanced at the tank fishnet leaning on the wall, too flimsy; at the bucket, lightweight plastic. He would cut me, and I'd suffer it because the fear he instilled in me was worse than anything he was about to do.

'Come.' He waggled the knife in front of my face. 'Best remove some clothes. I might go too deep if I have to cut you through them.'

'Yes, I'll...'

I reached down as if to undo the bottom button on my lab coat, picked up the bucket and hurled water into his face. He bellowed. I ran past him. Gone Puss's limbs slithered over and around his head.

Through the room's double doors. I heard them open again behind me as I hit the next pair. Out into reception, I thumped the buzzer button on the desk as I ran past. I twisted the door lock. He was in the room behind me, cussing me in a language I didn't know.

The door wrenched open. I slipped through into the car-park. I wouldn't reach my car in time. I found buttons on my keys. The wrong one, pushing again: the right one. Indicators flashed. I still wouldn't make it, unless... The door clicked closed behind me. I heard him scrabble at it.

...but it had locked again. He would have to go back to the desk. I was at my car, in it and slamming the ignition button as the door opened and he bundled out. I lurched forward, screeched in the tightest lock the car was capable of, belted out of the exit and through the Science Park.

✻ ✻ ✻

I parked up on a long dimly lit lay-by just outside Cambridge. Ten minutes, maybe more, had gone by, but my heart was still clamouring to leave my chest, my hands wouldn't still. I was trying to assimilate what had just happened. If George hadn't killed women himself, he had ordered it or been involved in some way. Word of my meddling had reached him – hell, my stupid words were everywhere – and he had reacted to close me down. He knew someone who knew me well enough to know about Harry being at Helen's. What now? I had escaped being cut, but the threat I still felt was palpable.

My escape was purely down to the luck that Gone Puss had

stayed in the bucket; not a very octopussy thing to do. I wasn't consciously aware of that at the time. My mind had closed down in the face of George's unemotional evil. It had rationalised that a few warning scars would save Harry and me from worse.

What had then changed? His suggestion that I remove some clothing to help him cut me more effectively, had sparked something. It wasn't that I thought he'd get some perverted thrill out of the situation. It was the utter demeaning certainty that he wouldn't. It was a purely practical consideration. To him, I was just a piece of meat to cut and control. His scorn had torn away my compliance.

I had to make some calls and top of the list was Kotryna. She didn't answer. She wouldn't pick up my call, I realised. I texted her: 'Help! a big brute just tried to cut me. He said he'd scarred you too. Why? Who is he? Sho.'

I called Webby. I took a deep breath and clicked. 'I've got something to tell you. Where are you?'

'Out of Cambridge. I've been at the cottage. I'm away now. Tell me what?'

'There's some primeval beast, probably Eastern European. He just tried to knife me,' I said. 'He said he had previously scarred Kotryna. Is he a friend of Toke's?'

'Jesus Fuck! That's Martini! Enough, Sho. You're on your own.'

'Does he work for Toke?'

'Other way 'round, more like. You don't understand. That man is the scourge of Kotty's life. He damaged her. He damaged her in ways you don't want to know about. He still gives her nightmares. Christ, he gives me nightmares.'

'Add me to the list.'

'If Martini's involved, Toke can't help you.' Webby's breath sounded ragged.

'He has to. This monster is threatening Harry.'

'He threatens everybody. Kotty warned me to stay out of it. If she hears Martini's involved, she'll leave. She'll just vanish into the night, back to Lithuania.'

I couldn't unsend my text, so I bit my tongue. 'We've got to finish this now, Webby. I'm going to meet with Toke – now, tonight.'

'Shon –'

I tapped off, dialled Shouty.

'How's Toke?' I asked when he answered.

'Hang on, Lotte,' he said in a staged shout, moving out of others' earshot. 'It's loud in here.'

I couldn't wait for his dissembling, 'Well?'

'Morose. He just received a call. No idea who from, but it didn't cheer him up.'

'I can guess. I need to speak to him.'

'You so don't.'

'Please Shouty. Just put Toke on.'

There was quite a delay before Toke came on. 'Shona, my lovely,' the soft voice drifted over the hubbub, 'Scott tells me you want a word.' I had been expecting belligerence and I was being fed saccharine smarm.

'We need to talk, Toke.'

'You've had several opportunities to do just that, but you didn't seem keen. As far as I know I'm still blocked from calling you. It doesn't help comms.'

'Remember, I didn't originally know it was you who attacked me or sent that text.' I slipped too easily on to the defensive.

'I didn't attack anyone. In fact, it wasn't actually me that sent the text. I thought you'd realised that now, what with all your amateur sleuthing. Only this morning, I recall, you were proclaiming my innocence, Shona. All over Facebook, I heard.' He sounded exactly like the cultured jovial man I played tennis with. 'And, as we both know, I didn't murder anyone.'

Toke was a good bridge player. I didn't hold many cards and I needed to use one to finesse this conversation. 'I have new information since then.'

'My reputation dies a little every time you open your mouth. Info about what now?'

'For starters: about that goon you sent round to intimidate

me.'

'Oh dear! More unsubstantiated ramblings. You don't learn, do you? Poor Scott, white as a sheet, trembling when he handed me this phone, Hugo's marriage has hit the buffers, I'm being kept from my preferred drinking establishments. William's been dragged in and wants out. Best stop soon, Shona, while there's anyone left in Hartsdell who'll still talk to you.'

'This fake guard you sent round with a knife spoke to me – a little too much. I need convincing that if I stay quiet, he stays away from Harry and me. I either meet with the police for that assurance or I meet with you, which?'

'When?' he asked wearily.

'Right now.'

'Extremely inconvenient. Where?'

I described the lay-by I was in. He knew it and estimated it would take 15 minutes to get there. I said I'd only wait for 15 and if he was any longer, or if he wasn't alone, I'd be gone. Then I added: 'One last thing, give your phone to Shouty now.'

A laugh, 'That's not happening.'

'I'm deadly serious. I've survived one run-in with George or Martini; I don't want another one. I'm not having you phoning him to join our discussion.'

'I really have no idea what you're bleating about, but I'll give Scott my phone if it salves your paranoia.'

'Right, clock's ticking, you better get here.'

I called Shouty back. 'Is he gone?'

'Yeah. Says he's going to meet with you. I know you've got a plan, Shona. I can't see it working.'

'Maybe not, but it's the only plan in town. Did he give you his phone?'

'Yes. He wasn't happy about it.'

'Christ. I hope this works. You've got a job to do. Best get Hugo home now.'

'On our way. I know Toke seems a dashing old chancer, but his back's against a wall. You can't trust him.'

'I know.' I hung up.

＊ ＊ ＊

More calls. I determined that I had no alternative but to alarm Helen. I told her that I'd had 'threats at work,' and to ensure all the doors and windows were locked tonight. The police were aware, it was only a precaution. I then spent ten minutes going over in my mind what I would say to Toke if he turned up.

A text flashed up from Kotryna. 'I don't know this man. U don't know what u do. Stay away from me, stay away from Webby. My advice: leave Hartsdell. You swim with sharks.'

Don't mess with marine life was a message that had reached me too late in life. Kotryna wasn't helpful but reading between the lines it confirmed my own view of George/Martini. She also confirmed everyone's opinion that I didn't know what I had gotten into or what I was doing. I included myself in that ever-lengthening list.

Something else Kotryna had said to me on Wednesday made more sense now. I texted Webby: 'Kotryna told me that "she knew", what did she mean? Call me later.' I put my phone away. Webby was driving to Hartsdell. Shouty would be bundling a disgruntled Hugo into a car. I was on my own – at least that was a situation I was familiar with.

Could Toke have a second phone on him? If so, he could still call George? How would I be sure that Toke was really alone in the car and that George wouldn't be lying down on the back seat, clutching his knife in his massive gloved fist?

Sweat broke out on my forehead. I had never been sure that my call to meet with Toke was smart, but after my altercation with George, it had felt necessary. Now it felt ridiculous. I was close to a panic attack. I checked my car-boot for items that I'd pitched into it earlier as potentially useful in the event of an attack. None of them would be of any help if George was in Toke's car.

I'd created my own murder mystery party for one, set out all the clever clues, but missed the big one – I was the victim. I needed a saviour.

I pulled out my phone, found Ant and hit the call button.

'Miss Patterson.' Ant spoke my name as if it was a wrong answer in a lame quiz show but he was still there for me. This man's patience was infinite.

I told him about 'George' waiting for me at work, that he was there to hurt me and shut me up. I told him I had recorded George making threats to me on my phone. I went big on George's knife and willingness to cut Gone Puss and me into bits like so much calamari.

Ant listened without interrupting but with, I suspected, a growing sense of disbelief at my ability to generate trouble and place myself at its centre. 'Where are you now?'

'On a lay-by outside Cambridge.'

'You need to go to the police station in Cambridge, Miss Patterson. Get safe and report this.'

'I can't. I've arranged to meet Mr Toakley here. I can't have these monsters threatening my son.'

'No, far better to get my colleagues to apprehend this fake guard now, while he's leaving Cambridge. He could be the murderer Hossein's looking for.'

'Or Toke sent him after me, while he gave himself an alibi. I need Toke to stop this.'

'It's more likely he'll finish what he's started.'

'That's why I called, Ant, I was just been thinking he could bring this George with him.'

'Exactly. Remember when I told you I have a nose for danger? It's glowing now, it's gone nova.'

'Oh shit, they're here!' A silver saloon was indicating to enter the far end of the lay-by.

'Just get out of there, Miss P... Shona – drive!' As usual, Ant spoke sense. I pulled open the car door, leapt in and sped off, on to the dark almost empty road. 'I'm on my way, heading south, Ant, towards you.'

'Put the phone on speaker. I'll intercept you on the Linbourn by-pass.'

I put the phone on the car-seat, engaging speaker phone at my third attempt. I was on my usual route home. I saw the silver saloon slip back onto the road behind me. It all seemed horribly familiar. The car behind me flashed its lights twice. I ignored them. The few times the car passed under street lights, I could only make-out one figure in the car. I assumed it must be Toke.

'The other car's coming after me,' I shouted at the phone, bouncing on the passenger seat.

'How many in it?' asked Ant. He was running, he sounded breathless.

'As far as I can see, only one.'

Heading towards the railway crossing, I panicked. Suppose its gates came down before I got to it. Something flashed red ahead. It could have been the gates descending or it may have been car brake lights, but it was enough to send me screeching off west on to the minor rural road. I was on the same route as the previous night. Still all too familiar.

I assumed Toke was following. I decided to repeat my escape manoeuvre from last night. I turned into the quarry again. I sped up after the sharp bend. Cut my lights and swerved into the quarry entrance. The buddleia bushes formed looming, grabbing shadows ahead and to the sides of me. Some of them took on the bearish appearance of George.

Nervous of crashing, I flicked my lights to see a path through them. I was straying off what passed for the main track – a couple of chalky ruts – so swerved to get back on to it. There was a low chain across with a notice on it. I had driven through it before I could correct my skid. The ground was bumpier and sloped down more precipitously than my car or driving skills were comfortable with. I remembered the drop into a water-filled quarry ahead of me. I swung back to point uphill and hit the brakes. The car shuddered to a halt, three or four lengths from the quarry edge. There was barely enough light in the sky to make out the drop or the still water brooding darkly beyond.

I was on a slope. My engine was dead. The car lights were off. My chest heaved. I lowered my passenger window and listened.

It was a mistake. The mournful dirge of the reeds drifted into the car. I recalled Harry's response to this place. His mindless urgent fear. Why had I been drawn back here again?

'There's nothing to worry about'

'There is.' What had he sensed in its stillness? What fate had revealed itself to him?

'What's that?'

'It's just reeds.'

But it wasn't. The reeds' rustle hid another sound. A car engine. I made out movement. A car rolled to a halt ten metres from the side of mine. Lights blazed; scowling beams lit up my car.

Grabbing the phone, I whispered loudly for Ant.

'Here,' he sounded busy and fretful, probably driving.

'Change of plan,' I hissed. 'I thought the crossing gates were coming down, so I turned off west.

'Shit. Has he followed you?'

'Yes. I'm in that old quarry with the lake. He's found me.'

'What? What possessed you to go there?'

'I was hoping to lose him. I'm going to reason with him. I'll keep the phone on.'

'Shona. For pity's sake. I'm 20 minutes away from you. Stay in the car. Lock the doors. Drive. Get out of there.'

Something in his faraway fear, brought back Harry's tremulous keening. 'Go, mummy, go, go.'

'He could ram me; I'm too close to the quarry. Stay quiet, Ant. You'll hear everything. I'll get him to confess.'

'This isn't a movie, Sh –'

I stepped out of my car. The phone buried halfway under a sleeve. The other car's headlights blinded me. Its engine was still a throaty roar, but my senses knew that someone had got out of it.

He left the engine going. Perhaps he was concerned I might yet drive away. A man stepped into the light beams, a hawkish silhouette.

'Well,' he called above the throb, 'this wasn't on my sat-nav's prior destinations. You seem to have dragged us to the skanky end of nowhere.'

'I wasn't sure you were alone.' I stepped round to the passenger side of the car so he could see I wasn't going to dive back in and drive off. We were here now. I had to have this out.

'As ever, quite alone. And, finally, we're alone.' It was Toke. 'Shona, my dear, you have deposited us both deep in a special hell of your making. How do you propose to make it go away?' His voice was sing-song. His anger, barely chained, strained beneath it.

'I can't. If I proclaim your innocence, it makes things worse. Anyway, the evidence is too stacked against you. It's out of my hands.'

'You say evidence. To me it's just bizarre coincidences and baseless rumours.' He perched on his throbbing bonnet with exaggerated casualness. I felt sure it had been him last night outside my cottage.

'I want you to call off your fake guard, George, or whatever his real name is.'

'I don't think I know any "Georges". They tell me there's a murderer out there somewhere. I imagine your naive Facebook posts upset him. Your capacity for prattling on about things that you – of all people – ought to keep shtum about, has probably ruffled the feathers of some scary people. My guess, one of them is trying to shut you down.'

'Call him off or I go to the police.' It sounded an empty threat.

'I really don't control these people. They are outside my circle of influence.'

If he was bluffing, he sounded convincing. Ant, if he was still listening, would probably be turning around and heading back home.

'You attack women. Sooner or later that always gets out of hand.'

'Not that old chestnut again. If you're so convinced I'm a murderer, why bring me to a disused quarry. Have you got a death-wish?'

'You were worried enough to send your thug George round to silence me.'

'So you claim.'

'So he claimed,' I needed to get more creative. 'He pulled a knife on me, told me you needed him to shut me up. He would have done it too. I recorded it all.'

Toke shrugged.

I pulled my phone out of my sleeve, 'You want to listen?'

'No.' He started up, off the car bonnet. He was leaving.

I tried something I hoped would shock him out of his complacency. 'I haven't yet told the police about Lindi Mills. Call George off and I won't.'

Amusement infected his answer. 'Lindi Mills? What about her?'

'You murdered her.'

He chuckled. His head shook in the reflected light of the car beams. 'Wide of the mark again, Shona. You really need to check your facts. I'm astonished the police listen to your wild theories. Lindi Mills isn't dead.'

'She was lying headless in a ditch. That usually does it. I am a biologist. I know about these things.' Nothing I said provoked him.

'I suspect we both know that's not true.'

'We'll know soon enough. I have a DNA match.'

'This really is beyond desperate, Shona.' He moved back to his car door. I noticed he, too, was wearing gloves.

'Is it? Where's your handkerchief?'

The silhouette stopped and turned back. A long telling moment, before, 'What handkerchief?'

'Someone waited for me by my cottage last night,' I said. 'They dropped a hankie.'

'I did not drop a hankie.'

'So, it was you.'

'I'd already lost my handke –'

'It turned out to have blood on it. Two sets of DNA: the hankie owner's and someone else.'

'Whose?' His blasé confidence vanished.

'A bloody tissue I took from Lindi's kitchen has got the same two sets of DNA on it.'

'What does that mean?' He was processing now, working it out.

'What I think? The blood of the murdered woman was mopped up in the kitchen by the same person who owns that hankie.'

Toke's dark shape nodded its expressionless head. 'You see, I stupidly thought you were here to sort things out. No, you're the same crazy bitch you always were.' He came for me.

'Stay back,' I shouted, ineffectively warding him off with my phone. 'I'm recording all this.'

'You're going to keep throwing stuff at me until something sticks. Convince the police with some crap out of a test-tube.'

'Stay back, Toke.' My foot caught on something. I looked down. A worn-out child's shoe was etched in his headlights. Footsteps scrunched towards me.

'Let's see if your cheap phone survives a dip in the quarry.' He was a giant shadow in the car headlights, his right hand out of sight.

'What have you got behind your back?... Toke?' Whatever it was, it would do me harm. I cringed back against my passenger door. 'What's in... Toke?'

'Not a thing.' He kept coming.

'No, please don't...' I screamed.

A shrill echo of Harry's scream.

From all those years ago.

As if he'd seen all this play out.

As if he'd known.

The phone was wrenched from my hand. It flew. A dark thing

streaking away low into the bushes. Ant's shrill warnings silenced by the distance.

24 MURDER

February 21 2019 Murder 1

Lindi watched while Boy and Toke conversed on the pavement outside the cottage. Across the darkening road, the neighbours' curtains twitched, their dog barked testily.

Eventually Boy alone approached her door. Lindi saw Toke pick at his phone. She wondered who would be answering that call.

Lindi opened the door and locked it behind Boy. 'What's Toke doing here?'

'Fretting; he thinks you're gunning for us.'

'That man's vile. Why would you trust him to finesse your scam?'

'It didn't start off as a scam, Lindi. Can I explain?'

She led him into the kitchen. 'Don't bother. I see exactly how it played out. I understand that you did the work in good faith. That doesn't stop it being fraud. Mitch is the victim here. He doesn't deserve it.'

'Yes, you're right, on every count. Toke is a nightmare. Shouty warned me. But his opportunity looked too good to turn down. Toke brought a perfect client to my table. Carl Brindle of PLS had all the credentials and his business strategy made sense. It was he who insisted Toke sat in the middle of the deal as the broker. I've since been informed by their finance guy that Toke had something on Brindle and used that to drive things through when they hit stumbling blocks. Whatever Toke had, Brindle couldn't convince his father to follow through on the contract.'

'You know what? Sod the sordid detail. What hurts is that you used me, employed me as your patsy. And now I'm totally compromised: I either shop you – costing you over £6m and a nasty legal record – or I'm party to your fraud.'

'I know. I have a small bit of mitigation.'

She snorted.

'Mitch is a friend as well as a rival, but he's an aggressive businessman. He originally talked up an exit figure that began with an eight. His cunning plan was that bad debts would pull the final deal down, but he's not too upset about the final pay-out. Some of the work we did on PLS is beyond anything he and the Yanks have got. That's how he's managed to sell it to his US bosses.'

'That's Mitch, not me.'

'Well, as you pointed out, I could have pulled in anyone to book-keep and work on the bad debts. I hunted you down because I found myself thinking about you. I wanted an excuse to get back in touch. Initially you were a fantasy, top of my wish-list, but I expected to find you working as CEO of some thriving paint company. When you weren't, my curiosity took over. I wanted to help put you back where you should be.'

'In other words, a charity case. Boy, whatever you say now, it's too late. You should have trusted me before you knew I knew.'

'I did something else three days ago, before I knew you knew.'

'What?'

Two United Airline tickets came from his jacket pocket and snapped on to the worktop. Boy's and Lindi's names were booked on a flight in 36 hours' time – a flight to Buenos Aires.

'I booked these.'

'Without asking me. What about Candi? When were you

going to tell her?'

'In a way, you did that, last night.'

'Oh, Christ, the poor girl.'

'I know. I was trying to find the right time. She's not taking my calls. You should know that she wasn't going to join me there anyway.'

'Because she's pregnant?'

Hurt mixed with surprise on Boy's features. 'How?'

'Hugo.'

'That figures. Well, Hugo's wrong. The pregnancy's a complete fiction. She convinced me she was pregnant six weeks ago. Maybe she convinced herself. It forced me to ask myself some hard questions about our relationship.'

'And?'

'I didn't see it going that way.' A shake of the head. 'Cand had sensed I was cooling – perhaps before I did. I think it was a reaction to that. She admitted to me two days ago that there was no pregnancy. She'd known for a while. By then the pregnancy news had slipped out to a few friends. She wanted to tell people it was a false alarm in her own way, she said, but she hasn't yet got around to it. You're only the third person to know it's not true. Webby had his ear bent about "her pregnancy" all last night.'

'You made her that desperate?' Lindi was pacing the tiny space.

'Seems so. At Christmas, I stopped mentioning Patagonia to her. I think because she didn't feel like part of my trip any more.'

Lindi's hands sprung apart. 'You have so screwed this up, everything. Can we *please* get rid of Toke? He's evil.'

'Slippery maybe, hardly evil.'

'You have no idea. Just get rid of him. I can't concentrate knowing he's out there, plotting.'

'Toke needs to know you're happy. He suspects something because he knows PLS wouldn't originally pay. He knows I registered a shadow company. He had to, as he was its named director. I threatened I'd shop him for blackmailing Brindle. It wasn't much of a threat, I didn't know the details. The carrot was that I would try to find a way to still pay the £30K finder's fee I'd agreed with him, if he played ball and kept his head down.

'At first he thought I had settled by dealing with the Brindles directly. He's realised for a while that I didn't but can't get his head around the scam. He's sure you've worked it out, though. I've said he only gets paid if my deal with Mitch goes through. He doesn't trust me not to disappear to Argentina and not pay him. Plus, he's paranoid that if you shop us to Mitch, he loses £30K and finds the police at his door.'

'Don't tempt me. He's toxic.' Lindi stared out into the road. 'It's like dealing with a vulture trying to find the fastest way into your corpse. He told me he'd help find Ash but, instead, threatened to maim him.'

'Toke did?'

'Boy, wake up, for fu... You don't know how poisonous he is. You said yourself, he blackmailed Brindle. His business involves sex trade property and legal highs. His hobby is extortion. He boasts about knowing murder details that were never made public. Your friends know; why don't you?'

'I've never been that close to him. I thought he was an old-school charmer whose dad left him too many farms. Alright, I'll go out and placate him.'

Boy left. Lindi watched as Boy and Toke conversed by the cars, before Boy returned. 'He wants to hear it from you. He doesn't trust me but believes you'll give it to him straight.'

'He's not coming in this house. I won't lie to him for you.'

'I know that. Whatever you decide, that's fine.'

'Warn him I'll lay into him, if he comes close.'

Boy went to relay her message. Lindi grabbed a winter jacket. Toke was leaning against the silver car. His features pinched with cold. There would be a frost.

'Well?' said Lindi, hands thrust into opposing sleeves where one gripped her phone. 'What do you want to ask me?'

'Lindi, my dear, one thing has become clear during our brief acquaintance. You are a peculiarly principled lady. You seem to be holding a few aces and I want to know how you intend playing them.'

'I said you'd never get your hands on any of Boy's money.'

'You did, but in the heat of the moment.'

'I meant it. I left last night determined to shop you to Mitch. But it's Boy's business. If he wants to honour his deal with you, even though you screwed up, that's up to him. My condition is that you have nothing more to do with Boy, or me or my son.'

'Naturally I'm devastated, Lindi, but if those are your terms,' Toke's smile was sly. 'And what will you tell our American cousins?'

'Stay clear of us. I won't need to talk to them at all.' Lindi was surprised how certain she sounded, how little it had taken for her to burn her principles. Did she really mean it?

She saw Boy breathe out in the cold air.

'I'll take you on trust, Lindi,' Toke said, but immediately negated the words. 'You know Mart will pay you and Ash a visit should you give me cause. Don't think your lad's safe in Karachi.'

'I'm done with your threats, Toakley. I've reported you to the police alre –'

She broke off as a sporty car bounded around the corner into the quiet cul-de-sac. It skidded on the slick surface and rode up over the verge. A screech and it stopped askew next to Toke's saloon, blocking the road. Candi threw open the door and leapt out.

'You callous bastard, Boy Compton.' Her words frosted the air. Candi wriggled between the cars. Lindi already had her back to the onslaught; she was retreating to her front door.

'And you, you two-faced bitch.' Candi raced after Lindi. 'Kiss goodbye to your marketing.'

She caught up with her by the entrance. A violent push sent Lindi through the door. Candi followed her in. 'You were just going to fly-off on *my* trip. Can't get your own man, you, you conniving cow.'

Lindi stumbled through the hall and ducked into the small kitchen. She turned to shut the door, but Candi's momentum carried her through. Lindi heard urgent steps in the hall. Boy's lie came, 'Cand, this is nothing to do with Lindi.'

Candi rounded on Boy, as the two men entered the room. Her grey eyes glistened. 'All our plans!' she sobbed. 'Our start-up, the house, our family, the dreams we had.'

'I only...' Boy started uselessly, 'I never intended it to end this way, Cand.'

'Her son is with Isis!' She flung an arm at Lindi.

'Calm down, Candice,' said Toke. 'You're here to talk, remember.'

Lindi realised Toke must have called her. She had no idea why: mischief, an ally, a diversion?

'Shut up, Toke. I know all about you, blackmailing people.'

'Let's focus on Boy,' said Toke.

'Oh, he's going down. You all are, when I'm through with you. Fraudsters, blackmailers, rapists, terrorists; whores, what a fucking village!'

'I can make it up to you,' Boy promised.

He couldn't.

And then it was too late.

Candi's eyes fixed on the flight tickets on the worktop. She snatched them up, saw the names, screamed and hurled them at Boy. She seized the breadknife off its heavy wooden board. It waved dementedly in her hand as she brandished it at Boy.

Boy backed to the wall. Toke ducked and ran around the worktop.

'I'd waited so, so long.' Candi's keening unhinged tone unnerved Lindi.

She stepped towards Candi, who spun at the movement. Lindi grabbed the heavy breadboard and lashed out, catching Candi's temple. The woman flailed, fell backwards, her feet tangling with one of the wooden bar-stools, her head whipping back against the granite worktop as she went down. The breadknife clattered to the floor.

Lindi stared mortified. Candi was still, then she moaned. Lindi burst past Boy and ran for the stairs. Behind her she heard Boy yell at Toke, 'Get an ambulance. I'll go after her.'

Upstairs, Lindi dived into the bathroom and flicked the bolt.

'It was self-defence, Lindi,' Boy shouted as he raced upstairs. Then outside the door, 'She's conscious; she's going to be OK.'

Lindi stumbled back onto the loo seat, dropping heavily. 'Come out, please. The last person at fault here is you. Candi will be OK. Toke's calling an ambulance.'

Boy continued to plead with her. She had no words.

She heard Boy shout down to Toke. A reply came but she couldn't make it out. Boy's desperation increased, and after a few minutes she heard him shoulder the door. A moment later a second attempt saw the lock fly off. The door burst open. Her hands flew up, 'Don't!' she didn't want him to touch her, to comfort her.

'I didn't know if you were...' his concerns were obvious but unspoken. 'We need to go downstairs. Toke says she's coming 'round. I don't want to leave her with him.'

'Get her to hospital,' implored Lindi. 'I'll tell them it was me.'

Downstairs they found Candi on the floor sitting up. There was no pool of blood. She was holding a glass of water in unsteady hands.

'She came to pretty quickly,' said Toke. 'Says no to an ambulance.'

'I'm OK,' Candi croaked. Tentative fingers probed a vivid bump visible through her dyed black-red hair. Lindi winced at the split in the skin. There was another on her forehead. Neither bled profusely. Toke had been administering to her. Several bloodied tissues were distributed around the floor. A dampened hankie was scrunched beside a dessert bowl of water.

'I'll run you to the hospital,' said Boy, 'Lister's 20 minutes.'

'I'm not going anywhere with you,' Candi mumbled as if hunting for the memory of their fall out.

'I've got it,' said Toke, pulling Candi to her feet. 'We've finished our business and you two probably need to pack. Come on, Candice.'

Candi's head had been down. Toke's words wormed through into her muddled thoughts. She shook her head, grimaced at the pain and stared wildly around the kitchen.

Of all the inane things for him to have said, thought Lindi. 'Boy,' she urged, 'you should take her.'

'Let me,' offered Boy moving towards Candi.

'No, don't you dare,' she shied from him and through the kitchen door. At the front door, she shook free of Toke's support and turned on Boy. 'You won't get away with this. You screwed Shona over. You're not doing the same to me.

'I know enough to put you all away.' She stumbled out on to the path.

'Even if Toke drives her,' Lindi grabbed Boy, 'we've got to follow.'

'I'll get my keys,' he said.

But as Toke tried to support her through the gate, Candi lashed out, 'Get away from me, Toakley.' She struck his arm and his car keys went flying. As he turned to retrieve them, Candi half-ran half-stumbled to her own car. Its door was still open. Her keys waited in the ignition. Slumping down on the seat, she closed and locked the door before Toke could try it. She started the car, remembered it was a cul-de-sac and attempted a three-point turn. Toke's car received a glancing blow. Candi rode the kerb and drove away.

Cursing, Toke was quickly into his own car, 'I'll go after her,' he shouted. 'She's a danger to herself,' His saloon turned and thundered off in pursuit.

'Stay here' Boy took Lindi by the shoulders. 'Please stay here, I've got to go.'

'Go!'

He finally claimed his keys, returned to the car and turned it around.

Boy was back 20 minutes later. 'Lost them,' he said. 'I've

searched as far as the A1, nothing. They could have gone north or south. I've tried her phone. It's off. I just called Toke, nothing; I've left texts for them both.'

'We need to involve the police,' said Lindi. She'd tidied up perfunctorily with a dust-pan, binning some of the bloodied tissues Toke had been using.

'Alright,' said Boy unconvinced.

'Quite apart from her losing consciousness, there's possible internal bleeding. But mainly, I'm scared that it's Toke that's gone after her.'

'You're worried that he'll... what?'

'Candi threatened to report his blackmailing and your joint fraud. I've witnessed Toke's instinct for self-preservation, first hand. I know you don't believe it, but he's involved with such awful people. He's dangerous, Boy.'

A text pinged on Boy's phone. 'It's Toke,' he said, reading: 'I'm on Candi. Leave it with me.'

'Don't trust him,' Lindi warned.

'What can I do?'

'Tell the police.'

Before he could respond, another text pinged up. 'It's from Candi.'

He read the text. 'I'm OK but going to hospl. Get Toke off my tail, first. I don't want him hanging round A&E.'

'Get him back here, now,' said Lindi. 'Threaten whatever you have to.'

Boy clicked on Toke's name and texted, 'Get back to mine. We need to talk NOW! If you're not here in 5, Lindi'll call the cops.'

'OK, f's sake.'

Toke drove up seven minutes later and joined them in the kitchen. 'Candice is round your bloody ex's,' he told them. 'I don't know what's going on at Shona's. Webby in the cottage with them. He's hiding in one of the front rooms. I saw him, and he saw me. You should have seen his face when he did.'

'That's weird.' Boy couldn't hide his surprise. 'Sho's talked some sense into her then. I've just had a text. Candi's heading for the hospital.'

'Don't be so sure,' said Toke, 'Candice will be persuading Shona into a conspiracy against us. I'm going back there.'

'Leave it!' Lindi stepped in front of the door. 'Let her be. Whether she goes to the hospital or police station, we can't stop her.'

'Maybe not,' said Toke, 'but I aim to be forewarned.'

They did their best to delay him further but within another few minutes he had left.

A text was waiting from Candi, 'Thanks, on my way.'

Boy tried Shona's landline but without an answer. He told Lindi he'd pop round there on his way home.

❋ ❋ ❋

The next day Boy arrived at Dell End cottage mid-morning. He showed Lindi two texts from Candi. One timed at midnight, read, 'Discharged from A&E. 2 lumps on my head, but OK. Don't call. Don't fuss.' A picture showing a bloody lump on her head made them both wince.

'I'm hoping that's the "before" picture,' said Boy.

The second text timed at 6.30 in the morning. 'We're so over. I NEVER want to see you again. I'm taking a break from everything. Just LEAVE me alone.'

Lindi was so relieved after her tormented night that she let Boy persuade her to take up the plane ticket. Part of her reasoning, she told herself, was that Boy had been so unnerved by events, was so far removed from his usual boisterous self, she didn't think he'd cope on his own. She called Ash to say she was going to Argentina for a fortnight, maybe a month, maybe more, but she'd keep in close contact. As soon as he wanted to come home from Karachi, she'd be back there for him. Lindi would leave Chester Toakley, the unhelpful police, the clever fraud and her assault on Candi here in Hartsdell. She would go to Patagonia, try and make a splash.

Murder 2
Friday night May 24 2019
The old dark blue van free-wheeled slowly and softly down the slope towards the quarry. Its lights and engine were off. Its driver's door was already open. The only radiance came from an interior light.

March 2019 Argentina
The first week in Argentina was slow and awkward. Boy wasn't himself, Lindi was adjusting to the tumultuous change in her life. However, Boy's refusal to plan meant they made it up as they went along and got to know each other a little better each day.

A much rehearsed, carefully worded email to Candi received a terse text response a few hours later: 'Don't ever contact me again – I mean it. I'm taking a break from work, from everything. But especially YOU! Don't text, don't call. It's over!'

They didn't.

Toke messaged Boy. They both blocked him.

They called and Skyped their respective sons without mentioning they were away together. Lindi wasn't sure where things stood with Ayan. Boy knew exactly how things stood with Shona. Neither of them was yet sure what they meant to each other.

April 2019 Chile
Three weeks into April, Boy announced something had come up in the UK that demanded his presence. He would be going back for a few days. Did Lindi want to join him?

She said she'd stay on. Eight weeks away had sluiced the misery and confusion of events in Hartsdell out of her head. She wasn't ready to invite them back.

They had travelled through Argentina to Chile, close to its wildly fragmented west coast but within 50km of the largest regional airport. Flights required transfers in Santiago and Madrid. In theory, the UK was two days away; in practice, with travelling and airport bureaucracy, three. Boy apologised but he'd be away over a week. Lindi pointed to the small pile of airport books she had barely started, at the expensive view on offer from their hotel room window, she retrieved and waved the leaflets of tourist excursions Boy had refused to go on.

She had survived without him for nearly six years, she reminded him; eight to ten days was do-able.

He left. She was fine without him. He didn't fill up her heart. He relaxed her. And that was a relief.

* * May 2019 Chile * *

On the 4th of May, two days before Boy was due back, the phone in Lindi's hotel room rang. A woman's voice on the line said: 'Hello, I don't know who you are, but we need a wee chat. Set up a new Skype account under the name "The Innocent Flower". Be online in 40 minutes.' The phone went dead.

Lindi thought she recognised the voice. The weird instructions captured her curiosity. Her new account was called at 7pm. The caller's alter-ego was 'The Serpent Under it'. The woman's face shuffled closer on the screen. It was Shona. She took a moment to take Lindi's picture in. 'So, you're the mystery woman, eh, very bonnie.'

'Er...'

'Do I know you? Don't answer that. I'm not giving you my mobile number and I don't want yours. There can be no record of us ever having been in contact. I've checked; it's very hard to trace and replay Skype conversations, but let's be careful. I've got some bad news for you. News, I intended never to tell anyone.'

'Is it Boy?'

'No, it's his former squeeze.'

'Candi? Don't say Candi's had a relapse.'

'Worse. I'm afraid she's dead. She never recovered.'

'Never recovered from what? How do you mean?'

'Back in February, Candi appeared at mine. She was barely

conscious, raving about Boy and some woman – presumably you – who had hit her on the head. She said she had come around on the floor with Toke trying to smother her.

'She wasn't coherent, but mainly she was adamant that I had to stop you and Boy flying away together. Boy was her man; she wasn't letting him go. All her friends thought she was going to Patagonia with him. It wasn't right. She was in a bad way, but she'd come to the wrong woman for sympathy.

'Then, she clutched her head and keeled over in my kitchen. I tried to resuscitate her. Believe it or not, I tried everything I knew. Finally, I gave up. Her pulse had stopped.'

'Candi's dead? She's been dead over two months?' Lindi couldn't take it in. She thought she had escaped Hartsdell, but The Hart's curse had followed her. It had reached across to the far side of another continent to claim her.

'For all of two and a bit months, since the night of 21st of Feb.'

'She can't be. Why haven't we heard before now?'

The swell of this news had been travelling for over two months, building in the deeps of the South Atlantic Ocean. Candi's death crashed over Lindi. She was still fighting for air when its backwash dragged her under, it was the realisation that she had struck the fatal blow. She'd killed a woman. Candi was dead and, a mere day-and-a-half later, Lindi had fled the country.

'I'll be arrested. How is it I haven't already been arrested?'

'Quite simply,' the face on the screen answered her, 'because I panicked. I had a woman, who everyone knew I held a grudge against, lying dead in my kitchen. She'd obviously been battered about the head. I made a spur-of-the-moment decision to remove her body.'

'What!? How? To where?'

'Best you don't know.'

'Has Boy been questioned about it?'

'No, because no-one kens Candi's missing. She didn't have any immediate family.'

'Her friends...?'

'They assume she's in Patagonia with Boy. A few work col-
leagues, a close ex-school friend, some couples in and around
Peterborough; they stay in touch on Facebook, text and email.
She lives in a small village without close neighbours.'

'Oh Christ is that where her body is?'

'No, it's not. Boy doesn't know anything. We need to keep it
that way.'

'I can't be party to that. I won't lie. Why are you telling me
this now?'

'Because a man called Toakley's putting two and two together. He doesn't know Candi well but he's pretty certain
that she's not in South America.'

'I can't keep this secret, Shona. I don't know how you're
doing it. Boy will see it on my face.'

'You have to. The way he is now, this news would break him.'

'The way he is now? Why? Shona, what's happened?'

'You'll find out when he gets back. He'll want to return to the
UK. You can't let that happen. No-one here knows you're together. We need to keep up the pretence that Candi is with Boy
in deepest Patagonia. Only Toke thinks otherwise and he can't
prove a thing while you and Boy are there. I need you to buy
me another two-to-three weeks.'

'You're only delaying the inevitable. It's bound to come out.
We'll both be sharing a cell when it does.'

'No, we won't be suspected. Just do this. Please don't screw
up.' Shona arranged a future call and quit the app.

When he returned to Chile, Boy was pale and drawn. 'I've got
a problem,' he confessed on the first night. She waited with a
pretence of patience. 'It's Toke. He's coming after me. In fact,
he's going after everyone. Since we left, he seems to have been
on a mission.'

'You shouldn't have met with him.'

'I didn't. I wouldn't. I met with Shouty, though; he warned
me of Toke's threat. Shouty's furious with Toke, anyway. It
seems Toke's always been a sleeping partner in Shouty's in-
vestment business. He's woken up. Toke's activated a share-

holder's agreement clause. Shouty would rather close his business down than let Toke loose on his investors and start-ups.'

'Like giving the fox the keys to the chicken coop,' said Lindi.

'I heard some more earthy analogies. There's all kind of implied threats flying around. Shouty's at the end of his tether. He can't see a way out. Toke's insistent that even walking away isn't an option. 'Shouty said Toke also mentioned that I'm in his sights. Says he's going to spill the beans about my deal blowing up.'

'To who? He's bluffing.' Lindi didn't feel as certain as she tried to sound.

'Is he? Mitch and I had lunch in London. Mitch said this guy, Toakley, was pestering him for a meeting. He asked me who he was.'

'What did you say?'

'I warned Mitch off. I said I'd made the mistake of dealing with Toke, that he's a bandit and I wouldn't go near him again. I said I'd sort it when I go back at the end of June.'

'Good, we're not going to let Toakley ruin our time here. Just two months ago, he was frantic, remember, making threats, desperate that I'd mention anything to Mitch. What's changed?'

'Toke has apparently. Shouty says it's like his restraining chip was disabled when we left. Toke's gunning for everyone. Ranting that people have been walking all over him. I picked up Harry for a day. Shona said Webby's catching it from Toke about something. It's stressing him out.'

'Someone needs to put that man away,' said Lindi remembering Shona's parting words.

** Friday night May 24 2019 **

Ahead of the van an empty car vibrated, engine buzzing angrily. Its full beams displayed a tableau: a man confronting a woman.

She stood defiantly by the passenger door of her own car. The van stopped, not intruding into the beams. The man's back was to the van. The pulse of his own car engine meant he hadn't noticed its approach.

** May 2019 Argentina **

Boy wanted to return to face down Toke's threat. Lindi hid her fear behind bluster. Every day she re-ran her arguments that leaving Toke to stew in silence was the best policy. They shouldn't go back to the UK early.

When alone, Lindi signed on to Facebook. Ayan holding a young Ash beamed out from her account cover photo. She tracked down Candi and scrolled through numerous posts.

In early March, Candi had been posting about Buenos Aires. Her phone had been stolen, said one post. Boy wanted to go to Chile, claimed another. They'd separated. Candi travelled alone to visit the Iguazú Falls. Post followed fantastical post. Envious friends commented, liked, loved, emoted, pleaded that she get a new phone, they wanted to call. Lindi marvelled at this dead woman enjoying a life so wildly, exotically, imaginatively different from the one she had actually lived.

A second Skype session with Shona was squeezed in while Boy was swimming. Lindi had to keep it short.

'There's a plan,' began Shona. 'I only need to discredit Toke. If I neuter him, he can't speak out.'

'This was a murder, Shona.' Lindi was aghast. 'He's not going to stay quiet. He knows I did it.'

'Strictly speaking, it's manslaughter. But we can make it look like murder.'

Lindi voice broke. 'Y-you already have.'

'Remember, Toke was the last person to see Candi alive.'

'Apart from you.'

'No-one knows that. I've only got to draw the police's attention to Toke somehow. I have to make him believe the police would suspect him first, rather than you.'

'How? It won't work. He knows I hit her. Boy knows.'

'I'm staging something. It will label Toke as a sexual predator. I'm deciding who I can get to help – it can't be you, obviously – someone who knows Toke.'

One name suggested itself.

'Do you know Shouty?'

'Scott, you mean, Scott Hadleigh? Lotte's ex?'

'Shouty'll help. He needs Toke out of his life, right now.'

'You're sure? Shouty and Toke are close. Too close for Shouty to pin Toke for murder. Oh, and Harry saw you in the background when he was Skyping his dad.'

'Oh no, I'll try...'

'Nae bother; he thought you must be Candi. Luckily, I never let him meet her.'

Lindi's resolve faltered after the third Skype session with Shona. It was 11pm UK time on the 15th of May. Shona had been drinking.

'Trap's set,' the Scottish woman laughed uneasily. 'I've kept it simple. It all depends on Toke fancying me enough to seduce me at a party. I'm going to make it look like he attacked me; laced my drink with Rohypnol; do something that ties him to Candi in some way.'

'That will just force Toke's hand.'

'No, I'll complain to the police, then refuse to press charges, but he'll be on their radar. He won't dare make a move.'

'Shona, don't put yourself in that situation. Toke's involved with some seriously scary people.'

'Webby's told me. That's why I need to act now: Webby's falling apart. Toke's threatening all-sorts, demanding Webby blabs.'

'What's Webby got to do –' and then Lindi dredged up a detail from the 21st of February, 'Webby was there, at your cottage that night.'

'True. I persuaded him to help me hide the body.'

'Webby had sex with Candi the night before.' Lindi remembered them leaving the party together, remembered Kotryna's accusation. 'When Candi spoke about a rapist – she meant Webby.'

'That's not how Webby sees it, but he did say she was in a right old state.'

'No wonder Webby helped you. He had to distance himself from Candi's body. In fact, he, more than anyone, needed her to disappear.'

'But it wasn't Webby who killed her,' Shona reminded.

'I don't understand how your plan works.'

'We just need Toke to go to this party. After that, it's all down to my allure. There are a lot of variables and most of it I have to make up as I go along.'

'What? This is the rest of our lives you're playing with.'

'I'm aware. I'm setting Toke up. It's a tiger trap. Toke's the tiger and I'm kind of the goat, but in a skimpy red party dress.'

'Is this the drink talking? Shona, who's got the gun?'

Shona laughed but it came up short. 'Good question. Most of Toke's business associates, according to Webby.'

'Shona, no. It can't just be you and the village butcher versus the Baltic mafia. I can –'

'Stay put. Shouty's in. You were right, he desperately needs leverage over Toke. But you *must* remain under wraps in Patagonia for this to work. Boy has to be far away too. I couldn't protect him from that woman when she was alive, now I'm saving him from her dead.'

'This is such a mess.'

'I've got to go, it's late and I've got to be at work tomorrow. Alright for you fun-seekers. Love to Boy. Only kidding.' Shona clicked off.

They returned close to Buenos Aires. Lindi felt she had to do something. Shona had absolutely no idea what kind of people she'd be dealing with. Boy was eyeing up a bike ride that involved three rustic overnight stops. Lindi said: 'You go. I'm going to pop back to the UK for a few days. Help out Evelyn.'

She called Evelyn and was scolded for being nearly three months away from the gallery. Her business acumen was urgently needed. Lindi said that she would be adopting an extremely low profile given all the turmoil over Ash. Evelyn couldn't tell anyone else she was back. The gallery owner insisted Lindi stayed with her.

'I have no problem closeting you in my spare bedroom and making you work for your keep,' Evelyn informed her. 'Modern slavery is booming here.'

** Friday Night May 24 2019 **

The van was about 12 metres from the man, directly behind him.

'No please, just don't...' The threatened woman screamed and then she hurled her phone away from the man. It bounced into the distant scrub. Her hands scrunched into the material of her summery dress as she cowered away against her car.

The van's ignition turned. The engine gunned.

'What the..?' The man spun in shock, which increased when he saw a woman with sandy hair behind the van's wheel.

He barked his astonishment, 'Oh lordy!'

** Wednesday May 22 England **

Disguised under a hat and neck-scarf, Lindi took her cab onto the Old Chapel Gallery's new block-paving apron. Over afternoon coffee, while they went through the plans for the gallery website, Evelyn took a phone call.

'You won't believe this,' she said in an aside to Lindi, 'but someone's been arrested in the village bar, Benedicts. It's to do with a murder according to Vanessa.'

Lindi didn't trust herself with her coffee cup. It chattered out her nervousness as she returned it to the table.

'Who?' she mouthed at Evelyn, convinced it must be Shona. It was a few moments more before the phone was put down.

'A man I know. In fact, everyone knows Chester Toakley, the rogue,' Evelyn reported. 'I can't see that Toke'd ever murder anyone, though. Two police cars are now parked up outside Boy's ex-partner's house, now too. That Scottish woman. Does he ever mention her?'

Lindi groaned and put her head in her hands.

'Lindi,' Evelyn's sharp mind barely skipped a beat, 'do tell.'

'You can't tell anyone, if I do, Evelyn, seriously, not ever.'

'The de Brets came over with the Norman Conquest, my dear.

We take secrets to our graves.'

Lindi explained the other reason she was here incognito. She had met Toke in January. She knew what he and his business associates were capable of. They had threatened Ash, specifically saying that they would remove his head and hands. Lindi felt at the time that it was a reference to the murder near Derby, but the police weren't interested.

'And Shona?'

'She must be on to Toke, somehow, but she won't know about his links to sex traffickers. If she's involved, she's in danger. I have to help her.'

Evelyn's initial disbelief was replaced with: 'And this is happening in Hartsdell, of all places? When I was a girl it was widely assumed that accountants led dull lives. That was one reason I took up with an artist.'

'We do lead dull lives,' Lindi said.

'Hardly. What is your plan?'

'I don't have one. I've barely met Shona, and not for over six years. She can't know I'm in Hartsdell. These people she's trying to expose, I wasn't brave enough to take them on. If she's aiming to, I should help her if I can; just keep an eye on her, maybe.'

'You know, I have an old van. It's a tatty dark blue Austin Maestro,' said Evelyn. 'Would you like to use it in your covert surveillance? It's in one of my garages. It's exactly the kind of thing a spy would use, no-one ever notices it.'

'Evelyn, you're a treasure.'

'I most certainly am *not* a treasure. But I'd hate for murder to be going on in Hartsdell and not be involved. How exciting!'

Later that Wednesday afternoon, Lindi parked up Evelyn's old blue van 50 metres on from Shona's cottage, under the shade of the trees. Shona was inside, presumably with the occupants of the dark blue BMW parked on her drive.

When Shona left, Lindi followed her car to the Cambridge Science Park, where Shona entered a deserted laboratory car-park. Lindi gave Shona time to get inside the building before entering and parked in the furthest corner. An hour on, a silver saloon screeched up, halting close to the lab doors. Lindi slunk down in the van as she saw Toke leap out and hammer against the door. Eight minutes later, still furious, he drove away.

Whatever Shona had tried to engineer, hadn't stuck, the police had let Toke go.

Shona didn't leave until well after midnight. Lindi followed at what she hoped was a discreet distance, expecting Shona's car to be assailed by Toke's at any moment. There wasn't much traffic. When Shona drove into a garage, Lindi doused her lights and parked up on a turn-off slip road.

She realised she'd spooked Shona when her quarry bolted out of the garage a moment later. Lindi followed, but lost her on the back-roads. She continued to Hartsdell and parked up, without lights, in the same spot, 50m from Shona's cottage. Hugo's wife Esther came out and peered suspiciously in the van's direction. Lindi turned it around and drove away.

** Friday Night May 24 2019 **

The man couldn't say more because Shona had fished a crow-bar from the open window of her car and lashed him, violently, across the side of his head. Toke groaned and collapsed to his knees. Shocked more than stunned, he lowered his head muttering incoherent curses. Shona looked up in astonishment as the newcomer in the van engaged the clutch and floored the accelerator.

Shona darted two steps to the left and jumped. Toke had neither the time nor lucidity to rise. The radiator, bumper and beaked bonnet of the old blue van rocketed into him. It mashed his head and chest against and into the side of Shona's car.

** Thursday May 23 **

On Thursday morning, Evelyn bought Lindi a copy of the newspaper and a mug of strong coffee.

'You'll need this,' she lifted the mug; 'when you read this,' she dropped the paper down. 'You were right about Hartsdell being murder-central.'

While Evelyn waited, Lindi read the morning reports about a man who was arrested in Hartsdell and interviewed about the 'The Doll Killer' murders.

'It doesn't say the murder suspect was Toke,' Evelyn said when Lindi had finished.

'Nor that they've released him,' said Lindi.

'Perhaps he has an alibi. Toke doesn't strike me as evil – well, perhaps some of his jokes...'

'If it's not him, it could be that brutal associate of his.'

Lindi researched the story online. She learnt a murdered woman's body was discovered the week following her departure for Argentina. Her astonishment escalated with every account.

It had to be Candi, but how had Shona managed it? How had she made it identical to a previous murder near Derby in October? Only, perhaps, because Webby had been given all the particulars of that murder, courtesy of Toke's boasting about his sex trade contacts.

Lindi tried to get her head around the stuff about the bruise. Why had Shona engineered that? What on earth was she planning next?

Boy Skyped. Lindi told him about Shona being involved with the police and the bruise story. Candi wasn't mentioned. Boy promised not to tell anyone that Lindi was back in the UK. She elected not to follow Shona's car during the day, her quarry would spot her too easily. An impromptu visit to view Dell End Cottage after lunch, almost led to her running into Shona. Lindi found Shona's car parked up on the narrow road. She couldn't understand why Shona was inside her former home.

Reversing away, Lindi returned to Evelyn's.

Evelyn reported seeing Shona in Webbs. 'I heard her say she's working nights,' Evelyn shook her head. 'They do that in rubbish TV series, put themselves in needless danger. Your woman seems completely scatty. They'll be checking the ditches tomorrow.'

'What work does she do?'

'She mentioned "a fish lab" – laboratory, I suppose.'

Armed with a printout note, Lindi waited until Shona left for work, then slid it into her letterbox. It read: 'I don't know what the hell you think you are doing. But STOP!'

That night Lindi repeated her stake-out at the lab. She again followed Shona home but at a greater distance. Despite more traffic Shona was still alert enough to spot her tail, cautious enough not to be caught stationary at the train crossing, and shrewd enough to lose Lindi on the back lanes. Having lost her quarry again, Lindi drove to Shona's darkened cottage to find Shona and another car parked up. A dark shape was moving towards Shona's vehicle – a man but she couldn't see who. She suspected Toke. He stopped at Lindi's arrival. Having second thoughts, he returned to his car and drove off.

* * Friday Night May 24 2019 * *

Dazed and bloodied, Lindi unclipped the safety belt, stumbled out of the crippled van and threw up. Shona was on all-fours in the scrub. She didn't glance at the mangled wreckage that had been Toke, but gaped at Lindi.

'You're OK!?' Lindi slumped forward, 'Thank Christ.'

'What the...?!'

'New plan,' wheezed Lindi, slipping to her knees. 'Is he..?'

'Must be,' gasped Shona. 'No-one could survive that.' She tried to stand. 'The police will be here soon.'

* * May 24 Friday * *

Friday started with more revelations about the 'Iona Cross woman' in the later editions of the papers. They reported that police had discounted Toakley as a suspect. Mid-morning one of Evelyn's circle called her to report a strange post from Shona on the Hartsdell Facebook page. Evelyn drew Lindi's attention to it. Shona had posted, declaring Toakley innocent. They shared a look of bafflement.

Evelyn tapped one of the comments on screen, 'I know that Fidel Castrol. She's in Stitch n' Bitch. She can't knit for toffee, but when it comes to people, she's rarely wrong.'

Later, Evelyn said she'd seen Shona in the village shop. 'She was skulking among the cereals, jumping at her own shadow.'

Lindi started to despair. 'Whatever Shona's up to, it's clearly not working.'

'If Toakley's the murderer, why would she proclaim him innocent?' The gallery owner was captivated by the machinations of the story unfolding in her quiet village.

'He must have turned the tables on her.'

'Do we even know who Shona thinks was murdered? You said she was poking around your old cottage yesterday. Oh great heavens, Lindi, does she think you're the victim?'

Lindi was stumped for a reply. 'I disappeared to Patagonia without telling anyone. She may think it's me.'

If Evelyn's expression could have been caught on canvas, the gallery's fortunes would have been made.

Using Evelyn's laptop, Lindi logged on to her anonymous Facebook account, Hartsmuch, and posted, 'Toke ISN'T innocent. The Cops should ask him about Big Mart in Derby.'

During the afternoon, Lindi heard Shona's voice downstairs. She had come to talk to Evelyn. Luckily the Austin Maestro van was locked away in one of Evelyn's three garages.

Evelyn was still in a state of astonishment when she took Lindi through the conversation. 'She ranted away into her phone. Almost scared off my customers. And, you were right, by the way, she really does think you've been murdered. If this is representative of her powers of deduction...?'

She passed Lindi a phone number with a laugh of amazement. 'If you're alive, she wants you to call her. Will you?'

'I won't. I think it's best if I stay dead for now. Anyway, I daren't use my phone, here.'

'This pretending to be murdered isn't a tax thing, is it?' Evelyn gave a conspiratorial shake of the head. 'You accountants...'

Lindi set off to Cambridge early that evening. Armed with Shona's number and Evelyn's borrowed mobile, she parked in her usual spot before the daytime work-force left.

At 5.45pm a large grey van pulled up and a burly man in a brown shirt leapt out with a sprightliness that belied his size. Lindi hadn't seen that figure for four months – Mart, the pimp, who'd threatened her in Peterborough. Shona arrived nearly an hour later. Lindi watched, heart in mouth, as the two interacted in reception but it passed off without incident. Shona disappeared into the main part of the building. The man lounged in reception, checking his phone.

A little after 9pm the man came out into the car park. He looked around and focussed on her van. Lindi twisted the ignition and sped out of the car park. In her mirrors she saw him watching her go. He looked puzzled.

Driving out of the Science Park, Lindi drove around a few blocks to make sure the grey van wasn't following. Tentatively, she returned and parked in another company's deserted parking area. She would see any vehicles that left Shona's lab.

She didn't know how to proceed. Mart had been checking the surroundings were clear, she felt sure. Shona's plan was about to be aggressively derailed.

She texted the number Shona had given Evelyn that afternoon. 'Get out of there now. No questions. You're in danger. Just get out.'

Lindi waited. Minutes passed like eons. Lindi's finger hovered over the 'nines' on her phone. Just as she felt she had to act, she saw Shona's car burst from the lab entrance and race away down the road. Lindi sped after it, not waiting to see if the large grey van would follow, not caring if Shona spotted her in the half-light.

Shona stopped on a long lay-by beyond the outskirts of Cambridge. It was on her route home. Hedges and bushes separated the road from wide fields on either side. Shona was out of her car and on her phone as Lindi pulled up, as far away and unobtrusively as she could, by another car in the lay-by. The calls continued for a few minutes before Esther's mobile went off in the van passenger seat.

'You texted me,' came Shona's voice. 'Who is this?'

'It's Lindi. Are you OK?'

'I'm unscathed – but purely down to luck! That gorilla in there tried to knife me.'

'Oh Christ. I suspected the worst.'

'Thanks for the warning.'

'He's a monster,' said Lindi. 'I had to do something, even if it meant blowing my cover.'

'I'd kind of guessed you were here.'

'How?'

'Innate Scottish witchiness. You're in Leroy's wee van?'

'The blue one. It's Evelyn's van. I've been following you for two nights.'

'That was you? I've had to bring forward my annual knickers-wash because of your antics. So, is this your phone?'

'No, Evelyn's.'

'Right, this isn't my real phone either, it's a burner. So, in call-tracking terms we're still not in contact. That may be useful. Stay in the van. We can't be seen talking to each-other.'

'Did Toakley take your skimpy red dress bait?'

'No. Despite all Shouty's carnal inducements, he never showed. Toke decided a meeting with some dodgy business contact in Ely was a more attractive proposition.'

Lindi's faint hopes drained, 'Then how...?'

'Shouty told me Toke wouldn't make it. I played Webby as a "ringer" in a devil costume, and caught a few lucky breaks. Shouty's been a big help, but he doesn't know I'm pinning Toke for murder.'

'So, what now? Are the police involved?'

'They will be. I've started writing a manuscript about my investigation, too.'

'What? Shona, these people are dangerous, evil. You need to take this seriously.'

'Oh, I do. Don't forget I've been living with this since you sent a half-dead woman to my door.'

'Is there still a plan?'

Shona's voice was defensive. 'Yes, well kinda. That fake guard may actually have helped. Toke'll be here in five minutes. Webby says Toke likes boasting about the murder in Derby. I'm going to lead him somewhere quiet, provoke him into admitting something incriminating about it and record him.'

Lindi flushed with anger. 'Is that it? That's hardly going to wash.'

'There's more but I don't have time to explain. Could you follow us surreptitiously in case Toke turns nasty? You could be an additional witness. I'm heading for the same quarry where I lost you last night.'

'You're aiming to put Toakley in prison, right?'

'For attacking me, yes, at the very least, hopefully more,' said Shona.

'You've not got nearly enough.'

'All I need is the admission and if I get that, we hit him with everything else.'

'He's hardly going to go quietly. Toke knows it was me who struck Candi, who effectively killed her. You said he already suspects you and Webby are involved. He knows vicious people, like that guard. They will pile the pressure on Webby. More so if Toke's put away. Boy and Shouty will go down with him.'

Lindi needed to put Toke somewhere he could never threaten Ash again. It wouldn't be met by Shona's crazy scheme.

'Lindi, in case you've forgotten, you're supposed to be on the other side of the Atlantic. You aren't part of this. Leave it to the lass from Glasgae. I've got to make another call. Keep your head down and have some faith.'

Lindi watched as Shona busied herself on her phone and with her car boot. Other vehicles flashed past, searing lights broadcasting over the countryside. She saw Shona, still on the phone, take sudden fright and race into her car. Lindi ducked down. As Shona drove away, a pale saloon, indicators flashing, pulled on to the lay-by, rolled forward and then lurched back out on to the road after Shona. It's angry full-beam headlights locked on to her rear bumper.

Lindi followed at a distance. Shona left the highway for the back roads. Lindi, lights off, turned a sharp corner just in time to see the silver saloon swing into a redundant opening between tall hedges.

Now what? How long should she wait? Long enough for Shona to record a confession? Long enough for Toke to really attack Shona?

Shona was still in danger. Toke would be livid. He'd tried to confront her twice already. Was he even alone in that car? What was he capable of? He had threatened Ash, menaced her, extorted money from the Webbs, blackmailed the PLS director and planned to do the same to Boy. Shona reported that Candi had claimed Toke tried to smother her. He'd sent his vicious animal, Mart, to Cambridge to knife Shona. Toke was a walking malignity.

Lindi had decided. She turned into the opening and headed towards the distant flare of radiance. She showed no lights, cut her engine, opened her door and drifted gently to a halt twelve metres behind Toke's back.

** Friday Night May 24 2019 **

Lindi saw Shona scramble to the driver's side of her car. It took a moment to open the back door. She pulled on a pair of lab gloves. Next a plastic bag was taken out.

Kneeling beside what had been Toke, she took a moment to find his right hand in the ruin of body and bonnet. She felt for a pulse but shook her head. From the bag she removed a hefty meat cleaver. It was eased beneath the body, close to a limp gloved hand.

Lindi, still kneeling, watched through barely comprehending eyes. Scurrying to Toke's car, Shona removed a tatty piece of crumpled kitchen towel from the bag and hid it under the passenger seat. The last item to emerge was a silvery ring sealed in a food bag. Shona opened the boot and placed it at the bottom of a tennis hold-all, be-

neath towels, rackets and sports kit. She closed the boot.

Shona sat down in the dust by the sobbing Lindi. She used a second phone she had plucked from the driver side of her car. She put it on speaker phone as she pulled a thick plastic bag from her pocket. Her call was answered instantly but no one spoke.

'You all set?' Shona asked.

Lindi heard the answering voice. It came uncertainly. 'Oh shit! You... you managed it...? Toke's incapacitated?' She recognised the voice as Webby's.

'I've done what we needed to. Go in now. Don't leave any evidence of you in that barn of his.'

'I know. I know. I've got your glove things and suit on. I'm driving up by Toke's place as we speak.'

'You've got everything?'

'I've got Shouty's keys to Toke's barns. Your doll's head and hands are here. This whole thing creeps me out. It was an effort of will like you wouldn't believe to enter Candi's cottage. I still have nightmares about that night as it is. I get sick just looking at my old mincer.'

Shona noticed Lindi's stare of disbelief. She put a hand over the phone. 'We had to use Webby's industrial mincer for her head. Trust me, had there been any other way...'

'I never believed your mad plan could work,' Webby's voice rushed on. 'Have you got the other stuff in his car? Has he said anything incriminating?'

'We've got him. The cops are coming.'

'This'll get him put down, won't it?'

'For a good long while.'

'You're sure he doesn't have an alibi?'

'The police haven't got a clear date or time of death, remember, I told you. Anyway, we know where he was that night.'

'Yeah, OK, it's just—' his breathing sounding ragged. 'I've arrived.'

'Good. Where's your fancy dress devil outfit?'

'Got it with me, wrapped up, washed twice. I'll leave it here somewhere.'

Shona hurried on. 'Lock the barn after. Walk to the rendezvous *asap. Return the barn keys to Shouty. Call when you're done.'*

The call ended.

Shona had Lindi's phone. The sim card was removed and bent into quarters. It, and the phone, went into the plastic bag. The crowbar hammered them to pieces.

'That's Evelyn's.' Lindi was too drained to resist.

'We'll buy her a new one. I'll do the same to my burner phone. Then phones, gloves and crowbar are all going into the bag, and into the lake.'

'I don't understand what's go –' Shona cupped Lindi's head in her gloved hands.

'Lindi, concentrate, it's important. You must tell the police that the last time you and Boy saw or heard anything about Candi, Toke was following her in his car, away from your place. He'd promised to take her to Lister Hospital. Otherwise, keep to the truth.'

Shona's phone vibrated. Busy, she clicked it on. Shouty's voice came through. It was careful. 'How're things?'

'It's done.'

'What. Really?' Lindi overheard surprise battling with relief. 'That's… uh, astonishing, frankly. Just dropped Hugo off home. I'm heading to the rendezvous now. I take it Webby's planted his devil suit at Toke's?'

'He'll be leaving there about now.'

'You reckon this attack on you is enough to bring Toke to heel?'

'No, but add in the hankie DNA link to that murder he knows way too much about… Trust me, he won't be saying or doing anything to upset you, Boy or Webby, ever again.'

'Sho, you're a miracle-worker. When I nicked Toke's hankie and borrowed his phone to send that text on Tuesday, I thought your plan was a busted flush….'

'There has been a minor change of plan. But keep your head down now, no matter what. And lose the phone. Gotta go, sirens in the distance.'

'Go.'

The instant he signed off, the phone buzzed again.

Webby: 'All done. Her car's in his barn. I hid Candi's phone and lap-

top inside Toke's desk. Her keys are on top of it. The red devil suit's in a cupboard.'

'Get out of there.'

'I know. It's all locked. I'm walking to rendezvous with Shouty, then I'll have to pick up my car from her village. There's one thing though...'

'What.'

'Her finger. The one you cut off and kept. When it came to putting it in his fridge-freezer, I couldn't find it. I must have put it down somewhere...'

'Finger?' blurted Lindi.

Shona motioned her to silence.

'OK Webby, it probably doesn't matter as long as it's there somewhere. If you find you still have it, burn it or bury it, somewhere far away from you. Be sure you get the message to Boy. Tell him what to say. If he gets it wrong, I'll be put away. Lindi too, tell him. Do it before the cops contact him. Then lose the phone. Any calls to my burner will lead to awkward questions.'

'Yeah-OK. About your text earlier: Kotty knows everything. We can trust her.'

'Everything?' echoed Shona.

'She knows it was you who killed Candi. She knows you did it for me.'

Lindi mentally replayed the image of Shona smashing the crowbar into Toke's head. Her sobs stopped. She stared. She started retching again.

EPILOGUE

The Manuscript

'OK, I've checked the draft. It definitely reads "Patterson".' The familiar desiccated cough, followed. 'The publishers love your title, "The Doll with a Bruise,". It's great. But they think "The Girl with the Cross" is stronger.'

'I'm just glad it's not "The Girl with the Octopus Tattoo."'

'Exactly,' Shelby's wheezing chuckle escaped her phone. It stopped with a gulp of breath. 'I'm not sure we've nailed the title; I don't suppose you'd –'

'No Steve.'

'Not even remembering that Gone Puss saved your life…?'

'Biologists don't do tattoos.'

'Pity. About your manuscript ending. It's so powerful: the Cambridge police – alerted by Sergeant de Clerc and your man, Leroy – screeching to a halt in the quarry to find you and Ms Mills retching and sobbing on your knees, barely moments after she'd saved your life; emotive stuff.'

'I sense a but…'

'We have several bits and pieces to add to the manuscript: Candice Egan's car, laptop and phone being kept in Toakley's barn, and the blood-soaked bathroom in her cottage where the decapitation was performed.'

'But those are things I know nothing about. It's my story and I wasn't involved in any of that.'

'Even so, here's what we need: the police searching Toakley's barn complex, finding Candi's car in it with your doll's head and hands hidden in its boot. There's the box Boy took from your dad's store-room being discovered in Candi's cottage and the butcher...' he hunted for a name.

'Webb.'

'Thanks, yeah Webb, lending Toakley an industrial mincer, supposedly for a deer carcass he'd found.' Shelby was consulting a list.

'Go on, I suspect there's more.'

'Fraid so. We need to explain that Toakley used Candi's own phone and her laptop to fabricate the Facebook pages and keep in touch with her friends. Posting from the Harty Fare Café's wifi, meant it couldn't be traced to his router.

'Which brings me to the finger. This is so gloriously macabre – he must have kept her finger in a freezer to fingerprint access her phone and laptop. Who does that? It all speaks to the evil genius behind that poor girl's murder.'

'The finger was never found, though.'

'No, pity that; it's the only loose end in the entire case.'

'What do the publishers say about DCI Hossein's comments, his refusal to believe Toke was the Doll Killer, or that he had murdered that first victim?'

'Well, your butcher... Webb's statement sorted that. When he said that Toakley had confided in him about a "C" being carved in the women's calf,' Shelby coughed up a laugh. 'That put the police on the spot. It forced the DCI to admit that both victims did indeed have a "C" slashed into their calves, but the police had previously held back that info. That was the clincher. His superiors closed down his objections, after that.

'The publishers agree with me, Hossein's reaction just adds to the publicity campaign. You succeeded where two police forces failed.'

'Hossein will never forgive me for undermining his reputation.'

'I kind of like, "C for Chester". Is that a title?'

'Unless the "C" stood for "*chiulpedra*". Toke was involved in Lithuanian drug running and sex slaves.'

'Good point. We need a chapter on the subsequent police investigations. That they believe Martini – or Martinaitus – has fled back to Lithuania. There's Ms Mills's evidence that Candi had threatened to expose Toakley's drug and sex-trade connections. It was probably why he killed her, although there's still forensic evidence suggesting Candi had endured rough sex shortly before she was killed.'

'It all good stuff but you should write it. I only know about crosses.'

'How about "The Double Cross Girl"?'

'Not going to happen.'

'OK, there's one more scene I'd love to get in.'

'Steve, enough.'

'Boy's reaction when Webb called him and said you and Lindi had been detained for killing Toakley. The moment when Boy realised he'd sent the Doll Killer after his injured ex-girlfriend. Imagine that.'

'As you well know, Boy and Lindi disown my account. Since the inquest returned a justifiable homicide verdict, they've made it clear they want nothing to do with it. Nothing to do with me.'

Acknowledgements: thanks to **Agnieszka Ryling** for beta reading, making comments and being a critical enthusiast – every book should have one. Thanks too, to **Jenny Thomson**, who did a brilliant job of proof-reading the final book and finding all my grammar blind-spots. The other readers who read, commented and helped make sense of my tricksy plot: **Nicola Freeman, John Patterson, Simon Cassia**. Thanks to **Cath-**

erine Harrison and **Margaret Harrison** who added biological insight. And to the talented writers of **Cottered Writers** group and the **Curtis Brown** school of 2019 under author Simon Wroe who got stuck into and improved key chapters.

Fans of this novel may want to try Interact Publishing's forthcoming 'The Language of Hedge', which we would summarise as 'Pride and Prejudice meets His Dark Materials'.

Printed in Great Britain
by Amazon